DENISE HUNTER

MENDING
PLACES

A Novel

HOWARD BOOKS
A DIVISION OF SIMON & SCHUSTER
New York London Toronto Sydney

THE NEW HEIGHTS SERIES

About the Author

 Denise Hunter is the award-winning author of five novels and three novellas. A voracious reader, she began writing a Christian romance novel in 1996, and it was published two years later. Her husband, Kevin, claims he provides all her romantic material, but Denise insists a good imagination helps too. She and Kevin live in Indiana with their three sons, where they are very active in a new church.

You can visit Denise's Web site at www.denisehunterbooks.com.

Books by Denise Hunter

Kansas Brides
Stranger's Bride
Never a Bride
Bittersweet Bride
His Brother's Bride

Novellas

Reunions "Truth or Dare"
Aloha "Game of Love"
Blind Dates "The Perfect Match"

Our purpose at Howard Books is to:

- *Increase faith* in the hearts of growing Christians
- *Inspire holiness* in the lives of believers
- *Instill hope* in the hearts of struggling people everywhere

Because He's coming again!

Published by Howard Books, a division of Simon & Schuster
1230 Avenue of the Americas, New York, NY 10020

HOWARD BOOKS   *Mending Places* © 2004 by Denise Hunter

www.howardpublishing.com

Library of Congress Cataloging-in-Publication Data

Hunter, Denise, 1968–
    Mending places : a novel / Denise Hunter.
    p. cm. — (The new heights series)
    ISBN: 978-1-58229-358-5
    1. Teton Range (Wyo. and Idaho)—Fiction. 2. Mountaineering guides (Persons)—Fiction.
3. Family-owned business enterprises—Fiction. 4. Mountain resorts—Fiction. I. Title.

PS3608.U5935M46 2004
813'.6—dc22

                                                                        2003067766

10 9 8 7 6 5

HOWARD is a registered trademark of Simon & Schuster, Inc.

Manufactured in the United States of America

For information regarding special discounts for bulk purchases, please contact Simon & Schuster
Special Sales at 1-800-456-6798 or business@simonandschuster.com

Edited by Ramona Richards
Interior design by John Mark Luke Designs
Cover design by David Carlson Design

ACKNOWLEDGMENTS

"Write what you know" is usually the first piece of advice new writers receive. It's a good general rule, but at some point a writer like me finds herself up to her chin in something she knows little about. That's where research comes in, and usually it involves begging the help of friends, family, and complete strangers.

I was blessed to have the help of several people during the course of writing this novel, and a hearty thank-you goes out to each of them! Any errors in this work of fiction are completely mine.

Roxanne and Lorren Henke for taking me through the ins and outs of banking.

Beth Moore for writing wonderful words in her study guides that draw me closer to God.

Kim Peterson for sharing her expertise in divorce procedures.

Donna Prewitt for providing details in the area of social work.

Tyler Sinclair for explanations on the game of chess.

Dan Tressler for offering firsthand information on climbing Mount Moran (so I didn't have to climb it myself!).

Also, a huge thank-you to my agent, Pamela Hardy; my editors, Philis Boultinghouse and Ramona Richards; and my critique partners, Colleen Coble and Kristin Billerbeck.

Finally, thanks to my husband, Kevin, who amazes me more each day with his love for Christ and devotion to our family.

CHAPTER
ONE

Hanna Landin maneuvered her 4x4 through Jackson, Wyoming, sighing when the upcoming light turned red. She hated being late. Not only was it rude but it smacked of irresponsibility, an attribute she did not wish to demonstrate, today of all days. Her stomach twisted in knots. What if Keith said no? She suppressed the thought. Failure was not an option.

She drummed her bare, blunt-cut nails on the steering wheel, willing the light to change. Suddenly church bells pealed in the distance, invading her vehicle with their liquid notes. She choked down the bile in her throat. Jamming the radio volume up, she drowned out the bitter reminder of her tardiness with gospel music. Still, revulsion burned like acid in her stomach. She mustn't think about it now. Had to concentrate on her meeting with Keith. A horn blared behind her, and she accelerated through the green light, shoving down the old memory that threatened to surface once again.

When she finally reached the bank, she spotted her brother-in-law at his desk and hurried on shaky legs across the highly polished floor. "Good morning, Keith. Sorry I'm late."

He clasped her extended hand. "That's okay, Hanna, have a seat." He gestured to a vinyl chair opposite his cluttered desk. "Natalie said you're thinking of refinancing the lodge and taking out an equity loan. Is that right?"

"Yes, that's right." She placed her folders on the desk, catching one as it slid off the mound. She wondered if Natalie had told Keith the extent of their financial problems.

Hanna cleared her throat, hoping to eliminate the quiver in her voice. "I'd like to initiate an advertising campaign and provide additional services for our guests. Business has been down the last few years, especially with all the improvements on the Majestic."

Keith reached for a folder. "May I?"

"Of course." Noting he'd immediately reached for the profit-and-loss statement, Hanna began her appeal. "Gram and I feel that Higher Grounds isn't living up to its potential. Other lodges in the area might be more upscale, but we think we can capitalize on Higher Grounds' rustic appeal."

His silence urged her on. "What we've lacked in the past is marketing. Grandpop did things the old-fashioned way, relying on word of mouth and fliers for business. But if Higher Grounds is to compete with the Majestic, we need to advertise nationally. Show people another way to vacation in the Tetons."

"I'm a little surprised by the loss you've shown the last three years. Nat told me things were rough, but I had no idea . . ."

Panic swelled in her leaden stomach. "That's why this campaign is so important. I've already listed the lodge in the *Christian Bed-and-Breakfast Directory*. That alone should draw new customers."

She handed him the marketing folder. As he skimmed the pages, she toyed with her grandma's ring, zinging it along the gold chain. She watched the frown lines pucker under his receding hairline and felt another surge of panic. No other bank would loan them the money or even refinance for that matter. Keith was their last chance. She knew it was a lot to ask, even of family. But still, she had to try.

"Your plans to increase business might work. Then again, they might not."

She dropped the ring and opened her mouth to speak. He held her off with a raised hand.

"When your grandfather built Higher Grounds, it was a risk. But there was no other lodging in the area. Now you're competing with the Majestic."

"They do have more to offer, but you can't deny our lodge is located on prime property. And with some changes, we can provide activities for our guests too." She handed him another folder. "I'd like to hire a trekking guide. Tourists from the city want to explore the Tetons, but many are afraid to venture off by themselves. We have a beautiful lake we're not utilizing, as well. I'd like to purchase some watercraft. Also, a shuttle to and from the airport would be nice."

Her breath froze in her lungs while he scrutinized the pages. What would she do if the lodge failed? Her eyes scanned his face, and she thought it seemed thinner, as if he'd lost some weight.

"Your plans are sound, and you've been meticulous with your detail. But you've been in the red for three years, Hanna."

Stuffing down the anxiety, she rushed on. "If you'll turn to page 4, you'll see my projections for increased business, which the advertising is sure to provide. With the income from additional guests, we'll easily be able to afford the payments."

Keith continued reading, flipping through the pages slowly until Hanna thought she'd expire from anticipation. Higher Grounds couldn't survive another season like the previous three. They'd already made every possible cutback. If she couldn't find a way to increase profits, the lodge didn't stand a chance. She resisted the urge to massage her temples.

Keith cleared his throat and ran a hand through his thinning hair. His expression divulged the dreaded answer. "Given the lack of profit over the last three years, no bank could take this risk. I'm sorry, Hanna, I don't see how I can do this." Regret seasoned his words but did little to lessen their impact.

"Isn't there something you can do? I know I can increase business if I just had the capital to advertise, but I can't do that without the loan."

"Does your grandmother have anything put away?"

She'd already jogged down that path. Gram had a pittance for retirement, and the way things were going, she'd need every bit of it. Hanna's parents were in no shape to contribute either, and neither of her sisters was in a position to help. Paula and her husband, David, were too deeply in debt with that huge house of theirs, and Natalie and Keith had their own bills as well, especially since Natalie had quit work to stay home with their boys. Hanna shook her head, searching his eyes for some sign of concession and not finding it. "Gram's not doing well." She winced inwardly. She'd promised herself she wouldn't resort to this.

His forehead furrowed again. "Is she sick? Why didn't you say something, Hanna?"

Guilt flooded over her. She ducked her head, toying with her leather purse strap. "No. I shouldn't have said anything. She just hasn't been herself lately." A glance at his face revealed skepticism. "Really, it's nothing to worry about."

What would she do now? How could she go home and tell Gram it was over? That Higher Grounds couldn't pay its bills, that they had no money in reserve, that the business her grandparents had started would go under?

She couldn't.

"We've never been late with a payment, Keith; you know we have excellent credit." She hated to beg, but the thought of facing Gram emboldened her.

"I know you do, but—" He paused and released a sigh that seemed to come from his toes, then he flipped to another page and studied the numbers.

Her breathing stopped. Was he reconsidering?

"Are you sure Gram isn't willing to sell?" he asked. "The profit would be enough for her to live very comfortably."

"No. She wants me to save it. It's important to her. To me. And she wants the property to be passed on to me and Nat and Paula. As an inheritance."

He rubbed his hand over his jaw line. "I'll tell you what. I'll give it some thought, talk to my loan committee and see what we can do. But I can't make any promises, Hanna."

Tingles darted through her as oxygen once again pumped through her body in massive doses. She extended her hand across the desk. "Thank you, Keith. I really appreciate this."

He stood, returning her handshake. "I should have an answer for you in a few days."

"I'll be waiting."

❖

Hanna tried to be patient, but the next couple of days were agonizing. She stayed busy, though. The chores around the lodge kept her hopping. She cleared away the layer of dead aspen leaves and raked flotsam from the beach area. She was toting a basket of sheets through the main room when the phone rang. She picked it up at the front desk.

"Higher Grounds. May I help you?"

"Yes, this is Meg Dodier from Star One Realty. I was wondering if I might speak with the owner of the lodge, please."

"This is Hanna Landin. My grandmother is the owner, but I'm the manager. How can I help you?"

"Well, I've recently acquired a client who's expressed an interest in your property. I was wondering if you'd ever considered selling."

"Well, no, not really."

"I see. Well my client is prepared to offer quite a bit for the property, Ms. Landin." The woman named an amount that pushed Hanna's eyebrows up a notch. "Would you at least consider the idea?"

"I don't think so, but thanks for calling."

"I'd appreciate it if you'd run the offer past the owner. She might feel differently."

"She doesn't. I do wish you the best of luck with your client, though."

She hung up the phone, but before she could even retrieve the laundry basket, the phone rang again. This time it was her sister.

"Hey," Nat said. "Just wanted to let you know I talked to Keith last night about the loan thing."

"What'd he say? I've been dying over here."

"He's been quiet the last couple of days, and I couldn't get much out of him. Doesn't like to talk about work with me anyway, so . . . anyhow, last night he seemed really pessimistic when I brought up the lodge. Said things didn't look good as far as profits and all that."

Hanna's mood took a dive. "Oh no. It doesn't sound like he's going to do it."

"Well, wait a minute. After that, I started talking all about your plan for the lodge, the advertising and trekker and everything. I told him about how good you are at that stuff, about how you were always in charge of planning activities and fund-raisers in high school. Remember that mega–garage sale fund-raiser? Anyway, I told him how successful you were and how you always achieved everything you put your mind to."

"What'd he say?"

"Well, mostly he just kept reading the newspaper, but I think he heard some of it. He seemed more optimistic about it when I turned in for the night."

"Oh, I hope so. Hey, would you believe a Realtor just called? Someone is interested in buying this property."

"Really? I wonder why someone would want an old lodge that's in the red. No offense."

"Thanks. No, I think they just wanted the property. They'd probably rip the building right down." She told Nat the offer.

Nat gasped. "Wow, Hanna, are you sure you don't want to at least consider that?"

"I can't believe you'd even say that."

A click sounded on the phone.

"Oh, I have another call," Nat said. "You know I didn't mean anything by that, right?"

"I know. I'm just stressing."

They said good-bye, then Hanna grabbed the laundry basket and started toward the laundry room.

A glossy brochure on the edge of the dining room table caught her attention. The words *Majestic Mountain Retreat* stopped her. Hanna dropped the basket and reached for the pamphlet. She flipped through the pages, absently counting them as she went. Color photos and graphics of the Tetons and Jenny Lake arranged in eye-appealing order lay flat on the page, interspersed with recommendations of former guests. It was wonderful. It was awful.

"Mrs. Eddlestein?" Hanna called absently into the kitchen, then began reading the introductory paragraph on page 2. *Founded in 1982 . . . privately owned . . .*

She raised her voice a notch. "Mrs. Eddlestein?" The housekeeper was kneading a lump of dough, a denim apron hugging her Aunt Bee figure.

"Mrs. Eddlestein!"

The woman turned with a surprised smile. "No need to shout, dear."

Hanna's emotions teetered between aggravation and amusement. She bellowed her question. "Where did this brochure come from?"

The housekeeper swept a knuckle across her cheek, leaving a trail of flour. "The Wilmingtons left it behind."

Great, they'll probably stay there next trip. And why not? The ad was impressive. Four pages, full-color, the works.

She breathed a prayer that her plan for increasing business this summer would work. "Maybe we should have a new brochure done up."

"We have a brochure?"

Hanna sighed. "The one on green paper."

"That's not a brochure, dear; that's a flier."

She scanned the list of amenities and services on the back cover. Two restaurants and a lounge, an indoor and outdoor pool, laundry facilities, a children's program, horseback riding, planned activities. No wonder everyone visiting the Tetons stayed there. *She* wanted to stay there.

"Any word on the loan, dear?"

Hanna shook her head. "I'm starting to get worried."

The woman shook her head and turned back to her dough.

"What's wrong?" Hanna asked.

Mrs. Eddlestein's eyes skittered to the Majestic brochure in Hanna's hands, then she sighed. "Honey, do you really think it's worth it? Taking out that big loan? The Majestic is so popular, and I just worry that you and your Gram have taken on too much."

"You know how much this lodge means to us. It's worth everything we're risking and more."

Hanna flung the offending piece of literature onto the table. "Besides, what would we do without you around to cook and dispense advice?"

Mrs. Eddlestein flopped a flour-coated hand in her direction. "Oh posh, you'd get along just fine without me."

Hanna smiled, then hefted the basket and strode to the laundry room. She pulled the washer knob with a click, starting the flow of water, and carefully dispensed a capful of detergent.

Her grandmother appeared with a wad of sheets and began stuffing them in the washer. "No sense in doing half a load, I always say." Her voice crackled with age.

"Thanks, Gram."

The woman patted her granddaughter's back, then disappeared into the kitchen.

She heard Gram address Mrs. Eddlestein over the gush of water. "I'm going to get the mail."

Hanna cringed; Gram had gotten the mail twenty minutes ago.

The phone rang as she closed the washer lid.

"It's for you, Hanna," Mrs. Eddlestein said. In a stage whisper, she added, "I think it's that brother-in-law of yours."

Gram was slipping into her cardigan, and Hanna laid a hand on her arm. "Today's mail is on the table, Gram."

Hanna picked up the phone. "Hello?"

"Hi, Hanna, it's Keith."

Her stomach slid down to her toes. "Hi there." She gripped the phone and squeezed her eyes shut. "Please tell me you have good news."

"Well, you're in luck. I do. The committee approved. We just have to sign all the papers."

The breath she didn't know she'd held rushed from her lungs. "You're kidding."

"Nope. It's going to happen."

"Oh, Keith, thank you so much. I know no other bank would do this for me."

"Don't be too thankful, Hanna. The loan committee wants to shorten the mortgage to twenty years instead of thirty. So even though you're getting a killer interest rate, your payments will actually go up."

Her nerves faltered. "Oh."

"It's a risk. You'll have to increase business by about 38 percent over last year. If you can't make your payments, you'll be worse off than ever because you'll lose the lodge altogether."

"I know, but that won't happen."

They talked about a few details, set up a time to sign papers, then she thanked Keith again before hanging up.

"We got it?" Gram asked.

"We got it!"

Mrs. Eddlestein came over for a group hug, and they all ended up with flour on their clothes.

"What were you talking to Keith about when you said, 'That won't happen'?" Gram asked.

"He was just reminding me what would occur if we can't make our payments. But don't worry; we'll be fine."

She refused to even consider the thought. Because the consequences were too awful.

CHAPTER TWO

Micah Gallagher stowed his gear in the equipment shed and followed the bald path that led to his secluded cabin. The mammoth Tetons formed a backdrop for the cottage, rising from the valley floor, their snowcapped peaks beckoning the tourists. The distant view awed him, but nothing compared to the thrill of scaling the rocky inclines to the crests.

He entered his one-room cabin, unbuttoning his shirt as he went. Silence hung in the stale air, and he remembered his roommate was gone on his own climb for a couple of days.

He slid out of his dusty jeans and turned on the shower full blast. Stepping under the spray, he let four days of grit swirl down the drain.

When his boss had asked him to lead the Majestic's owner and his son on an expedition up Grand Teton, he'd had no idea what he was in for. The men had expected him to cater to them like a nanny, but serving with a smile had worn a hole in his dignity.

He'd been handpicked for the excursion, though, so he couldn't afford to disappoint his boss. Mr. Woodrow was set on impressing the owner with every facet of the well-oiled Majestic. Micah had done his job well, and Mr. Woodrow would be pleased. The owner and his son had sung his praises all the way back to the hotel and were no doubt soaking in the hot tub of their owner's suite at this very moment.

He stood under the warm spray, reveling in the hot prickles that massaged his skin. The temperature was just the way he liked it—hot enough to soften tar. Feeling clean was a luxury he missed on overnight trips. After a quick shave, he'd be a new man. A flick of the knob stopped the flow of water, and he stepped through the billowing steam, securing a big Majestic towel around his waist. Shoving aside Gregg's toiletries, he swiped at the foggy mirror and towel-dried his black hair. Soon the electric razor's buzzing filled the tiny bathroom, and four days' worth of stubble were whisked off his jaw. He finger-combed his hair as he stepped across the threshold into the main room, his mind already fixed on lunch.

A woman posed on the sofa. He stopped cold. Fran's red hair caught the lamplight, sending copper highlights dancing with each slight movement. Her silky blouse dipped low on her bosom, showing more than he had a right to see.

He clutched his towel, suddenly afraid it would slip off and leave him exposed.

"Hope you don't mind me letting myself in," she said.

"What are you doing here?" He tucked the towel firmly at his waist.

Mrs. Woodrow stood and pressed imaginary wrinkles from her slacks. Her earrings glittered in the light. "Did you miss me?"

"Nothing's changed, Fran. I want you to leave." He walked to the door and opened it.

She approached, but stopped directly in front of him. "No, you don't." The cloying scent of her perfume brushed his nostrils.

"You're a married woman." He skirted her and walked to the closet, trying to put space between them. Once there, he ripped a T-shirt from a wire hanger.

She followed. "Why don't you forget all that religious stuff for once, hmm, Micah? You won't regret it."

He felt the heat of her body on his bare back. His mouth tasted of sand, gritty and dry. There was a time he'd have bedded her before she'd issued a vocal invitation. The look she'd given him would've been enough, married or not. But that was before. He turned and addressed her firmly. "Go home, Fran."

Desperation glimmered in her emerald eyes, and her full lips puckered in a red, sensuous pout. "Go home to what? Ben doesn't care about me. All he cares about is that boring hotel. I'm just shriveling there, with nothing to do all day. I want some intelligent company—someone who appreciates me, someone to hold me."

He may as well have been holding her, as close as she was standing. He draped the shirt over his shoulder and grasped her arms firmly, hoping to get through to her. "You've got to stop this."

Instead, her fingers slithered from his abdomen to his chest in a quick, suggestive move.

"Micah?" A deep voice boomed through the open doorway.

He abruptly released Fran's arms. Judging by her sudden gasp, she'd recognized the squat silhouette of her husband filling the doorway.

Micah's feet seemed to be cemented to the floor even as Fran stepped away.

The manager's body stiffened, though Micah couldn't read his expression, silhouetted in the door as he was.

"How ironic," Mr. Woodrow's voice was disturbingly calm. "I'd come to tell you what a good job you did, Micah. It seems you've been doing a good job on my wife as well."

"Really, Benjamin—"

"Save your breath, Fran," his manager said. He nailed Micah with a look. "Pack your bags. I want you out of here tonight."

Hanna picked up the receiver and greeted the caller, who turned out to be a woman wanting to reserve two rooms the following week. Over the past several weeks, her national advertising had been placed and calls were trickling in steadily.

Hanna answered the woman's questions, and when Gram entered the office, setting a mug of coffee at her fingertips, she smiled her thanks. She marked the reservations calendar with the woman's name and returned the phone to its cradle.

"Another reservation? Wonderful!" Gram said.

"Umm."

"What's the matter?"

She'd thought their problems were over now that the bank had extended a loan. Instead, she felt the pressure of the higher payment like a vise around her throat.

"Mrs. Leavenworth, the lady on the phone, was interested in a guided mountain trip. She saw our ad in the *Travel America* magazine, the one that promoted our trekking guide. Her husband and three teenage boys want to do an overnighter up Grand Teton next week."

"Still haven't found anyone?"

She tucked in the corner of her mouth. "You saw them, Gram. One of them was barely out of adolescence, with no experience, and that Hank guy gave me the creeps. I haven't found someone to oversee the watercraft either."

"We still have another week before the season starts. Are the help-wanted ads still running?"

"Yes." Hanna took a sip of coffee. "We might be able to make do without the watercraft person for a while, but we need the trekker right away."

Gram patted her arm. "God will provide the right man, child."

"Well, he's not going to blow in on the wind, so I guess I'd better figure out something quick."

"Hello?" The deep voice rumbled into the office from the lobby.

She rounded the corner and stopped short. The man was as masculine as his voice. A strong jaw line rescued his face from mediocrity, and his body looked as if it had been chiseled from Petzoldt Ridge. She squelched the automatic rush of anxiety. "May I help you?"

"Hope so. I'd like to talk to the manager."

She smiled. "That would be me." She extended a hand over the counter. "I'm Hanna Landin."

He set down his bags and enveloped her hand. "Micah Gallagher."

"What can I do for you?"

His eyes left hers to roam the lodge. She saw it as it would appear to him, the wooden cedar planks weathered to a gray patina, the scarred wooden floor she'd been wanting to refinish. His gaze returned to absorb her in a sea of gray. "I'm looking for work. I'm a mountain guide. I know you don't have a trekker on staff, but I wondered if you'd ever considered it."

Hanna sucked in a breath. She stood for moments in shock while he continued.

"The rates customers pay practically pay a trekker's wages, and it's a big draw for tourists." He seemed to notice her astonishment. "Sorry if I sound pushy—"

"No, not at all." She heard Gram stifling a laugh behind her and introduced her. "Why don't we go into the office?"

Gram caught her eye as she passed. "I think I'll go shut the door." She winked at Hanna. "Seems it's getting mighty windy out there."

Hanna led him into the office. There was strength and control in his movements, a certain masculine grace that showed body awareness. Bulk was one thing, grace another, and he had both in abundance.

She seated herself behind the desk. "It just so happens I've been looking for a climbing guide. Do you have a résumé?"

"No, sorry, I don't. I just stopped here on a whim, but I can tell you I have five years' experience at the Majestic, and I've been lead climber the last three. I can give you references."

She handed him a pad of paper and ink pen. "Please do." She studied him as he wrote awkwardly with a left-handed grip. He had the dark coloring of someone who worked outdoors, and his black lashes swept the top of his cheekbone giving him a boyish appearance.

A WWJD bracelet dangled from his wrist. A Christian. This seemed too good to be true, his stopping by just when she was in desperate need of a mountain guide. *Thank You, God.*

"May I ask why you left your job at the Majestic?"

His pen stopped midword, and his countenance fell as his eyes flickered with something akin to anxiety. He rubbed his jaw. She didn't need to be an expert in body language to see that the question had caught him off guard.

"I have a good track record at the Majestic and never had a customer complaint, but . . ." He looked at the pen he rolled between his fingers. "Although my reviews were excellent, the manager and I had some . . . personal differences."

Personal differences? What did that mean? Her mind spun with suspicion.

"I'd prefer you not call him for a reference."

She weighed the suspicious information against the bracelet, evidence of his Christianity. For all she knew, he could be a thief or worse. She couldn't hire him to work with her guests when he was so evasive. She needed someone she could trust implicitly; after all, he would be taking her guests on overnight trips. A wave of disappointment swept over her.

"Look, I can see you're uncomfortable about this, so I'll just tell you straight out." He took a deep breath and let it out in a puff. "The manager's wife had a . . . a thing for me."

She quirked a brow and watched a flush climb from the crew neck of his black T-shirt to his cheekbones.

He held his hands palm out. "I never touched the woman, at least, not in that way, but she showed up in my room, and Mr. Woodrow caught her there and just assumed . . . well, you can imagine."

He ducked his head, avoiding her gaze, but instead of evasiveness, she sensed embarrassment. The man could probably have his pick of women. She wondered if he had considered his boss's wife off-limits or if he had merely found her unattractive. If he was even telling the truth. She watched him rub his jaw again. Sympathy tugged at her heart. A man who blushed so easily couldn't be that bad. Still, she only had his word.

He finished writing on the pad and handed it to her. "Here's my references. I included two of the climbers at the Majestic so you can get a feel for my abilities. I've climbed many times with both of them. I also included my pastor's number and the man who used to be my foster father."

She took the pad, feeling a smidge better about him.

"Either way, I still need a room for tonight. If you'd like, you can make those calls and let me know later."

"That sounds fine." She led him back to the front desk, signed him in, and gave him a room key. When he left, she went back to her office and looked at the paper again. Even his writing slanted darkly with strength. Her eyes skimmed across the last name on the list. His foster father. She wondered what had become of his real parents.

CHAPTER
THREE

Natalie Coombs flipped the dishwasher lever, sealing the door, and pushed the metal button. As the appliance whirred into action, she lifted Taylor from his high chair and set him down on the other side of the safety gate. "Here you go, baby." She handed him his sipper cup and peeked around the corner to make sure Alex was not into any mischief before heading upstairs to straighten the rooms.

She stooped to retrieve Cheerios along the way, smiling at the way they led to Alex's room like a treasure-hunt trail. A few of them had already been reduced to Cheerio dust by small, bare feet, and she made a mental note to vacuum later in the day. She threw the handful of cereal away in Alex's trash pail, then frowned at the mini Lego blocks scattered across the carpet. For a moment she considered calling him to clean up the mess, then just as quickly dismissed the idea. By the time she convinced him to do it, she could have done it herself and moved on to other things.

After gathering the blocks, she closed the gaping drawers and picked up the pajamas that had Bob the Builder splashed across the fabric. Resisting the urge to remake the lumpy bed, she went to the nursery and changed the crib bedding. That done, she moved on to her bedroom, deposited the dirty laundry into the hamper, and made her own bed. As usual, Keith's side was in chaos, the flat sheet pulled up from the bottom, and the fitted sheet pulled loose from the corner.

Her own side of the king-sized bed hardly looked like anyone had slept in it.

As she placed the last throw pillow on the bed, Taylor squealed unhappily, and she went to peek over the loft rail. "Alex, give him back his blankie."

Her four-year-old turned his wide blue eyes on her. "But, Mommy, Bear wants to take a nap," he protested, pointing at the stuffed animal he'd laid on a pillow on the floor.

"That's Taylor's blanket. You'll have to use something else."

Alex held the blanket out of Taylor's reach, and the baby began crying in earnest.

"Give him back the blanket and get a towel from the closet."

For once Alex obeyed without arguing, and Taylor toddled across the room with his blanket as if nothing had happened.

Natalie retrieved a cotton diaper from the linen closet and returned to her room to dust the light oak furniture. She lifted an eight-by-ten photo of the boys that had been taken the previous summer at Higher Grounds. The Tetons rose in the distance like guardians overlooking the lodge. Taylor was cuddled up on Aunt Hanna's lap, and Alex was behind Aunt Paula with his little hands covering her eyes. The picture had captured such a mix of charm and mischief on Alex's face that she'd had the photo enlarged.

Natalie finished dusting the chest of drawers, then moved on to the window seat, which was not so much a seat as it was a convenient place for Keith to throw his clothes as he undressed. She sighed. She'd promised herself a week ago she was not going to pick up his clothes anymore, but the sight of the growing pile was more than she could take.

She grabbed the shirt on top and began folding. She really shouldn't complain. Keith was a good father and a decent husband. If discarding his clothes in piles was the worst thing he did, she didn't have much to complain about.

She grabbed a handful of plastic hangers and started on the pants, throwing aside a pair that had wrinkled under the pile. She'd never regretted giving up her job as an obstetrics nurse to become a full-time mom. There would be time enough to explore her profession when the boys were grown, or at least in school. She was just glad Keith earned enough at the bank for her to put her career on hold for a few years, although Keith had made it clear he resented her quitting.

Her entire day revolved around the boys, and she knew that Keith sometimes thought her completely out of touch with the rest of the world. How had that happened in four short years? How was it that her identity now seemed to be totally wrapped up in her children?

It seemed Keith had managed to keep his individual self. Of course, he had the bank, which consumed more of his time than she liked.

Their marriage had suffered the most. Somewhere along the way, they had ceased being each other's partner. Sometimes it seemed as if they were simply two people committed to the raising of their children, as if they were more like roommates than marriage partners.

Natalie breathed a laugh and shook her head. For heaven's sake, what right did she have to complain? So her marriage was lacking in the intimacy department. All relationships went through ups and downs, and this was such a busy time in their lives. It was only natural their relationship would suffer a little. Between Keith's work schedule, Alex's swimming classes, and her own involvement in Marriage Enrichment, just getting together was a feat. To say nothing of going out on a date. Who had time to find a responsible sitter?

She finally reached the bottom of the pile and retrieved hangers for the last two pair of pants. Picking up the khakis she'd bought him for Christmas, she folded the pants at the creases and slung them over the hanger, arranging them just so. As she did, something fell to the ground, plunking softly on the carpet. She held the pants aside and looked down. It only took a moment for her to recognize the small square package between her stockinged feet. Disbelief fanned from her stomach outward to every nerve in her body, and the brand name printed on the white package blurred as every part of her body screamed in denial.

Micah kicked off his boots, swept back the quilted cover, and fell onto the crisp, white sheets. When his head sank into the pillow, he grabbed the one beside it and stacked. The mattress was soft for a hotel bed, much softer than the one in his cabin had been.

He allowed himself a moment of self-pity. He'd still be at his cabin if not for Fran. The woman just didn't know how to take no for an answer. Lord knew, he'd used the word often enough where she was concerned. So much for integrity. It had gotten him nothing but fired. Five long years he'd put in at the Majestic, and what did he have to show for it? Not even a reference.

He hadn't planned to stop here after he'd packed up and driven off; he had planned to go into Jackson and buy a newspaper. But something had pulled him here. *Do You have some purpose for me here?* He paused, staring at the beamed ceiling, waiting for an answer. None came.

Probably not. He'd seen the skepticism all over the manager's face. She didn't trust him, and he couldn't blame her. Maybe he shouldn't have told her about the situation with his former boss, but if he hadn't, she would've either called Ben or turned him down. The way he saw it, he hadn't had much choice.

Oh well, it's in Your hands now, God. If there were some purpose for him here, he'd get the job. If not, he'd drive into Jackson tomorrow and comb the help-wanted ads. He wasn't too worried. He had money in the bank, enough to last a few months anyway.

Besides, he wasn't sure how he felt about working for a woman. An attractive one at that. Several years ago he'd have loved the situation, would've taken advantage of it. But he was different now.

When his stomach rumbled, he realized he'd missed lunch. He sat up and rooted through his duffel bag for the apple he'd stuffed inside. Before he found it, he saw his Recovery Journal and pulled it out for later. His weekly meeting was tomorrow night, and he still hadn't completed his assignment—had been dreading it all week. He'd come to realize that getting over his past meant reliving things he'd rather forget, digging up the memories piece by piece and dissecting them until they were no longer painful. But it was hard. Agonizing. By now you'd think he'd have worked through it all, but there always seemed to be more sludge beneath the still waters.

He bit off a chunk of apple and forced himself to think about the weekly topic. His earliest memory. He didn't need to think long. It had been just after his fifth birthday, at Christmastime.

He'd ripped a branch from a straggly pine and scurried back to his building, taking the stairs as fast as his legs would carry him. The stale odor of cigarettes barely registered in his brain as he passed through the tiny apartment. Once in the kitchen, he clambered onto the counter and rooted through the cabinets for a clean glass. Finding none, he grabbed a plastic cup from the sink, filled it with water, then set the cup on the counter.

When he inserted the branch, the cup toppled, sloshing water over the counter. Maybe he needed a heavier vase. He rifled through the dirty dishes and, not finding anything, opened the refrigerator door. Kitchen light flooded into the dark compartment, and his eyes spied a brown bottle on the bottom shelf. A smile tugged at his lips as he withdrew it and opened it expertly with a bottle opener. Pouring the amber liquid into the sink, he watched in fascination as foam bubbled up around the drain. After filling the bottle with water, he stuffed the pine bough through the narrow neck and smiled in satisfaction when it remained upright.

He held it aloft. "What do you think, Toby?" His mom got mad when he talked to his friend, but that was only because she couldn't see him.

Micah carried his treasure to the floor-model TV and set it carefully on top. Perfect. Now for some decorations. He rummaged through drawers and found thread, scissors, paper, and crayons. "We'll just make our own things. I'll use the scissors first, then you can have them." He pulled out a chair for Toby and sat down beside him.

21

A short time later, Micah stood back from the tree admiring his work. "Not bad, huh, Toby?" Crayon-waxed paper stars and candy canes dangled by thread from the branches. His smile widened with approval. He wondered if the baby would be born by Christmas and if it would like looking at his tree.

He watched TV the remainder of the afternoon, occasionally glancing up to admire his tree. When the news came on, Micah knew it was almost time for his mother to come home. At the first commercial break, he heard the keys twist easily in the lock. Had he forgotten to bolt the door?

His mother appeared, her brown hair damp and frizzy with rain and her tan coat splotched with wet dots. Her big belly poked out between the buttons. "How many times have I told you not to leave this apartment?"

"I just went out for a minute. Look what I—"

"Not now, Micah."

She dropped her purse and went straight to the kitchen. He heard the sucking sound of the refrigerator door opening, followed by rattling sounds as she knocked around its contents. Her work shoes tapped across the linoleum. She rounded the corner and glared at him. "Where is it? I know I had another beer in there. What did you do with it?" Her words were laced with frenzy.

Fear stiffened his spine. He'd heard that tone often enough to know he was in trouble. Why had he forgotten she always wanted a drink after work? Why had he used her last one? Maybe when she saw the tree, she wouldn't be angry anymore. "Look, Mommy. I made a Christmas tree for the baby."

Her wild eyes found his creation. She walked with slow, deliberate steps to the TV and snatched up the bottle, flinging the branch to the floor. The paper ornaments fluttered behind the branch like a kite tail.

She held the bottle to her nose and inhaled. "What did you do with the beer?"

"I . . . I poured it in the sink."

Her eyes narrowed, and her mouth twisted in that way he hated. "That was my last beer! I don't get paid 'til Thursday, you know that, and you wasted my last beer."

When she turned and strolled to her purse, he held his breath. She thrust her hand inside and withdrew a cigarette. As she lit it, the tip flickered with an angry orange light. His mother smirked, her eyes slicing into him like a cold knife as she puffed a stream of smoke.

Fear snaked through his body. He stood slowly to his feet. She advanced, mute anger blazing in her eyes. His feet propelled him backward, until his back connected with the wall. When she inhaled again, his gaze fixed on the flaming eye. As he stared, it blurred into a fiery glow. His breath came in short gasps. Micah squeezed his eyes shut, tried futilely to embed himself into the wall, scarcely felt the warm, wet flow down his legs.

The rest of the memory had been mercifully blocked from his mind, but his body still carried the scars from that day. He forced himself to grab the pen off the nightstand and relive the memory again.

CHAPTER
FOUR

Hanna settled into her desk chair and started a to-do list: help with dinner cleanup, get groceries, cancel the help-wanted ad for the trekker.

Satisfaction flowed through her as she mentally checked off the task of finding a guide. That was one big burden off her mind. And the phone calls she'd made this afternoon totally relieved her of all skepticism about Micah Gallagher. The pastor had great things to say about the man. Words like *integrity* and *hardworking* had been used to describe him. And the fact that he attended church every week further convinced her that he wasn't a thief or mass murderer.

She had almost decided against calling the foster father, but her inner sense of security demanded she be extradiligent about screening her new climber. The foster father had reiterated everything the pastor had said and had added *independent* and *loyal* to the list of adjectives describing him. Micah's climber friends were both away on trips of their own, but the receptionist confirmed that Micah had been lead trekker for the past few years.

She would offer Micah the job this afternoon if she saw him again. He obviously needed a place to stay, so she'd just need to subtract the cost of lodging from the figure she'd planned to pay. Having him right on site was a positive, anyway. If guests decided on a spur-of-the-moment trip, he'd be available. He might not even want the job when he heard what she paid. His salary was probably higher at the Majestic than she could afford.

Part of her almost wished he would turn down the job—the part of her that was drawn to him. It had been a long time since she'd been drawn to any man, and her one and only experience with a relationship made her even more timid about having Micah around all the time. In many ways it had been a typical college romance, but Hanna had only been able to open her heart to a point. Jess had been patient, but even after a year's time, she'd not been able to endure his touch. Understandably, Jess grew weary of feeling rejected.

The relationship likely would have ended on its own, but when Gram needed help with the lodge, she'd taken the opportunity to escape, putting college on hold indefinitely. Jess had seemed almost relieved, but not nearly as relieved as she had been. It had been too soon, she told herself. She just needed time.

Avoiding relationships had been easy these past few years at the lodge. There weren't many young, single men around, and those who did come stayed briefly. Even her church lacked eligible bachelors and was filled with seniors and middle-aged married couples. No, there hadn't been much opportunity for dating, and Hanna was glad.

But now that would change. At least it would if Micah took the job. He'd be living on the grounds, eating meals with them when he wasn't on a climb. What worried her the most was this attraction she felt.

She breathed a laugh. She'd just been without a male companion for too long. Maybe she'd forgotten what it was like to be around a man. But she knew it was more than that. Micah had a certain presence. A strength. And that strength drew her and repelled her at the same time.

You're thinking too hard, girl. She suddenly remembered her intentions to work on the van and added it to the list. She had to get the thing running before next week when she started shuttling guests to and from the airport. Almost every registrant had requested the service when she offered it. And she'd gotten the used van for a bargain, knowing she could fix the problem.

After dinner Hanna gathered her tools and went to work.

Micah slowed to a walk and took his heart rate. He was within his zone. His body had long ago acclimated to the high altitude, and now he could easily run five miles a day. Except for days when he climbed. That was a workout in itself.

He liked the Higher Grounds property. The still lake and lack of people gave an ambience of solitude and peace. Birch, willow, and oak trees dotted the area, and a fresh cushion of pine needles layered the ground. It was a refreshing change from the bustling Majestic property. He wondered if this would be his last day here or if it would be the first of many. He didn't like having his future up in the air and was anxious to know what Hanna had decided. He'd checked the office before his run, but she wasn't there.

When he came to the drive, he turned and slowed his pace a bit, allowing his heart rate to come down gradually. The gravel crunched under his running shoes, joining the orchestra of warbling bird calls.

Rounding a bend, he saw a pair of denim-clad legs protruding from beneath a Chevy van. Maybe he would know where Micah could find the manager. "Excuse me." The body inched from under the vehicle. "Could you tell me where I can find—" The body had a head, and it was a woman's. Hanna's. "Oh. It's you."

She smiled, and the streak of grease settled into the crease on one side of her mouth. "Hi." She sat up, wiped her hands on a rag, and took the hand up he offered. "I'm glad I caught you. I wanted to talk to you about the job."

Her face was devoid of makeup, a fact he'd missed earlier. But her dark complexion and wide eyes didn't need it. "Yeah, that's what I wanted to talk to you about."

"I called your references, and you come highly recommended."

She sounded like there was a *but* coming, so he said nothing as her lashes swept down over golden green eyes.

"But I'm afraid I won't be able to pay you what you're worth." She met his gaze firmly. "I can offer room and board, of course, but the additional income won't be what you're used to." She quoted a figure, and Micah noted the way she crossed her arms defensively. She was expecting him to turn down her offer or perhaps dicker with her over his salary.

"Actually, I don't need much. A roof over my head, food to eat, and very little else. I accept your offer."

Surprise was evident in the way her finely arched brows inched upward. "Oh." Then a grin tugged at her lips. "Well, let's get you settled then."

He followed her to the lodge, his eyes skimming her trim figure from the ponytail to her Levi's. Long legs for her petite stature.

He forced himself to look away. At the big oak, at the rustic lodge, at anything but the alluring sight in front of him. Maybe taking this job wasn't such a good idea. The last thing he wanted was an attachment. When they reached the office, he took a seat across from the desk and watched while she opened her reservations book.

"Your first trip will be next week. I have a family who wants to hike up Grand Teton."

He nodded. He could do that trip blindfolded. "Did you want to have a regular weekly schedule or just go with reservations?"

She asked how they worked it at the Majestic, and he explained their regular schedules.

"That sounds fine. Why don't you work up a tentative schedule with both day trips and overnighters, the most popular treks, and I'll take a look at it. How did you schedule days off?"

"I have a standing appointment on Thursday nights, so I always had Thursdays off. Sundays too."

"Why don't you work the schedule around those two days, then, if that's all right with you." She handed him employee papers to fill out.

"Fine." He began filling out the forms.

The phone rang, and she grabbed the cordless. "Higher Grounds, may I help you?"

Micah jotted down his social security number.

"What's wrong, Nat?"

He looked up, and Hanna placed her hand over the mouthpiece and whispered, "Just leave them on my desk when you're done." Then she slipped out the door.

Hanna entered the empty kitchen, letting the louvered doors swing shut behind her. By the sound of her sister's voice, she could tell Natalie was fighting tears. Nat had been rambling about tidying up after lunch, but hadn't yet gotten to the point.

"And it fell out of his pants, right there on the floor. I couldn't believe it when I saw it, Hanna. Why would he do it?" She sounded hysterical.

Hanna's mind spun as she tried to decipher some kind of meaning from her sister's meandering words. "Now, wait, Nat. What fell out of his pants? I'm not following."

"A condom!" The word brought on a flood of tears and sniffles.

Hanna paused in the taut silence.

"I'm on the pill, Hanna!"

Hanna wilted and squeezed her eyes shut. "Oh, Nat."

"We haven't been very close lately. He's been so busy at the bank, and I've been busy with the kids and church, but . . . an affair? How could he?"

She heard the torment in her sister's voice, wished she could take it away. What could she say? "Maybe it hasn't gotten that far yet. The package wasn't empty, was it?"

"No." She sniffled again, and Hanna heard the baby squealing unhappily in the background, then a muffled, "Alex, get off him!"

Nat just didn't deserve this. She would never dream of having an affair. Hanna could hardly believe Keith would either.

"Do you really think he hasn't done anything yet?" Nat asked. "Who could it be? He's never home, and I thought he was working. But what if he wasn't working at all? What if he was spending all that time with *her*?"

Hanna smiled stiffly when Mrs. Eddlestein entered the kitchen, then lowered her voice, ensuring that the hard-of-hearing woman wouldn't hear. "I don't know, sweetie. Could it be someone at the bank?" Hanna tried to recall if she'd seen anyone at the bank when she'd gone to sign papers. No particular woman stood out in her mind.

"There are plenty of women there, but most of them are married or overweight. And you know how Keith feels about extra pounds. At least, on me." She sighed into the phone. "He's lost weight lately himself, and he's been wearing cologne every day!" she said, as if she'd just put two and two together. "Why didn't I see this coming?"

"You had no way of knowing. Your mind doesn't work that way. What about at church? Is there anyone there you can think of?"

"Church? Keith hasn't been to church in weeks." A fresh wave of tears started. "Oh, Hanna, he went out of town two weeks ago! What if he was really with *her*?"

How could You let this happen to Nat, God? And to the boys? "Are you going to ask him?"

"What if he's in love with her? What if he wants to leave us?"

Hanna didn't know what to say. She wasn't married, had never even come close. Who was she to give advice? "Have you thought of calling Mom and Dad? Or Paula?"

"I can't do that. Mom and Dad would never forgive Keith, and he'd never be able to face them again if they knew. And Paula's not exactly the most sympathetic ear in the world. I need advice; that's why I called you."

"I don't know what to say, Nat." Silence crackled between them. She watched Mrs. Eddlestein taking a fresh batch of crescent rolls to the dining room. "You're going to have to ask him what's going on. Maybe there's some other explanation." She could hardly fathom that the man who had risked a sizable loan for her would betray his own wife.

"Do I tell him what I found, or should I just ask if something's going on?"

She rubbed her temple with her free hand. "If you started a discussion about your relationship, do you think he'd open up?"

"He's been so distant lately. Why didn't I see this coming? I can't believe this is happening."

"Let's assume nothing has happened yet. Maybe the relationship has just been heading in that direction, and he wanted to carry protection just to be on the safe side."

"I need to confront him about it. Tell him what I found and see what he says."

Sympathy swelled in Hanna, and she wished she were there to hold her sister and let her cry on her shoulder. "Do you want me to come over?"

She heard Alex begin to wail in the background. "I gotta go, Hanna. Alex bumped his head. I'll call you later."

She said good-bye, then jabbed the off button. *Oh, God. You have to help her.* The words jammed in her mind like cars in rush-hour traffic.

Later that night as Hanna sat behind the computer, she wondered how Nat was doing. Was she confronting Keith even now? *Help her, Lord. Give her the words and the strength she needs to handle this.*

She kept remembering Keith's kindness to her in extending the loan. She knew his loan committee must have looked at it unfavorably, and yet he'd done it anyway. Life could be so complex. She dragged her hands over her face.

The screen saver kicked on, and she realized she'd hardly gotten a thing done. She continued transferring the reservations from the book to their old computer, Methuselah. Even though it was ancient by today's standards, it still worked and even allowed her to access the Internet through free software. She'd recently invested in a program that allowed her to see at a glance how booked they were for any given week or month. Soon, she'd put all the guest information directly into the computer when she took reservations and use the book for backup only.

Gram entered the office. "How are we doing for June?"

Hanna paused her tapping and clicked on the button that would show June. "Here we are." She pointed at the screen. "We're half booked most nights and sold out for the third weekend. Not bad, huh?" Well on the way to the 38 percent increase they needed over last year.

"That's wonderful!" She squeezed Hanna's shoulders. "This is going to work out just fine. All your ideas were just the thing. Thank God for giving me such a brilliant granddaughter!"

"If I were brilliant, I would've done this two years ago."

"Oh, I almost forgot." Gram grabbed a paper from the desk and handed it to her. "There was a young man in while you were grocery shopping. He was interested in the watercraft position, and I had him fill out a . . . oh drat, what's the word?"

"Application?"

"That's it. Anyway, I skimmed it, and it looked pretty good, so I asked him to come back at seven tonight for an interview. I hope that's all right with you."

"Sure, that's great, Gram, thanks." Her grandmother went to the front desk to check in a guest, and Hanna studied the form. Devon Garret was a third-year business student at Central Wyoming and was seeking employment for the summer. That would work out fine since business slowed once fall arrived. He'd been employed at various businesses during previous summers. Why in the world was he interested in the Higher Grounds position? He was overqualified to oversee the watercraft and run the shuttle. When he heard what they were paying, he'd probably scoot right back to the accounting firm where he'd worked last summer. But if he didn't, it would be their gain.

She finished keying in all the guest information and, before she knew it, seven o'clock rolled around. A golden-haired young man arrived, looking to be about her own age and wearing a baby blue polo with white Dockers shorts.

He extended a hand. "Hi, I'm Devon Garret, and I have an appointment with Hanna Landin."

31

She shook his hand, noting his smooth, cool palm. "I'm Hanna. Nice to meet you, Devon. Why don't you come back to the office, and we'll talk."

She took a seat behind the desk and gestured toward an opposite chair. "My grandmother gave me your application, and I've had a chance to review it. Did she fill you in on the nature of the job?"

"I'd be responsible for maintaining the boats and arranging for their rental. I think your ad said something about running an airport shuttle?"

"That's right. Not all the guests require this service. Some of them rent a car and, of course, some of them drive here from their homes. I'm assuming you have a driver's license, and there would be no problem with that?"

His lips curved into a smile. "No problem at all. You'll notice I have experience working with the public."

"Yes, I see that." She set his form aside. "Look, I have to be honest. This job doesn't pay much." She named the figure and noticed he didn't seem surprised. "You've held good positions every summer."

"I've been very lucky in summers past. But this summer is my last break before entering the business world and, quite frankly, I had a heavy course load last semester and will have another heavy load in the fall. I'd really like to take on something less . . . challenging my last free summer."

"Good enough. Do you have your own accommodations, or will you need a room?"

"I have my own."

This was turning out better than she thought. Yesterday she was fretting because she was short two employees, and now the positions were filled with men who were overqualified for their jobs. "I haven't had a chance to call your references, so why don't I just plan on calling you tomorrow and letting you know."

He stood and extended a hand. "Sounds great."

As she watched Devon walk out the door, Hanna felt a great sense of relief. Finally, things seemed to be going their way.

Natalie laid Taylor in his crib and wound up the stuffed bear that would play lullabies for several minutes. "Night-night, baby." She put up the crib rail and walked out, blowing a kiss before she shut the door. Going through the motions.

She'd been doing it all day. Reading books to the boys, doing laundry, kissing boo-boos. Her body was doing all the right things, but her mind was numb. Somehow she'd held the tears at bay. After her phone call with Hanna, she'd pulled herself together and had gone from one activity to the next. Her mind had churned all afternoon with questions. Who could *she* be? When had it started? How far had it gone? How could she have been so blind?

She, volunteer director of Marriage Enrichment. What a laugh. She was arranging for couples to spend weekends away learning how to develop a better marriage, and hers was falling apart at the seams.

How could she have been so stupid? She picked up Alex's clothes from the floor and threw them in the laundry basket. She almost wished she'd kept the boys up for a while. Normally she welcomed the quiet after a hectic day, but tonight she dreaded it. She would have time to think, really think, about what Keith was doing. Was he with her even now? She'd called his private line at seven o'clock, and there had been no answer. Her throat clogged with tears she refused to shed.

How dare he. She'd done nothing but be a good wife and mother. She'd never even looked at another man. No one had been more faithful than she'd been.

She poured herself a glass of orange juice, knowing she needed something in her empty stomach, and headed back to the family room. A framed eight-by-ten of her and Keith on their wedding day caught her eye. She paused to stare disgustedly at it. How naive she'd been. Standing there, face to face with Keith, with rosy cheeks and adoring eyes. And him. Look at him, staring at her with promise in his eyes, making pledges he was now mocking.

She tore the picture from the wall and flung it across the room, spilling her juice in the process. The photo hit the brick fireplace and shattered. Her heart thudded heavily in her chest. She suddenly understood why cartoon characters had smoke coming from their ears when they were angry. There was so much heat and fury in her, it was a wonder her own ears weren't steaming.

"Mommy?" Alex called from his room.

She took a deep breath. "It's all right, honey. Mommy just dropped something. Go to sleep."

"Okay."

Nothing was all right. Her world was falling apart and, with it, the boys' world too. What would become of them if Keith left? She'd have to return to work, for starters.

The mantel clock struck nine and began its chiming. Lately Keith didn't come home until ten or even eleven. When he did, she could never hide her anger. It either manifested itself through barbed replies or stony silence. Neither worked. She could recite his excuses as well as he. *Do you think I want to work this late? Don't you think I'd rather be home, sacked out in front of the TV? Successful businesses don't just happen on their own, you know. I'm doing this for you.*

Ha! What a joke. Rage tore through her like a violent wind, and she set down her half-empty glass before she threw it too. After fishing a towel from the drawer, she got down on the floor to mop up the mess.

What would she say when he came home? How would he react? Would he tell her the truth? Would he tell her who it was? Did she know the woman? *Oh, please, God, don't let it be someone I know.*

She tossed the towel in the washer and went to clean up the shards of glass on the hearth. She picked up the big pieces first, then moved on to the tiny fragments, almost wishing she'd cut her hand. Anything to take her mind off the internal pain she was feeling. She retrieved a broom and trash can and swept the last of the glass slivers into it. If only cleaning up her marriage could be accomplished as easily.

Headlights chased across the expansive living room wall, then she heard the familiar squeak of the garage-door opener. Natalie settled herself on the couch. *Help me, God, please help me.*

The door clicked open, and she waited in silence until Keith rounded the corner. "Hi," he muttered, then proceeded to empty his pockets of change and business cards onto the desk.

Her mind flew back a scarce twelve hours ago when *it* had fallen from his pocket. It seemed like days ago, not hours. She wondered if he had one in his pocket now. *No,* she thought bitterly. *He'd probably already used it.* She observed him with new eyes. Suspicious eyes. His pants hung loosely on his hips, and even his face seemed thinner. Had he lost weight for *her?*

Keith went to the kitchen, and she heard him grabbing a can of soda from the fridge. When he returned, he collapsed in his La-Z-Boy, kicking out the footrest, and flicked on the TV with the remote. Didn't he notice how quiet she was? Did he think her silence was of the I'm-angry-you're-late variety? Couldn't he feel the difference? Couldn't he feel the cold vibrations in the air?

Apparently not. He was already absorbed in a baseball game.

A commercial came on. "Is there anything to eat in there? I'm starving."

"There's meatloaf in the fridge." If he thought she was going to wait on him, he'd better think again. He was just in the kitchen himself, why couldn't he get his own? How could he even talk about food when he was betraying her?

Her hand reached down, and she felt for the evidence in her pocket. A visual aid, in case he claimed ignorance. How should she start? With an accusation? What if by some miracle he had another logical reason for carrying around a condom?

No, not an accusation. If she were somehow mistaken, he would never forgive her.

"I hung up your clothes in the bedroom today." Somehow her voice sounded normal, though her heart felt as though it might explode.

He took a sip of Coke. "Is that what's got you so upset?"

She gave him an ounce of credit for noticing something was wrong. "Look, I'll try to do better, okay?"

"Something fell out of your pants." She didn't look at him but saw him go still in her peripheral vision.

"What's that?"

She fished into her pocket and withdrew the packet, then held it up and met his eyes.

His lips parted, surprise flashed in his eyes. Fear. Just for a moment, then defenses kicked in. "Hey, Nat, it's not what you think."

"It's not a condom?" Sarcasm wormed into her tone. "Gosh, I must've misread the package." She looked closely at it, pretending to read it. "Ultra thin latex condom. Nope, guess not." Fury seasoned her words, and she reined it in. Get the confession first, then she'd turn loose on him. Maybe if she remained calm, he'd be more likely to confess.

"That's not what I meant. I meant it's not mine."

"Those weren't your pants?"

"Of course, they were my pants. The condom's not mine."

"Then whose is it?"

Did he falter for a moment, or was it her imagination? "It's Dale's."

"What are you doing with it?"

"We played racquetball last week, remember? It fell out of his wallet when we were getting dressed, then by the time I found it on the floor, he'd already left to go on his date. I tried to catch up with him in the parking lot, but he'd already driven away."

She wanted to believe it. It was an unlikely story, but, oh, how she wanted to believe it. "Why don't we give Dale a call and straighten this out?"

"He's in Dallas this week, and I don't have his number."

How convenient. And no doubt Keith will get hold of Dale before I have a chance to question him. Why won't he just tell me the truth and get it over with?

Keith snapped in the footrest and came to her, sinking into the sofa beside her. She refrained from looking at him. Doubt swelled in her mind, and she refused to give in to the hope that hovered just above the surface of her heart. She forced herself to be objective. It was unlikely he was telling the truth. Yet she couldn't condemn him outright. What if she was wrong?

"Look at me, doll." His voice rumbled deeply with the pet name she loved. The one he hadn't called her for years.

She turned and met his gaze, seeing him through a veil of tears.

"I'm not seeing someone else. I swear." His blue eyes penetrated her. "I've just been working long hours. You know things have been rough at the bank. If you can just hang in there awhile longer . . ."

He looked so sincere, sounded so genuine. She looked away. She couldn't forget the moment she'd seen the condom between her feet. If it had been Dale's, why would Keith have kept it? Why not just toss it? Besides, Dale was not one to sleep around. And he'd only just begun dating the woman a few weeks ago.

She drilled him with her gaze. "I called your private line tonight, and you weren't there."

He looked guilty. "I had to go to the store. We were out of coffee filters."

"What time did you go?"

His mouth tightened in a straight line. "I don't know, Nat. Man, you sound like a shrew." He jumped off the couch and snatched up his Coke, storming toward the kitchen.

So much for the loving patience he'd demonstrated moments ago. Now he was angry and defensive. And he hadn't given her an answer about the time of his errand.

Moments later he stormed up the stairs without a word, and Natalie knew she would get no answers tonight.

CHAPTER FIVE

Micah held the door open for Hanna, and she slipped through, waiting for him to follow. She surveyed the vast array of sporting equipment, overwhelmed by the size of the store and the variety of goods.

She followed him with a shopping cart back to the camping area, stopping just short of bumping him in the back. "Sorry."

"Do you have a list?" he asked.

She tucked in one side of her mouth. "I was hoping you could show me what we need."

"Sure." He led her to a wall crowded with backpacks, then proceeded to point out the advantages and disadvantages of styles and brands.

Hanna flipped over a price tag and winced at the price. "We're kind of on a budget here, but I want the gear to be safe and durable."

They settled on backpacks, then Hanna went to get the flashlights while Micah moved on to the climbing gear. She stared at the shelves stacked with flashlights. Good grief. There was such a thing as having too many choices. Should she get the big six-volt ones, or would they be too heavy to lug around? Maybe she should get the industrial-sized one for Micah and smaller ones for the guests. She took a step toward the sporting-goods area, intent on asking Micah, when she noticed a woman standing with him.

She stopped and watched for a moment, wondering who the woman was. Micah's back was to her, but she could see the lady's face. Her red hair was set in a style popular among the twenties crowd, but

Hanna suspected the woman was well into her thirties. The tennis outfit she wore showed off a pair of legs that could've passed for a teenager's.
The woman laughed and laid a hand on Micah's bicep, where it lingered
too long to be a friends-only gesture.

Just then, Micah turned and pointed to Hanna, and she quickly
grabbed a flashlight and pretended to read the label. She felt heat infuse
her face as she realized they'd probably seen her staring. A quick glance
showed that the couple was once again engaged in conversation. Was *she*
Micah's Thursday night appointment? He'd never mentioned a girlfriend, but they hadn't really talked about their personal lives.

The woman had moved closer to Micah and was brushing something off his sleeve. Micah repositioned his arm causing hers to fall away.
The smile fell from the woman's face, and her chin raised a notch.

Stop being so nosy, Hanna. Honestly. She forced her attention back to
the shelves in front of her but couldn't miss the rumble of Micah's voice,
then the hiss of an angry woman. *Don't look. It's none of your business.*

Big flashlights, little flashlights, waterproof flashlights . . . batteries.
Don't forget the batteries.

The low, angry tones of the woman's voice reached her; then, in her
peripheral vision, she saw the woman storm away. What's this? A lover's
quarrel? *None of my business, none of my business.*

Minutes later, Micah approached and dumped an armful of ropes
and harnesses in the cart. He helped her select the flashlights, then they
moved on to the tents.

It was a much quieter Micah on the ride back to the lodge. During
the silence Hanna sought for a way to ask him who the woman was.
Why do you care so much anyway?

The thought jerked her mind to a momentary standstill. *Yeah, why
do I care so much?*

Hanna tossed to her other side and squinted at the red digital numbers
on her alarm clock. Twelve-sixteen. She kicked off the covers and

flopped to her stomach. She felt like she was in junior high and tomorrow was her first day of school. *It's just Memorial Day weekend, Hanna, get a grip.*

But it was much more than that. It was the beginning of tourist season, and the lodge was booked fully for the first time in almost two years. It had always been one of the most popular weekends, but this one marked a new start. Tomorrow they would kick off the plan they'd been working on for six months, ready or not.

And they *were* ready. So why did she feel uneasy? Devon was scheduled to pick up the guests from the airport. Micah wouldn't have his first climb until Monday, when he would do a two-dayer up Mount Moran, but his schedule was set and advertised in the front lobby. She and Gram had prepared all the empty rooms today—make that yesterday—and Mrs. Eddlestein had made scones and biscotti to be served at tea in the afternoon. The van was up and running, and she had finished entering all the customer data into the computer.

The computer. Had she saved all the information she'd entered on disk? Surely she had. She'd been burned before, so she *always* saved now. It was routine for her; that's why she didn't remember doing it.

But could she honestly recall putting in the disk and clicking on save? She glared at the clock. Twelve-seventeen. She knew she wouldn't go to sleep until she checked. At any rate, she wasn't sleepy, so she crept out of bed and slipped into her terry robe. Once out in the living room of the suite she shared with Gram, she peeked in on her, pleased to see that the excitement of the new season hadn't kept her grandmother awake.

Hanna grabbed the key off the hook and closed the door softly behind her. She pulled her collar tight, feeling awkward about traipsing around the hallway in her nightclothes. There were only two guests for the night, though, and they'd turned in before Hanna.

Night sounds seeped through the log walls, reminding Hanna she was alone. The hall shone dimly with the Exit sign at the end of the corridor, but she turned into the main room of the lodge and headed toward her office. The Exit light by the main door was burned out, leaving the room in darkness. Her heart rate automatically accelerated, and she pushed back the terror that clung to her like a wet cloth.

Thwack! Her thigh bumped what she assumed was the end table, causing the lamp to teeter. She reached out and managed to grab the shade before the whole thing toppled over, then rubbed the spot just over her knee.

When she rounded the counter, she saw a dim light sweeping across the office. She stopped short. Then she breathed a laugh of relief. Of course. It was only the light of the screen saver flashing on the shadowed walls.

She flipped the light switch, grateful for the overhead light that flickered on. She took a seat behind the desk and clicked on the program's icon. The gentle hum of the computer, unnoticed during the busier daytime hours, seemed unnaturally loud in the quiet of the night. She heard a car pass on the road outside and wondered what someone was doing out at this hour on a weeknight. Finally, she retrieved the information she'd typed in and slipped a disk into the drive to save it.

A thump sounded in the main room, and her hand stilled on the mouse. What was that? A shuffling sound sent her heart into wild palpitations. It was probably just a guest getting up for a snack or getting something from his car. *At this hour?* her thoughts demanded.

Her mind flashed back to the previous night when she'd checked in Mr. Humphry, a middle-aged man whose flirting wink and lingering touches had made her shudder. His overt behavior would have been offensive enough even if he hadn't been wearing a wedding band.

Her ears tuned in sharply. Even the crickets outside had hushed, and only the hum of the computer filled the night air. She could almost hear the beating of her own heart. What if Mr. Humphry had seen her leave her room and followed her? What if he meant to attack her? She'd worried about it before. After all, she and Gram knew nothing about their guests except their names and addresses. How many criminals had they unknowingly harbored under their roof in the past? A psycho could check in, and they wouldn't know it.

Her eyes scanned the room for a possible weapon. A stapler, a stack of disks, and a paperweight. She reached for the latter and stood, letting the chair roll back silently on the floor.

Should she go out and investigate or stay here and wait? Her body, too scared to move, made the decision for her. She was at a severe disadvantage, here in the brightly lit room with only darkness beyond the doorframe. Even if she did go out there, her eyes would need time to adjust. And she would be visible to whomever was there.

She stared at the doorway. A creak sounded. There was definitely someone there, and he was just to the left of the register where the floorboard was squeaky. She raised the granite weight over her head as a shadowed figure loomed in the doorway. She froze. Her breathing came in shallow rasps.

"Hanna?"

There was no mistaking the deep voice. "Micah." She lowered the paperweight. Relief gushed through her veins like water through a dam. A hand went to her chest as if to still her riotous heart. "You scared me silly."

"Sorry," Micah said. "Heard someone moving around out here and wanted to make sure everything was okay."

She sank back into her chair, suddenly feeling weak and shaky. "It's just me."

He looked around the office, as the fluorescent light flickered. "You do lock this up at night, don't you?"

She shook her head. "There's not even a lock on the door. Besides, there's nothing in here worth stealing."

"There's a lucrative market for office equipment. A guest could make a copy of your entry key and rip you off one night."

She blinked. "Oh. I guess you're right."

He shuffled for a moment, then backed up. "Guess I'll head back to bed. Good night. Sorry I scared you," he added as an afterthought.

"That's all right. Good night."

She stared at the doorway after he'd disappeared. Man, but he'd given her a fright! She hated feeling scared. Hated how helpless it made her feel. Reminded her too much of another time when she'd been scared and helpless.

Hanna shook her head as if to dismantle the thought. She scooted up to the desk, clicked on the save button, closed the program, and removed the disk. Her short errand had turned into an adrenaline-pumping fright that would probably keep her awake for hours.

It wasn't until after she padded back to her room and snuggled up in bed that a disturbing thought jolted through her mind: When she'd seen Micah, she'd not been afraid. She'd been relieved.

⁂

Micah lay on his back staring up into the vast darkness. He knew the nightstand clock must read after one o'clock, but he felt as if he'd just had half a dozen cups of coffee. His mind kept racing back to the moment he'd discovered Hanna in the office. He'd been relieved that it was her and slightly amused at the sight of her in her bulky robe with that useless paperweight suspended over her head. But in the flickering light of the office, he'd read the fear in her eyes and felt her immense relief in the lowering of the weight, in the sudden sagging of her shoulders. She'd been relieved to see him.

Relieved. What a wonder that was. If it had been several years ago, meeting him alone at night might've been her worst nightmare. Micah flipped on his side and turned his face into the pillow. Thinking about those years, it almost seemed like it was someone else. Not him. How could he have sunk so low? How could he have been so cruel when he, of all people, knew what it was to hurt? *When will I forget, Lord? When will Your forgiveness be enough?*

CHAPTER
SIX

A week later Gram dropped onto the recliner and leaned her head back. "My goodness, I'd forgotten what it was like to clean all those rooms."

Hanna looked at the clock and saw it was almost check-in time. According to the books, they had three parties checking in for the weekend, which would fill the lodge again. The season had officially begun. "Can you believe we're almost booked solid? I guess advertising does pay."

"That, and a little prayer, goes a long way."

"How about a cup of tea before we have to worry about checking in more guests?"

Gram agreed, and Hanna went to the kitchen to start the tea, but the kettle wasn't in its usual spot at the back of the stove. "Gram? Do you know where the teakettle is?"

"You know, I couldn't find it yesterday, either," she called from the great room.

Hanna checked the cupboards but couldn't find it. Just then, Mrs. Eddlestein entered the kitchen, tying an apron around her waist. "Mrs. Eddlestein, do you know where the teakettle is?"

"What, dear?"

Hanna repeated the question louder, and the woman looked toward the stove, then the sink. "I surely don't. It was here yesterday, I think."

Hanna heard the front door open and looked around the corner to see Micah and the Sawyer group, three teenage boys and their father, returning from their three-day trip up Mount Moran.

"How was the trip?" she asked.

"Sweet!"

"Cool!"

Mr. Sawyer gave a thumbs-up, while the shortest teen simply smiled and nodded.

Micah's hair was damp around the collar, and his clothes were smeared with dirt.

"I'm starving," said the oldest boy.

"Me too!" chimed his brother.

"You guys are always starving." Mr. Sawyer tousled their heads and pointed them toward their room for a shower.

"Thanks, Micah!" One of them said, with no prompting whatsoever. "This has been the coolest vacation ever."

"You guys did great. Now go get a shower so I don't have to smell you anymore."

They snickered and returned the compliment.

"They're probably right," Micah said. "It's been a pleasure, Dave." He shook Mr. Sawyer's hand. "See you at dinner."

Hanna had a feeling Mr. Sawyer was hanging behind to talk to her, and she was right.

"Ms. Landin, I just wanted you to know what a treasure of an employee you have there. He told us it was his first trip with Higher Grounds."

"Thanks for telling me. That's good to hear."

"I own my own business, and I know how hard it is to find reliable people. Just wanted you to know he's a keeper."

Hanna laughed. "Well, thanks. I appreciate it."

He left, presumably for a shower of his own.

"I knew he was the right choice," Gram said from her spot on the chair. "God doesn't make mistakes."

Hanna released a long breath. She'd believed all along Micah would be great with the customers, but hearing it firsthand eased her mind. That was the last untried aspect of her plan, and now it seemed

45

everything was right on track for a successful season. "I think we're going to be all right, Gram."

"Speak for yourself, child. Personally, I'm dying for that cup of tea."

Hanna laughed. "Oh, Gram."

Micah entered from the hall, still in his hiking wear, and carrying the silver kettle. "Is someone missing something?"

"There it is," Hanna said, going to retrieve it.

"Where on earth was it?" Gram asked.

"Would you believe on my nightstand?"

"Oh my. How did it get there?"

Hanna felt the smile leave her face. Gram had cleaned Micah's room yesterday morning and had undoubtedly brought it in there.

"Let's just be glad we found it," Hanna said and felt Micah's intense perusal.

"I'm the only one who's been in your room, so it must've been me," Gram said. Her brows drew down over her eyes and formed a crease between them. "Now, why in the world would I have brought a kettle in there?"

Micah squeezed Gram's shoulder. "I've been known to sleepwalk," he said with a smile. "Maybe I decided to have a cup of tea in the middle of night."

It was a nice try, but Hanna knew he was just trying to ease Gram's mind. She didn't know about the sleepwalking, but he didn't even drink tea. He kidded around with Gram for a moment until she seemed to forget the incident, then went off to take his shower. The way he'd handled Gram touched her heart.

Hanna watched him go and wondered how else he would surprise her.

❧

Natalie checked her watch, noting that a whole three minutes had passed since the last time she checked. She sipped her Diet Coke.

The waiter appeared again. "Would you like to continue to wait or go ahead and order?"

"I'll wait." Her smile was forced, her lips stiff.

Leave it to Keith to be late for their first date in over a year. Hanna, bless her heart, had offered to watch the boys, and Natalie had been too desperate to refuse.

In the two weeks since the confrontation, she'd gotten nowhere trying to discover the truth. Keith's pants became a crime scene as she rooted through pockets prior to tossing them in the laundry. Each night as she lay in bed, she quietly picked up the bedroom receiver and listened to see if he was using the downstairs extension. She went even further than that. Every night she dialed the weather number before he came home, then, in the morning she hit the redial button. Only once had a different number come up. She'd written it down but hadn't had the nerve to call it yet.

Paranoid. That's what she'd become. But who could blame her? Living in uncertainty and dread was taking a toll on her. This week she'd decided to do something about it. Something constructive. Whether Keith was having an affair or not, their marriage was in trouble. She couldn't do anything about his behavior, but she could do something about her own. She'd bought a marriage book at the Cottage Christian Bookstore and had discovered plenty of things she could improve. Number one on her list was a date night.

And here she sat alone. He'd said he could leave the bank at closing, but where was he? Was work his only mistress, or was there someone else? Why couldn't he just tell her the truth and put her out of her misery? Not knowing was awful.

She dabbed at the corner of her eye with the starchy cloth napkin. *Stop thinking like that before all your makeup runs off your face.* Blinking to clear her vision, she glanced around the busy dining room. No one seemed to have noticed her emotional lapse. She wanted to keep things light tonight, have fun like they used to when they were dating.

Suddenly Keith slipped into the chair across from her, and she choked back the reprimand that formed on her lips

He held out his hand, palm up. "I know. I'm sorry. An emergency came up." He picked up the menu. "Have you seen these prices?"

Only for about a half hour. "They've always been high." *And you never complained when we dated.*

He closed the menu and sipped the iced tea she'd ordered him. As he brought the glass to his lips, she saw it.

A long black hair hanging from the stark whiteness of his sleeve. She froze. Every muscle, every fiber of her being froze. Except her heart, which throbbed fiercely. She looked at his face as every doubt from the last week seared her memory with the same ferocity as the moment she'd found the condom on the floor.

He noticed. "What?" he asked with annoying innocence.

What? How about, "I found a condom in your pants two weeks ago"? What about, "You're never at work when I call"? Or, "You have another woman's hair dangling from your sleeve"? Her eyes filled with tears again.

"What?" he asked again, this time with a measure of irritation.

The waiter appeared out of nowhere. "Are you ready to order?"

She shifted her gaze to the peach tablecloth and blinked rapidly.

"We need a few minutes," Keith said.

The waiter disappeared, and she dabbed at her eyes again.

"Do you mind telling me what this is all about? I thought this was supposed to be a nice evening out."

"That was before I saw *that*." She gestured to the hair, which now clung to the tablecloth.

He looked down at the table, then his shirt. "What?"

"The hair." She hated the tremble in her voice.

His gaze found the evidence. He plucked it off. "You're upset about a hair on the tablecloth?" His eyes mocked her.

"It was on your shirt." She sniffed.

Keith flicked the hair onto the floor, then lowered his voice to a whisper. "Have you lost it, Nat? I work in a bank, for crying out loud. There are women who work there, you know. Not to mention the customers."

She wavered. Was she being overly suspicious? She didn't know what to believe anymore. Her eyes glazed over, and she felt a sob rise in her chest. She was on the edge of losing it. She covered her mouth.

He cursed, then reached into his wallet and withdrew some bills, flinging them onto the table. Then he threw his napkin down and rose to his feet. "If this is your idea of a good time out, I'd just as soon be at work."

Every eye in the room except hers seemed to follow him out the door.

⋯◆⋯

"Hey, Hanna," Devon called from the office door in his typical greeting. "Boats are all locked up for the night. Do you have my shuttle schedule ready?" His gaze dragged down her body, then back up.

She shifted uneasily, then slid the advertising proof back on the desk. "Not yet; just a sec." She pulled up the page with tomorrow's reservations. "How did today go?"

"Great except for the tipping incident."

He'd told Hanna at lunchtime about the three teenage girls who'd tipped over their canoe in the middle of the lake. "They probably did it on purpose, just to get you to rescue them."

"Nah, they were just fooling around."

Hanna stared at the reservations calendar. "That's odd."

"What's wrong?"

She got up and leaned her head around the corner to the dining room where Gram was doing a crossword puzzle. "Gram, do you know why there's fewer rooms booked than there were last night? I'm sure we were full."

"Yes, honey, we had some cancellations today."

"Were they part of the same group?"

"No, I don't think so."

Hanna went back to her desk. Three rooms empty. That meant they'd received three cancellations in one day. Odd. "Well, let's just hope that doesn't happen too often."

"What's that?"

"Nothing to worry about, just a few cancellations. You still have three parties to pick up at the airport." She wrote down the times and handed him the paper.

"Thanks. See you tomorrow." He winked.

Hanna looked away from him and studied the calendar. She'd taken two cancellations herself in the last week but had thought nothing of it. The schedule was still pretty full, though. *It's just a fluke. Nothing to worry about.*

Later that day, as she talked with Natalie on the phone, she realized there were plenty of other things to worry about.

"Give me the number. I'll call it," Hanna said.

Through the phone she heard Nat sigh. "I don't know. Part of me is afraid to know for sure."

After a long pause, Nat agreed. "All right, do it." She rattled off the number, and Hanna jotted it down.

"I'll call you right back," Hanna said, then hung up.

She punched in the number, wondering what she'd say. The number was probably only a friend of Keith's or something. There was every—

"Hello?"

The voice was female, but she sounded too young to worry about.

"I'm sorry, I probably have the wrong number, but do you know a Keith Coombs?"

She waited for a reply. The pause stretched too long.

"Who is this?" the woman asked.

The question caught Hanna off guard. And made her stomach tighten in a knot. "Do you know Keith?"

There was a noise in the background, a TV maybe. "Don't call here again."

The phone clicked in her ear.

Hanna dropped into her chair. That didn't sound good. Though the woman hardly admitted knowing Keith, she hadn't denied it either.

She picked up the phone again, this time dreading what she'd have to tell Natalie.

CHAPTER
SEVEN

Hanna was running through the woods, the branches around her blurring in her rush. *Hurry, you're going to be late.* Late for what? She didn't know, but it was something important. The path ahead forked. *Which way, which way?* She looked over her shoulder and saw nothing but shadows.

She turned, taking the fork to the right. *Where am I?* The woods seemed an endless maze of trees and bushes. Then she saw light ahead and knew where she was. It was the woods behind the lodge. She was almost there.

She entered the light and stopped. Suddenly the sun was shining, casting a beautiful glow across the lake. White wooden chairs, filled with guests, formed a large block in the sun-dappled yard. Her grandfather approached, wearing a suit and tie, and extended his hand. She put one glove-encased hand in his and smoothed her wedding gown with the other.

"It's time," he said.

She smiled, barely able to contain the joy bubbling in her soul. He tucked her hand through his arm and walked her down the center aisle. She felt as if she were floating, flying almost. It was her day, and everything was perfect. She looked sideways at Grandpop and smiled. He winked, and they continued walking.

Halfway down the aisle, she turned her attention to her groom. He faced the preacher, his back to her. *Turn around,* she urged. He filled out his suit, from the broad shoulders, to the tapered waist and long legs. *Turn around so I can see your face.*

As if reading her mind, he turned.

Her feet stopped. She sucked in her breath. *Micah. There must be some mistake.*

"It can't be—"

Grandpop squeezed her arm. "It's true."

But he wasn't her groom, was he? She couldn't remember who it was supposed to be, but it wasn't Micah. Was it?

"This isn't right."

He leaned closer and whispered in her ear. "Yes, darling girl."

Reassured by his words, she started forward. She met Micah's gaze, and he smiled as if for her eyes only. Peace flowed through her veins like a refreshing mountain spring. Yes. It was all right. She heard the buzz of a bee nearby. It grew louder, and she wished it would stop. Micah was holding his hand out to her, and she wanted desperately to reach him. But the buzzing continued.

Her eyes popped open, and she looked around, lost for a moment. Then she realized her alarm was buzzing. She reached over and fumbled with the button, finally shutting it off.

She flung herself down on her pillows and tried to recapture her dream. Micah. Good grief, where did that come from?

But why a wedding? Her gaze fell on her Bible on her nightstand. She'd been reading about the bridegroom coming for his church, and that must've planted thoughts of a wedding. She smiled as she remembered Grandpop in her dream. He'd looked exactly like himself, except he had been missing his walnut cane.

Silly, silly dream.

But later, as she and Gram arranged breakfast on the credenza, the dream replayed in her mind.

"Hanna." Gram touched her sleeve, and Hanna got the impression it wasn't the first time her name had been called.

"Sorry, Gram, what is it?"

"Mercy, child, where are you this morning?"

Hanna covered the crescent rolls with a towel. "I had the strangest dream last night and can't get it out of my head."

"What was it about?"

Hanna laughed. "It's so silly. I was running through the woods and when I came out, I was somehow at my wedding."

"Really . . ."

"Grandpop was there. He escorted me down the aisle. Don't ask me where Dad was."

Gram retrieved a clean tablecloth, and they worked together to spread it across the long table. "And who, may I ask, was the groom at this wedding?"

Hanna grew warm just thinking about it. "It's too silly to even mention."

"If it's so silly, why are you afraid to tell me?" Gram's eyes twinkled mischievously.

"All right, it was Micah. See, I told you it was silly." She glanced Gram's way, but the older woman continued smoothing the linen as if she'd said nothing strange at all.

"I don't see why that's so silly," Gram said.

"Really, Gram. You weren't there—well, I guess I wasn't either." She giggled. "But it was all so odd, you know how dreams are. When I saw that Micah was the groom, I balked, but Grandpop was just so sure. Then Micah reached out his hand, and everything in me wanted to reach him, but I woke up."

Gram glanced over her shoulder. "Morning, Micah."

Hanna squeezed her eyes shut. She couldn't look. Was Gram putting her on? *Please, please, please.*

"'Morning, Mrs. Landin." His bass voice strummed across the chords of her nerves. "Hanna, I need to talk to you when you get a minute."

"All right," she said, without turning.

She heard him exit through the front door, and only then did she open her eyes. "Oh, Gram, that was so embarrassing," she whispered.

Gram giggled like a teenage girl. "I thought it was mighty amusing, myself."

Hanna picked up the towel covering the bread and swatted her grandmother, which only provoked more giggles.

The chance to talk to Micah didn't come until late that afternoon when he returned from a day trip. Which suited Hanna just fine, since she was still feeling awkward about this morning's incident.

He stopped in at the office where she'd been signing paychecks. "Got a minute?"

"Sure." She turned over the checks and invited him in. An action she regretted when he seemed to fill the room.

"I was looking over next week's schedule and saw there are seven people signed up for the Grand Teton trip. Normally, I could handle seven fine, but three of them are kids, so I wondered if you wanted me to make some cuts."

"Will the parents be going?"

"Yeah, it's a family of five, plus another couple, newlyweds, I think. But the point is that I can't take kids on that climb, much less in a group that size."

"Hmm. What about doing the Mount Moran trip instead? That would be easier with the kids."

He shrugged. "Sure, but it still doesn't help the fact that the trip is overbooked."

She scowled. She hated to cancel a trip. The customers would be disappointed, and she would lose money. She supposed she could go along to help. With seven customers gone, she was sure Gram and Mrs. Eddlestein could handle the lodge. *Do I really want to be that close to Micah for three days?* Of course, she could. He was just another man. She had to put that crazy dream out of her head. "I guess *I* could go. It's been years since I've done the trip, but my grandpa and I used to go every summer."

Micah's brows rose. "Oh. I hadn't thought of that."

He seemed less than thrilled. Well, that was too bad. She wasn't going to lose income just because he liked his independence. "Go ahead and plan on my going with you." She blocked out the dates on her personal calendar and made a note to notify the guests of the change while Micah left the office. *See, I'm not afraid of being near him.* But somewhere in the recesses of her brain, the dream replayed hauntingly.

The next day Hanna browsed through the schedule for the remainder of June. She just didn't get it. They had been booked almost full for the last three weeks in June, and now they had openings every night. Some days were only half-full. Their budget has been fine so far, but with the cancellations she feared they wouldn't make June's payment.

The phone rang, and she snapped it up. "Higher Grounds Mountain Lodge, how may I help you?"

"Hi, this is Delia Hampton."

"Mrs. Hampton, hello. I was just looking over the schedule and see that we have you booked for the last week in June as usual."

A moment of silence passed. "That's what I was calling about, dear. It seems we won't need a room after all."

Hanna winced. "I hope everything's okay."

"Oh yes, just fine."

Maybe she was just going to have to ask and find out what was going on. Maybe Mrs. Hampton knew something she didn't. "Mrs. Hampton, may I ask you something?"

"Certainly, what is it?"

"Have you been unhappy with Higher Grounds's service? Is your cancellation a reflection of your dissatisfaction?"

"Oh, not at all, dear! Why, we've always had a wonderful time there. It's just, you see . . . we've always admired that big, beautiful hotel down the way from you, but it's way out of our budget. But with the special they're having, well, we could hardly pass it up. I hope our cancellation doesn't put you in a bind."

"You mean the Majestic? They're having some kind of special discount?"

"Oh yes. We couldn't afford to stay there otherwise. Fifty-nine dollars a night. And that includes all their activities and even the meals."

"Yes, yes, I understand perfectly," Hanna mumbled, then got off the phone.

How could the Majestic afford those rates? Their normal rates were over two hundred dollars a night, and that was just for a standard room. This was peak season, so why would they be giving their rooms away at such a discount?

Hanna walked to the kitchen where Gram and Mrs. Eddlestein were making strawberry pies.

"Gram, have you heard anything about the Majestic having a rate special this summer?"

"No, dear, why do you ask?"

"I just got off the phone with Delia Hampton. She cancelled her reservation, said the Majestic was offering a rate of fifty-nine dollars and that it included meals and activities."

"That can't be right."

"That's what she said. Do you think that's why we've been having these cancellations?"

Gram stopped crimping the edges of the pie dough. "Wait a minute, did you say Delia Hampton? Isn't she that eccentric woman who brings all her photos and knickknacks from home and sets them up all over her room?"

"Yes, but that hardly—"

"Delia Hampton, you say?" Mrs. Eddlestein cocked an ear.

Gram raised her voice. "Yes, yes, that woman from New Jersey that comes in June."

Mrs. Eddlestein rolled her eyes. "She told me last year all three of her grown kids were in the U.S. Senate. I mean, really, who would believe that?"

Hanna didn't know what to believe now. Had Delia told her the truth about the Majestic rates? Why would she lie?

That night Hanna drove home from the grocery store and turned into the lodge's parking lot. Only the street lamp lit the parking lot as she gathered the two sacks and trudged up the sidewalk and steps to the lodge. The oscillating buzz of cicadas filled the warm night air, joined by the chirping crickets. She'd always found the nighttime music relaxing—peaceful—but the darkness that accompanied it terrified her.

No light shone from the porch, casting the walk from the sidewalk to the lodge in darkness. Hanna hurried as quickly as she could toward the lodge's door. The bags grew heavy, and she shifted them while digging in her pocket for the key.

<hr />

Micah slowed to a walk as he neared the lodge, letting his heart rate fall. Tonight's class had been rough, and when he'd returned, he'd felt the need to release some pent-up energy. The counselor of his group knew what he was doing; he was a pro at digging out the putrid junk Micah didn't even know was there. When his foster father, Jim, had first told Micah about the Children of Alcoholics group meeting at his church, Micah had thought the whole thing was a bunch of psychobabble. But Jim had convinced him to give it a try. It was encouraging to know others had gone through the same stuff he had, but when they started getting into issues that hurt, Micah dropped out. Jim, a marriage counselor, stepped in once again and convinced him to go back. No Pain, No Gain was Jim's motto, and it had become Micah's too. Now he was determined not to let his past determine his future. Whatever it took, he would get over the pain of his past.

He stepped onto the porch, breathing steadily now, and fished in his pocket for the key. Just then Hanna rounded the corner, and they collided.

A shrill scream left her mouth. He jumped, then reached out to steady her. Two bags of groceries dropped on his toes as Hanna batted his hands away from her.

"Hey, it's—" A fist connected with his chest, then another.

He reached out and took hold of her hands.

She squealed and tried to jerk away, her eyes wide under the unlit porch.

"Hanna, it's me."

She stopped struggling, her chest heaving in the darkness.

"It's all right."

She put a hand to her heart. "Micah." The word carried a load of relief.

"Sorry I spooked you."

She closed her eyes and seemed to be recovering from the adrenaline surge. "You okay?"

"Yeah, yeah, I'm fine."

She stooped down and began gathering the groceries. Micah did the same and noticed her hands trembling.

The porch light flickered on, then her grandma opened the door. "Hanna? You all right?"

"Fine, Gram. Micah startled me, that's all."

After the groceries were packed up again, Micah said good night and headed toward his room. He flipped on the shower and undressed. No doubt anyone would've been startled to come upon someone else so suddenly, but Hanna had been terrified. The way she fought him, it was as if she'd expected him to attack her.

He stepped under the hot water and remembered the incident a couple of weeks ago when he'd frightened her in the office. She sure did scare easily. Embarrassed easily too. He could tell she'd been embarrassed when he'd walked in on her talking about her dream. He smiled. She hadn't even turned around to face him. He was glad. The smile slipped from his lips. He didn't want to encourage her. Tempting though she was, he was determined to stay clear of women.

Then why is it you keep thinking about her? He frowned and rinsed the suds from his hair, imagining the water was washing away all thoughts of Hanna. What was it about her anyway? She was attractive enough in a very natural way, but he'd been around plenty of attractive women and been able to maintain his hands-off policy. It wasn't as if she were coming on to him the way Fran had.

God, help me to get my thought life in order. I don't want a relationship with Hanna or any other woman. Help me to get her out of my head.

Micah dried off and dressed in his gray sweatpants. He had to do something, anything, to get her off his mind. His gaze fell on the Recovery Journal, still on his bed where he'd dropped it. He groaned. He had a whole week to complete the assignment, but at least that would get his mind off Hanna.

He snatched it up, grabbed the pen off the nightstand, then leaned back against the headboard and thought about the discussion in the group tonight. They'd talked about pivotal points during their childhood. He knew what that was for him.

He'd been in first grade. He liked his teacher, Mrs. Winters, because she had a soft voice. One day she was reading to the class when his stomach began to itch. And every time he scratched, it itched more. He couldn't even pay attention to what Mrs. Winters was reading. Finally, she closed the book, and the class divided into groups for their reading circles. But instead of joining his group by the aquarium, he walked up to his teacher's wooden desk.

"What's wrong, Micah. Did you forget to bring your book?"

"No. My stomach itches." He scratched. "Right here, and it won't stop. I think a skeeter bit me."

Mrs. Winters stood and circled her desk, then squatted down in front of him. "Well, now, those skeeter bites can itch pretty bad. Let's see what we have here." She lifted his T-shirt.

Micah watched her eyes grow wide.

"Oh, my! That's no mosquito bite, sweetie. I think you have chicken pox."

"Really?" A smile stretched his lips. Just about everyone else in his class had already had the chicken pox, and he thought he'd never get it. But he didn't know it would itch this much.

"You'll need to go to the nurse's office and show her your stomach. While you're waiting for your mom to come get you, I'll put together a packet of the work you'll miss over the next week or so."

His smile fell from his face. He didn't know he'd have to miss a whole week of school. He would have to stay at home all day with no one to play with.

Mrs. Newburg, the school nurse, was walking a girl out the door when Micah entered the office. She said good-bye to her, then turned to him. "Hi, there. Not feeling well?"

"My stomach itches. Mrs. Winters said I have chicken pox."

"You're Micah, aren't you?"

"Uh-huh." His bangs flopped over his forehead, caught in his eyelashes, and bounced each time he blinked.

"I'm Mrs. Newburg." She lifted his T-shirt. "I think you visited me a few months ago."

He nodded. "I had a temperature."

"Yes, I remember," she said while examining him. "Well, you do have the chicken pox, young man. We'll need to call your mom or dad to come and get you. Are they at home or work?"

"My mom's at work."

"Do you know her number?"

"Uh-huh."

She showed Micah to the phone, and he dialed his mom. When he told her he had chicken pox, she cursed and huffed but finally said she'd come.

"Is she coming?" Mrs. Newburg asked.

"She said she'd be here in a while." He scratched his stomach.

She smiled gently. "I've got just the thing for that itch. Come sit here." She patted the vinyl bed and shook a pink bottle. "Why don't you take off your shirt, and I'll put this on."

He hesitated for a moment. He didn't want anyone to see his back.

"I can see you're a very smart boy, Micah; it's good that you're careful of who you undress in front of. But I'm a nurse so, just like at the doctor's office, it's okay to take off your shirt."

He swallowed, suddenly dry mouthed, then peeled off his shirt. He held still as she dabbed pink lotion on each spot. "There. It should stop itching real soon, but be careful not to scratch or you'll rub the medicine away. "Turn around, and let's see how your back looks."

Micah froze.

"You probably have some on your back even if they aren't itching yet." She reached out and helped him turn on the bed. Micah closed his eyes.

He heard her gasp. The clown on the wall in front of Micah blurred as his eyes filled with tears. Nobody except his mom had ever seen him without his shirt on; he'd made sure of it. He'd tried so hard to be good in school. To make sure he obeyed his teacher so she'd like him. And now it was all ruined. His secret was out, and she would tell everyone the truth: He was a bad boy.

Stop crying! You're such a baby. He counted the polka dots on the clown's outfit to distract himself. *One, two, three, four* . . .

"You only have a few spots on your shoulders."

Micah felt the cold lotion as she dabbed it on.

"There. Why don't you sit here for a few minutes and let it dry. I'll be right back."

Micah put his shirt back on. He didn't care about the wet lotion; he didn't want anyone else to see the burn marks. Stretching out on the bed, he lay on his side and pillowed his head with his arm. Would Mrs. Newburg tell his teacher he'd been bad? Is that where she'd gone?

For what seemed like hours, Micah lay on the bed. He didn't like the way his skin stuck to his shirt. He'd already studied all the pictures on the walls. A clown, holding a fistful of round balloons, a chart they used to test eyes, and one of the food groups like they'd studied in class a few weeks ago. He reached out and played with the fingers of the fake skeleton hanging in the corner. Sitting up, he grasped the fingers in a handshake. "Nice to meet you, Mr. Bones." He giggled, then inspected the hand. Were there really that many bones in his hand? He held his own next to it and flexed his fingers. Neato.

He heard the outer office door shut, then voices. Micah dropped the bony hand and listened.

"Can you tell me . . ."

He leaned closer to the door, but could only hear pieces of conversation.

"And I've seen them before. I'm certain . . ."

"Did you question him about . . ."

"His mom is coming . . ."

A moment of silence followed, then the door to the clinic opened. He leaned back against the wall. A lady dressed in fancy clothes stepped in, followed by Mrs. Newburg, who closed the door behind her.

"Hi, there, Micah. I'm Nancy." She put her notebook down and extended her hand.

He shook it, then stared at his shoes. They were untied again, and the laces were dirty from being dragged along the ground.

"I hear you have a case of the chicken pox. My little boy had them last year, and he was itching all over. Is that how you feel?" She sat beside him on the cot.

He studied her face. She had the skinniest nose he'd ever seen, but she had kind eyes and a nice smile. "Just my stomach. Is my mom here yet?"

"Not yet. Can I have a look at those itchy spots?"

She didn't want to look at his chicken pox. The nurse had told her about his marks, and she wanted to see them too.

"It's okay, Micah, I'm here to help you."

He didn't know why, but he trusted her eyes. He lifted his shirt, and she looked at his stomach.

"Yes, I'd say that's chicken pox, all right." She met his gaze and smiled gently. "Mrs. Newburg said you have marks on your back. May I take a look?"

Fear seeped into Micah's bones. He was right. The lady just wanted to see the sores. And then she would know he was bad too. What did they do to bad boys?

"It's all right, Micah. I'm here to help you."

Reluctantly, he lifted his shirt and turned away from her. He flinched when he felt her fingers run over the marks.

"Do they hurt?"

"No."

"But they must've hurt a whole lot when you got them, huh?" She lowered his shirt.

Micah turned to face the door again. He didn't want to answer any more questions. "I want to go home."

"Your mom is on her way. Does your dad work too?"

"I don't have a dad."

"How about brothers or sisters?"

"A little sister."

The lady wrote something down on her paper. "So the two of you just live with your mom?"

"Uh-huh." Why was she asking all these questions?

"Where does your mom work?"

"At a restaurant."

The lady smiled. "I used to work at a restaurant too. But now I have a different, very important job. Do you want to know what I do, Micah?"

He looked at her face. She was still smiling. If she thought he was bad, wouldn't she be mad at him? "Guess so."

"I keep children safe. My job is to make sure children are not hurt by anyone. Do you know a child who gets hurt by someone?"

Micah studied the lady's face. Then his gaze went back to his shoelaces. Was his mom in trouble for hurting him?

"Sometimes children are hurt by a parent, grandparent, or baby-sitter. Sometimes grownups have a bad day and do things that are not right. That's a very sad thing. When a child tells someone he trusts, it's my job to make sure nobody hurts him again."

He heard the bell ring out in the hall and then the shuffling feet and locker doors being opened and shut. He wished he were with his class.

"Can you tell me how you got those marks on your back?"

Micah felt hot. He scratched his stomach. He itched again. What would they do if he told the truth? Could she really stop his mom from hurting him? He didn't want to get his mom in trouble.

"Can you tell me how you got them?"

He wished she would stop asking. He didn't want to think about that. He could still feel the scalding tip on his skin, still remember the smell. He closed his eyes.

"Grownups make mistakes sometimes, Micah, and I don't want anyone to hurt you."

Micah opened his eyes and looked at Mrs. Newburg through a glaze of tears.

"It's okay, honey," the nurse said. "Tell Nancy what happened."

He looked at the lady. She patted his hand. "Sometimes my mom gets mad. I do bad things." He sniffed, and Mrs. Newburg handed him a tissue.

"Go on, Micah."

"It burned." Fat, wet drops rolled down his cheeks, and he held back the sob that rose in his throat.

"It's going to be all right, sweetie," Nancy said. She stood and whispered something to the nurse and left the room.

Mrs. Newburg sat beside him and put her arm around his shoulders. He wiped his face. "Is my mom here yet? I wanna go home."

"You'll be able to leave soon."

They waited side by side for what seemed like hours. Micah's stomach rumbled, and the nurse went to get him a peanut butter and jelly sandwich. When he finished it, he balled the plastic wrapper and practiced shooting it into the trash can in the corner.

Finally, Nancy opened the door and came in followed by a policeman. Micah's eyes widened. He looked at Nancy, then the policeman. Suddenly he was very thirsty, but he didn't care. All he could think about was the policeman, how big he was and how he had a gun in his holster.

He'd had it now. Why did he say those things to Nancy? She told the police, and now he was in trouble. What did they do to bad kids? He didn't want to go to jail!

"Hi, Micah, I'm Officer Dan." He held out his hand, and Micah shook it.

Then he asked a question. Micah remembered his teacher talking about honesty. She always said telling the truth was the right choice. Looking at the big policeman, he wondered if she was right. Maybe they wouldn't be as mad at him if he told the truth. He'd already told Nancy and the nurse anyway.

He answered question after question until the officer stepped out of the room.

Nancy knelt in front of him. "Micah, remember how I said—"

"What's going on here?" his mom's voice carried in from the office. "Where's my boy?"

A quieter voice rumbled, in words he couldn't hear.

"You said I was to come get him, now you're telling me I can't take him? I had to leave work—"

The door burst open. His mom came toward him.

The policeman stopped her.

Nancy took Micah's arm and pulled him out of the room, then through the office. "Where are we going?" The policeman walked on his other side. No one answered his question. *Where are they taking me?*

His mom's voice carried through the glass doors. "Micah! You can't just take him! He's my kid!"

Micah looked at his mom, then turned back and ran. The officer caught him and snatched him up. "Mommy!" he screamed. Tears ran like a river down his face. His mom blurred as he bounced on the policeman's shoulder. "Mommy!" He beat the man with his fists. "Put me down!"

"Let him go!" His mom screamed. The nurse was trying to hold her back. "You can't just take him!"

They burst through the exit doors. The sunlight stung his eyes. "Mommy! I want my mommy!"

He was dropped into a car. He looked frantically around. He was in a police car. Fear spiraled through him, strangling his words, choking his breath. *I don't want to go to jail! Mommy! Help me, Mommy!*

CHAPTER
EIGHT

Natalie closed the book. *His Needs, Her Needs* had revealed problems within their marriage. They'd been just floating along, expecting the current of life to carry them together in the right direction. Especially since the boys had been born. After meeting their needs all day, she'd hardly had the energy or desire to worry about Keith's needs.

And her own needs had been neglected as well. No wonder their marriage wasn't working. She couldn't make Keith meet her needs, but she could try to meet his. Starting with what the book said is often a husband's number-one need: sexual fulfillment.

Natalie thought about the woman Hanna had called. Was she having an affair with Keith? She shook off the thought. Tonight she'd think only about her marriage.

What had happened to their sex life? It used to be good. Satisfying. Keith used to want her all the time, but it had been months since he'd shown a real interest. She suspected she'd turned him away one too many times, tired from the daily demands of motherhood.

But that was easy enough to fix. With her boys at her parents' house for the night, she had a plan to set her marriage back on the right track. She went to the master bedroom and rooted through her lingerie drawer. Somewhere in there was a sexy nightie or two. Way in the back corner, her hand found the garment. She pulled it out and shook out the wrinkles. She'd worn it on their honeymoon and several more times after she'd seen Keith's approval.

She tossed it in the dryer to smooth out the silky, black material, then rounded up various-sized candles. For a moment she debated whether she should light them yet. Keith might not be home for hours. On the other hand, he could come home any minute. She lit them, silently imploring them to burn slowly, and placed them randomly around the bedroom and bathroom. The bathwater would have to wait, but she removed the boys' water toys and set out the only bottle of bath bubbles she could find, a yellow container shaped in the form of Big Bird.

She removed the negligee from the dryer, pleased when she saw it was wrinkle free. She laid it on the bed, then went to the refrigerator and peeked inside. A half-empty jug of grape juice sat in the back, and she pulled it out, poured it into two fluted glasses, then set them back in the fridge to keep them cold.

Back in the bedroom, she shimmied out of her jeans and T-shirt and into the flimsy negligee, relieved that it still fit. She walked to the floor-length mirror and tried to view herself objectively. She was fortunate she'd inherited a fast metabolism that kept her thin without much effort. *I sure need some sun, though.* Her long legs, though pale, were her best feature, and the French-cut legs of the garment made them seem even longer, but her knees were as knobby as ever. Squared shoulders and an ample bustline balanced out her hips nicely, but as she turned to the side, she admitted her stomach was no longer flat. *Well, with two pregnancies, what can I expect?*

All in all, not bad. Especially if she dimmed the lights. She twisted her hair up and secured it with a clip, pulling down tendrils around her face. She glanced at her watch, then slipped under the covers with a novel.

Time passed slowly. She didn't know if the book was boring or if she was simply too anxious to give it her full attention.

Finally she heard the overhead garage door, and she jumped out of bed to retrieve the goblets from the fridge. She'd just made it back to bed when the garage door clicked open. She heard the clink of coins being emptied out of his pockets.

Natalie folded down the covers to expose her full body, then propped a pillow against the backboard and lay back. She heard the TV snap on, followed by a sports commentator analyzing a play. Would he even come find her? She heard him tap across the kitchen's tile floor and open the refrigerator. She looked at the goblets on the nightstand and decided to stop him before he grabbed a Coke. "Keith?"

"Huh?" The fridge's door snapped shut.

"Can you come here a minute?"

She heard his footsteps as he crossed the house. Her heart thudded like it had on their wedding night. She felt heat prickles under her arms and at the back of her neck.

Keith appeared in the doorway. He stopped, his eyes widening slightly at the sight of her. His gaze took in the candles, then swept back over her.

Her nerves clattered in the strange language of expectation. She sucked in her stomach, then deliberately curled one leg behind as she rolled on her side.

"What's this all about?" He loosened his tie and dropped it on the window seat.

"Isn't it obvious?" Her lips curled in what she hoped was a seductive smile, but he wasn't looking.

He sighed. "It's nice to see this side of you, Nat, but I'm kind of tired. It was a long day."

Disappointment snagged at her, but she was determined not to give up.

He sat on his side of the bed and removed his shoes.

Quickly, before he could get up, Natalie scooted over behind him. She let her hands roam his shoulders. "How about a backrub? There, how does that feel?" On her knees, she kneaded with both hands, noting the tight muscles in his shoulders.

He sighed deeply, then let his shoulders sag in relaxation.

"Why don't you tell me about your day?"

"Not much to tell. Same old stuff."

She worked his neck with her fingers. "Do you remember the first time I wore this?"

She took his grunt for a no.

"It was on our honeymoon. Remember the night you were on the terrace overlooking the falls, and I came to the patio door? I still remember your words. You said, 'I've never seen a more beautiful sight.' I thought you were talking about the falls at first." She slipped her arms around his chest and pressed herself against his back. She kissed the tip of his ear while her hands roamed his chest.

Suddenly he pulled her hands away and stood. "That felt great, thanks."

Her hope faltered again. "Come back to bed, Keith." The request came out like a plea.

"I told you, Nat, I'm tired. I just want to kick back and relax." He started for the door.

She scurried after him and turned him toward her. "How about taking a bath with me then. It's been years since we've done that." She slipped one hand in his and turned his face toward hers with the other. "Come on, Keith," she coaxed, pulling his hand as she started toward the bathroom.

He jerked his hand from hers. "No, Nat. I said I'm tired; now leave me alone!"

She watched, shivering, as he left the room. Icy fingers of dread crept through her veins, freezing her to the core.

He was cheating. He was being satisfied by someone else. Darts of pain pierced her heart at the thought. She covered her trembling lips with her fingers as a sob threatened to escape.

Please, God, no. She slipped on one of Keith's dress shirts and followed him into the living room. He lounged in his recliner, his face intent on the TV. She drew the two ends of the shirt together, suddenly feeling naked. "It's true, isn't it?" Her deadpan voice barely sounded over the TV. "Isn't it?" she bit out.

"What?" he snapped.

"Who is she, Keith?"

The animosity in his gaze didn't impede her desire, her need, to know the truth.

"I know there's someone else; stop playing games with me!"

His gaze returned to the screen.

"Who is it?"

A commercial came on, and he began surfing the channels.

She grabbed the remote and flung it across the room. "Stop it! I want to know the truth! Why won't you just say it? Say it, Keith!"

He kicked in the footrest and stood. "Fine, it's true! All right? There *is* someone else! Are you happy now?"

His words sliced her whole being. As if a truckload of tar had been poured on her, she sunk to the floor and collapsed.

Tears poured as a moan tore from her soul and pierced the air. *Why? Why?* Sobs, wrenched from the deepest part of her, erupted. *Why, God?*

"Who is it?" The words raked across her throat, sounding nothing like her own voice.

Silence met her plea. She found the strength to lift her head. He wasn't there. She pulled herself up and staggered through the house. When she reached the bedroom, she saw him. Putting on his shoes as if it was just another day. As if he weren't betraying her. "Who is she?" She spewed the words with a bitterness she didn't know she was capable of.

"You should know; you called her, didn't you?"

"Called her?" Nat's mind spun at a dizzying speed. "That was Hanna, not me. Who is she? Why are you doing this? How could you do this?"

He sprung off the bed and started past her.

Malignant fury seized her. She grabbed his arm and spun him around, pummeling his chest with her fists. "Who is she?" She cursed, blinded by the vicious assault of emotions. "Tell me!"

He grabbed her hands hard. "It's over, Nat! Do you hear me, it's over."

Terror surged through her, dark and overwhelming. "You don't mean that."

He turned and walked to the living room, pocketing his wallet and keys.

"Where are you going?" She followed, wiping at the wetness on her face.

"To somebody who cares."

"I care!" She caught up with him and clutched his arms. "Can't you see? I've been trying!"

He shook her off. "It's too little, too late, Nat." Then he opened the door to leave.

"Don't go!"

The door slammed.

"Don't go!" She pounded the door, sliding weightlessly to the cold ceramic as sobs shook her frame. "Don't go!"

*

CHAPTER
NINE

Hanna pulled the sheet up around her shoulders and sighed. Sleep eluded her tonight, and it was no wonder. It seemed she had more problems than she could handle. Nat's marriage problems weighed on her. Gram's forgetfulness worried her. She'd seen enough TV programs on Alzheimer's disease to know Gram had some of the symptoms. She needed to tell her dad. More importantly, she needed to convince Gram to make a doctor's appointment.

And then there were the cancellations. Another one had been called in today. As if the other concerns weren't enough, she was also dealing with her own issues. Her mind flashed back to earlier in the evening when she'd taken a canoe out on the lake. Devon had been there, finishing up for the day, and had shown her to the red canoe. When she'd stepped down into it, her foot had slipped on the wet dock, and she'd nearly gone into the lake. But he'd reached out and grabbed her around the middle.

She shuddered at the suffocating feel his grasp had provoked. From the time he'd grabbed her, she'd wanted loose, even if that meant falling into the lake, and it wasn't just because he'd held her longer than necessary. Whether it was a shoe salesman or a hug at church, she was repelled by a man's touch. When would she get over it?

Lord, I feel so many burdens right now. Help me to give them over to You. Heal my spirit in the place that's wounded. Make me ready for the day when You bring a man into my life. Prepare my heart and take away these feelings of fear, Lord.

Hanna stopped and tied the laces of her hiking boots. Her muscles ached, but almost in a good way. She'd been inside too long. Out here, breathing the moist air laden with the scent of pine and creosote, she felt alive and refreshed. Despite the two layers of socks she'd put on that morning, she could already feel a blister forming on the back of her heel. She'd taken this trip many times with her grandfather but hadn't gone since she was a teenager. And her body felt it. She hadn't known she was in such sorry shape. The canoe trip to the base of the mountain was as much fun as she remembered, but the steep footpaths drained her of energy.

They took frequent water breaks, more often than Hanna suspected was usual, since three adolescent Schaeffer boys were in the group. Their parents walked in front along with Micah, and she could hear him educating them about the wilderness and Grand Teton National Park. The boys trailed after them, followed by Mr. and Mrs. Thompson. Hanna, who rounded up the group, shook her head. Even through the sweaty, dirty climbs, the honeymooners had scarcely let go of one another.

Occasionally, Micah would give the boys a pop quiz on safety or point out a tree, plant, or animal, challenging them to find another like it.

Judging by her watch, dinnertime was nearing. She wondered how Gram and Mrs. Eddlestein were getting along. At church the previous day, Hanna had talked to her dad about Gram. His face had sobered when she told him of his mom's forgetfulness, but he'd admitted he'd seen the signs also. They'd had lunch together with Paula, and he'd talked with Gram about scheduling an appointment with the doctor.

Hanna had thought she would put up a fuss. Her easy acquiescence left Hanna thinking that Gram had been concerned about her behavior too. She didn't even want to think about a possible diagnosis of Alzheimer's. An elderly man at church had it, and she saw his wife dealing with the final stages. So sad. *Please, Lord, help the doctor to get to the bottom of this. If it is Alzheimer's, I pray that You'd give us the strength to cope.*

Later that night they settled at the deserted CMC campsite. Micah explained to the campers that the campsite was named after the Chicago Mountaineering Club, the first group to ascend Mount Moran in 1941. He began supper, cooking chipped beef and gravy over the propane stove while Hanna combined powdered milk and water with an instant pudding mix and set it in the shallow edge of the spring to set. The campers struggled to set up their A-frame tents. Hanna and Micah laughed when the boys' tent collapsed on them, then Hanna went to help.

After dinner Micah showed them how to use biodegradable soap and a scrub pad to scour the pots and utensils. By the time they'd cleaned up, the pudding was set, and they ate it as they watched the sun slip over the horizon.

After dessert Hanna removed her boots and socks. The red spot on her heel burned hot, but the blister had already burst.

"Blisters?" Micah had sneaked up behind her.

"So much for two pairs of socks."

"You might want to wash it off." He dug the first-aid kit from his backpack and knelt down beside her. "Ever used moleskin?"

She wrinkled her nose. "Sounds gross."

He cut a circle from the material while she washed her heel with the leftover water and soap, then she returned to her log. Turning her heel out, she showed him the sore spot, and he cut a smaller hole in the center of the circle, making a donut shape. Hanna felt awkward letting him treat her sweaty feet, but consoled herself that no one else smelled any better than she did.

Micah peeled off the plastic backing and placed the moleskin on her heel, pressing hard to ensure a tight grip. His hands felt cool on her warm feet. "This should keep the friction off. If you develop another sore spot tomorrow, let me know, and I can treat it before a blister forms."

She smiled her thanks, then he went to doctor one of the boys' blisters.

Hanna didn't know about everyone else, but fatigue began to claim her body once she finally relaxed. Micah prepared a fire as dusk settled quickly around them. The adults discussed their hometowns and occupations while the boys talked among themselves, mostly about girls, from what Hanna could gather. The Thompsons cuddled up on a log, sharing secret glances and whispers.

When darkness covered the land and the fire crackled with life, Hanna fished in her backpack for the marshmallows she'd brought.

"Anyone for roasted marshmallows?"

The youngest boy's eyes lit up, but his parents announced it was time for all of them to turn in.

Groans and complaints sounded, but Mr. Schaeffer reminded them they'd be rising at dawn, and that seemed to smother further argument.

Hanna and Micah said good night as the Thompsons rose, arm and arm, and announced they were retiring too.

The night air, already abuzz with crickets and cicadas, was filled with the zipping of tent flaps and the rumble of muted conversation.

Hanna found a long, skinny stick, slipped two marshmallows on the end, and held it out over the fire with Micah's.

The heat warmed her face and arms, and she slipped out of her light jacket.

"It's burning," Micah said from across the fire.

She pulled it out and blew at the flames. "Actually, I like them burned." She pulled off a gooey, char-crusted confection and tasted. "Umm. It's been years since I've had roasted marshmallows."

"Too bad we don't have some chocolate and graham crackers."

She gave him a mock glare. "Don't even get me going."

The first ones tasted so good, she thought she could eat half the bag, but by the time she'd had four, the sweet taste had grown old.

"I think I'll turn in now," she said. "Want me to help put out the fire?"

"No, you go on. I'm going to stay up a bit longer."

Taking her flashlight, she slipped into the pup tent and unrolled her sleeping bag. She settled into it, then grabbed her clothing bag and flattened it for a pillow. Night sounds seeped through the tent fabric, lulling her mind and her already-weary body. She left the flashlight on, flipping it upside down, then turned to her back.

Thank You, Lord, for the beauty of nature. Thank You for Your protection and provision. She closed her eyes, and moments later she succumbed to the beckoning call of sleep.

The next morning Hanna woke to the faint light of dawn. She pulled the bag up over her shoulders, seeking warmth in the crisp morning air and longing for the jacket she'd taken off by the fire the previous night. She used to sleep soundly on these trips with her grandfather, but last night she'd tossed and turned, trying to find a soft spot. It seemed the ground had gotten harder over the years.

She sat up and stretched, rolling her shoulders around and tilting her head to each side. Silence permeated the campsite, and she thought she must be the first one up. But when she pulled back the flap, she saw Micah sitting on a log reading a book. On closer observation she realized it was a Bible, a little New Testament. She'd known he went to church on Sundays and said grace before he ate, but watching him in his quiet time with God stirred her heart.

Micah closed the Bible and knelt on the ground, propping his forearm on one knee, his head bowed in reverence. Something about seeing such a masculine man submitting himself to God affected her in a powerful way.

She remembered her dream, and suddenly it didn't seem so absurd anymore. In fact, it seemed . . . intriguing.

She dropped the tent flap and fell back on her heels. She'd been asking God to prepare her heart for her chosen mate. Could it be that it was Micah?

But I'm not ready for this, God.

And he works for me. He's my employee, Lord.

Not to mention he'd never given any indication that he was attracted to her.

The excuses fell silently around her. She sighed quietly. *Well, if this is Your will, God, maybe You'd better let him in on it too.*

After a breakfast made with dehydrated hash browns and sausage, the group tore down camp and started toward the summit. Hanna's gaze repeatedly found Micah's back as he led the group. He'd proven his expertise on the job, and now she found herself admiring his strong faith. *Is he the one, Lord?* Maybe she was just imagining it all.

And if he was what God wanted for her, how did she go about getting it . . . er, him? She'd never been the aggressive type and had no desire to start now.

She glanced at him again, watching as he helped the youngest teen across a crevasse in the rocks. His biceps bulged under his T-shirt as he caught the boy.

When she reached the fissure, he waited on the other side for her, his arms outstretched. "Ready?"

She nodded, then jumped, and he caught her in his arms. A quiver of pleasure rippled through her stomach. She met his gaze, felt his warm breath on her forehead, then flushed at the intense look in his smoky eyes. Slowly, she slid from his embrace, still feeling the heat of his gaze. "Thanks," she said, avoiding his eyes, certain he would be able to read her heart.

Hanna watched as he jogged to the front of the group. When she'd been in his arms, she'd felt no repulsion. To the contrary, she'd wanted to stay there longer. And, if she wasn't mistaken, he'd wanted her to stay as well. *Okay, God, maybe You do know what You're doing.* Hanna breathed a laugh. Of course, God knew what He was doing. He'd made all these awesome mountains; surely He could handle a little thing like her love life.

By midmorning, rivulets of perspiration ran down her temples. With a vigorous workout like this, she wondered why Micah felt he needed to jog every day. She knew from experience this second day was the most wearing part of the climb, but also the most exciting part, as she was always driven with eagerness to reach the summit. The footpaths grew steeper and claimed her undivided attention.

When they neared Half Dome, their pace slowed as they faced climbing the slabs. Micah handled the group with the aptitude of someone who'd done this many times. As for Hanna, the last part of the climb seemed much steeper and longer than it had when she was younger.

By the time they reached the summit, it was well past lunchtime. Once they'd all admired the impressive view, they sat down and replenished their energy. After the meal the family of five and the newlyweds posed for pictures with the majestic view in the background. The whipping wind tugged on Hanna's ponytail and shirt, cooling her off. Micah hurried the group, reminding them they had to make it back to the CMC site before dark.

The descent was easier and provided a beautiful view. When they reached the campsite, they repeated last night's rituals, and soon they were relaxing around a campfire while darkness closed in around them. All the water Hanna had drunk during dinner was having its effect, and nature's call beckoned. The area outside of the fire's light was an ambiguous black hole. Why hadn't she thought to go before night fell?

For a moment she considered asking the ladies if one of them needed to go, but decided against it when she realized they might think she was afraid of the dark.

She slipped quietly away, flicking on her flashlight when she reached the shadowed edge of the campsite. As dark as it was, she wouldn't have to go far, at least. Leaves and gravel crunched under her feet. Insects ceased their chirping as she invaded their space. Off in the distance, an owl hooted. Her heart thudded heavily in her chest. Mentally, she knew there was nothing out there, but the vast darkness beyond the ring of the flashlight terrified her. When she finished, she scurried back to camp, then settled once again on her log, waiting for her heart to settle.

The Thompsons turned in, followed by the Schaeffers. Once again, she and Micah were left alone at the fire.

Hanna brought out the marshmallows. "Want some?"

"Sure."

They found sticks and began skewering them. It took Micah twice as long to roast his because he held it above the flames, rotating it until it was golden brown. He teased her about her preference for charred marshmallows, and when one of his caught fire, he brought it to her.

"Thanks." She slipped it carefully off the stick.

He sat on the log next to hers. "How long have you worked at Higher Grounds?"

"Three years. I dropped out of college when Gram needed help, and I've been there ever since."

The firelight washed his face in a golden glow, settling softly on the uppermost planes and casting shadows in the cradle of his cheekbones and jaw line. "Are you the only grandchild or just the only one who could help at the time?"

"I have two sisters. But Natalie's married with two little ones, and Paula works full-time. Not that I minded helping out. I love the mountains, and Higher Grounds is like a second home to me. How did you become a climbing guide?"

"When I first joined my church, the singles took a guided trip up Grand Teton. I went along and haven't stopped climbing since."

"Any brothers or sisters?"

He looked away, toward the heat of the flames. His jaw twitched.

She remembered he had a foster father and bit the inside of her mouth. He might not want to talk about family.

"A little sister."

She searched her memory for another subject, but the churning wheels turned up nothing. The awkward silence stretched longer, becoming more natural as time passed. Finally, Micah asked about her church, and once again they were chatting.

Time rushed by as they sat in the fiery glow of the light talking and getting to know one another. Micah didn't talk much about himself until she asked him about his foster father, and then he opened up about his foster family. She didn't know anything of his life before that point, and he skirted around his early adulthood.

She was reluctant to turn in, but as the fire died low, she knew she needed to get some sleep before dawn crept up on them.

❖ ✦ ❖

Hanna hurried through the woods, her eyes searching frantically for safety as she heard footfalls behind her. The steps neared. She broke into a run. Branches clawed at her skin, tore at her clothes. *Please, God, help me!* The bells of Saint Jude pealed in the distance.

He grabbed her from behind and dragged her deeper into the woods. His hand clamped over her mouth. She kicked at him, flailing her arms, pushing at him. He was too strong. Whimpers tore at her throat.

She smelled the sickening odor of alcohol on his breath. Her stomach churned with sour acid. He pushed her to the ground. A scream tore from her lips. "No! No!"

He grabbed her by the upper arms and shook her until she thought she was going to be sick or faint. "No!" She wrestled with him, this unseen monster whose face was hidden by the cloak of darkness. But he was too strong.

❖ ✦ ❖

Something had stirred Micah from the arms of sleep, but what? He propped his weight on an elbow and listened. Probably just a marmot or chipmunk looking for food.

Whimpers whispered through the tent, and he sat up. That was no animal. He felt for his flashlight, unzipped the tent flap, and stepped out into the brisk air. He tracked the whimpers to Hanna's tent, which was dimly lit from the inside. She must be having a nightmare.

81

He hesitated. He should probably just go back to bed. She wouldn't want him trespassing on her personal space. But what if it wasn't a nightmare? What if she was in danger?

A quiet sob reached him, followed by muffled words. His feet went into action. "Hanna," he whispered from outside the tent, not wanting to wake the others. The mumbling continued, punctuated by the sound of her thrashing about in her nylon bag. "Hanna!" he said as loudly as he dared.

"No . . . no . . . !" The words were moaned.

He unzipped her tent and slipped inside. Her flashlight lay on its side, its beam focused on the tent side in a tight circle. He dropped his and touched her arm. "Hanna."

She was shaking her head, and perspiration dampened her bangs. Her face scrunched up. A tear flowed into her hairline.

The childhood nightmares he'd been plagued with pierced his memory. He had to wake her. He took hold of her upper arms and shook. "Hanna!"

She wrestled with him, pushing at his chest, crying out.

"Hanna. It's Micah, wake up!"

Her eyes snapped open wide, their shadowed depths flashing a terror he knew only too well. Her breaths came in shallow gulps. Her fingers bit into the flesh of his arms.

"It's okay. It's just a nightmare."

One last shuddered breath, then her face crumpled. As the nightmare's memory slammed into her, she covered her face with both hands and sobbed. Hard, racking sobs.

Her vulnerability tore at him. "Hey," he murmured, pulling her into his arms. "It's all right. It was just a dream." Her body was stiff and trembling. He stroked her back, remembering the many foster homes where he'd received no comfort, no solace, from the terror of his dreams. Only Jim had sat with him in the wee hours of morning until he slept again.

When her weeping stopped, she pulled herself awkwardly from his arms. "I'm sorry." She wiped her face with her sleeve, reminding him of a child. "I'm not usually such a baby."

"You have nightmares a lot?"

"Not for a while." She was avoiding his gaze. "What time is it?"

He pushed up the layers of sleeves and held his watch out to catch the light. "Almost four-thirty."

"Sorry I woke you."

"You going to be all right?"

"Sure, I'm fine."

For all her bravado, he knew the fear a nightmare seared into one's mind. The fear would cling to her until morning's light washed it away. He'd been overwhelmed with relief when Jim stayed with him. But he could hardly remain in Hanna's tent.

She settled back in her bag. "Thanks."

He took his cue to leave, slipping quietly through the opening and zipping the flap into place, glad she had the light on to chase away the darkness.

C H A P T E R
T E N

Natalie picked up the clutter in the living room, putting her nervous energy to work. Hanna was coming over and, finally, she would have someone to bare her soul to. The past few days she'd spent in silent torture, trying to feign normalcy for the boys. Her mind had been in another place, a dark, overwhelming place. After crying most of Saturday night, the last thing she'd felt like was attending church the next morning. But she was meeting her boys and parents there, so she'd applied eyeliner to hide her puffy eyelids as best she could.

What she would give for just a few minutes' respite from the grief and rage that washed alternatively over her like tidal waves. Sunday she'd been too steeped in depression to talk to anyone, but by Monday she was ready. And Hanna had been away. Her sister was the only one she could trust with the news of Keith's awful betrayal. All her friends were mutual friends of Keith's, and she couldn't tell her parents. Paula would have heard her out, but her sister could be critical and unfeeling at times. Natalie didn't think she could bear that right now.

She felt like one of the water balloons she made for the boys. Dark emotions filled her, and if she didn't release some of it soon, she would burst. She'd evaded questions from Alex on the whereabouts of Daddy. She didn't even know where he was. Evenings, in the privacy of her bedroom, she'd let loose all the ugliness pouring from her innermost parts.

But somehow, the ugliness never drained away. It filled her up, gnawing at her insides like termites.

Where was God? She didn't feel Him, couldn't feel anything but the crushing weight of betrayal. *Where are You, God? I need You!*

A soft rapping sounded at the door. Finally, Hanna. She wiped her eyes and opened the door. "Thanks for coming."

Hanna stepped inside. "What's happened?"

"Oh, Hanna." She covered her mouth as if she could hold back the sobs. "He left me."

Hanna embraced her, and Natalie wilted, letting herself lean physically and emotionally on her younger sister. Hanna simply held her, murmuring comforting words while Natalie sobbed. Then Hanna took her hand and led her to the couch. "What happened?"

Natalie wiped her nose with the tissues she now kept in her pocket. "He's having an affair. I found out Saturday, and he left that night. I haven't seen him since."

"Who is it?" Hanna's eyes teared, sympathy written clearly on her face.

"I don't know. He said I didn't know her, but I think it was that woman you called. Oh, Hanna, what if he doesn't come back? What am I going to tell the boys? What am I going to do?"

"He hasn't called or anything?"

"He came over Sunday while we were at church. I only know because I noticed some of his clothes missing. I called him yesterday at work, but they said he was busy." She dabbed at her leaking eyes. "He's avoiding me. I was trying so hard, and then he told me, and now it hurts so bad I just want to die."

"Oh, Nat, I'm so sorry." Hanna held her, letting her cry.

"Why is he doing this? Doesn't he love me anymore? I don't want a divorce. I want him back, but I'm so *angry* with him! One minute I want to kill him, and the next I want to beg him to come back."

Hanna took the tissue and wiped Natalie's cheeks. "What have you told the boys?"

"I just told them he's away for a while. I don't even know where he is. He's probably staying with *her*."

"Have you tried going to see him at work? It's not fair of him to leave you in the dark."

"I haven't had the nerve to go there. What if everyone knows? What if they're laughing at how gullible I am?"

"Why don't you keep trying to reach him at work? You can ask him to meet you here so you can talk privately."

"The boys—"

"I'll watch the boys. Just let me know when, and I'll come get them and take them to the park or something, okay?"

Natalie felt her lip trembling. "Thanks, Hanna."

"Maybe you can talk him into going with you for marriage counseling."

"Yes. I think that's a good idea." She blew her nose, stuffing the tissue back in her pocket. "I keep remembering what Dad said when we got engaged. Remember? About Keith's dad being an alcoholic and a womanizer? I thought since Keith had sworn off alcohol, everything would be different. But look at the example he had growing up. He watched his dad have affair after affair, and now he's doing the same thing."

Hanna tucked a strand of Natalie's hair behind her ear. It felt so good for someone else to be caring for her.

"Can I pray for you?" Hanna asked.

She nodded, and Hanna took her hand.

"Dear Lord . . ." Her sister paused as if searching for words. "Nat's hurting so much right now, Lord. I pray You'd comfort her. Give her strength and wisdom to do what she needs to do. Help Keith, God. He's on a path he has no business being on. Show him the way back to Nat and back to You. Restore his love for his wife. Direct Nat through this difficult time. Be with her and the boys. Help her to seek You even in the midst of her pain. For it's in Christ's name, amen."

Hanna held her again, and they talked long into the night. By the time she left, Natalie felt better. She had a plan now, at least, to contact Keith and set up a meeting. She wondered if he would return her phone calls. If he didn't, she'd be forced to go to the bank. And she would. Even if she *had* been the last to know, there was no shame in that.

Keith was the one who should feel ashamed.

"Anyone for a game of chess?" Hanna asked.

Gram paused in her task of clearing the table and shot her a strange look. Mrs. Eddlestein hadn't even heard the question.

Micah pushed in his chair. "Sure, sounds good. I'll go set it up."

After he left, Hanna helped clear the table.

"What was that about?" asked Gram.

Heat crept up her neck, suffusing her cheeks. Neither Gram nor Mrs. Eddlestein played chess or had any interest in learning. Hanna had asked before, missing the games of chess she'd played with her college roommate, but the two older ladies preferred to stick to Scrabble.

"I just felt like playing."

Gram's lips curled in a knowing smile.

"Can't a girl just want a game of chess?" Hanna muttered as she slipped out of the kitchen through the swinging doors.

She heard Gram chuckle as she headed for the great room. Micah was lining up the pieces.

She'd avoided him since their return from the mountain two days ago, embarrassed about clinging to him in the middle of the night. But as she'd prayed about her own healing and asked God to make her ready for a relationship, Micah had once again come to mind. She'd surrendered it to God during her quiet time and decided to take steps to build a relationship with Micah. She could use a friend, and she figured he could too. He'd mentioned on the trip that he played chess, so . . .

Hanna sat across from him on the floor and helped him set up the pieces. "I'm out of practice. I haven't played since college."

"You first." He gestured for her to start.

She made her move, then settled back against the sofa front. She wondered what his background was and how it affected him. She couldn't help but think of Keith and how his father's behavior had seemingly affected him.

Micah moved a rook, and she reached out to move her knight. He was playing to win, and there was nothing she liked better than a good competition.

Micah watched Hanna from across the chessboard as she made her third move. Her legs curled to the side, one leg folded under the other. Her long, straight hair hung on both sides of her face, and she casually tucked it behind her ears. She analyzed the board, her lashes sweeping the tops of her cheeks, lashes that looked soft and supple, not the kind that sprung stiffly with clumps of black makeup. In fact, he couldn't see a trace of makeup on her face. Her lips were rosy pink but—

"Micah."

"Huh?"

"It's your turn."

Her cheeks were flushed with pink, and he realized she'd caught him staring. He made a move with a knight and resolved to keep his eyes on the board. He'd thought about her a lot lately. Especially after her nightmare. She was independent and capable, but the vulnerability he'd sensed in her that night drew him.

She was a beautiful woman. The natural kind of beauty that you see on soap commercials. But it was more than outward beauty that attracted him. She was beautiful on the inside too. She'd been raised in a nice, Christian family, the kind that went on drives in the country and picnics in the summer. Her parents had been her biggest fans when she'd played volleyball in high school and sung solos at church. Their backgrounds couldn't be more different.

She cleared her throat loudly.

"My turn again?"

Her smile wrapped around him like a hug. "Where are you tonight?"

"Sorry. I'll do better." He moved his rook, trapping her queen.

"Hey, how'd you do that? You're not even paying attention."

"I multitask well."

"Man, I can't do two things at once to save my life. Take that pat-your-head, rub-your-belly thing. I can't do it. If I pat with my left hand, I pat with my right."

"But you can play volleyball."

She shrugged. "That's different."

"Have you ever thought about setting up a net behind the lodge in that big, grassy area?"

She paused in moving a knight. "That's a great idea. We could have a volleyball night and get all the guests involved."

"Sure. I think it'd be fun."

She spoke as if to herself. "We have enough guests now—at least, if the cancellations stop."

"Cancellations?"

"Lately we've had a lot of them. It's odd."

"Hmm."

"Have you ever known the Majestic to run ridiculously low rates during the summer to attract tourists?" She blocked his move.

"Sorry. I didn't get involved in that aspect of the business."

It would be strange if the Majestic was trying to attract Higher Grounds customers. The hotel had always bustled with business during the summer.

Hanna concentrated on the game, remaining quiet. He observed her as she tucked in the corner of her mouth and squinted at the board. She was too appealing. Dangerously appealing. He was already attracted to her, and now he was beginning to get emotionally involved.

Watch it, Gallagher. He didn't need the reminder. He'd been careless until now, but he was determined to keep the relationship on a professional level. She was his boss, and he needed to keep it that way.

At last Hanna made a final move, winning the game. That was fine. He didn't mind losing a game to a woman. But he wouldn't lose his heart to one. Not at any cost.

CHAPTER
ELEVEN

Hanna started the mower and surged forward across the backyard. It was an old relic, her grandfather's, but it was a ride-on model, and she was glad for that, given the size of the property. The sun warmed her skin, while a light breeze cooled her off and carried the smell of cut grass.

She actually enjoyed the chore, delighted in having time to think. And she could use a few minutes' thinking time today. Something was not right with Micah. The amiable Micah was gone, replaced by an indifferent, aloof one. Well, that wasn't entirely true. He seemed his normal self with the customers and Gram. Namely, everyone but her.

What had happened after the chess game two days ago? She thought of every time she'd seen him since. There weren't many instances since he'd done two-day trips, but there was a difference in his behavior toward her. He wasn't rude or mean, just indifferent. Professional. Business only.

Just with her, though. She'd seen him joking with Mrs. Eddlestein and high-fiving the customers. Had she done something to upset him?

She edged around a tree and continued along the wood line, glancing at the large, open area of the backyard. She'd purchased a volleyball set yesterday, and Devon had volunteered to set it up.

Devon. He was a nice enough guy, but he was becoming a problem. When she'd expressed interest in volleyball, he'd asked if she wanted to go watch Central Wyoming play sometime. She'd responded ambivalently, but she knew he'd ask again.

She shook her head. The guy she wasn't interested in was all over her, and the one she wanted ignored her. She'd have to put an end to Devon's interest, but she couldn't use the you're-an-employee line. After all, she wanted to pursue a relationship with Micah, and he was an employee too.

As she turned the mower back toward the lodge, Micah rounded the corner with an armful of backpacks. He balked when he saw her, then nodded in greeting as he continued on toward the barn.

Hanna watched him go and wondered again what was wrong. So much for building a relationship. It was going backward instead of forward. *I could use a little help here, God.*

Micah emerged from the barn, and she waited until he neared, then shut off the mower. "Micah."

He turned, brows raised.

"Are you all right? Have I done something to upset you?"

His tucked his hands in his pockets. "No, not at all."

"You seem, I don't know, different."

He shook his head. "I'm fine. Hey, do you know where the dehydrated meat is? I looked in the pantry, but it wasn't there."

Hanna's spirits sank at the change of topics. "You might ask Mrs. Eddlestein."

He continued toward the lodge, and Hanna mechanically turned over the key. For whatever reason, he'd decided to keep their relationship professional. She tried not to take it personally. She wasn't successful. *Was I wrong, Lord? Was this just my own silly thoughts? Before Micah, I didn't even want to have a relationship with a man, much less be the pursuer. I'm no good at it, God. If this is what You want, please show it to Micah.*

That night, after a dinner with Micah the Polite, she retired to her room for her quiet time. She was working her way through the Old Testament and was now in the book of Ruth. Ruth had lost her husband

and had traveled to Moab with her mother-in-law, Naomi, who wanted to find a husband for her. Her instructions were clear:

> "Wash and perfume yourself, and put on your best clothes. Then go down to the threshing floor, but don't let him know you are there until he has finished eating and drinking. When he lies down, note the place where he is lying. Then go and uncover his feet and lie down. He will tell you what to do."
>
> "I will do whatever you say," Ruth answered.

Hanna continued reading and saw that Ruth had indeed done the forward thing her mother-in-law had asked of her. When Boaz discovered Ruth lying at his feet, he asked who she was.

"I am your servant Ruth," she said. "Spread the corner of your garment over me, since you are a kinsmen-redeemer."

Hanna searched for the explanation of the verse at the bottom of the page. She knew a kinsman-redeemer was the closest male relative, who was responsible for marrying a widow. Her eyes found the answer to her question in the study notes.

Spread the corner of your garment over me. A request for marriage.

Wow. The woman literally asked Boaz to marry her. Goose flesh tightened the skin on Hanna's arms, and her heart tripped. Micah came to mind, and she shoved the thought away.

Oh no. No way, God, I am not asking Micah to marry me. Please tell me You're not asking that.

She reread the verses and closed her eyes, listening more than praying. Her heart had not stopped its rhythmic pounding since she'd read the verses. Anxiety had sucked the moisture from her mouth, and she sipped from the ice water on her nightstand.

The words of the verses stirred in her mind, not settling anywhere, just floating aimlessly around. There was meaning in the story, a meaning for her, but it couldn't be what she'd originally thought. *Okay, let's think this through in a left-brained manner. Naomi knew what was sup-*

posed to happen, and she told Ruth what she needed to do. In Ruth's case Naomi knew Ruth needed a husband. *So, what do I know? I know I feel drawn to Micah, and I know he needs a friend.* Her dream of their wedding day surfaced, but she shrugged it off.

She felt God wanted them together for some purpose. *It's a little hard to accomplish that, God, when only one of us is aware of it.*

Bingo.

The thought hit her like a sledgehammer. *That's it. I'm aware of what God wants, but Micah isn't.*

The story pieces settled at last, though in a pattern she wasn't entirely comfortable with. *You want me to tell him? Oh, Lord, wouldn't it just be easier if You told him?*

She squirmed uncomfortably. People didn't just go up to others and say, "We're supposed to be together." *He'll think I'm a fruit loop, Lord! A real nutso. People just don't do that.* The Bible story flashed like a neon sign in her mind. *Well, they don't do it anymore.*

Hanna closed her Bible and lay back against her pillows. How could she just walk up to him and say that? And for goodness' sake, not only did he show no signs of being attracted to her, he didn't even want to be around her!

She looked grimly at her Bible as if the Book were at fault. *If I agree to this, Lord, I'm going to need the courage of Ruth. And it would help if You'd maybe prepare his heart to be open to what I say. And speaking of what I'll say . . . I guess I'm going to need some help there too.*

She breathed a laugh. *See, Lord, don't You think it'd be easier to do it Yourself?*

She should've done it herself. Hanna looked at the volleyball net, drew a deep breath, and sighed. The net sagged in the middle, and the poles poked outward from the ground like metal antennas. She fetched the volleyball from the barn, then came back and threw the ball into the net. It sank into the meshing and plopped onto the ground.

For all Devon's ambition, he tended to do things halfway. She looked at the horizon and gauged she had about half an hour before it would be too dark to work. Time enough to get started.

After digging around in the barn, she came back with a shovel and pulled the poles from the ground. She went six inches beyond the tiny hole and began scooping dirt from the packed ground. She wanted the net to stretch tautly from pole to pole, and she wanted the poles upright and solidly in the ground.

Hanna had plenty of time yesterday to think about Micah and how to approach him. Only problem was, she hadn't come to an answer about what to say. How did one go about this sort of thing? He would probably think her message had nothing to do with God, that it was some fantasy of her own making.

Her skin heated, and she knew it was the thought, not the exercise, that was causing it. He'd think she was enamored with him and had some illusion about it being God's plan. How could she convince him that it was not something she'd even wanted? That she, personally, had no desire for a relationship with him?

She stopped herself. Okay, maybe there was an attraction, but she certainly hadn't dreamed up this notion of a relationship with him. Actually, it scared her to death. What if she wasn't ready for a relationship? What if she couldn't bear to be touched?

The memory of Micah holding her in the tent skittered across her mind. She hadn't minded it then. *Is that what this is all about, God? Getting me over this fear of men?*

And, her feelings aside, how was she going to convince Micah? He might have a girlfriend, for all she knew. He'd never mentioned one, but there was that woman in the sporting-goods store. She'd definitely seemed proprietary toward him. And there was that Thursday night appointment he never missed. How dumb would she sound with her announcement if he had a girlfriend?

You are taking care of all this, God, right?

She leaned against the shovel for a breather. *How in the world am I supposed to pass this information on to him?*

Micah, we're meant to be together.

Micah, God has plans for us.

Micah, spread the corner of your garment over me.

She laughed and covered her face, embarrassed at the thought. She could just see herself huddling at the foot of his bed, saying those words. In today's culture they'd have a very different connotation. Maybe she wouldn't have to say anything to him. After all, if God really wanted her to do this Ruth thing, wouldn't He provide the opportunity? Micah had been as scarce as a snow flurry in July.

"What's wrong?" Micah's unmistakable voice pierced her thoughts—her very embarrassing thoughts.

She uncovered her face, exposing the blush that was surely there. "Nothing. I'm just trying to get these poles in the ground."

"Your grandma said you needed some help." His reluctance to be there was evident in the evasive gaze.

Good ol' Gram, undoubtedly with an ulterior motive.

He held out his hand for the shovel. "Want me to dig?"

She straightened her spine and opened her mouth.

He held his hand as if to ward off her words. "I know you're per-fectly capable, but it's getting dark, and we can get it done faster if we work together."

He had a point. She relinquished the shovel and went to the barn for the rusty one. His presence, even if reluctant, did something to her insides. She wished for the camaraderie they'd shared on the climb. If only he would relax again, and they could become friends in a natural way. *As opposed to flinging myself at him. Are You listening, God?*

Hanna plucked the other pole from the ground and began shovel-ing. They worked in silence until he called her over to steady the pole while he packed the dirt around it. She was conscious of the sweat trick-ling down her neck. He didn't even seem flushed, much less sweaty.

He packed in the last of the dirt with his feet and tested the pole. It didn't budge. They moved to the other hole, and he finished digging while she watched him work under the veil of her lashes. Was now the time for the conversation she'd been dreading? Had God sent him out here for just that reason?

Twilight was falling like a sheer curtain, giving a sense of anonymity she found comforting. Wouldn't she rather confront him about it now when he could barely see her than in the stark light of day?

"I've been wanting to talk to you about something." *Oh, boy, there's no turning back now.*

He continued to dig. "What's that?"

The moment was here, and she didn't know what to say. Words flew frantically around her mind.

The odd silence drew his attention.

Help me, God.

He quirked a brow.

"I have a feeling about us."

He waited.

She took a deep breath. "It might sound strange. In fact, I know it'll sound strange, but . . . look, you're a Christian, too, so I'm just going to say it outright. God has impressed on me that He wants us together for some . . . purpose."

He stiffened, then thrust the shovel into the ground and left it standing upright. "You're mistaken."

Hanna let out the breath she'd been holding. She'd expected him to laugh. To roll his eyes. To tell her she was nuts. Anything but this. "I thought so, too, at first but—"

"It's a bad idea." He stabbed the pole into the ground.

"If you're already involved with someone—"

"There's no one else. I'm just not interested." His bass voice vibrated through the night air.

Hanna's face heated, and she was grateful for the cloak of dusk. *Well. He couldn't have been any plainer than that.* She kicked dirt around the pole, more to cover her mortification than to fill the hole.

"Look, I didn't mean it that way."

Sure he didn't. *What am I supposed to do now, God? I've done what You asked, and what good has it done? It's done nothing but humiliate—*

"You're my employer."

She let silence be her answer.

"You don't even know me, my past."

"That can be changed."

"You wouldn't like what you found."

"I'm willing to take that chance."

He impaled her with a steely look that penetrated the murky air. "I'm not." He stomped on the dirt twice more, then walked away.

Micah shut his door behind him and leaned against it. Fear. He could taste it in his mouth, the sour, biting taste he'd thought he'd conquered. It left him feeling weak and vulnerable, two emotions he'd sworn he was through with. He sat on the sofa, not bothering to turn on a light.

Hanna. The words she'd said nearly knocked him backward. They'd sent shivers up his spine and uncoiled a length of fear in his gut. He was afraid to listen to her words, afraid to acknowledge the truth in them, afraid to turn this over to God.

I don't want a woman in my life. I thought we had an understanding, Father. I don't want a relationship; I don't want love; and I don't want more pain. Haven't I had enough of that?

His heart was still pumping furiously as if he were scaling West Horn instead of lounging on the couch. It was bad enough that he was attracted to Hanna. That he genuinely liked her. That her presence was unavoidable.

And now she had some notion they were meant for each other.

Maybe you are.

He deflected the words from his heart. It wasn't true. God wouldn't ask that of him. And he wouldn't ask that of himself. Ever.

He knew he'd hurt Hanna with his adamancy, but he wanted to be very clear that it wasn't going to happen. *They* weren't going to happen. What good would he be in a relationship? What did he have to offer but a heart that had withered and rotted before it had a chance to grow?

His three-day climb started tomorrow, and for that he was grateful. Maybe by the time he returned, Hanna would be over this absurd idea. Maybe with time she would see he was no good for her.

CHAPTER
TWELVE

"Come here, Alex; let's fix your shirt." Natalie tucked it in and adjusted his elastic-waisted shorts. His hair stuck up on top, and she feathered his bangs with her fingers. "There you go." She patted his behind and went to straighten up the living room.

She'd purposely told Hanna to come a few minutes after she expected Keith. It wouldn't hurt him to see the boys, to see how much they missed him. She had one goal tonight, and seeing the boys might give her that one little push she needed.

Keith had picked up the boys on Saturday to spend some time with them. They didn't understand why Daddy wasn't staying at their house. Neither did Natalie. He'd told her he was at the Comfort Inn, and she'd confirmed it when she'd called to arrange tonight's meeting. Why wasn't he staying with *her*? Was *she* married too? Whoever *she* was. He'd told her nothing, given her no clue who he was breaking his vows with. She shook her head. She would not give in to her anger tonight. It would defeat her purpose.

She picked up the stack of magazines and papers that had accumulated over the past few weeks. Her Bible-study workbook, *A Woman's Heart,* was at the bottom of the pile. She felt a pang of guilt. She'd started the study with her women's group at church a week before she'd found out about the affair. And she hadn't opened it since.

You've had your mind on other things. Your life has fallen apart. Of course the routines are going to be broken.

"Dink. Dink." Taylor held up his sipper cup; she took it and filled it with juice.

The clock chimed the hour, and she dashed to the bathroom to take a final peek at her own appearance. She'd taken time with her makeup and hair. All the books she'd read said a husband wants his wife to take care of her appearance. It was an area she'd slacked off in.

"Daddy!"

She heard Alex's squeal preceded by Taylor's as they ran to the window to watch him come in.

"Remember, you can spend a few minutes with Daddy, then Aunt Hanna's going to come and pick you up."

"I want to stay with Daddy!" Alex said.

"I know, sweetheart, but Aunt Hanna's going to take you to the soda fountain and the park. You'll have so much fun." She injected her voice with enthusiasm and breathed a sigh when they seemed to buy it.

She opened the front door and forced a smile to her lips. "Hi, Keith."

The boys barraged their dad before he could return her greeting. He picked up Alex and gave him a hug.

"I missed you, Daddy! Are you back? Are you sleeping here tonight?"

Keith opened his mouth, then shut it again.

"Me! Me!"

Keith laughed as Taylor danced on his feet with his arms outstretched toward his father. Keith knelt down and swooped him up. "Hi, buddy."

Natalie felt her eyes burn as she watched him kiss his sons.

"Hanna's coming to get them while we talk."

"Are you staying, Daddy?" Alex wanted to know.

"We'll see, tiger."

He set them down, and they ran to get the pictures they'd painted at church.

"Does Hanna know everything?"

She nodded.

His jaw twitched.

"I had to talk to someone."

The boys returned and showed their artwork. Keith gave them his full attention, smiling and tickling and just enjoying them. He did love the boys. They had that going for them.

Moments later, she heard a car in the drive. Keith sent her a panicked glance, and she knew he didn't want to face Hanna. For a moment she reveled in the thought of his having to face his shame, but she shoved the feeling aside and gathered the boys.

They said good-bye to their dad, and she led them down the sidewalk just as Hanna exited her car. Natalie installed Taylor's car seat, buckled them in, and shut the door. She offered Hanna a twenty-dollar bill, but her sister refused.

"I'll be praying for you," Hanna said.

"Thanks. I'll need it."

"I'll give you a couple of hours, all right?"

"Sure, that'll be plenty of time.

Hanna got in the car.

"Hanna."

Her sister looked at her expectantly.

"Thank you. For taking the boys."

Hanna smiled and pulled out of the driveway.

Natalie took a deep breath, feeling her tight rib cage expand as if she'd been taking shallow breaths all day. *Help me, God. Give me the words to say. Don't let my temper take over.*

She turned and went back to face her husband.

Keith was still standing when she entered the house. His gaze was taking in the appearance of the house. He turned when the door swung shut behind her, "The house looks nice."

"Thanks."

They stood several feet apart, looking everywhere except at each other. There were so many questions she wanted answers to. Who was she? When did it start? How far have things gone? Do you love her? Do you love *me*? Are you leaving us? And the one that kept her awake at nights: *why?*

Questions she wanted to ask; answers she dreaded to hear. But none of that mattered right now. She must stay focused on her goal, not let her emotions take over.

Natalie sat on the sofa hoping Keith would follow her lead. *Don't make me ask you to sit as if you're a guest.*

He didn't. He rested his elbows on his knees, and she watched him twiddle his fingers. He always did that when he was nervous.

She started with the heavy artillery. "The boys miss you."

"I miss them too."

"*I* miss you."

The silence was deafening.

She cleared her throat. "I'm not sure why you felt you had to leave, but I want you to know I'm willing to fix whatever's broken in our relationship. Obviously our marriage isn't meeting your needs."

His eyes met hers, then darted away. "It might be too late."

Her stomach bottomed out. "We won't know until we try." She walked to him on trembling legs and knelt at his feet. "Remember when we first met? I was lying there in the snow seeing stars dance around in my head, then you appeared." A smile lifted her lips. "I thought I was imagining you. You asked if I was okay, then you helped me to my feet." She took his hand. She felt a bolt of joy when she saw he was still wearing his wedding band. "I swear I could feel the heat of your skin through our gloves."

"I remember."

"You asked me back to the lodge for a cup of cocoa, and we talked the whole afternoon. After we married you said you knew I was the one for you that day. Do you remember how we felt then? How we felt every time we were together?"

"That's gone now."

"You can't expect those heady, romantic feelings to last. They go away, but they're replaced by a more mature love." She took a breath and let it out slowly. The next sentence needed to be tempered with love. "Whatever you're feeling with . . . her . . . it'll go away in time. And then what'll you do? Leave her too?"

He shook his head. "This isn't what I expected today."

She knew what he meant. He'd expected accusations and demands, had probably come expecting to be on the defensive. "Would you consider moving back home?"

Skepticism filled his face.

She appealed to the tightwad in him. "What sense does it make to pay for a hotel when you have a home?"

"This is about more than money."

"I know. But the boys don't understand. I don't know what to tell them." She pressed closer. "They deserve a father, Keith. We can work on whatever's broken. We can make our relationship better. I can still make you happy."

He stared out the window. Was he seeing the newly mowed grass, the annuals she'd planted last week? Was he seeing the swing on the porch where they'd spent many hours talking and laughing? Was he seeing the sidewalk where he'd taught Alex to ride without training wheels?

If she could just get him to move back home. She couldn't win him back if he wasn't here. If he saw how hard she was trying, if she made him happy again, maybe he'd forget this other woman. He would need to stop seeing her. They would surely need counseling. But all that would come later, after he agreed to come back. One step at a time.

"If I agree to come back, that's no guarantee. You need to understand that."

It was less than she'd hoped for. "I understand."

His eyes found the boys' portrait hanging on the wall. She forced herself to wait patiently, while her heart poised as if on the edge of a cliff.

Finally, his head nodded slightly. "All right."

Joy bubbled within her, but she suppressed the giddiness. She didn't want to scare him away. "I'm glad. The boys will be ecstatic."

He stood. "I'll go get my things packed up, check out."

"All right."

"When's Hanna bringing them back?"

She looked at her watch. Had it really only been twenty minutes since they'd left? "About an hour and a half."

"I'll be back in a couple of hours."

The hotel was only a few miles away. It shouldn't take that long. Was he going to see *her*? Going to tell her he was moving back home? She bit the inside of her mouth until she tasted blood.

He slipped out the door, and she shut it behind him. She closed her eyes as she leaned back against the door and allowed the relief she felt to wash over her. *Thank You, God. Thank You.* They had a long way to go, but it was a start.

She went to the kitchen and took the sirloin strips from the freezer. She would make dinner while she waited for Hanna. She'd bought all the ingredients for beef stroganoff for just this occasion. It was Keith's favorite.

While she defrosted the meat, she thought about the boys. They would be so glad to have their father home. They'd asked about him every day. Even Taylor, who hadn't combined two words yet, had given his daddy's name an inflection that left no doubt he was inquiring about his father's whereabouts.

Whatever she did, she could not blow this opportunity. Keith would be home, and she must not make him angry—make him regret his decision to come back. It would be hard when her heart longed to rage at him for what he'd done. When her mind wanted answers to the dozens of questions that swam through her head all day.

But that was goal number two: counseling. If he would agree to counseling, she could get her answers in the safe presence of an adviser, who could keep the conversations from getting wildly out of control. If only he would agree.

She knew Pastor Richards counseled married couples, but she didn't think Keith would want to go to him. She opened the junk drawer and pulled out the phone book. In the yellow pages, she found "Marriage Counselors." How did one go about choosing the person who would help them put their marriage back together? She didn't know anyone who'd gone to counseling to ask for a reference. Maybe she could ask Pastor Richards. But what if Keith didn't want anyone to know what was going on? If Pastor knew, Keith would never go back to church.

By the time the stroganoff was bubbling in the skillet, the doorbell rang. She let Hanna and the boys in, and Alex began rambling about doing the monkey bars while Taylor pranced in place saying, "Daddy? Daddy?"

"Daddy will be home in a few minutes."

She met Hanna's gaze and smiled. "Alex, take Taylor and wash your hands. It's almost dinnertime."

They disappeared around the corner.

"He's coming back to stay?"

"Yes. I'm so relieved."

"Of course, you are." She drew Natalie into an embrace. "Oh, I'm so glad."

"He made sure I understood it's no guarantee. This is far from over. I still don't know who it is or if he's willing to give her up."

They parted, and she asked Hanna to follow her into the kitchen so she could continue making dinner. "We have a long way to go. I'm so angry, Hanna. Angry at him. Angry at her. Sometimes the rage fills me, and I have horrible thoughts. Thoughts I never dreamed I was capable of."

Hanna stirred the noodles. "I'm sure that's normal."

"And other times I'm terrified. Of losing him, of being a single parent . . . I don't know what I'll do if that happens."

"We'll just pray it doesn't happen. He's willing to come back home; that says something."

Nat heard the boys playing in the water in the bathroom, but decided to let it go.

"I think we should get some counseling."

Hanna nodded. "That's a good idea."

"Do you know anyone who's had counseling? I want a Christian counselor, someone who won't suggest a divorce when things get heavy. And preferably a man. I think Keith would respond better to a man."

"I don't know of anyone who's had . . . just a minute. I think Micah mentioned his foster father is a marriage counselor. And I know he's a Christian."

"Micah—your climbing guide?"

"Yeah, I think I told you about him." Hanna sniffed and rubbed her nose, a sure sign of discomfort.

"What's this? Is there something going on between you and Micah?" She smiled as Hanna's face flushed.

"There *is* something going on."

"It's more like *nothing* is going on."

"Despite your wishes? What about—do you feel like you're ready?" Hanna nodded. "He's not, though."

"If he has any sense, he'll snatch you up while he can."

"Anyway, I know he said his foster father is a counselor."

Natalie smirked. "Nice change of subject."

"Thanks," Hanna said, without pause. "I'll ask Micah about it and get his name and number, all right?"

Nat hugged her sister. "Thanks, Hanna."

"I wish I could do more, make this whole mess go away."

"Me too." She checked the microwave clock. "I don't mean to rush you, but he's going to be home any minute, and I think he's afraid to face you."

Hanna crossed her arms and narrowed her eyes. "He should be."

"You're sounding more like an older sister than a younger one." Natalie smiled.

"Sorry. I guess I'm angry with him myself."

"Thanks for sticking up for me." They embraced again, then Natalie let her out the door. "Pray for us."

"You know I will."

Natalie watched her go, then went to the bathroom where the boys had undoubtedly created a pond in the basin of the pedestal sink.

CHAPTER
THIRTEEN

"Why don't you go out there and join them?" Gram asked.

Hanna shrugged and stepped away from the office window where she'd been watching Micah and Devon playing volleyball with several families.

"All right, now, what's the matter? I can see there's something going on between you and Micah. Did you two have a spat?"

"No, Gram, nothing like that." She sat in her desk chair, and Gram sat across from her. Hanna sighed deeply. What would Gram say if she knew how Hanna had been feeling, how she was convinced God had a plan for her and Micah? How she'd boldly confronted him about it? Then she remembered something Gram had once told her and gathered the courage to be honest.

"I guess if anyone would understand, it would be you. You've said you knew Grandpop was the one for you when you met him, right?"

Gram nodded, tender patience filling her eyes.

"I've got that same feeling with Micah. It's like God has put his name on my heart. I didn't even want a relationship with a man; you know that. But I just have this feeling . . ."

She waited for Gram to say something, but the older woman just tipped her lips in a smile and waited.

"God may have let me know what He wants, but apparently He hasn't clued Micah in." She went on to explain how he'd rejected her four days ago. The sting of it was still fresh, and she felt as if her face were on fire as she talked. "He has no interest in me or a relationship."

"Either that, or he's running from it. Sometimes what we want and what God wants are two different things. Maybe Micah's just fighting it."

"I guess that's possible."

"How do you feel about him?"

Nothing like getting right to the point. "I enjoy his company. At least, I did before he clammed up. And I am attracted to him."

"What about—has he ever touched you?"

"Yes." A smile played at her lips. "Nothing serious, you know, but I wasn't afraid, not even a little. In fact, he made me feel . . . safe."

"It sounds like you've made progress since your last relationship."

"Either that, or it's just that Micah affects me differently." She absently slid Gram's ring along her necklace. "I don't know what to do. If he's fighting it, how can I get him to change his mind?"

"Only God can change the heart, but you're not exactly making His job easy."

"What do you mean?"

Gram cocked her head. "Well, how's he supposed to be tempted by you if you're never together? Get out there, child, and show him what he's missing!"

Hanna chuckled. "Has anyone told you you're an awesome grandma?"

Gram took on a self-sacrificing look. "It *has* been a while . . ."

She hugged her grandma, "You're the best, Gram."

Hanna changed into her tennis shoes and walked around the lodge to the backyard. Gram was a good listener. When she'd been in high school, she used to tell Gram about all her secret crushes. *Too bad Natalie can't bring herself to tell Gram about their marriage problems. She could probably give good advice, what with her fifty-plus years of marriage experience.*

She heard the volleyball players cheering and laughing from the distance. It had been a long time since she'd played, and her footsteps quickened in anticipation. *Don't forget your main purpose for being out here.* Maybe she could finagle her way onto Micah's team. Proximity and all that.

When she rounded the corner, an athletic-looking teen served the ball overhand straight into the net. His team ragged on him as they passed the ball to the other side, Micah's team.

"Hey, Hanna," Devon shouted. "Come give us a hand! We're dying over here."

"All right." *Shoot, wrong team. Oh, well, at least we'll be across from one another.*

Devon moved over and motioned for her to fill the gap on the back row. The game got under way again, and teams cheered their teammates, calling "set!" when they were in position to spike. Hanna hadn't hit the ball yet, but she watched eagerly for her chance.

Then a man on the other team hit the ball right to her. She clasped her hands together and got in position.

Whomp! She was knocked sideways, and the ball connected with Devon's hands instead of hers. She stumbled, barely keeping her footing.

The ball stayed in play. She shot Devon an annoyed look that went unnoticed.

By the time she'd made it to the front row, her team was ahead fourteen to eight, and she still hadn't hit the ball. Not that it hadn't come to her. *Ball hog,* she thought, as Devon once again claimed a ball that had her name on it. The teen who'd mis-served was up again.

"Hey, man, get it over!" Devon called.

"Game point!" someone called.

His serve cleared the net, and the ball was volleyed back and forth. Micah was directly across from her, and Hanna hoped she wouldn't have to block a shot from him. *Not much chance of that with Devon around.*

Hanna's team's front row sent the ball to Micah right over the net, a perfect set for a spike. Devon was still in the back corner where he'd dived for the last ball. Hanna clasped her hands to dig the spike. But Micah simply tapped the ball to her, and she set the middle-aged man beside her. She looked at Micah. He could've spiked that.

But she knew why he hadn't. He wouldn't take the chance of nailing a woman in the face. The thought pleased and annoyed her at the same time. She could handle herself; she didn't need to be mollycoddled.

The ball was still in action, and it was heading toward the kid beside Micah. "Get it, Josh!" Micah called. Micah was close enough to snag it himself, but he let the boy try. The ball ricocheted off the boy's hands and flew out of bounds.

"We won!" Devon said. "That's three for us."

The players talked for a few minutes, then began wandering off in different directions.

"Hey, Hanna." Devon appeared beside her. "How 'bout taking a boat out on the lake?"

"Oh, sorry. I have some work to do." She escaped to her office before he tried to cajole her into going. She did have work to do, and she wanted to check how booked the lodge was for July.

Later, Hanna stopped tapping on the keyboard and stared at the screen. Those cancellations hadn't stopped, and they were in trouble. They would be able to make June's payment, maybe even July's. But August was half-empty, and there was no way they could make the mortgage like that. She didn't even want to think about the early fall.

She saw Micah pass the office, carrying his empty cake plate to the kitchen. Earlier Gram had offered him a slice of her carrot cake, and he knew a good deal when he saw one.

When he passed by again, Hanna listened until she heard the rustle of newspaper in the great room. It was something he did almost every evening after dinner. She debated whether she should join him. He was just as indifferent toward her as ever, maybe even more so after she'd made a fool of herself. *What am I supposed to do now, God? If I go in there, I'll probably just scare him away.*

So what? She'd already been humiliated once, what did she have to lose? She picked up her coffee mug and left her office just as Gram entered the great room with a plate of carrot cake.

"Here, Micah," Gram said. "How about a slice of my famous carrot cake?"

He opened his mouth, then shut it again before smiling kindly. "Sure, Mrs. Landin, that sounds great." He took the plate.

Gram patted Hanna's shoulder as she passed. "None for you, child, not with your allergies."

It was true; she was allergic to nuts, but that was the last thing on her mind. Hanna rested her elbows on the counter and watched Micah. He set down the paper and started eating in what could only be described as a reluctant manner.

Suddenly he looked up, as if becoming aware of her presence. "Hi."

"Hi." She was vaguely aware of the smile curling her lips, and she knew the warmth she felt for Micah must be spilling from her gaze.

He set the fork on the plate. "Stop looking at me like that."

"Like what?"

His brows knotted together in the center of his forehead. "Like I'm a hot fudge sundae, and you've been dieting all week."

Heat singed her cheeks. "I wasn't."

He raised a single brow, silently refuting her denial. After a moment he dug into his cake while reading the paper in his lap.

"I saw what you just did."

He glanced in her direction, then away, as if he planned to ignore her comment.

"You're a nice man, Micah Gallagher."

His expression hardened, his eyes narrowed. In a somber voice, he said, "If you knew some of the things I've done, you wouldn't say that."

What could he have done that was so bad? She'd seen him with the customers, with her grandmother, with the kids. Was he just trying to scare her away? "I've seen the kind of man you are."

"You're seeing what you want to see." He took the last bite of cake and carried his plate past her to the kitchen. When he returned, it was only to collect the paper and retire to his room. She returned his goodnight and watched him walk around the corner.

He was every bit the man she thought he was. Her mother's saying flashed into her mind. "If it acts like a duck, looks like a duck, and walks like a duck, it's probably a duck."

You can't scare me away, Micah Gallagher.

⟡

Hanna and Gram grabbed breakfast off the sideboard before heading to church. Fortunately, Sunday mornings were slow at the lodge, and Mrs. Eddlestein always covered the desk while she and Gram attended church.

They were discussing the week's menu when Micah rounded the corner. His hair was damp, and he was in his Sunday clothes, a pair of black jeans and a polo shirt.

"Mornin'," he said.

They returned his greeting. Gram looked at her watch. "You're running a mite late, aren't you?" Micah always left for church by the time she and Gram sat down for breakfast.

"Overslept."

Gram slathered jam on a piece of toast. "Why don't you join us this morning?"

Hanna met Gram's gaze just in time to see the wink she tossed her way.

"By the time you finish eating, your church will be starting. Besides, it's been years since I walked into church on the arm of a handsome young man. It'll make Gerdy jealous as can be."

"Well . . ." Micah sat beside Gram with a plate of food and looked at his watch. "I suppose you're right. I just might do that."

"Splendid," Gram said. "You'll be in Hanna's Sunday-school class. It's for the singles. Just you make certain to watch out for Amy Lipenschiemer. That gal will have you hitched with a ring on your finger before you can turn around and say howdy-do."

Hanna laughed. "She's not that bad, Gram."

The older woman sipped her tea and tossed Micah a look. "Don't say I didn't warn you."

Hanna watched Micah across from her, noticing the way he blew on his oatmeal before sliding it in his mouth. His lips were tinged with pink, and when he blew, they puckered up slightly, sending the steam in a swirl around his face. She could almost feel the softness of his lips against hers. The thought sent a wave of heat coursing through her veins.

His mouth curled upward at the corners and, with a stab of dread, she met his stare. His eyes held a hint of amusement. She flushed but couldn't seem to look away. She was melded to the warmth in his eyes. The heat within her seemed to settle in a liquid pool in her stomach as the smile fell from his lips. She drowned in the molten silver of his eyes.

Gram cleared her throat. "I guess I'll get that." Humor tempered Gram's words. She left the table, and Hanna realized the phone had been ringing.

She grabbed her orange juice and sipped, more to busy herself than anything else. An awkward silence filled the air. She'd seen it in his eyes. He was drawn to her, too, whether he denied it or not. She hadn't been out of circulation so long that she didn't recognize attraction when she saw it. And she'd more than seen it. She'd *felt* it. *My, oh, my.* She resisted the urge to fan her face.

Soon Gram returned, and they finished breakfast in silence. Hanna drove them to church in her 4x4 and, once they got inside, she and Micah proceeded to her Sunday-school class. It wasn't a large class, only ten or fifteen on any given Sunday, but the group knew her well enough to be surprised when she walked in with a man. A few pairs of eyebrows lifted as she introduced him as the lodge's climbing guide. They'd arrived right on time, and Hanna was glad the class started before anyone started quizzing them about their relationship.

Afterward, they made their way back to the sanctuary and met up with Gram in the hallway. Somehow, as they filed into the short pew, Hanna wound up beside Micah, a feat she hadn't manipulated, but certainly didn't mind.

They spread out as much as they could on the pew, but when Gerdy passed by, Gram called out to her. "Gerdy, come sit with us."

Hanna looked at the few inches between each of them and back at Gerdy, whose sedentary job as a police-station secretary left her hips on the wide side.

"Not enough room," Gerdy said.

"Sure there is," Gram said. "Scoot over, you two."

Micah wedged into the corner, and Hanna scooted closer. But when Gerdy sat down, Gram was forced to almost sit on Hanna, so she slid even closer to Micah. Her thighs were flush with his, and she could feel the heat of his leg through his jeans. She crossed her legs, but she was still pressed up against him, shoulder to shoulder, thigh to thigh.

Oh, well, this isn't so bad. She stifled a giggle. She couldn't have planned it better herself. Her gaze met Gram's, and her grandmother winked.

Hanna's mom and dad took a seat in front of them, and Hanna reintroduced them to Micah, whom they'd met on one other occasion. Several greeters worked their way over to shake their hands and meet Micah. Paula and David squeezed in beside her parents, and Hanna introduced them to Micah.

"She looks familiar," Micah whispered, after Paula had turned back around in the pew.

Micah was still looking at Paula, and Hanna felt a twinge of jealousy at her sister's glamorous red hair and immaculate style. "You've probably seen her on Channel 3 News."

The music director stepped forward then, and they began a medley of choruses, using the big screen. Micah's bass voice resonated beside her as she sang melody, and she thought their voices blended nicely. She closed her eyes and sang the words to her Father, riding on the swell of harmony.

After a lengthy time of singing, they took their seats and listened to the announcements. Next came the silent prayer time.

Pastor Richards took the podium. "I don't do this often, but I wonder if we could join hands in unity as we go to the Lord in silent prayer."

The congregation joined hands, moving across the narrow aisles to connect with each other. Micah moved out and grasped the hand of a preschooler, then grasped Hanna's hand.

She slid her fingers around his hand and felt his fingers tighten on hers. His skin was warm and rough against hers. The kind of hand that could perform tasks of strength as well as deeds of kindness, gentleness.

The heat grew between their palms, and she felt as if fire licked at her skin. *Next thing you know, you'll have sweaty palms.*

She forced herself to think about something else, like . . . Gram. She had a doctor's appointment coming up later in the week, and Hanna was anxious about it. *Lord, help the doctors to know what to do, what kinds of tests to perform. Help Gram; give her strength and peace. Give our whole family peace as we seek an answer. She's so dear to us, Lord, it's hard to imagine losing her slowly to Alzheimer's.* Hanna stroked Gram's hand with her thumb. *If it's within Your will for a complete healing, Lord, I pray that it would be so. But if she's diagnosed with Alzheimer's or some other disease, I pray that You'd give us the strength to cope. Bless her, Lord with Your—*

Suddenly, Hanna realized what she was doing.

As she caressed Gram's hand with one thumb, she was caressing Micah's with the other.

All fingers ceased movement. She cringed. *Oh, Lord! Please. Just let me melt into a lava puddle and flow out the back door. That stupid little quirk of mine. Why can't one side of my body do something without the other side following suit? He must think I'm completely shameless!*

She squeezed her eyes tightly shut, never wanting to open them again. *Oh, God, right now would be a great time for the Rapture, don't You think?*

Micah bowed his head as the pastor called for silent prayer. Hanna's hand felt cold in his. Cold and small. But soft as a rose petal. He concentrated on keeping his hand perfectly still, but the more he thought about it, the more his muscles seemed to twitch. He imagined her hand stroking his face, his mouth. All he could think about was their twined hands inches from his body. *Get a grip, Gallagher. Think about something else.* He began a prayer but didn't get far. The child on his other side was getting antsy and began swinging their hands back and forth.

The pastor began praying aloud.

Then he felt it. A barely discernible movement that grew into a full-blown caress. His breath caught. A shiver wiggled up his spine sending tingles through all his limbs. *Have mercy.* She was . . . she was stroking his hand, brushing her thumb gently across the back of his own. The movement stirred the tiny hairs on his thumb making his skin tingle with awareness. He felt every nuance. Every cell she touched. It accelerated his heart, his breathing. How could one little touch incite him to such—

Just as suddenly, she stopped. Her hand, her arm, stiffened against his. He squelched the urge to peek. But instantly he knew. She hadn't meant to do it. Somehow, she'd done it mindlessly, then stopped when she'd realized what she was doing.

The prayer ended, and as he glanced at Hanna, who avoided looking at him, he smothered the grin that tugged at his mouth. If he were a cruel man, he could have a lot of fun with this one.

CHAPTER
FOURTEEN

Natalie answered the phone, balancing it between her shoulder and ear.

Hanna greeted her. "Tonight's the big night, isn't it?"

"Yeah, and I'm feeling really nervous about it. But I'm glad Micah was able to recommend someone."

"Have you two talked about anything yet? Has Keith told you who the woman is?"

Natalie's stomach clenched the way it always did when she thought about her husband with another woman. "No. It's killing me, but I thought it'd be better if we waited until we were in Mr. Schmidt's office."

"Keith doesn't say anything? Is he still getting home late?"

The ache started in her midsection and radiated outward, the way it did every night as she waited for him to get home. "I don't know if he's working late or seeing her. I haven't wanted to know. I'm afraid if I knew the truth, I'd blow up at him and make him leave again."

Hanna sighed. "You're in such an awful spot, Nat. I wish I could do something."

"You can do something. Tell me how things are coming along with you and Micah."

"We don't have to talk about me. My problems are minuscule compared to what you're going through."

Nat felt a little smile tilt her lips. "Yes, but your problems are a lot more fun to talk about than mine. Please. Give me something else to think about for a few minutes."

"There's nothing exciting to report. He's busy ignoring me, and I'm busy making a fool of myself."

"Ooooh, you can't stop there. Details please."

Hanna breathed a self-deprecating laugh. "He went to church yesterday with me and Gram, and the pastor had everyone hold hands during the quiet time."

"And . . ."

"Oh, Nat, it was so embarrassing! Gram was on the other side of me, and I started caressing her hand, and you know how I tend to—"

"Oh no, you didn't."

"I did! I could've died."

Laughter bubbled up in Natalie's throat and spilled out.

"It's not funny."

Natalie couldn't seem to stop laughing, and it felt so good. It had been so long since she'd had a good laugh.

Her sister's voice rang with the pretense of irritation. "Fine. Go ahead and laugh at my humiliation; see if I care."

"What did he say afterward? Did you tell him you didn't mean to?" Natalie contained another chuckle.

"I didn't say anything. I was hoping he'd just forget the whole thing."

"And did he?"

"He had a smirk on his face the rest of the day. Like he was amused with my . . . my little *crush* on him. But the good news is that I think he cares too. Maybe he won't say so, but I see signs of it in the way he looks at me. There's so much heat in his expression, if I were ice cream, I'd melt. When he looks at me like that, I know he feels it too. I wish I knew what was holding him back."

"Maybe he had a bad relationship, got burned before, and is afraid to try again."

"I don't know. He keeps alluding to his dark past like he's trying to scare me away."

Natalie frowned. "What kind of past?" If he was interested in her sister, she wanted to know what kind of guy he was.

"Nothing to worry about, Nat. You should see him with Gram. Whenever she does something forgetful or loses something, he handles her so gently. And he's patient with the kids and great with the customers."

"It sounds like he might deserve you. Maybe."

Hanna laughed. "Spoken like a true sister."

Natalie heard a knock on the door. "Oh, gotta run, Hanna, the sitter's here."

"I'll be praying about your meeting."

They said good-bye, then Natalie went to let the sitter in.

Twenty minutes later, she followed the directions she'd taken from the secretary at One Accord Counseling. Slowing her Suburban, she slipped out of the rush-hour traffic and into the parking lot of the business complex.

When she saw the sign, she pulled into a parking space. The lot had two cars, and neither of them were Keith's. She glanced at her watch as she walked toward the door. She was five minutes early. She hoped Keith wouldn't be late but knew she shouldn't expect anything else.

She entered the lobby, looking around to get her bearings. The office behind the glass partition was dark and empty, but she saw a sign-in sheet and scribbled her name on the line. Apparently the secretary worked regular business hours, but Mr. Schmidt worked evenings when necessary.

She took a seat on an upholstered chair and clutched her purse in her lap like a lifeline. What would happen tonight? Would she find out who he was seeing? Would she find out her husband was in love with the woman?

Getting him to agree to counseling had been a taxing effort in itself. He'd claimed he was too busy to see a counselor every week, claimed it was a bunch of malarkey anyway. But after three days of gentle prodding, he'd agreed. To one session only, but it was a start.

She looked around the lobby. On the wallpapered walls hung prints of quiet outdoor scenes. The mauve carpeting looked fairly new, except for the path that was worn from the entry to the hallway. How many troubled marriages had been renewed within these walls? How many had ended?

A door opened down the hall and, moments later, a woman appeared. She avoided Natalie's eyes as she slipped out the door. Natalie watched her scurry down the walk and wondered if the woman's marriage had ended. Had her husband left her? Was he involved with another woman? The cloud of perfume she'd left behind carried no clues.

She heard another door open and took a deep breath. Would she have to face Mr. Schmidt alone, like she was the only one who cared about her marriage? *Maybe you are.*

The door beside her opened. Keith entered, and she smiled with relief. They exchanged greetings just before Mr. Schmidt rounded the corner. He introduced himself, insisting they call him Jim, then they followed him down the corridor. Relief at Keith's presence carried her to the office, but once they entered, fear twisted in her stomach as she wondered again what she would discover tonight.

The office looked like the living room or den of someone's home. The lighting was neither bright nor dim, and the furniture was the pillowed, comfy sort that beckoned you after a long day.

Mr. Schmidt gestured to them to take a seat. Natalie sat in the love seat, but Keith took the padded chair instead of sitting beside her.

"Now," Jim began, "what brings you to One Accord?" He slipped on a pair of round, frameless spectacles.

Natalie looked at Keith, whose arms lay folded across his chest. He looked toward her, then away.

How did she begin? She knew so little of what was going on. "We're having some problems." She cleared her throat. "I don't know where to start."

"How about starting when you first realized something was wrong," Jim said.

She glanced at her husband. Apparently he was only here to fill the chair. "I was putting away his clothes one day . . ." She continued the story from the time she found the condom to last week, when she asked Keith to move back home. Tears flowed freely down her face as she relived the moments, and Jim plucked a tissue from the box between them and handed it to her.

She wiped her face repeatedly, crumpling the tissue between trembling fingers in between. Keith remained impassive, a virtual wall of indifference. Finally she finished talking, ran out of things to say.

Jim looked at Keith. "Natalie doesn't seem to have the full picture. Maybe you can fill in the blanks?" Jim crossed his legs and leaned back against his chair.

The clock on the wall ticked off time. The silence thickened. Natalie watched Keith's jaw twitch and knew he didn't want to talk. Didn't even want to be here.

Somewhere in the building a vacuum cleaner roared to life.

"How are you feeling right now, Keith?"

"Mad. Cornered! I feel like a trap's been set for me, and you're both just waiting for me to reach in for the cheese."

Interesting that you compared yourself to a rat, Natalie thought.

"Would you agree that your marriage has problems?" Jim asked.

Keith cursed. "Isn't that why we're here?"

Natalie watched her fingers fold the tissue, then unfold it. She avoided Jim's eyes. He was a Christian; what must he think of Keith with his belligerent attitude and filthy mouth?

"You've admitted to having an affair, yet Natalie seems to know little about the details," Jim said. "Are you willing to answer her questions?"

Keith shifted in his chair. "Depends on what she wants to know."

"Natalie?" Jim turned the floor over to her.

Oh, God, it's time to learn the truth. I don't know if I'm ready to hear it. I don't know if I can bear to know the details. She wiped away the tears that began flowing down her face. "I—I guess I want to know who it is. I *need* to know who it is."

Jim looked at Keith.

Keith crossed his arms again. "I already told you. You don't know her."

"Does she work at the bank? Live in the neighborhood? Work at the coffee shop? Tell me! I deserve to know that much, don't I?" The words scalded her throat.

He pressed his lips together. "She works at the bank."

His words sliced her heart, left an awful empty feeling in the pit of her stomach. *He's been with her every day for how long? Spending more time with her than me!* There was no stopping the tears now.

"How long?" she asked when she could talk again. "How long has this been going on?" She steeled herself for the answer.

"I don't know, awhile."

Anger nipped at her. "*Awhile?* How long is that? A few months? A year? How long?"

"Since around Christmas, all right?"

She sucked in a breath. Shock tumbled through her midsection in waves. Then the ache. The ache that had filled her to varying degrees for the last six weeks. "She's been working there for *six months*? You've been cheating for *six months*? How could you, Keith? How could you live with yourself? How could you face me, face the boys every night?"

"I didn't mean for it to happen."

"Well, it did! It did, and look where it's left us! Our marriage is in shambles."

She'd almost forgotten Jim's presence until he spoke. "Is there anything else you'd like to ask, Natalie?"

Her breaths came in gulps. She wiped her eyes and nose. She had dozens of questions, but none more important than this. "Are you in love with her?" The words squeaked from her throat. *Please, Lord, no.*

"I don't know." Keith raked a hand through his hair. "I'm confused. I don't know what to think anymore."

The answer both relieved and scared her. She bit her quivering lip until it stilled. "Do you still love me?"

"I don't know!" His voice was fraught with frustration.

How could he not know? Haven't I been a faithful wife? Haven't I taken care of him, cooked for him, done his laundry for seven years?

"Keith, why don't you tell us your side of the story?"

He looked at the ceiling as if for help, then studied his loafers. "Lindsey came to work for me late last year, part-time. She's a teller. One day she needed a ride home, and we started talking. Nothing big, just small talk. But I liked her. She listened when I talk, really listened." He shot Natalie a look as if comparing her unfavorably.

Natalie's stomach clenched with pain. *I'd listen, too, if only you'd talk to me!*

"I started giving her rides home sometimes, began to enjoy her company, anticipating the time we'd have together. We weren't doing anything wrong, just talking."

Jim interrupted. "At some point that changed?"

Keith scratched the back of his neck. "Around Christmastime I was taking her home. She told me how she felt. Somehow . . . somehow that changed everything. My feelings grew over the months until I wasn't sure who I loved anymore." He looked at Natalie, really looked at her, for the first time since they'd walked in the door. "I'm sorry, Nat. I never meant for this to happen."

She wept. Covering her face with her hands, the hurt poured from her in wracking sobs. *Why? Why? Why have you done this to us? I love you! How could you do this?* She struggled to pull herself together.

Jim handed her another tissue to replace the limp, shredded one in her hand. She wiped her face and tried to swallow the achy lump in her throat.

"You're both here," Jim said. "You want to fix your marriage?"

"Yes," she said.

Keith crossed his ankle over his knee. "I don't know what I want."

"Fair enough," Jim said. "Let's talk about your marriage."

CHAPTER
FIFTEEN

Hanna started the 4x4 and pulled out of the bank's parking lot. She was thankful she'd been able to avoid Keith and relieved that she was able to make the June payment on their loan. There wasn't much money left in their account, only enough to cover the necessities. What if the refrigerator broke down or one of the water heaters needed to be replaced? Operating on a week-by-week basis was scary. But what could she do about the cancellations?

The phone call she'd received from that Realtor flashed in her mind. Her client had wanted to buy Higher Grounds. Could that person somehow be behind this?

As she drove back to the lodge, she tried to jog her memory. What was the agent's name? She couldn't remember, hadn't paid much attention since she wasn't interested in selling.

Maybe someone was starting rumors about the lodge to scare customers away. Or maybe someone was luring them away somehow. But how would they know who had reservations?

You really ought to keep this office door locked. Micah's words haunted her. *There's a lucrative market for office equipment. A former guest could make a copy of your entry key and rip you off.*

Had someone done just that? Stayed as a guest, made a copy of the entry key, and come back to steal her customer files? It was possible, and if that's what had happened, she had made it easy. How could she have been so naive? She made a mental note to call a locksmith.

This afternoon was Gram's doctor appointment, and Hanna's heart clenched at the thought. The test results wouldn't be available immediately, she was sure, but this was a start. *Lord, help them find what's wrong, and give us all the strength to cope with whatever it is.*

When she pulled into the lodge's parking lot, she saw Micah tinkering with his motorcycle. She pulled into the space next to his and walked around the 4x4. He was revving the engine, an open box of tools at his feet.

"Problems?" she asked.

He stopped revving the engine. "It's making a noise. Not sure what it is."

"What kind of noise?"

Looking her in the eye, he said, "That's right. You're the resident mechanic." Hope clung to his solemn face. "It's a knocking noise. Seemed loud when I was driving earlier, but when I gave it gas just now, I could hardly hear it. You familiar with Honda cycles?"

She smiled. "I cut my teeth on them. Dad used to collect bikes." She listened as he revved the motor again. "It could be the bearings," she said over the noise. "I'd have to take a ride to know for sure."

He let off the gas. "Oh. Well . . . I don't know . . ." Finally his gaze settled on the helmet. "I only have one helmet."

It was an excuse, she knew. He didn't want her on the back of his bike, snuggled against him. She smothered a smirk. "I'll ride without one; we won't go far." She helped him put his tools away.

"Look, you don't have to. I can take it apart and check it out."

"Don't be silly. If it's the bearings, I'll be able to tell in just a few minutes." She hopped on the back of the bike while he set his toolbox aside.

He took the helmet off the cycle and handed it to her. "You can have it."

She fastened the helmet while he straddled the seat in front of her. His body leaned forward at an unnatural angle.

He turned the bike around, and off they went. Micah settled into a more natural position as they leaned into the turn onto the main road.

Hanna slipped her arms around his waist. She felt him stiffen at her touch. His sides felt hard beneath the cotton T-shirt, and she resisted the urge to lay her palms flat against him. Her arms ached to tighten, to hold him against her. When had she ever felt such a yearning for a man's touch?

Never. And it wasn't just physical attraction. She had almost daily contact with young men, customers who came and went, and she'd never felt this way. Even Devon was handsome, well built, but she wasn't attracted to him. No, it wasn't just physical with Micah. She liked the whole package, inside and out.

When he accelerated, she leaned into his back to shield her face from the wind. His shoulders were broad and high, topping her head by an inch or two. Heat radiated from his back and through her blouse. She shivered. *Oh, God, what a fine specimen of a man You've made.*

❧

Micah struggled to keep his mind on the road. It was hard with Hanna pressed up against his back. *How could an innocent touch do so much to my insides?* She shifted her arms, and his insides twisted. Ah, sweet agony. What would it be like to have her as his own? To hold her, kiss her whenever he felt the desire? He ached for more.

Knock it off, Gallagher. He gripped the handlebars with tight fists. *Think about something else. Something other than her hands lying against your ribs, her arms wrapped around you.* His heart tripped. *Lord, have mercy.*

"It's getting louder; hear it?"

What, my heart?

"I'm pretty sure it's . . ." the wind carried away her words.

He turned his head to hear better. "What?"

"It's the bearings," she said, her lips near his ear. "The knocking is getting louder because the engine is getting hot."

That's not the only thing that's getting hot.

"Put on the brake and free the clutch."

He did.

"Yep. Better head back, shouldn't be riding on it this way."

He did a U-turn and headed back to the lodge. Gladly.

Every inch was maddening. What he would have done in his earlier days . . . pulled off the road, found a nice secluded spot . . .

Don't go there. His intention to avoid a relationship had never seemed so exasperating.

He pulled into the lot and swung the bike into the shaded parking space. The shadowed air offered immediate relief from the sun's heat. When Hanna hopped off the bike, his body sagged with relief.

"If you've caught it early," she said, "you'll only need to change the bearings."

"But if I haven't, the crankshaft will need replacing."

"Right." She handed him his helmet.

He went for his tools, opening the box and laying out what he'd need. "Need any help?"

"Nope. I can handle it. Thanks." The last thing he needed was her tempting presence.

She stood there watching, and every cell in his body was aware of her. Aware of her denim-encased legs inches away. Aware of her stare burning his skin. He wiped away the trickle of sweat that coursed down his forehead.

"Did you need something else?" he asked.

She waited until he looked her in the eye. "Why do you keep doing that?"

"Doing what?"

"Pretending you don't feel it."

He gathered his tools and hunkered down by his bike. "Feel what?"

"This . . . *thing* between us."

He began disassembling the bike, cringing when his distracted mind made him reach for the wrong tool. "You're a woman. I'm a man. It's no big deal."

Itty bits of gravel crunched as she sat down on the pavement close beside him. Too close. "You feel this with every woman?" Her voice teemed with amusement.

He peeked at her. Couldn't resist. It was going to be a quick look, just to read her face, but he couldn't stop there. Once he saw how close she was, saw the mirth in her eyes, the warmth in her cheeks, the little smile tilting her lips, he didn't want to look away. Couldn't look away. The stirring started again in his gut, clenching and churning in a head-spinning dance of emotion. She was so tempting. Too tempting.

He forced his eyes away. He didn't want to go there. Would *never* go there. "Look, maybe I should just explain the way it is. I'm never getting married." He enforced his words with his eyes. "And we both know physical intimacy outside of marriage is wrong. So there's really no point in dating or relationships. That would just lead a woman to believe something that's not true."

Her cheeks colored at his words. "Why not?"

"Why not what?"

"Why don't you want to marry?"

"Why—" He'd never had to answer that one. Had never been asked. "I have my reasons. Just consider me like Paul." He jumped all over the excuse. "He remained single all his life. I'm going to do the same." He tossed a tool back in the box.

"What a waste."

His eyes darted to hers, and he blushed. Sassy woman.

He took advantage of her silence. "So, if you want to know the truth, yes, I do feel something with you."

She looked at him, and her lips parted to speak.

"But," he said, before she could say anything. "It's not going anywhere, I don't want it to go anywhere, so it'd be best if we just kept things on a professional level." He returned his attention to his bike, but he couldn't help wondering what was going on behind those beguiling eyes.

Hanna watched Micah take apart the bike, assessing his words, deciphering his meaning. Why would a perfectly healthy male want no part of the female species? Especially when there were such sparks between the two of them. Such promise.

Maybe Natalie was right when she suggested he might have had a bad relationship. Or maybe his parents had a bad relationship, and he'd decided he wanted—

No, that can't be right. He had a foster father, which meant that both parents had been out of the picture. But for how long? And did that have something to do with his decision to remain single?

Maybe someday she'd know him well enough to ask. But how could she get to know him if he didn't want her company. He was gone on treks most of the time, and when he was here, he didn't—

An idea blossomed in her mind, one that brought hope to her heart and a smile to her lips.

Hanna was checking the wording of her brochure when the phone rang. "Higher Grounds, may I help you?"

"Hi, Hanna, it's Nat."

"I've been waiting to hear from you." She walked into the office for privacy. "How'd your session go?"

Her sister sighed. "Well, I know it's someone at the bank. And I know it's been going on since Christmas."

Hanna's stomach tightened. "Oh, Nat, that must be so hard."

"I've had a few days to get used to it, but—" Her sister resumed only when she seemed to have collected herself. "It's hard knowing that every day when he goes to work he's with her. He wouldn't commit to ending it. And he was resistant to the idea of continuing therapy."

"What are you going to do?"

"I made another appointment for next week. I don't know if Keith will show up or not, but I need it. I need someone to help me deal with these emotions. Someone who knows what I'm supposed to do, how I'm supposed to win my husband back."

Hanna suppressed the desire to belittle Keith. It wouldn't do Natalie any good to hear her opinion of Keith. Her sister went into the specifics of the counseling session, breaking down twice more.

When the other line rang, Hanna decided not to interrupt her sister, but Natalie heard it ringing and insisted she answer it.

On the other line was a man who wanted to make reservations for the entire next week. Taking reservations, especially for weeklong stays, always delighted her. She went to the front desk and marked the reservation on the books, then hung up the phone.

A family entered the lodge, each toting suitcases and duffel bags. They clustered around the front desk, and she checked them in. The oldest boy read the dry-erase board announcing the guided mountain-trek schedule and pointed it out to his parents.

"I didn't realize you offered anything like this," Mrs. Nettleworth said.

"It's a new service we're offering guests, and it's been very popular so far. Would you like to sign up for a trip?"

They discussed the cost and difficulty of each climb before deciding on the Mount Moran trip, which began the following Monday. Hanna smothered a grin as she found the appropriate clipboard and saw there were already five signed up for the climb.

She handed the clipboard to Mrs. Nettleworth. "Just sign your names and ages."

Micah passed the desk, presumably on his way to dinner.

"The trip leaves Monday morning at seven," Hanna said. "And there's a meeting the night before at seven to pack the backpacks and discuss climbing techniques and safety."

Micah, nearly to the dining room, turned and ambled back to the desk.

The woman handed her the clipboard, and she felt Micah's gaze over her shoulder.

"I'll just bill the trip to your room, if that's okay with you."

Mrs. Nettleworth agreed, then the family disappeared around the corner with their luggage in a clamor of chatter.

"Hanna, can I have a word with you?"

"Sure." She turned expectantly, only to see Micah eyeing the couple talking on the couch and Mrs. Eddlestein dusting the bookshelves.

"In the office?" he said.

She led the way and shut the door behind him. He wore a navy T-shirt that called attention to his muscular arms when he crossed them over his chest.

"What is it?" she asked.

"You signed those people up for the Mount Moran trip. It's overbooked. I can't take on six more people." He had those twin lines between his brows and several days of stubble that accentuated his square jaw.

"I thought I would go along again."

Skepticism and opposition flared in his expression. He looked away, then drilled her with his gaze. He was reading her. She tilted up her chin ever so slightly and met his look with defiance. He didn't want her to go. She didn't have to be a mind reader to know that. But she *was* the boss, and if he didn't like it—

"You're playing with fire, Hanna."

His acknowledgment of their attraction sucked the moisture from her mouth. "I like the heat."

Something flickered in the steely depths of his gray eyes. Desire? Challenge? His eyelids swooped shut in a blink that erased the emotion as effectively as a cloth clears a dry-erase board.

"Stop it, Hanna," he said.

She studied his face, the bone structure that was as harsh as his attitude. "I've been doing some thinking lately, about why God is drawing me to you. I think you're afraid to open up to anyone, especially a woman."

His lips parted in protest.

"And I'm good at drawing people out. You need me."

His eyes narrowed. "I don't need anyone." His bass voice rumbled with conviction.

"You think that, but God knows differently. And so do I."

"Why can't you leave this alone?"

"Why can't *you* take a chance?"

He looked away, his body stiffening in stubborn resistance. Finally, he started at her in an open challenge. "You keep this up, you're going to get hurt."

Her lips twitched. "I'm a big girl."

His eyes brushed over her figure. An involuntary reaction, she realized. As if he was agreeing with her previous statement. She smothered a grin. He liked what he saw, whether he wanted her to know it or not.

With a disgruntled huff, he turned and left the office, and Hanna freed her barely contained smile.

CHAPTER
SIXTEEN

"Looks like it's you and me," Hanna said.

She watched Micah take a survey of the guests: a family of six, a young couple, and two college roommates. They assembled in natural groups of two in front of the canoes, leaving Micah and Hanna together.

He harrumphed as he picked up one end of the canoe.

Hanna grabbed the other end, and they toted it to the shore of String Lake. After a briefing on canoe handling, the groups of two settled in their boats, with Micah and Hanna leading the pack.

Across the lake, Mount Moran rose from the earth like a big volcanic cone. Hanna took in the sight, anticipating the challenges ahead. Both the challenge of the climb and the challenge of breaking down Micah's resistance. She was hoping to draw him closer in the next three days. He was pretty much stuck with her, and she intended to take full opportunity of it.

The bow of the canoe sliced silently through the water with the help of their paddles. She and Micah worked in tandem, each experienced with handling the watercraft. When they gained a lead, they pulled their paddles from the water and waited for the others to catch up.

Already the July morning promised a scorching day, and Hanna made a note to herself to slosh some water on her clothes before she started the climb. As the other groups neared, she and Micah began paddling once again. Laughter floated to them from the other canoes as the brothers and sisters of the Nettleworth family teased one another.

Jeff, one of the college boys, begged to trade partners, claiming Dave was going to drown them both. He made his preference for a partner clear. "Come on, Hanna, be my partner. Dave can't paddle, and he's ugly to boot."

Hanna just shook her head and laughed. Dave was far from ugly. It was going to be a lively three days.

When they reached the portage to Leigh Lake, Hanna saw a bald eagle watching from its perch on Boulder Island. "Look." She pointed out the bird to Micah and watched him pause in appreciation of the sight.

As they paddled on, Hanna's mind turned to the lodge. "Did you notice I had a lock put on the office door?"

"Single-bolt or deadbolt?"

"Single. I wanted a thumb-turn on the lock in case the keys got lost. At least then we could break in the window and open the door."

He grunted his approval.

"The way Gram's losing things lately, that's a real possibility." She pulled the paddle from the water and let the canoe glide on Micah's strokes alone. "Dad took her for tests last week and, so far, they don't look good. They ruled out other causes of dementia, and next they're going to do some kind of interview and cognitive testing. Alzheimer's is looking more likely."

He switched his paddle to the other side. "She definitely has the signs."

She knew Micah wasn't one to gloss over the facts, but a word of encouragement would have been nice. She turned in her seat to face him. "Sheesh, tell me what you really think," she said.

His biceps bulged with each stroke. His eyes met hers, then darted away. "I say what I mean and mean what I say. It's who I am."

She let the words take root. He was one who saw things negatively; she was one who saw things positively. Her dad had always compared her to Tigger from *Winnie the Pooh*. If she was like Tigger, Micah was like—she stifled a giggle. Unsuccessfully.

That got his attention. His brows furrowed over serious eyes. "What?"

"I just thought of a nickname for you. Eeyore." She giggled again.

"Who's that?"

"You don't know who Eeyore is? In *Winnie the Pooh*, the donkey." He's all doom and gloom, you know, pessimistic."

His lips curled down. "I prefer to call it realism."

He would. It was a fundamental difference in the way they saw things. She looked for the silver lining; he looked for the rain cloud. "We're very different, you and I."

Meeting her stare, he replied, "Exactly."

Her stomach quivered with his look. All he had to do was look at her, and she was helpless to stop the reaction that jolted through her body. She hoped he felt it too. "Think what a good influence we'd be on each other."

He pulled the paddle effortlessly though the water. "You can teach me how to look at life through rosy lenses, and I can teach you how to pull your own weight." He glanced pointedly at the paddle resting on her lap.

She turned back around and put the paddle to work. "Don't think you're off the hook."

She heard him grumble something unintelligible, which only fed the smile on her face.

Later, as they tied up their canoe at the base of Falling Ice Glacier, the group gaped in awe at the massive mountain, clicking pictures with automatic cameras. They sloshed water on their clothes in preparation for the next part of the trip, a thirty-five-hundred-foot climb in less than two miles. Not only was the climb steep, but there was no discernible trail.

Dave and Jeff went out of their way trying to help Hanna, who was actually a better climber than both of them combined. Especially Jeff, who was a bit klutzy. When they stopped for a midmorning break, Dave

sank to his knees beside Hanna and asked her where she'd attended college and what she'd majored in.

She watched Micah drink from his canteen and apply moleskin to
the heels of those developing blisters. Afterward, he watched the
Nettleworth teens razz one another as Dave droned on beside her.
Micah was an observer by nature, she'd at least learned that about him.
As a result he read people well. If only she could read him. But she
thought she'd guessed correctly about his fear of relationships. He hadn't
admitted it, but he hadn't denied it either.

"Hello?" Dave waved a hand in front of her face.

She laughed. "Sorry, what did you say?"

Her laughter drew Micah's attention. A scowl lined his face, and she
wondered at its cause before turning back to Dave and answering his
question. She'd no sooner answered it than Micah announced they
needed to move on.

Hanna was pleased with her energy level compared to the last time
she made the climb. The day passed quickly, and it helped that she had
Dave and Jeff to talk to, both of whom were outgoing and gregarious.

They made camp at the CMC campsite, and Hanna and Micah
settled into the same jobs they'd had on the last trip while the campers
hurried to set up their tents before dark.

After dinner they settled on logs around the campfire. As the cloak
of darkness seeped in around the camp, the group chattered. The young
couple sat to one side of Hanna, and they were the first to turn in. The
Nettleworths followed, and Hanna thought they'd better get a good
night's rest, as they were clearly worn out.

By the time the rustle of sleeping bags and zippers hushed, Jeff had
joined her and Dave, taking up residence on her left. While they
shared marshmallows, Micah scowled from across the fire. Twice Dave
had tried to include him in the conversation only to be given abrupt
answers. She couldn't help feeling that her goal of growing closer to
Micah was faltering.

Micah watched Hanna over the flickering campfire. The white of her teeth glowed with each smile, and he'd seen them plenty of times in the last hour.

He gritted his teeth and forced himself to look away. The three of them had carried on like long-lost pals, chattering and laughing about everything from roommate pet peeves to Jeff's lack of coordination. Hanna's face was animated as she talked. Jeff was only being friendly, but Micah read the interest on Dave's face, in his body language. If he touched Hanna's arm one more time, Micah was going to leap across the fire and slug him.

He poked the logs with his stick and the fire crackled, sending sparks of light into the air. He had no right to Hanna. She was free to have a relationship with anyone she chose. So why did he feel so possessive? He glanced across the fire, clenching his jaw when Dave touched her yet again.

Didn't the man need some sleep? He glanced at his watch and saw it was past eleven. It was a good thing Micah was a night owl because he wasn't about to turn in and leave Hanna alone with these guys, no matter how nice they seemed.

Soon Jeff retired to his tent, and Micah looked at Dave, hoping he'd take the hint and go too. No such luck. He and Hanna picked up right where they'd left off, albeit more quietly now that the comic had left.

He took a novel from his backpack and read by the light of the fire. Five minutes passed, then ten. Finally, at eleven-thirty, Dave got up and said his good-nights. Micah exhaled loudly when the zipper sealed the tent flap.

Across the fire Hanna had removed one of her boots and was scrutinizing her heel. "I think I've got a blister after all."

Micah fished the moleskin out of his pack and joined her on the log, willing to help but still peeved about Dave. "I was beginning to think he was going to sleep out here." He couldn't keep the gruffness from his voice. He felt her watching him as he cut the circle out of the material.

"What's your problem tonight?" she whispered, as if worried the words might leak through the tent walls.

He peeled off the backing and centered it over her blister. "I don't have a problem." He pressed the moleskin against her skin, then put the first-aid kit away.

"You were short with Dave earlier. It's not like you to be rude to the guests."

"It's not like *you* to flirt with them."

"I wasn't!" she hissed, stiffening defensively.

He pinned her with a glare.

"I was just being friendly." She crossed her arms and raised her chin a notch.

"You may think you're being friendly, but guys like that take it as interest. And they're only after one thing."

"How do you know what they're after?"

"Because I used to be one of those guys." He picked up her stick and poked at a log. "I've seen the way Dave's been looking at you. It's no coincidence he walked behind you today. He's been checking out your rear end all day."

She drew in a breath, and her cheeks became tinged with a pink that had nothing to do with the fire's heat. "He was not."

"He was. He's looking for a good time, and if you weren't so naive, you'd know it."

Her mouth opened and closed several times before she recovered enough to turn away from him and stare into the fire. Her face was set, her color high. "Why are you so interested anyway?" When she faced him, her eyes flickered with anger. "You wanted me to leave you alone, and that's what I've done all day. Isn't that what you wanted?"

He didn't know what to say. He did want her to leave him alone. But at the same time, he was drawn to her. He couldn't understand himself, much less explain it.

"Why won't you give in to it?" she asked. "This stuff about staying single all your life, it's just an excuse for someone who's afraid to take a chance."

He watched the fire lick at the logs, feeling the heat from it, from the woman sitting too close beside him. She laid her fingers artlessly on his knee, and he nearly jumped from the jolt that coursed through his leg. His breath caught in his throat.

"Take a chance on me," she said.

He looked at her eyes, shining with boldness. She was so innocent, so pure. She needed to understand they were wrong for each other, that he didn't deserve her. "You don't want me, Hanna. I'm not like you."

Her fingers tightened on his knee in a squeeze that almost sent him scampering across the campsite. "What's that got to do with anything?"

He dropped his leg straight, breaking the contact with her hand. He'd just have to convince her. Convince her that she didn't want him. "You're probably just as innocent as you seem, aren't you? Been saving yourself for your husband someday, right?"

Color heightened her cheeks, but to her credit she didn't flinch at his expression. "So?"

"How many partners do you think I've had?"

She looked away. "I don't know. That's none of my business."

He watched her use a twig to draw circles in the dirt.

"I don't know either," he said.

The stick stopped twirling as she looked at him.

"I've had so many women, used so many woman, I have no idea how many."

Her head snapped toward the stick, which she flicked in the dirt again. "Stop it."

His heart tightened, and he was surprised how much it hurt to tell her the truth about himself. "Not very appealing, is it? Knowing I've been with women I barely knew."

"Stop it!" She looked at him again, tears sparkling in her eyes.

His stomach clenched. Those wide eyes accused him, not of being immoral, but of trying to hurt her. He was guilty. Suddenly he couldn't think. Couldn't breathe. All he could do was feel. Feel the dance of pleasure in his gut, the rush of adrenaline through his limbs. He looked at her trembling lips. He'd never wanted anyone so badly.

He leaned forward, wanting desperately to soothe the hurt he'd caused. When his lips touched hers, he gave in to the desire he felt. Never had a woman driven him to such distraction. He felt her lips move innocently against his and knew he'd never felt such passion. And he didn't think it was abstinence alone that stoked the fire in his gut. That a simple kiss could so move him terrified him.

The tiny moan that tore from her throat nearly drove him over the edge. *Sweet Jesus, help me.*

Hanna had seen the promise in his eyes through her veil of tears before he'd drawn close. The moment was suspended in time, drawing out deliciously as she savored the way he looked at her. Not like a man afraid to take a chance, but like a man who had no choice.

His lips met hers, tentatively at first. Tasting, testing with a gentleness that melted her heart. Their breath mingled in a swirl of heat that seemed to come from deep within her. Of their own will, her arms slid to his shoulders. She buried her fingers in the silky softness of his hair and almost moaned when he drew her closer.

Sweet bliss, this meeting of hearts. She never wanted him to let her go.

He wrenched his mouth from hers and stood in the same motion. In two strides he was in front of the fire, running a hand through the hair she'd combed with her fingers. His body blocked the heat and light from the fire.

She tried to swallow but found her mouth dry as dirt. So that's what all the fuss was about. Jess's kisses had never been like that. It was like comparing tomatoes and jalapeños. Her heart still thudded in her chest at twice the normal pace.

Why had he broken the kiss? Why did he stand with his back to her instead of looking her in the eye?

A sudden thought sent her stomach tumbling in a heavy heap. What if he'd found her touch repulsive or inexperienced? Of course, he could affect her with his kisses—he'd already admitted to plenty of practice. But she could count on one hand the times she'd been kissed. Had her attempts seemed fumbling and inept compared to the practiced women he'd been with? She shivered.

He cleared his throat. "I shouldn't have done that."

What was left of her confidence sagged hopelessly to the ground. The optimist in her wanted to ask why. Why shouldn't he have done that? The coward in her wanted to run to her tent and lick her wounds in private.

The choice was taken from her when he walked to his tent and disappeared inside.

CHAPTER
SEVENTEEN

Hanna turned onto Natalie's street, braking for the squirrel that scampered across the road. It was a nice, upper-class area with roomy, two-story cedar and log homes and yards shaded with mature trees. She slowed her 4x4 as she neared her sister's home. Everything looked so nice on the outside: a neatly trimmed yard, flowers sprouting a rainbow of colors from freshly mulched areas, a large house perched on a hill at the base of a butte. It was hard to believe that the orderly estate housed a shattered family.

Hanna parked in the driveway and grabbed the carpet cleaner from the backseat. Alex burst through the door and hugged her legs, paralyzing her for a moment. "Whoa there, fella! How's my boy?"

Natalie smiled at her from the doorway. "You didn't have to dress up on my account."

Hanna spun in a pirouette, as best she could with the carpet cleaner in tow. In truth she wore her scroungiest T-shirt and denim shorts.

"You're just in time for lunch. I made my lasagna and homemade breadsticks."

Hanna brushed by her and set the cleaner on the floor. "What did I do to deserve that?"

Natalie gave a wry grin. "When you see the carpet, you'll know. If you thought it was dirty last year . . ."

"Uh-oh, has someone been spilling drinks on the floor?" She gave Alex a mock glare.

"I didn't mean to," Alex said.

Hanna laughed and picked up Taylor for a hug.

After lunch Natalie put Taylor down for his nap, and she moved furniture around while Hanna cleaned the downstairs carpet. When Hanna stopped for a break, Natalie took over for a while. Before long, the entire downstairs carpeting was damp but clean.

Natalie sent Alex to the backyard to play while she and Hanna sat down at the bar for a cup of coffee.

"So, how are you and Keith doing? Have you had another counseling session?"

Natalie stirred the creamer into her coffee and laid the spoon on the bar. "I don't know, Hanna. I had a session this week, but Keith didn't come. And when he's here, it's like he's not even my husband."

"Do you think he's still seeing her?"

"He sees her every day. How can he help it when she works with him?" She picked up her mug with trembling fingers and took a sip. "He's still getting home late, so I'm pretty sure he's spending time with her outside of work." She blinked back tears. "And he's not interested in me sexually; he hasn't been for a long time. I should've seen it coming."

"I'm so sorry, Nat." She squeezed her sister's hand.

"I sit on the couch watching cars turn onto our street, watching their headlights approach and pass our drive, wishing it would be him."

Hanna glanced out the window to see Alex pushing another boy on the swing.

"In my last appointment with our counselor, he asked me if I could tolerate Keith seeing her while he's living here."

Hanna watched her sister struggle to keep control, and it broke her heart. She reached over and embraced her in a sideways hug.

"I won't. I can't tolerate that. I can't stand knowing he's with her, knowing what they're doing."

"What are you going to do?"

"Jim said I need to tell him how I feel. That I need him to stop seeing her if we're going to try and work things out." She got up for a tissue and returned, dabbing at the corner of her eyes.

"What do you think he'll say?"

"I'm afraid to guess. But he left before, after I confronted him about the affair."

Hanna couldn't say it, but she thought Keith would leave, too, if Natalie gave him an ultimatum. But he couldn't have them both. It was tearing Nat apart.

"You know, you see it on TV all the time—people having affairs. Especially on the soap operas, even the one I watched. But it's nothing to make light of—it hurts so much." Her face crumpled, and she sobbed into her hands.

Hanna held her for a moment, wishing she could do something more.

Her sister straightened in her seat and wiped the tears off her face. "You'd think I'd be out of tears by now."

Alex came in and asked if he and his friend could have a Popsicle, so Nat took two from the freezer and gave them to the boys, who sat on the patio with them.

Natalie returned to the barstool. "Okay, enough about my dreary life. How are things progressing with Micah?"

The memory of the kiss they'd shared by the campfire ignited a flame in her heart once again. She'd relived the moment repeatedly and never grew tired of it.

"What's this? Do I see a blush on those cheeks?"

Hanna smiled. "You know I went on his climb earlier this week . . . Well, the first night, after everyone went to bed, he kissed me."

Natalie's lips parted in a smile. "That is progress. Tell me more."

"The kiss itself was . . . well . . . indescribable. I've never felt such fire, such passion. It was overwhelming." Her stomach lurched as it always did when she remembered the moments following the kiss. She told Nat how Micah had regretted kissing her. "He told me he'd been

DENISE HUNTER

with a lot of women before he became a Christian, and you know how
little experience I have. I don't think I measured up."

A smirk curled her sister's lips, matching the teasing light in her
eyes. "That's not what it sounds like to me."

"What do you mean?" If she'd interpreted Micah's reaction
wrongly—and she hoped she had—she wanted to know about it.

"You said Micah wants to remain single, right?"

"Yeah . . . and I also have reason to believe you were right about his
being afraid of having a relationship."

"Then it makes even more sense."

"Explain."

"Okay, imagine that he's attracted to you. You and he have to be
around each other a lot. He's fighting it because he doesn't want a relationship. But, when he's stuck with you all day on the trip—"

"Thanks a lot."

"Hey, I'm trying to look at this from Micah's point of view. So, he's
stuck with you on this trip, he can't keep his eyes off you, and I'm sure
you weren't exactly trying to avoid him."

"Actually, I spent most of my time talking to a couple of guys on the
trip. They were—"

"Young and cute?"

"Natalie. I was going to say they were outgoing and we had a lot in
common."

"And they were young and cute?" Natalie said.

"All right, they were."

"Aha!"

"Aha?" Hanna echoed.

"He was jealous. Micah was not only around you nonstop, but he
had to see two handsome guys paying you lots of attention."

It had occurred to Hanna before, especially with the way he'd
reacted to Dave, but she thought it was just wishful thinking. "Do you
really think so?"

"It makes perfect sense. He was feeling attracted and trying to deny it. Add to that he was jealous, and he finally gave in to his feelings and kissed you." Natalie sat back on the barstool and crossed her arms over her chest.

Hanna thought through Micah's behavior over the past few weeks. Is that why he'd pulled away from their initial friendship? Had he been attracted to her even then and distanced himself trying to stall his developing feelings?

"I can see I've given you something to think about. Why would he have kissed you if he wasn't attracted to you?" Natalie's delighted grin leaked confidence.

"I hope you're right."

"I'm sure of it. Why would God put him on your heart if Micah wasn't interested? God's probably dealing with Micah, too, but maybe he's too stubborn to give in."

It did make sense. That would explain his behavior, the way he'd said he regretted the kiss, the way he's distanced himself from her since then. "But now what do I do? If he's determined to fight it, how do I change his mind?"

"Hmmm. I'll have to think about that one."

Taylor let out a squeal from his crib, and Natalie went to get him.

Hanna's spirits were buoyed. Sometime through all of this, feelings for Micah had taken root in her heart. And if what Natalie said was true, there was hope after all. Eventually he'd have to give in, especially if God was in it. She smiled as she picked up her mug and rinsed it out in the sink.

After Natalie tucked in the boys, she went downstairs to pick up the day's mess. Amazing how many things got out of place during the course of a day. She loaded the dinner dishes in the dishwasher, letting her mind wander to the evening ahead.

She would confront him tonight, she'd decided. If he was in a decent mood. She'd even fixed a roast with carrots and potatoes to warm for him when he got home. He always said he was too busy to eat at work.

Her hands trembled as she touched up her makeup. The mirror of the compact showed tiny lines around eyes that had lost their sparkle. She applied fresh lipstick and tucked in the blouse she'd worn all day. Frowning at the lasagna stain, she went to her closet and selected a clean one in a flattering shade of lavender. Next, she twisted her hair up in a quick French knot.

The garage door sounded its warning, and her heart accelerated automatically. What would happen tonight? Would it be the seed of renewal for their marriage or the kernel of death? That familiar ache started in the pit of her stomach and spread to every limb. She was tired of hurting. *Please, God, let this work out. Give me the words.*

She didn't even have the words for a prayer, much less for the confrontation that was about to happen. Where had God been these last weeks? He was supposed to carry her through times such as these, wasn't He? Why couldn't she feel His comfort?

She met Keith at the door and surprised him with a kiss on the cheek. "Hi."

"Something smells good." He slipped past her.

She tried not to be disheartened by the way he ignored her gesture. "I made a roast. You haven't eaten, have you?"

"No." He emptied his pockets and loosened his tie while she warmed his food.

"How was your day?" she asked, once he was seated at the table shoveling food in his mouth. The normalcy of her words were canceled by the quivering note of her voice.

"Fine."

"How are things going at the bank?"

He looked at her curiously. "All right."

How did she start? How did she say what she needed to say? What had the counselor said? *Start with an "I" statement.* She sorted through a dozen possible starters, rejecting each one as threatening or pathetic.

Fear coiled in her heart. Was this his last dinner here? Would he refuse to give up the other woman?

"What?" His defensive tone caught her attention.

She'd been staring at him, head propped on hand. "Just thinking." She got up to pour him a glass of milk and set it by his plate.

Seating herself across from him again, she steeled herself to say the words. "In my counseling session with Jim this week, I said something to him that he felt I needed to say to you."

He glanced at her between bites.

"I was telling him how I didn't know if you were still seeing . . . Lindsey." She forced herself to say the name without the bitterness she felt. "He asked how I felt about that. And, of course, I told him I didn't want you to see her, that we didn't stand a chance of working things out if you continued to see her." She waited for an answer.

He took his time, swallowing a gulp of milk and sopping his next bite of beef in the dark gravy. "Of course, I see her. She works at the bank."

Natalie clenched her teeth. He knew what she meant; he was avoiding answering. Which told her all she needed to know.

He narrowed his gaze. "I'm not going to fire her."

She fixed her eyes on the teal tablecloth. Was she supposed to trust him to work with this woman every day? How could he expect that of her? She remembered a line Jim liked to use and decided it was the perfect one for now. "Let's deal with one thing at a time. Are you seeing her outside of work?" Her nerves gelled in a cold lump of fear. She tried to read his eyes. He was defensive and getting angry—she could tell by the way he stabbed at the meat.

After an uncomfortable, agonizing pause, he set his fork on the plate and leaned back in his chair. "I won't stop seeing her, Nat."

Her heart skipped a beat, and her stomach clenched in anticipation of worse news.

"I guess it's time I shoot straight with you." His eyes darted across the room, studying the floral print on the wall as if it held all of life's secrets. "I'm in love with her."

Nothing had prepared her for those words. Nothing could have. A rush of feelings assaulted her: terror, hurt, rage. Her senses couldn't assimilate it all. But she felt every emotion on a level she'd never experienced. Tears formed and coursed down her face but did little to assuage the pain. She could cry rivers, and it wouldn't even begin to rid her body of the ache his words induced.

How could you do this? What's going to happen to us? Why didn't you tell me? Questions jammed in her mind, a hopeless jumble of words she couldn't articulate.

As she stared at him through a film of tears, terror seized her heart. Her limbs felt weak, and she was grateful for the chair supporting her weight. "We can still work it out. Go with me for counseling. We can put our marriage back together." She hated the pleading note in her voice.

He took his plate to the sink, a rarity. He was only trying to avoid her.

"It's too late," he said.

"Lots of marriages go through this kind of thing. We can fix it if we try!"

"It's beyond that, Nat." He turned to face her, his hands on the sink ledge behind him. "I don't care enough to fix it. I've lost the desire to try."

Sobs worked their way up into her throat, but she choked them back. She blinked furiously trying to clear her vision, wanting to see his eyes when he answered the next question. "What about me? I love you, Keith. I know I've neglected some of your needs—I see that now—but I'm working on it! I can make you happy again." Her fingers frantically twisted the corner of the tablecloth.

She watched him. Watched his eyes as they softened. Watched his hands as they tucked themselves away in his pockets.

"I don't love you anymore, Nat."

The words slipped off his tongue and pierced her heart. The pain of it sucked her breath from her lungs. Her body was immobilized, but the agony of his words wrenched the deepest part of her. *Oh, God! Oh, God, help me!* Her heart cried out, but no words would form on her lips.

She released the sobs that surged to the surface. Her body shook with them. *Why? Why, God? What did I ever do? Why doesn't he love me anymore?* Lost in her own misery, she didn't hear Keith approach but felt the touch on her shoulder.

"I'm sorry, Nat." he said. "I didn't mean for it to happen, it just—" The words ended in an invisible shrug.

He's sorry? He's sorry? Rage tore through her like a violent whirlwind. She knocked his hand away and jerked around in her chair, standing with trembling knees. "How long have you known?" she shrieked.

His eyes widened.

How long?" she asked again, when he paused a second too long.

"I—I wasn't sure until just this week."

"Why did you ever come home again? Look what you're doing to us! To the boys! How am I supposed to explain this?"

"I can't help how I feel."

Her hand whipped through the air and connected with his cheek. "Neither can I."

A red, mottled flush climbed his neck.

She saw the red marks her fingers had left and knew she should feel remorse. But she felt only rage. The blow did nothing to diminish the fury bubbling in her gut. "How dare you! How dare you cheat on me? How many nights have you been with her while I waited for you to come home?" The poison of anger possessed her body, and her fists struck out at his chest. "How many?" She cursed him, calling him names that had never crossed her lips as the flood of tears poured down her face. Her hair came loose and flew wildly around her face, sticking to the wetness of her cheeks.

He grabbed her wrists. "Stop it, Nat!"

She pulled and twisted futilely, trying to loosen her hands from his grasp. He held them tight. "Stop it!"

Suddenly the fury drained from her body, taking her strength from her. Her legs went limp, and she sagged toward the ground.

Keith caught her around the waist. He pivoted into the chair, supporting her weight under her arms, but she sank lifelessly to the carpet. Blessed numbness flowed through her, making her dizzy. She steadied herself with a hand on the chair. Keith's knees jutted out inches from her face.

Hadn't he been sitting just as she was when he proposed to her? *Oh, God!* The emotions came back, this time anguish so powerful that her breaths came in quick rasps. Her lungs pulled in a rush of oxygen, and she forced it out, then drew in another breath. It hurt. Even breathing hurt. She closed her eyes, turning inward. She didn't want to look at him. She'd lost him, and he loved someone else.

Once again sobs raked across the achy lump in her throat. Her torso sagged as the floor dragged her downward. But Keith pulled her shoulders toward him. Her face fell against his leg. Waves of grief assaulted her, wrenching painful sobs from her body, as she lay with her head against the very one who'd betrayed her.

CHAPTER
EIGHTEEN

Micah stuffed his Recovery Journal in his knapsack and straddled his cycle, shoving the helmet on. He'd had trouble keeping his mind on the meeting tonight. Instead it was filled with Hanna. Hanna sitting across the campfire, Hanna with tears shimmering on her lashes, Hanna melting into his embrace.

Hanna ignoring him for the past three days.

That's what was bothering him the most. And the one thing he should be satisfied with. He turned the key and took off with a satisfactory squeal of tires. She'd spared him all but necessary conversation on the remainder of the climb, and today, his day off, she'd disappeared before lunch and hadn't returned when he'd left.

Micah dismissed the fact that he'd planned to disappear himself. His plan to remain detached was not working out. Sure, they were avoiding one another, but it seemed to be bothering him more than her. Everything would've been fine, if only he hadn't kissed her.

Ah, just the thought of it sent a pleasurable sensation coursing through his gut. He'd been angry that night at the way she'd spent time with Dave and Jeff. Frustrated that she was so innocent she didn't even see it for the come-on it was. And, he admitted to himself, jealous.

He'd never felt so jealous, and they weren't even dating. What right did he have to be so possessive? He was the one who refused to start a relationship. Who was he kidding? The relationship had already started. The feelings were there, feelings he'd wanted to avoid at all costs. *Lord,*

You know I wanted to avoid all this. Why is this happening, and how can I get it to stop?

And it had to stop. Not only was a relationship wrong for him, but it would be wrong for Hanna too. *He* was wrong for Hanna. He'd been surprised at her reaction when he'd told her about his past, about all the women he'd been with. Instead of the disgust he'd expected, there'd been hurt. Her eyes had widened and teared, and her lips had trembled.

And that's what had gotten him into trouble. Those perfect, soft lips of hers had just begged for comfort. Her reaction to the kiss, innocent and trusting, had almost been his undoing.

It was the trusting that had gotten him. She thought she knew him, thought she could trust him, but she didn't know about his past. Didn't know he'd committed crimes, served time in jail. And all those things paled in comparison to the one thing he could never forget. The one thing he could never excuse or forgive.

He pulled into Higher Grounds's parking lot, relieved that Hanna's 4x4 was gone. In his room the message light blinked on the phone, and he punched in the number and listened to Pastor Witte request a return phone call. He memorized the number, hung up, then redialed. Pastor Witte answered the phone on the second ring and thanked Micah for returning his call.

"Micah, I'm sure you're aware that William Zimmerman asked to be removed as a deacon several weeks ago, and that last Sunday our church body voted on a replacement."

"Yes sir, I remember." He'd voted himself, but couldn't imagine why Pastor Witte was calling him.

"Well, the fact is, the church voted for you to take his place, and . . ."

Pastor Witte continued on, but Micah lost the capacity to listen. They'd voted for *him*? There had to be some mistake.

"So, what do you think?"

"Uh, Pastor Witte, I don't see—"

"You're probably a bit surprised since you're single, but, although all our current deacons are married, I don't think there's any reason biblically or doctrinally why an unmarried man can't accept the position."

He went on to list the roles of deacons in the church, a leader, a servant, but Micah's inner voice seemed louder than his pastor's. *You're not worthy to be a deacon. They wouldn't want you if they knew the truth about you.* But Pastor Witte knew; he'd told him when he'd joined the church.

". . . respect you a lot, young man."

His pause seemed to require a response. "Uh, thank you."

"I'm sure you'll want some time to think and pray about this important decision."

"Yes sir."

They said good-bye, and Micah hung up, his thoughts a dark jumble of recriminations. It wasn't his crimes and jail time that nipped at his conscience. He'd made them right eventually, serving time for most of them, and even going as far as to repay those he'd stolen from. His conscience was clear when it came to that.

But there was one crime he'd never paid for. His gut tightened with remorse.

Micah expelled a heavy breath and got up to find something to eat. The gurgling in his stomach had given way to shaky hands, and if he didn't eat something soon, he'd turn into a major grouch. The clock told him it was time for dinner, so he slipped out the door and headed to the dining room.

When he reached the lobby, he heard voices and knew dinner was under way. He stopped short by the vending machines when he heard Hanna's voice. So much for dinner. He eyed the machines with distaste but dug around in his pockets for change.

He slid quarters into the machine, cringing at the clinking sound they made, and selected a granola bar and a bag of pretzels. The packages hit the vending machine bay in two distinct thuds. He eyed the two bags and knew it wouldn't be enough. After fishing a dollar from his wallet, he selected a bag of peanuts. He was trying to decide between sodas when he heard Hanna's voice float through the door.

"I'm getting worried. She's always home for dinner."

"Did she say anything about running other errands?" Mrs. Eddlestein asked.

"No, just the post office. Can you stay for a while and watch the lodge while I go look for her?" The squeak of a chair suggested she was getting up from the table.

"Oh, I'm sorry, Hanna. My grandkids are in a camp program tonight, and I promised I'd come."

Micah slid a quarter into the slot and froze when Hanna came through the door.

"Micah. There's food in there if you're hungry." She gestured toward the dining room.

Worry still lingered in her gaze, and he put in the other coins to avert his attention. "Just wanted a snack."

She surveyed the pile of snacks cradled in his arm and quirked a brow. He felt heat creep into his face and decided it was a good time for a change in subject.

"Is your grandma late?" He removed his Mountain Dew from behind the machine's flap.

"She's been gone for two hours, and I'm getting worried."

With the way the woman forgot and became confused, it was no wonder Hanna was fretful. And she was always here for dinner. Micah felt the stirrings of concern in his own stomach. What if she'd gotten lost, didn't know where she was? Didn't people with Alzheimer's lose their way?

"Could you watch the lodge for a while?" Her forehead wrinkled, her eyes pleaded.

"Hanna, I don't know much about taking reservations or anything— how about I go look for her instead?"

Relief flooded her features. "Would you?" She touched his arm, and his skin tingled uncomfortably.

"Sure." He pulled away. "Just let me drop this stuff in my room." He escaped down the hall, dumped the food on his bed, then came back to the lobby. Hanna told him her grandmother had gone to the post office and gave him a couple of ideas of other places she could've gone.

Micah left, hopping aboard his cycle with uneasiness as his companion. *She's probably just lost, wandering around somewhere.* As much as he liked to be a loner, it had been impossible to avoid getting attached to Mrs. Landin. People didn't come any gentler or more tender-hearted than she. Hanna was lucky to have a grandma like that. He'd always wanted one himself.

After he checked the post office, which was now closed, he stopped by the grocery, hair salon, and church. The 4x4 was nowhere to be seen in any of the parking lots, so Micah drove through town looking left and right. Jackson wasn't that big and didn't take long to cover. Where could she be? After searching a few side streets, he called the lodge from his cell phone, hoping she'd found her way home by now.

He heard the disappointment in Hanna's voice when he told her he'd seen no sign of her grandmother and would keep looking. Darkness was settling around town, making massive silhouettes of the buttes.

He flipped on his headlight and toured the main roads of Jackson once more. The vehicle seemed to have disappeared from the face of the earth. Turning north, he decided to check some streets off the main route. He drove down several streets a few blocks, then turned around and headed back to the main drag.

Hanna must be worried sick by now; he certainly was. Had the woman gotten lost? Been abducted? Had a heart attack?

The hospital. He turned the cycle around and headed toward Saint John Hospital. Maybe she'd had chest pains and driven herself there. Surely she'd have called home, though.

When he arrived, he drove down the rows of cars looking for the red 4x4. He huffed in frustration when the last row turned up nothing. Now what?

He called the lodge again to find a panicked Hanna wanting to call the police. He persuaded her to wait another hour and took off on his cycle once again. He drove away from town, not knowing what she'd be doing on the roads but knowing he was desperate.

As he rounded a bend, his headlights lit on a red vehicle pulled to the shoulder of the road. His breath caught. It was Hanna's. *Thank You, God.*

He pulled up behind her, leaving his headlight on, and walked to the driver's-side door. The car was running, and from a distance he could see Mrs. Landin slumped over the steering wheel. He rushed the remaining few feet.

The windows were up, so he pounded on the window. "Mrs. Landin!"

Her body flew upright, and fright covered her face as she cowered away from the door.

"It's Micah! Open up."

She fumbled with the buttons, and finally the window slid down. "Oh, Micah, I'm so glad to see you!" Relief etched itself in the lines of her face that was damp with tears. Her hair had come loose from her tidy bun and hung in strings around her face.

"Are you okay?" He leaned in through the window and opened the door.

"I am now. I was so frightened!" Tears coursed again down her cheeks from eyes that begged for comfort.

"What happened?" He awkwardly put an arm along the back of the seat.

She turned into him and clung to his T-shirt. "I couldn't find my way! I got in the car after I left the post office and started driving, and I was suddenly lost. Nothing looked familiar, so I just kept driving, thinking I'd find my way, but I couldn't. Oh, Micah, what's wrong with me?" She cried on his shoulder. "I was so scared."

"It's going to be all right." He patted her arm. Comforting was not his forte. Hanna should be here. She'd know just what to say. But the elderly woman didn't appear to need words of comfort, just his presence.

He let her cry for a few minutes, then fished in the console and pulled out a crumpled McDonald's napkin. She wiped her eyes and blew her nose.

"Let's get you back home. I'll call Hanna and let her know you're okay. She's awful worried."

"I knew she would be."

"Are you okay to drive? I can just leave my cycle here if—"

"No. No, I'll be fine, just let me follow you." Her eyes teared up again, but she straightened her shoulders as if to convince them both she was capable.

<hr />

Hanna paced the floor of the lodge, peeking through the sheers every few minutes. Where was she? There was no answer at her parents' house. She'd already called all of Gram's friends, and none of them had heard from her today. *Keep her safe, Father.*

She stopped by the window and pulled back the drapes. Darkness had fallen in the valley like a black, velvet cloak, and only the light in the parking lot lit up the night sky. She'd seen few headlights approach, and all of them had gone past the lodge. Was she lost? Hurt? She would've called by now if she could've; Hanna knew that much. She glanced at her watch. It had been forty-five minutes since Micah's last call.

Added to all this stress was the phone call she'd received from Gram's doctor's office earlier. All the questioning and testing he'd conducted pointed to Alzheimer's. She hadn't told Gram yet; she was waiting for the right time. The doctor suggested the tests be repeated by a neurologist and had recommended one. If this was Alzheimer's, tonight was just the beginning of a long, scary trip into complete senility.

The phone shattered the silence, and she grabbed it as though it were a lifeline, without even saying hello. "Micah? Did you find her?"

A great weight lifted when she heard his voice, and her body sagged. *Thank You, God,* she prayed, as she hung up and went to the window to wait. Headlights finally shimmered in the distance, and she was unable to stop the rapid pulsations of her heart. *Please, let it be Gram.* It seemed to take an eternity for the headlights to draw near. They disappeared momentarily, blocked by trees, and her heart faltered until they shone again in the distance.

She cupped her hands against the window. Was that three lights she saw? They grew nearer, and she saw that it was indeed three lights, with one ahead of the other two, and she knew it was Micah leading Gram home. They approached the lodge, and Hanna exhaled a heavy sigh when the vehicles pulled into the parking lot. She opened the door and walked along the porch, then saw Gram, followed by Micah, walking up the dim incline to the lodge.

"Gram, are you okay?" She reached out a hand to help her up the steps.

"Oh, I'm fine. I just got a little turned around." Her voice sounded strong.

But even in the dim porch light, Hanna thought she saw the evidence of tears. And her hair was in disarray. She sent Micah a questioning glance but received only a shrug in answer.

She took Gram's arm and led her to the door. "Let's get you inside and fix you some—"

"Now, don't fuss, child. I haven't forgotten how to feed myself." Gram patted her hand, then slipped through the screen door. "I can still smell that pot roast . . ." Her voice faded as the door fell shut.

Micah pulled the handle, and she stopped him with a hand on his arm. The porch light cast a silver glow over his features.

"Is she really okay? What happened?"

His hand fell from the handle. "I found her on Spring Gulch Road, pulled to the side. She'd lost her way, like she said."

"But how? She's lived here all her life. How could she get lost?" She knew the answer but didn't want to admit, even to herself, that Gram was losing her faculties.

Micah shook his head.

"What condition was she in when you found her? Was she worried, afraid?"

"Both, I suppose." His voice rumbled softly in the night air. "She was crying. I took a few minutes to calm her down before driving back."

A lump formed in her throat. What if Micah hadn't found her? What if she'd been lost all night? Anything could've happened to her. She met Micah's gaze briefly before he looked away. What an enigma, this man. Strong, harsh even, but gentle enough to console an old woman when she wept in fear. He could say anything he liked, but his actions were proof of the man he was.

Her hand reached up to cradle his jaw. It was rough with stubble and tightened at her touch. She leaned up on her tiptoes and kissed him on the cheek. The kiss landed on the soft corner of his lips. "Thank you," she whispered.

He didn't move, not a muscle, but she sensed the tightening of his body, saw the desire in his expression. What was she feeling, this pleasant emotion burning deep within her? It was more than attraction, more than . . . anything she'd ever felt. Love's tender sprouts were taking root in her heart, and there was nothing she could do to stop them.

She felt the heat from his body, only inches away. Why couldn't he take her in his arms? Why couldn't he kiss her like he did before? He wanted to. She could see it in his eyes. But she could also detect the iron will that held him back. The same will that had kept him distant, that had stopped their kiss before.

She sighed and broke eye contact, slipping through the door, brushing close to him purposely. He could fight it all he wanted, but she didn't have to make it easy for him.

Gram was coming through the swinging doors of the kitchen with a plate of food when Hanna entered the dining room. She took a deep breath and sat across from Gram. Hanna's emotions had been all over the board tonight from anxiety and fear to gratitude and passion.

But now only Gram mattered.

The woman bowed her head in silent prayer. She seemed smaller than she used to be. Had she lost weight? Her disheveled hair and puffy eyes were the only remnants of what must have been an evening fraught with worry and fear.

At last, Gram dug into her mashed potatoes, and Hanna wondered how to break the news she'd gotten earlier. Gram was no dummy. When she heard she needed to see a specialist, she'd put two and two together.

"Don't worry so, dear. I'm fine. Really."

Hanna's lips slanted in a smile. Tonight's fiasco had proved one thing. Gram could no longer drive anywhere alone, Alzheimer's or not. It just wasn't safe. But how could she convince her? Gram, who'd taken over the lodge fearlessly upon her husband's death. Gram, who prided herself in independence and courage. She might be angry with Hanna for suggesting it, and she might even refuse to comply. But Hanna had to try.

"You really had me worried tonight."

"I'm sorry, I know you must've been."

"I think . . . I think maybe it would be best if you took me or Mrs. Eddlestein with you when you run errands." Her heart beat out a frantic staccato. "At least for a while."

Gram calmly set her milk glass on the table. "Maybe you're right."

Hanna blinked.

"Don't look so surprised. You're not the only one who was worried tonight." Gram placed her wrinkled hand over Hanna's. "You've no idea how terrifying it is to be out somewhere and realize you have no clue where you are. To not recognize anything even though you know you've been there hundreds of times. To know everything should be familiar, but nothing *is* familiar. Believe me, I have no desire to go through that again."

Hanna breathed a sigh of relief as Gram squeezed her hand and continued eating. She'd handled that better than Hanna had expected, but the next news was even worse. How could she soften the information so as not to alarm Gram? Maybe if she handled it matter-of-factly, like it was no big deal.

"Your doctor's office called today. They suggested more testing and gave you a referral to another doctor. I went ahead and made an appointment for you."

Gram's loaded fork made a slow descent to her plate. The frown between her brows spoke of keen understanding. "So," she said, "the testing Doc did is pointing to Alzheimer's." She settled back against the wooden slats of the high-back chair.

"Well, he thought a neurologist might be better suited to conduct the . . . " Her voice trailed off as Gram shook her head.

"You don't have to beat around the bush, child. I've gotten pretty good at getting around on the Internet. I've been conducting my own investigation, and I know what this referral to a neurologist means."

Sadness bubbled up in Hanna's heart. How would it feel to be going senile and to know it would get worse until she was totally dependent on others for even the simplest tasks.

"Don't look so glum, Hanna. I've been walking with the Lord for sixty years, and He's not let me down yet. If I do have that dreaded disease, He'll be with me—with us—all the way through, giving us the strength we need to cope."

Gram's faith blew Hanna away. She was one of the few whose life was a living testimony to Christ's faithfulness. "There's still a chance you don't have Alzheimer's at all."

"And even if I do, it takes *years* for the illness to progress." Her eyes lit mischievously, and she winked at Hanna. "I have plenty of time to give everyone around me a hard time."

Hanna laughed and squeezed Gram's hand. It was true; they had years together, even if she did have Alzheimer's, and God would give them what they needed in the meantime.

<hr/>

Hanna stacked the clean towels in Micah's bathroom and picked up the dirty sheets from the floor. It was a lesson in temptation, cleaning his room. Not only did the spicy scent of his cologne linger in the air, but there were personal effects lying all over the room. Folded papers, mail, a leather-bound book that looked like a journal. Curiosity ate at her each week, but thankfully, she'd inherited her father's determination and had so far resisted the urge to peek into Micah's private life.

She stuffed the bedding into the hallway cart and pushed it into the storage closet. She needed to do laundry, but first, she wanted to check on reservations for the rest of July. She'd been keeping track of cancellations since she'd installed the lock on the office door, but if her hunch was right, they were still in trouble.

She was almost certain the cancellation she'd received that morning was for a reservation made *after* the lock was installed. Was someone breaking in and getting into their files?

The lodge was quiet this morning, several guests having checked out and several of the others gone for the all-day climb. She rounded the front desk and pushed open the office door.

Devon turned from his place at the computer, a startled look blanketing his face. "Hanna." The screen flickered to the home page.

She frowned, suspicion flowing like poison through her veins. "What are you doing?" She couldn't prevent accusation from tainting her words.

"Oh." He rolled the chair out and stood. "I was just checking on the shuttle schedule. You were busy cleaning, so I just . . ." He shrugged. "Hope you don't mind."

Hanna studied his face, wishing she could read people the way Micah did. He didn't look guilty. If anything, he looked embarrassed. "I left next week's schedule at the front desk as usual."

"Oh, I didn't even look. I thought you wouldn't have had time to—well, anyway, I'll go get it. Thanks." At the doorway he turned. "Hey, I was going to go to the Central Wyoming game next Friday; what about coming with me?"

Unfortunately she was free, and she didn't want to lie. Maybe it was time to set the record straight. "Thanks for asking, Devon, but I think it's best if we keep things on a professional level. Have fun at the game, though."

He tossed her a boyish grin. "No problem. See ya."

Hanna turned and watched him leave, closing the door behind him. He seemed to take that well. There was no attraction on Hanna's side, not to mention she was suspicious of him after finding him at the computer. Could Devon be sabotaging them? She'd never considered it could be one of her own employees.

She opened the file cabinet and pulled out the office lock receipt and compared it with the reservation that had just been canceled this morning.

Her stomach lurched. The reservation had been made *after* the lock was installed. Whoever was getting the information was not being deterred by a lock. She resolved to lock up during the day from this point on. Only she and Gram had a key, and hers was on her all the time. She would tell Gram to keep the key someplace safe.

⚬

Micah scurried up the last scree slope before coming to a good resting spot. The group with him, an overweight woman and her husband, a thirty-something man, and his foster father, Jim, sank to the ground for a moment's rest. Jim had always made a point of climbing with Micah several times a year.

"So, your job's going well?" Jim asked.

"Sure." Micah took a swig from his canteen. In all honesty he didn't know how much longer he could live under the same roof with Hanna. Regardless of his detachment, she wasn't giving up on the notion of a relationship. And a man could only take so much.

"What's wrong?"

Jim's profession as a counselor carried over into every other area of his life. He was known for his probing questions, and Micah wasn't sure he wanted to go there.

"It's a problem between my boss and me." Maybe he'd leave it alone.

"What kind of problem?"

Maybe not. Micah would ignore anyone else who pried into his life, but Jim was the only one who really cared what the answers were. That didn't mean Micah had to tell him everything, though. "We just have major differences of opinion."

Jim's lips twitched. "That's not the feeling I got this morning."

Hanna had invited Jim to have breakfast with the others before they'd left the lodge. And she'd made no secret of her feelings toward Micah. He watched the other three members of their group taking pictures from their panoramic spot.

"You're running scared, aren't you?" The sober look shadowing Jim's eyes checked the automatic defensiveness in Micah. "It's a normal reaction, Micah. The only woman in your childhood, your mother no less, mistreated you. You bounced from one foster home to another during your childhood, and in that time connected with no other female. The only female you were bonded with, your sister, was taken from your life too. That's bound to affect the way you feel about women."

It was nothing Micah hadn't thought about many times. Most of his group therapy centered around the effects of having an alcoholic parent. He thought of Jenna. At first his little sister had been placed in the same foster home with him. But somewhere along the line they'd been separated. Many times he'd wondered what had become of her. One day maybe he'd try to find her.

"Have you been using the journal I gave you?" Jim asked.

He nodded.

"The whole purpose of working through your past is to bring healing to your present. Man was not made to be alone. That's why God created Eve." He winked. "And I must admit, it was a great plan." The smile fell from his face. "At some point you're going to have to take the risk."

A part of him certainly wanted to. The part that shuddered with desire whenever Hanna looked at him with open longing in her eyes. The part that weakened with yearning whenever she listened to him like he was the only man in the world. The part that saw her playing with children and wondered what she'd look like carrying his child.

Micah shook his head, trying to clear the tempting image from his head. He took another drink from his canteen and urged the group into motion again. Jim filed silently into line, leaving Micah to think in peace.

As he climbed he came to a conclusion. He could either continue working at Higher Grounds and allow himself to enter a relationship with Hanna, or he could quit and move on. One thing was certain: He couldn't continue to be around Hanna and remain detached. His feelings for her were growing; avoiding her had not stopped it from happening. And if he stayed, he would only grow to love her.

Should he stay or should he go? That was the question of the hour, and the one he reflected on for the remainder of the day.

Once the group had settled around the campfire, their bellies full from dinner, Jim brought up the subject again. "So, what's this Hanna like?"

Micah sighed. She was very different from him. "Outgoing, caring." He huffed a laugh. "Stubborn."

Jim smiled. "You seem less than pleased about that."

"It puts us at odds when she's determined to have me, and I'm determined not to be had."

He laughed. "Ah, so that's how it is." Jim poked at the fire with a stick. "How much does she know about you?"

"I've dropped a hint or two about my past."

"To scare her off?"

Micah looked directly at Jim.

"Don't be so surprised. It's my job to be perceptive. So, did it work, scaring her off?"

He humphed. "Not hardly."

"Sounds like quite a woman."

She was. And he didn't deserve her.

"Just the kind of woman to keep you in line," Jim said, poking him in the elbow.

"All that stuff you did when you were younger doesn't matter anymore, you know," Jim whispered. "When Christ came in, He wiped the slate clean."

"I know."

"You know it in your head, but do you know it in your heart?"

How like Jim to get right to the point of the matter. How did he convince his heart? It was true he didn't feel completely forgiven, hadn't forgiven himself.

"I think you should do it."

Micah jerked his head sideways to look at Jim. "Do what?"

"I think you should go for it. With Hanna. She seems like a caring, Christian girl. And from everything you've said, she had a healthy childhood and an intact family. A relationship with her could be very healing for you, in more ways than one."

"How romantic," Micah said sarcastically.

Jim chuckled. "Sometimes we psychologists are way too clinical, aren't we?"

As Micah sat in the shadowed night watching the flames leap and shoot sparks, he had a sudden craving for toasted marshmallows and the woman he loved to share them with.

CHAPTER
NINETEEN

Natalie watched Hanna chase Taylor across the playground and smiled when she caught him up in her arms. His shrieks of joy caused Natalie another moment of guilt. It had been weeks since she'd really played with her boys. Every smile she gave them seemed pinned on her face. Could they tell how unhappy she was? Were her grief and anxiety rubbing off on them?

"Watch me, Mom!" Alex slid down the spiral slide on his belly. After seeing his mom's thumbs-up, he climbed back up the ladder.

It had been three days since Keith had left, and she hadn't heard from him. Was he going to file for divorce? What would she do? How would she support the boys? And worse, what if Keith filed for custody?

More questions. Would there never be an end to this mess? She'd decided to continue going to counseling. Even if Keith wasn't willing to stay, she needed to find a way to deal with all the emotions.

Hanna set Taylor in a baby swing and pushed him from the front, making faces and tickling his legs each time he neared. As if Natalie's marriage problems weren't enough, now she had Gram to worry about. Hanna had told her about Gram getting lost and about the next appointment being with a specialist. She'd only been around one person who'd had Alzheimer's, and that was Keith's great-aunt Sophie. They'd visited the woman in a nursing home last year, and she hadn't recognized Keith. She used to be a soft-spoken, gentle woman, but when they'd visited, she'd thrown a temper tantrum over the food on her dinner plate.

Natalie couldn't imagine that happening to Gram. Didn't even want to think about the possibility.

Hanna set Taylor on the ground, and he sat in the wood chips using a stick to dig. Hanna plopped on the bench with a loud sigh.

Natalie smiled as she watched Taylor throwing the chips up in the air by the handful. He'd definitely need his hair washed tonight.

"How are you doing?" Hanna asked. "You sounded so depressed on the phone the other night."

She sighed. "I go through bouts of depression and bouts of rage. And in between those two, I have bouts of self-pity. It's really weird. Not just the emotional mood swings, but the way my mind works. Every time I think of some event in the past, whether it's Taylor's last birthday or when I had my hair highlighted, I keep trying to organize everything by whether it was before or during the affair. I do it constantly. Isn't that weird?"

Hanna smiled sadly. "It's probably normal. I mean, you really had the rug pulled out from under you. I'm sure you must feel like you were duped."

"Exactly. It's like, since I didn't know what was going on then, I have to take all the information I have now and apply it to the past year."

"It probably has a lot to do with your personality. I mean, you're a very organized person, so it makes sense that you want to organize all this information."

Natalie felt a rush of understanding. "Right. Like I had all these events filed away under 'normal life,' and now I have to go through each event and decide where I need to refile it."

Hanna shook her head. "You are *sick*, woman."

Natalie laughed, and it felt good. They silently watched the boys play. Alex disappeared into a tunnel, and Taylor continued to dig in the wood chips.

"Have you heard from Keith?" Hanna asked.

She shook her head. "I feel so lost. I don't know if he's going to file for divorce. And if he does, what will happen with our finances? Do they freeze the assets or what? How are the bills going to get paid until all this is settled?"

"Maybe you should call an attorney and ask." Hanna was starting to wish she'd been able to get the lodge's mortgage through another bank. If Keith divorced Nat, it would be awkward dealing with him.

"The boys keep asking when Daddy's coming home."

Hanna put her arm around her and squeezed her shoulder.

"Can we talk about something else? I'm tired of crying."

"Sure. Hey, have I told you about the cancellations at the lodge?"

"Yeah, have you figured out why you're getting them?"

Hanna sighed. "Nope. Someone told me the Majestic is offering this really low rate. Have you heard any negative talk about the lodge?"

"No."

"I thought maybe someone had started a rumor or something. Remember that phone call I told you about—the Realtor whose client wanted to buy our property?"

"Yeah."

"I'm wondering if that's connected somehow. Oh. I forgot this part. Yesterday I found Devon at the computer. He said—"

"Devon?"

"The watercraft guy. Anyway, he said he was just getting the airport shuttle list, but I'd already printed it out for him."

"Hmm, I'll have to give this some thought."

"I'm no good at this detective stuff, and nothing illegal has been done that I can prove. But if I don't put an end to this, we're not going to be able to make July's payment."

"I wish I could help." Natalie didn't know how her own bills were going to get paid, much less those of Higher Grounds.

"You've got enough to worry about. But it wouldn't hurt to mention it in your prayers if you think of it."

"You got it."

Taylor went running for the ladder and began climbing. Natalie jumped up and went to spot him. So much was going on in their lives right now, and all of it seemed bad. *Lord, why do I feel like Job all of a sudden?*

Hanna opened the file drawer and pulled Devon's application. Her eyes skimmed the page for anything suspicious, but everything looked in order.

Who else could it be? A stranger who picked the lock in the middle of the night? The thought sent a shudder through her. Maybe she should have the entrance locks changed. Who else had access to the lodge?

Micah. The uneasy thought flashed through her mind. She fished through the files for his application, but she couldn't find it. She started at the front of the stuffed file and paged through the papers again, tossing out old papers as she went. His tax form was there and, right behind it, a half-sheet of paper with names and phone numbers scrawled on it.

That's right. He'd just stopped in, spur of the moment, and I didn't have him fill out an application. Her head spun. *No. This is silly, Hanna; he wouldn't do this. You know him. He's the man who found Gram, the man who stirs your heart, for heaven's sake.*

Hanna breathed a laugh. Of course Micah isn't doing this. What was she thinking? She shook her head, feeling a momentary pang of guilt. After all the things Micah had done for her, for Gram, for the lodge, and she was suspecting him of betrayal.

Rendering a mental apology to Micah, she tossed his references in the trash and went to the front desk to check out a couple. While she printed out their bill, Micah approached the desk and began looking over the sign-up sheets for this week's climbs. The couple chatted with her for a few moments and thanked her for her restaurant recommendations over the past few days. Micah remained at the desk, quietly scanning his papers. Finally the couple left.

"Hi," she said to Micah.

"How's it going?"

It was his typical greeting, and she knew by now he didn't expect a response. She reached under the counter for the register paper and began replacing the empty roll. She glanced at Micah. What was he doing? It only took a few moments to see how many were going on each trip. It was almost as if he were stalling, wanting to be there for some reason.

She harrumphed silently. Not a chance of that. He'd done nothing but avoid her since their kiss. One week ago today, she noted.

Micah cleared his throat, but a quick look at him showed his eyes were still fastened on the sign-up sheets.

"Did you want something?" she asked.

He glanced at her, then looked back at the papers as if studying them intensely. "No." He flipped the page, and Hanna noticed the corner of the pages quivering in his hands. "I just—well, I . . ." He cleared his throat again. "I'm going canoeing on Thursday. Want to come along?"

Hesitant joy bubbled within her. Unless she was fooled by his tricky semantics, she had to believe he was asking her out on a date. She waited for him to look at her, but he studied the page as if her answer were written there. Sudden suspicion smothered her elation. Why was he asking her out? He'd been avoiding her for weeks, especially the past week.

"Why?"

His eyebrows popped. "Why?"

"Yes, why are you suddenly interested in spending time with me?"

Color mottled his cheeks as he flipped through the pages in his hand.

It didn't take a genius to see he was embarrassed. Should she have put him on the spot that way? After all, she'd made her interest very clear over the past several weeks. He probably thought she'd jump at the chance. She longed to do so, but her impish, curious side wanted him to say it. She wanted him to admit he was asking her on a date and not making a casual, last-minute invitation as his words had suggested.

She watched him squirm and felt a prick of guilt. But just as she was about to accept his invitation, his chin jerked upward and hardened, drawing attention to the square planes of his jaw line.

He dropped the papers on the desktop and stuffed his hands in his pockets. "Fine. You want honesty, fine. I've had a change of heart. I want to get to know you better. I want to—to date you."

Except for the brief hesitation, he sounded adamant and confident. Her heart hammered inside her chest like a bass drum, vibrating through her body with rhythmic booms. She watched his cheeks redden despite his bold declaration. A wave of excitement rushed through her veins. He'd always been abrupt, but she hadn't expected such a direct statement. Suddenly it was she who was speechless.

His brow hiked up. "Cat got your tongue?" His voice rumbled through the air, bringing a pleasant sensation to her ears.

She loved his deep voice. Loved the way his jaw always sported a five o'clock shadow. Loved the way he was looking at her right now. An unbidden smile formed on her face. "I'm just a little surprised by your change of heart." A *lot* surprised, she corrected silently.

He leaned on the counter, placing his forearms against it and clasping his hands. The movement brought him within inches of her.

＊＊＊

Micah allowed his gaze to roam freely over Hanna's face. Her green eyes had flecks of gold in the center that sparkled when she was happy, such as now. That he'd shocked her with his invitation had been obvious. And he hadn't missed the fact that she had yet to answer.

It had taken him all day to get up his nerve. And trying to arrange it so he appeared casual had proven to be almost impossible. He'd asked out more women than he could count, but that had been years ago. And the purpose of his dates then had been altogether different. Maybe that's why his hands trembled like an old woman's.

Hanna wet her lips, drawing his attention to her mouth. "Well." He watched her lips form the words. "I guess it would be silly to turn you down, seeing as how I've hunted you like a hound dog for weeks." Her lips tipped into a smile.

He met her gaze. "We can do something else if you'd rather." He felt magnetically drawn to her. His eyes couldn't seem to look away from hers.

"I like canoeing. I haven't gone in years, except for that little trip crossing String Lake."

She looked at his lips, and desire singed every nerve in his body. He couldn't move, couldn't breathe.

The phone rang, shattering the moment. Hanna picked up the receiver, her eyes still trained on his. "Higher Grounds, may I help you?" The words, spoken in breathy distraction, brought a smile to his lips.

From her side of the conversation, it was clearly a prospective guest with lots of questions. He backed away from the counter and lifted a hand in a wave. His last view of her before he left was of her wiggling her fingers and smiling in return.

❈

Hanna dragged her paddle through the water as the canoe shifted away from the shore. She could hardly believe Thursday was here at last. The past three days had trudged by. Micah had been away on trips most of the time, and she'd looked forward to spending a whole day alone with him. She'd packed a cooler for the occasion, and Mrs. Eddlestein had included a big lunch for them, as well as snacks and soft drinks to last the day.

After trying on three different outfits and bemoaning her meager selection, she'd decided on a pair of khaki shorts and olive T-shirt over her swimsuit. After grabbing a bite to eat, they'd gone to the rental store, then put in at Pacific Creek Landing.

Now, as the canoe sluiced through the water of Snake River, she became conscious of the silence that had settled around them. No other boaters were in sight, though they'd likely run into groups along the way.

"I'm surprised you're not tired of canoeing," Hanna said to break the silence.

"Because I canoe on the Mount Moran trip?"

"Yeah, I wouldn't think it's something you'd want to do on your day off."

"You can't really compare the Snake River to String Lake."

Hanna heard the sarcasm in his voice. "Are you saying String Lake bores you?" she teased.

"Let's just say I like the challenge of Snake River."

Hanna turned and tossed him a smile. "Well, this is a first for me, so I guess I'm getting initiated."

"Yeah, well, just don't initiate us both with a good dunking."

Hanna tipped her chin. "I'm not a novice, you know. I think I can manage to stay dry." She paused pointedly. "If I have a decent stern paddler behind me."

Micah let the comment go, and soon they were talking about Hanna and her family. Before she knew it, she'd rattled on for the better part of an hour, pausing only to concentrate when they'd gone through rapids.

She was curious about his family. What had happened to his mom and dad that he'd ended up in the foster care system? She wanted to know; yet, she didn't feel they knew each other well enough to ask.

She'd just finished talking about her sisters when she thought of a neutral question for him. "What about you? Were you born in Jackson?"

She felt the pause, not only in conversation, but in the steady drifting of the canoe as he pulled his paddle from the water. "No."

She took his brevity as a hint that he didn't want to discuss himself and led the conversation on to where they attended high school. She shared that she'd been involved in student government and volleyball, but he'd said nothing except that he'd attended Kemmerer High School, about an hour south of Jackson.

"I'll bet you had a lot of boyfriends in high school," he said.

The comment surprised her. Not only because he rarely asked questions, but also because he thought she might have a lot of experience with the opposite sex. "I had a few, but nothing serious."

"What about in college?"

"I dated one guy. We were fairly serious."

"What happened?"

She shuddered when she thought of the times he'd tried to touch her. She thought of all the times she'd tried to endure it for Jess's sake, so he wouldn't feel rejected. But she didn't want to tell Micah about that.

"When Grandpop died, Gram needed help so . . . I dropped out of college and came here. I was majoring in business anyway, so it was right up my alley. Besides, I'd always loved the lodge. I spent a lot of time there as a kid."

The sun was high in the sky when they found a good spot to eat, and they paddled the canoe to shore. She wanted to ask him about relationships he'd had, but his comments from the previous week kept her quiet. He'd made it sound like he'd been physically involved with many women, and she didn't even want to think about that. From what she understood, he hadn't been a Christian then.

That brought up another question, and once they'd settled on the blanket with their food and said grace, she voiced it, "Tell me how you became a Christian."

She was startled when Micah choked on the bite of sandwich. He took a drink from his Mountain Dew, hacking a few more times before managing to swallow his food and gain his composure.

"Was it something I said?" she teased.

He looked at her, then away, and Hanna wondered if she hadn't stumbled upon something. What if he wasn't a Christian at all? Her heart tripped at the thought. True, he prayed and read the Bible, but what if he didn't have a real relationship with God?

"What?" she forced herself to ask. She had to know, and the sooner the better, if he wasn't a Christian at all.

"There's a lot you don't know about me." He picked at a potato chip, then tossed it back on his plate. "I guess I should just get this out of the way."

Her mind raced with one ridiculous thought after another as she watched him intently.

"I became a Christian while I was in jail."

Jail? She worked to keep her expression neutral. Her thoughts spun.

He continued. "I was a pretty rough kid. Had a few scrapes with the law." He shook his head. "I'm not sure how Jim and Jan put up with me. Anyway, when I turned eighteen, I took off. Thought I was better off on my own, making my own decisions."

Hanna wondered again why he'd been placed in a foster home and what effect that situation had on his troubled youth.

"I got a job at a gas station and did all right. But before long I got caught swiping some motorcycle parts from a repair shop. I was convicted of petty theft, but the judge was easy on me and I just got probation."

He looked away from her frequently as he spoke but always came back to study her intently, as if trying to read her. She wondered what he saw. Surprise maybe, but she hoped he saw the caring and empathy that filled her heart.

"I knew I'd gotten off easily and thought I was hot stuff. I made some friends—if you could call them that—at the gas station I worked at. We did some stupid stuff, but we didn't get caught."

Hanna saw the regret in his eyes and wanted to tell him it was okay, that God had forgiven him, and she did, too, but he seemed determined to finish.

"One night we decided to hold up a gas station. We were cocky, figured we'd never get caught, but someone had gotten the license of the car, and they tracked us. I got sentenced to eighteen months in jail."

When Micah looked at her, she allowed a smile of empathy to form on her lips.

"I was pretty rotten. Looking back now, I can see all the hatred I had in me, but at the time it just seemed like everyone was out to get me. No one knew I was in jail. I had no family to tell, and my friends were in jail too. I hated it. I despised being cooped up. I wound up in lots of fights."

Hanna thought of all the times she'd seen him jogging and knew he must've felt claustrophobic in jail. "I guess you didn't get paroled."

He gave a self-deprecating laugh. "You could say that." He took a long sip of his pop. "But after I'd been in jail awhile, a prison-ministry team came to visit the inmates." He smiled. "Imagine my surprise when Jim came to see me as part of the team."

"Your foster father?"

He nodded. "And if you think I was shocked, you should've seen his face. I'll never forget the disappointment in his eyes when he saw me there. He looked so old." Micah looked at Hanna, and she saw the weariness in his eyes. "It was the first time I really believed he cared. During the years I'd lived there, I thought he was just trying to control me. I thought he and Jan were like all the other foster parents I had, that they just wanted the government money."

Sympathy surged through Hanna's heart. How blessed she'd been to have godly parents when he didn't even have a taste of love until he was a young man. Her soul longed to touch his, to heal him. But then, God had already done that.

He drew a deep breath and grinned sheepishly. "Didn't mean to go on for so long, but anyway, that's how I became a Christian. Jim led me to the Lord."

Hanna reached over and squeezed his hand. "Thanks for telling me."

Micah shifted and gathered his trash. The quiet moment teemed with awkwardness, and Hanna gathered up her things too. She realized Micah must be feeling vulnerable, having spilled the details of his past. Embarrassed about the things he'd done, about the man he'd been. But as far as she was concerned, all that was in the past. She could easily fill the silence with reassurances but decided to let her actions speak for her. He would come to see that she respected him for the man he was today,

CHAPTER
TWENTY

Micah stuffed their trash in the cooler and lugged it through the underbrush to the canoe. His nerves were worn from the confessions he'd just made, but judging by Hanna's reaction, he'd done the right thing in coming clean. She seemed to accept him as he was. And that was comforting, knowing that he'd told her every shameful thing about his past.

Not everything.

She didn't have to know about that. He wasn't over it himself. How could he bare that raw issue?

Tell her.

He shoved the thought to the back of his mind. There would be time to tell her later. When he'd come to terms with it himself. When he felt some twinge of forgiveness. He'd been relieved when he'd told Pastor Witte on Sunday that he couldn't serve as a deacon. Micah hadn't given a reason, and Pastor Witte hadn't asked.

They silently stowed their belongings in the canoe and put on their life vests. As the boat began moving once again, so did conversation, and Micah was relieved that Hanna was easy to talk to. They worked as a team, growing quiet when they reached rapids. They maneuvered through them with ease, with Hanna paddling on the appropriate side while he used his oar as a rudder.

As they exited this last set of rapids, the most turbulent so far, Hanna tossed him a smile. "That was fun."

The canoe glided slowly into the still center of the river, and they rested, their oars lying across their laps as they caught their breath. The hottest part of the afternoon had descended upon them, and Micah wished he could take off his shirt.

Memories surfaced of the one time a woman had seen his scarred back. He'd picked her up in a bar, an exquisitely beautiful Asian woman, who'd known what he was after from the first. Even the haze of alcohol had never kept him from remembering to dim the lights when he was with a woman, but this one had surprised him. As they'd left the bed, she'd flipped on the overhead light. He hadn't turned soon enough to prevent her from seeing his scarred back. The revulsion on her face was a bitter reminder of the grotesque deformity of his skin.

The memory brought a shadow of anxiety, sucking the moisture from his mouth.

"Want a soda?" Hanna asked.

"You read my mind."

She turned in her seat and attempted to unzip the nylon cooler. The awkwardness of her position forced her to stand and turn.

"Here I'll get it," Micah said.

"I've got it." She stepped over her seat but lost her balance when her foot slipped against the wet, rounded side of the canoe. Her hand found the only hold, the side of the boat. The motion dipped the canoe precariously to the side.

Micah reached out to help steady her, but it was too late. The canoe flipped, and they plunged into the water.

Water rushed over his head, but the life vest carried him to the surface. He wiped the water from his eyes and looked for Hanna. Beyond the floating cooler, she bobbed, a dazed expression coating her features, but obviously unhurt.

He couldn't suppress the smile that tugged at his lips. "Do you know how many times I've gone down this river without tipping?"

He watched her collect herself. Finally, she blinked innocently. "Two or three?"

"Ha! Try dozens. *Dozens.*" He glanced at the canoe floating topsy-turvy beside them. "And I have *never* tipped."

She tilted her chin and lowered her lashes in a way that made him want to grab her and kiss her. "It's your fault," she said.

Kiss? He meant throttle. "My fault?"

"If you hadn't wanted a soda . . ."

He lunged through the water at her, hearing a squeal just before the water surged over his head. A game of chase ensued. Hanna turned and caught him with a wave of water to the face. He growled menacingly and pursued her again.

They splashed and chased in the refreshingly cool water, dunking one another when the moment provided itself—no easy feat in the buoyant orange vests. Hanna's laughter floated across the surface of the water as she caught him from behind.

He let her dunk him, then twisted under the water and came up facing her. He blinked the water away from his eyes and reveled in the impish expression on her face. Her wet hair was slicked back exposing the natural beauty of her face. Water-spiked lashes framed her sparkling eyes.

He watched a rivulet of water run down her sun-kissed cheek and past the corner of her lips. His gaze caught there, watching the smile fall from her mouth.

Far beneath the surface of the water, her feet found his and mingled with his calves. He read the desire in her eyes. Lord help him, but he'd never wanted a woman so badly. Not just physically. He wanted all of her, body, mind, and soul. He wanted their lives to mingle the way their feet did now.

Micah tugged her as close as their vests would allow. Water lapped gently against them as her hands found the front of his vest and clutched there. He lowered his mouth to hers, wanting her, needing her.

Catcalls echoed across the water surface. Micah looked up to see two teenager-guided canoes shooting out of the rapids. As he and Hanna parted, regret simmered within him like the glowing ashes of a campfire. They made small talk with the boys as they glided past, and one of them fished their errant oars from the water and tossed them back.

By the time the boys were gone, the intimate moment had been shattered. Hanna pushed the cooler to shore while he pushed the canoe and oars. They emerged from the water sopping wet.

Hanna removed her T-shirt, exposing a modest black tank suit, and wrung the water from it. She met his gaze and shook her head in good humor. "You may as well take off your shirt. We can lay them out to dry in the boat."

Muscles clenched in his abdomen, and his mind fought for an excuse. Instead, he began wringing the hem of his shirt. "Nah, it's fine. Feels cooler this way."

Soon they were gliding downriver again, but this time Micah had the tantalizing view of Hanna's square, tanned shoulders tapering down to a tiny waist.

They sailed through the remaining rapids, stopping two more times to rest and enjoy the scenery. By the time they reached the end, their clothes were barely damp, but their energy was depleted. After returning the canoe, they agreed to stop and eat on the way back to the lodge. Doing so guaranteed Micah missing his support-group meeting, but watching Hanna return his smile, he couldn't bring himself to care.

After dinner at the Shady Nook Café, they stopped at a quiet spot along the shores of Flat Creek. Micah didn't want the day to end and, apparently, neither did Hanna because she seemed content to sit at the water's edge and talk until dusk settled around them like a down quilt.

"How many are signed up for the climb tomorrow?" she asked.

"Just a few. Should be an easy group."

She picked a blade of grass and tore it in half. "Have you ever got caught in a snowstorm up in the mountains?"

"Nah. I watch the weather reports before I leave. It snows sometimes, but nothing dangerous."

"I'll have to take another trip with you soon."

A smile sneaked upon his lips. "I'd like that. I've been missing your marshmallows."

She smiled, and he stared out at the creek, remembering their first climb together. He'd hardly known her, but even then there had been something compelling about her. Suddenly he remembered the last night of that climb when she'd awakened him from his sleep with cries and whimpers. What had caused her nightmare? He remembered the flashlight left on all night in her tent. Was she—

"What?" Hanna laughed lightly. "You look so serious."

He studied her face. "I was just thinking about the night we were camping when you had that nightmare."

Her expression sobered, and she looked out into the gathering darkness.

"Do you have them often?"

"Not so often anymore." She gave a wan smile. "It's been such a nice day, I don't want to spoil it. Can we talk about something else?"

"Sure."

Beside him, Hanna picked up a flat stone and skipped it across the creek.

Ah, now there was something he could talk about.

She picked up another one and threw. "One, two, three," she counted the skips. "There, beat that." Her adorable chin nudged up defiantly.

Should he tell her he had an unfair advantage? Nah. He picked up a stone and hurled it. It skipped rapidly across the water like a bionic frog, disappearing in the distant darkness.

Hanna's back straightened. "Hey, how'd you do that?"

He tossed her an "aw shucks" grin. "Don't be too impressed. I've had lots of practice." No need to tell her he'd gotten it in the prison yard, skipping stones down a drainage ditch.

"So have I, but I've never seen a rock skip so many times. Show me."

He moved behind her, and picked up a flat stone. That he could've shown her from a distance occurred to him, but that wouldn't be as much fun.

Hanna leaned back against his chest while he showed her precisely how to hold the rock. When she had her fingers properly placed, he curled her arm and held her wrist, slowly repeating the flicking motion until she got the hang of it.

"Okay," she said. "Let me try."

He leaned back on his hands to give her room to maneuver and, after several practice throws, she flung the rock horizontally. It skipped four times before plunking into the water.

"That's better," he encouraged.

She turned, wearing a proud smile. "I did it."

Suddenly rocks were the last thing on his mind. Her hair had air-dried to a tousled mane of honey, and he reached out and smoothed it behind her ear. She settled back against his chest, and he wondered if she felt the beating of his heart through his shirt.

As if reading his mind, she laid her hand against his heart as if asking for permission to enter. Then her hand moved to the roughness of his jaw, and he thought he'd expire from the yearning. Her eyes asked a question. He answered.

His lips covered hers, tasting the sweet surrender of her heart. He nipped gently at her lips, wanting to treat her with the care she deserved. Her eager response sent pleasant sensations surging through his veins. Euphoric sensations that made him wonder what he'd ever done to deserve this moment.

She twisted in his arms, facing him, nestling in the curve of his chest. The kiss deepened, and the assault on his senses intensified. Passion swelled in him until he feared it would overtake him.

He broke the kiss and jumped to his feet in one motion. Hanna nearly fell at his departure but caught herself with her hands.

Heat still coursed through him, now flooding his face. He felt silly, jumping and running like there was a fire. He laughed derisively.

There was a fire, and it was in him.

One look at Hanna's confused face drained all humor from his thoughts.

"It's not—," he began. "Don't think—" He heaved a frustrated sigh.

"What's wrong?" Her voice was raspy, her hair tousled, her lips swollen. The sweet confusion on her face begged for an answer.

He dropped to his knees, keeping a safe distance. When he looked at her, she turned away, but not before he saw the tears shimmering in her eyes and read the hurt on her face.

Suddenly he remembered their last kiss, when he'd abruptly left her sitting by the fire, and knew with certainty Hanna was thinking about it too. Thinking about the way he'd fought the attraction and avoided her for days. But this wasn't like last time.

"No, Hanna, that's not it."

She continued to look the other way, but he could see her eyelashes fluttering quickly and knew she was trying not to cry. He could alleviate her suffering easily if only he could figure out how to say it. How could something that came so easily to him on paper come so hard with the spoken word?

"It's just that I—look, I've never had to—" He flipped a twig with his finger. How could he explain without humiliating himself? "Kissing you—it makes me want more, okay?"

Her head swung to meet his gaze. Her wide-eyed innocence forced him on.

"Always before, before I was a Christian, I never had to stop with just a kiss. See what I'm saying?"

She did, he could see it by the quick downward flutter of her lashes. She clutched her knees to her chest in a gesture that screamed vulnerability.

Great, now he'd made her feel inexperienced, like she couldn't compete with his past. As if you could even compare those shallow physical acts with the depth of feeling one kiss from Hanna provoked. How could he explain that it was hard to stop when he'd never had to before?

He tried again. "It's like—I was in the habit of going from zero to sixty, and it's hard to stop at twenty and go back to idling." His pitiful analogy stumbled and fell.

She had pity on him. "I know what you're saying."

Relief filled him. He gulped a breath and released it with a whoosh. Thank God he wouldn't have to explain that again.

"It's a sex thing, right?" she stated, clearly bothered that he'd had so many partners.

Not that he could blame her. "I guess you could say that." He tipped up her chin until she met his gaze. "Hanna, I regret that I was so promiscuous before I was saved."

She offered him a weak smile.

"If it makes you feel better, I haven't kissed a woman since then."

Her eyes widened. "Really?"

"Not in six years." He wanted to drown in the innocent pools of her eyes. "I haven't wanted to kiss a woman until you."

He watched a shy smile spread across her lips. Her lids lowered to half-mast, and the green of her eyes seemed to deepen in color. He practically felt the caress of her gaze. Her lips parted sweetly.

"If you don't stop looking at me like that," he said, "we're going to be right back where we started." The words lightened the moment, and with darkness closing in, they agreed to head back to the lodge. At her door he dropped a quick kiss on her lips and said good night.

Later that night as Micah lay in bed, his journal perched on his lap, he relived the day on paper, putting words to his feelings. After staring off into space, lost in the lingering afterglow of their day, he finished the entry.

It was only our first date, yet I'm already half in love with her. My soul hungers for her nurturing love, and I can't help but wonder if this is God's healing answer to my past.

CHAPTER
TWENTY-ONE

Natalie stuffed a pile of darks in the washer, pausing when her hands discovered a pair of Keith's pants in the bottom of the hamper. A myriad of emotions assaulted her as his own unique scent filled the cubicle.

Although he'd stopped to see the boys twice since he'd left, he'd dodged her questions about their future. She didn't know if he'd come back to them when he tired of Lindsey, but she clung to the thought day by day.

Taylor toddled by the laundry room, and a familiar, pungent odor wafted upward. She closed the lid on the washer and snapped up Taylor in her arms. "Come on, punkin', let's go change your diaper."

"Mommy, I don't want cereal; I want waffles," Alex called from the table.

"You asked for cereal, Alex."

She ignored his whining and carried Taylor to the nursery changing table. Her mind, seldom on what she was doing these days, wandered to the last time Keith had come to see the boys. She'd noticed the slimmer contours of his face. Was he losing weight because he was depressed or because he wanted to be more attractive for *her*? Natalie hoped he was as depressed as she was. Hoped he suffered the same mental anguish he was putting her through. Not simply for retaliation, but because if he was lost without them, maybe he would come home soon.

The doorbell rang, and she heard the patter of Alex's feet across the kitchen floor. "Don't answer the door, Alex. Wait for Mommy."

She rushed to stick the diaper tape, then began snapping the sleeper, abandoning her plan to dress him for the day. The doorbell pealed again. "Hold on," she said, as if the visitor could hear.

Taylor squirmed, kicking his feet in a game he liked to play while she struggled to snap his clothing. "Stay still."

Alex peeked in. "Mommy, get the door."

"I will, honey, as soon as I'm done. Lie still, Taylor!" He continued to kick his legs, so she held them down. Finally, she fastened the last snap and lifted the toddler down from the table.

The doorbell rang a third time just before she unlocked and opened it.

A sheriff—the new one she'd seen around town a time or two—stood on her porch. Her heart accelerated as a dozen scary possibilities entered her mind, none of which she wanted to entertain.

The man tipped his head. "Ma'am. I need to speak with Natalie Coombs."

"That's me." She struggled to keep a pleasant smile on her face. What was it with having a sheriff on your doorstep that reminded you of the dreaded visit to the principal's office?

Alex peeked around her legs. "Are you a real policeman?"

The sheriff nodded, and she sent Alex back to the table, barely aware of him as he scampered back to the kitchen.

"I have some papers for you."

Natalie had been served papers before when a man had sued Keith. Maybe it was something to do with the bank. "What kind of papers?"

The man's eyes softened under the shaded brim of his hat. "Divorce papers, ma'am." He held them out.

Cold fingers of dread twisted around her heart, freezing her, numbing her. She stared at the papers but refused to reach out and take them. To do so would be accepting this thing. And she didn't. Didn't want it. Didn't accept it.

"I'm sorry, ma'am." He nudged the papers her way. "You have to take these."

With one hand she accepted the papers. With the other she gripped the doorknob at her back. Her eyes scanned the page. It was a notice of a hearing or some such. She saw the words "Keith A. Coombs vs. Natalie A. Coombs." Had it truly come to this? They were enemies, she and her husband? He was suing her for divorce? Why hadn't she contacted an attorney?

Her legs buckled, but she caught herself.

"Are you all right, ma'am?" He steadied her with a hand.

In the whirlwind of her thoughts, she noticed a slight Tennessee twang and found it comforting. She met his gaze. "What do I do? I don't know what I'm supposed to do."

She saw sympathy in his eyes. "That's a court summons. What you want to do is hire a lawyer so you can appear in court by the date right here." He pointed to the date on the paper.

She couldn't believe it had reached this point. To courts, plaintiffs, and attorneys. He hadn't even had the decency to tell her himself. She'd had to find out from a stranger, who showed her more sympathy than her own husband.

"I'm sorry, ma'am." The sheriff backed off the porch. "You get yourself a lawyer, and you'll be fine. Best of luck to you."

She watched him go, forgetting for a moment the two children inside. It was just her and the papers.

Some time later, she shut the door and walked through the living room. Her hands trembled as she set the papers on the desk. Her gaze clung in shock to the words on the top paper: *Keith A. Coombs vs. Natalie A. Coombs.* The black ink blurred. He'd done it. He'd filed for divorce. Without even telling her.

Her stomach clenched with nausea.

"Uh-oh." Taylor's voice penetrated the fog of shock. "Uh-oh." He appeared from the hallway, and she swiped the tears from her eyes.

"Uh-oh." Taylor held a bottle of baby powder she'd received at a shower and had never used. White dust spattered his pajamas, and powdery footprints marked his journey from the nursery.

"Taylor!" A sob rose within in, but she choked it back. Tears fought for release and won. She grabbed the bottle from him, and a puff of white escaped as she inadvertently squeezed the container. "That's a no-no!"

She followed the trail, berating herself for forgetting to shut the nursery door. She stopped on the threshold. Frustration welled up, choking off the despair and bitterness for just a moment. The scene before her might have reminded her of a winter wonderland in a happier moment, but at the present time, all she saw was an impossible mess. He'd left no surface uncovered. Even the sheets of his crib and his beloved blankie were victims.

A sob worked its way up her throat and escaped. She covered her face and allowed it. Allowed the torrent of feelings to escape, hoping they would go away if she let them out. The ache in her midsection grew to a massive blob and coated everything within her with the dark stench of misery.

"Uh-oh." She barely heard him. "Uh-oh, Mama."

She drew a deep breath, then coughed when the talc-coated air permeated her lungs.

"Mommy," Alex called from the kitchen.

She couldn't summon the energy to answer. Could only stand and look at the mess in the room and realize it could represent the mess of her life. Would she be one of those divorcées that people at church talked about? Would everyone judge her? Hadn't she judged others?

"I don't like this cereal, Mommy!"

Numbly, she took Taylor's hand and left the room, shutting the door behind her this time. She would worry about it later.

She heard Alex's fist hitting the table in rebellious rhythm. "Wa-ffles, wa-ffles, wa-ffles."

"Stop it, Alex," she said, entering the kitchen and wiping away the evidence of tears. Her brain was glazed with confusion, and she fought to remember why she'd come to the kitchen. The papers sitting on the desk drew her attention.

"I want waffles!" He shoved his cereal bowl forcefully across the table, and it sloshed over the rim, making a puddle of milk. The sugary loops floated in the milky pool like colorful life preservers.

Her body moved automatically toward the paper towels. A shriek pierced the air. She moved to the living room where Taylor had gotten

191

stuck between the end table and couch. Mechanically, she lifted him out.

Alex tugged on her shirt. "Mommy . . . waffles . . ." The nasal whine grated across her nerves.

She pushed his hands from her shirt. "No! You said you wanted cereal; now go eat it!"

He pulled again at her shirt, jumping up and down, his face scrunching into a temper tantrum.

Suddenly all the irritating stimuli swelled to unbearable heights. A black pit of anger welled up within her. She pushed him away and grabbed his upper arms. "Stop it! Do you hear me? Stop it!" She shook him once. "Just listen for once, would you?"

Her hands stilled, and so did his body. His eyes bulged with tears. Fear flickered back at her. His face scrunched up again, this time in genuine despair. His shoulders heaved in sobs.

What have I done? Look at me! What is happening to me?

She watched her son cry as if from a distance. As if he wouldn't go through enough pain in the coming months, she had taken out her grief on him. His life would be irrevocably changed.

Natalie sank to her knees and gathered him in her arms. He came willingly, clinging to her as if she had not just been inexcusably rough with him.

"I'm sorry. I'm so sorry. Mommy shouldn't have—" Her voice broke as emotions strangled her words. She held her son and choked back her own tears. Keith had done this to her. To them. But she would not let them feel an ounce of her pain. They would have enough of their own. She must be there for them, hold them up, convince them of their value. She may not have a husband, but she had her boys, and she would fight the devil himself before letting them suffer needlessly.

CHAPTER TWENTY-TWO

Hanna punched the buttons on her desktop calculator and watched the green numbers light the display. Eighteen dollars and seventy-six cents. And that was without her taking a salary. A breath whooshed from her. She didn't know whether to be relieved they were still in the black or anxious about the piddling sum.

She began stamping the stack of bills with postage. They should be accustomed to operating without profit, they had done it for the past two years, but then they'd had Grandpop's insurance money to fall back on. Now that it was gone, there was no safety net.

And strangely enough, reservations had slowed down. July had always been one of their busiest months, and with the magazine ads she'd placed, they should still be getting calls. The worst time of year for the business was approaching, that time between the start of school and the first big snowfall when all the eager skiers headed to the slopes. But that wouldn't be until November. What would they do until then? She couldn't afford any more ads, and the ones she'd placed didn't seem to be doing any good.

Despite the office door being locked during the day, the cancellations continued. Just the thought that someone was breaking into her office gave her the creeps. She looked around the room. Had this person sat in her chair, rifled through the drawers? She shivered.

How was he or she getting in? Had someone made a copy of one of the keys? Was this person picking the lock? Whoever it was could be making copies of their customer files and sending them to someone via the Internet.

Bingo. She double-clicked the Internet icon and waited to get online. If they were e-mailing the information, a record of the post would be in her "sent" file. Could it be as simple as that?

The home page appeared, and she clicked on "read," then "sent." The list of sent mail appeared, and she scanned the column looking for an unfamiliar recipient over the last week.

Nothing. She searched the list again and sighed when she didn't find anything she hadn't sent herself. Her program only saved mail for one week, and besides, the interloper could have erased the transaction all together. If he was even using this method to transfer customer files. Who was doing this?

A list, that's what she needed. A list of everyone who had access to the office. She jotted down names. Me, Gram, Devon, Micah, even Mrs. Eddlestein could have gotten hold of a key.

Next she crossed her own name off the list. Her pencil began a line through Gram, then stopped. Was it possible Gram was doing something, then forgetting? Maybe it wasn't Alzheimer's she had, but some sort of mental illness. They would find out soon. She looked at the clock. In just a couple hours, in fact, when they were scheduled to meet with the neurologist who had performed the testing.

Back to the list. She made a question mark by Gram's name. Not likely, but with Gram's state of mind, she couldn't rule her out with absolute certainty.

Devon. She had caught him in the office once. She put a question mark by his name.

Micah. She hesitated. She wanted very much to draw a line through his name. They'd spent a lot of time together the past two weeks, and she felt she knew him well. She was definitely falling for him and hated to even consider that he'd be doing anything harmful to the business, but she forced herself to be completely objective. And it was technically possible that he'd been put up to ruining their business. That thought brought a host of questions about the validity of their relationship. She didn't even want to think about that. Reluctantly, she drew a question mark beside his name.

Mrs. Eddlestein. She'd had access to the key if she'd wanted it, could've somehow gotten it from Gram and used it while they were at church. But she had no motive, and she was perfectly sane. Hanna drew a line through her name.

Three possible suspects. Could a guest have made a copy of the front-door key? Not likely, since guests would also have to get a copy of the office key too.

She searched for any other ideas, any other people who might have a motive or access to her keys. No one came to mind. It had to be someone on the list, didn't it? Devon would be going back to school at the end of August. Just three weeks away. But next month they'd be in the red for sure, even if the cancellations stopped. And with the slow months of September and October coming, they would miss three months of payments. Enough to lose the lodge.

Hanna rubbed her temples. Between Natalie and Keith's divorce proceedings and Gram's health problems, she had enough to worry about without the financial problems and espionage. *All right, God, I'm fresh out of ideas. You're going to have to bail us out here.*

Two hours later she sat sandwiched between Gram and her dad in the neurologist's waiting room. When the office called yesterday, they'd set up the appointment to come in and discuss the results of the tests. Gram had taken the call and passed on the news to Hanna. Her first thought was that if the news was good, the nurse would've told her on the phone. Surely Gram had the same thought, but neither of them had voiced it.

Hanna thumbed a copy of *Ladies' Home Journal* while Gram cross-stitched with seemingly steady hands. In the car on the way over, Gram had patted her knee and winked as if she hadn't a worry in the world. Was she confident in a good test result, hiding her anxiety, or simply resting in the fact that God would take care of her regardless? It was hard to say, and Gram wasn't telling.

Ten minutes passed, then fifteen. Hanna looked around the waiting room and noted there was only one other woman who'd been here when they'd arrived. She flipped to a cover article on handling stress but gave up two paragraphs into the column.

Her dad walked to the receptionist desk and inquired how long it would be, then returned with news that it was almost their turn.

Gram tilted her head comfortably and resumed cross-stitching.

"How can you be so calm?" Hanna asked.

The older woman raised her head, a soft smile forming on her lips. "I'm concerned, child, believe me. But the way I figure, God already knows what's going on in this old body. He's known all along, and it will be no surprise to Him whatever the doctor says."

"Mrs. Landin." A nurse held open the door leading to the hallway of offices and examination rooms.

The trio rose as Gram stuffed her handwork into a satchel, and they followed the nurse to the end of the hallway. A baby shrieked from behind one of the closed doors.

The nurse showed them into a cozy office. "Dr. Matthews will be right with you." She shut the door leaving the three of them in silence.

Hanna studied the collage of certificates hanging behind his desk chair.

"Mercy, he sure has enough education." Gram gestured to the degrees.

"Let's just hope he learned a thing or two along the way," Hanna's dad said.

Hanna looked at him, not for the first time today, wondering how he was going to handle it if Gram had Alzheimer's. She noticed a heavy spattering of gray in his beard and hair that she hadn't noticed before. He slid his bifocals on his nose and read the brochure on neurological diseases.

The mahogany desk appeared cluttered at first glance but was actually arranged in neat piles. Family photos lined the desk, and a misshapen, clay paperweight hinted at a creation in an elementary art class.

The door clicked open, and Dr. Matthews entered with a manila file. "Hi, Mrs. Landin." He shook Gram's hand, then greeted Hanna and her dad before taking a seat behind the desk in a big leather chair.

"As my nurse undoubtedly told you on the phone, we've finished your clinical assessment. I explained before that there is no way of diagnosing Alzheimer's with 100 percent accuracy, short of examining brain tissue after someone has died." He folded his hands on top of the folder. "We can, however, diagnose the disease with 90 percent accuracy, and I'm very sorry to say, Mrs. Landin, that the test results do point to Alzheimer's disease."

Hanna's breath caught. She tore her eyes from the doctor's face and looked at Gram, who lowered her gaze.

"What do we do now?" her son asked.

"Well, the good news is that it was caught early. Most people exhibit signs for two years before they're diagnosed. You're in the mild stage of Alzheimer's, Mrs. Landin. A lot of research has been done in the last ten years or so. There are medications available that allow patients to hold on to cognitive skills longer and retain the ability to do basic activities."

"What about vitamin E?" Gram asked.

"In high doses it's been shown to prevent declines in functioning for about seven months, so yes, I would encourage you to begin taking it."

He wrote a scrip for a medication called Reminyl and gave Gram some pamphlets on the disease. Questions formed in her mind, and Hanna voiced them one after the other until she was satisfied she knew what to expect over the coming months and what the course of treatment would be. She would make sure they were doing everything possible to slow the disease's progress.

Looking up at the grand mountains rising up around her like a royal crown, Hanna didn't see her red-and-white bobber slip under the glassy surface of the water.

"You've got a bite," Micah said.

She turned in time to see the bobber surface, echoes of ripples ringing outward. She waited for it to go under again. And waited.

A magpie chirped somewhere behind her, and another answered its call. Her hair ruffled as a breeze blew across the lake, cooling her hot skin.

"I think he took my worm." Hanna reeled in her line to find an empty hook. She pulled a fat worm from the container and threaded it on the hook.

She'd started taking Thursdays as her day off, and they'd spent every one of them together. They'd gone hiking, had picnics, and spent hours talking in the lodge in front of the stone fireplace. He'd become an indispensable sounding board for her. Someone with whom she could talk about her fear of losing Gram to Alzheimer's. Someone with whom she could vent her anger about Keith without fear of upsetting anyone.

And today she'd finally told him about the lodge's financial trouble and her suspicion someone was sabotaging them. The genuine concern and confusion in his eyes erased all doubt of his loyalty from her heart.

She recast, rinsed her hands in the water, and continued their conversation where it'd left off moments ago. "So, when I sit down to do next month's bills, I don't see how we'll have enough to cover everything. One thing is certain: We can't miss three mortgage payments, or the bank'll foreclose on us. Keith'll have no choice."

"Your brother-in-law?"

"He refinanced the lodge when no other bank would. But there are other people at the bank he's accountable to. If we miss those payments, he'll have to foreclose."

Micah swatted away a fly. "You know, I've got a little money set back; it's not much, but—"

"No, Micah." His generosity softened her voice. "That's really sweet, but I don't want to do that. We've already drained my account and Gram's. I don't want to do that to you too."

"I thought you said a couple of months ago that business had picked up."

"It had, but then all the cancellations started coming in, and they've continued even though I've put a lock on the office door. I don't know what's happening."

His eyes jerked to hers. "Hanna, we have to find out who's doing this."

"I've been trying. But it's not so easy."

His brows furrowed and his jaw clenched. "We should go to the police."

"There's nothing they can do."

"But someone's been prowling around your office."

She shrugged. "I have no proof of that."

"So we're just supposed to wait until someone puts us out of business?"

Her heart warmed at the way he'd said "us," including himself as part of their family. "We're just going to have to figure out who it is or catch them in the act. I've taken precautions with the lock. But even if we keep all the reservations we've got, we're still in trouble." She told him about the lack of reservations for the coming months. "I don't get it. The magazine ads really started paying off right away, but now nobody's calling."

"Maybe you should cancel them."

"I think I will at the end of the month if we're still not getting any business from them." Hanna reeled in her line and set the pole aside. She hadn't been paying any attention to it anyway.

"I'll have to think about this. Maybe we can figure it out."

"Thanks."

"Anything to make you happy." His wink sent warm tingles up her spine. He laid his pole aside and scooted over next to her on the grass. "Anything else I can do to make you happy?"

The soft rumble of his bass voice stirred delicious flutters in her stomach. Her skin heated in anticipation. She studied his face, inches from her own, drew in the musky scent she'd come to recognize as his alone. His gray eyes twinkled playfully; his crooked smile offered an irresistible invitation.

She leaned forward and nuzzled his nose with her own. The closeness brought a dizzying sensation to her head. His eyes grew serious, and she felt the warmth of his hand as he cupped her jaw ever so gently. He tilted her face to his and brushed his lips across hers.

How had she ever lived without him? Without the sweet sensation of his touch. *Thank You, God.* Micah's lips claimed hers again. Heat kindled inside her belly and spread outward toward her limbs. His gentleness endeared him to her. She felt his restraint, sensed him holding back, being careful of the lure of desire.

When he drew back slightly, her trembling hand found his jaw. He turned his face into her hand and placed a kiss there. Their shaky breaths mingled, and Hanna knew in that instant she had fallen in love with this man. Fallen in love with his integrity, with his vulnerability, with his sense of honor.

A rebellious strand of hair had tumbled onto his forehead, and she brushed it back, loving the feel of his silky hair on her skin. A smile formed unconsciously on her lips.

"What?" he asked.

And his voice. She loved his voice too. But she didn't want to confess her feelings just yet. She wanted to savor them awhile longer. She ran a finger along his lips, and when he kissed it, her breath caught. "You're going to lose your bait," she whispered.

He tenderly captured her hand, his lips twitching. "That's not all I'm going to lose if you don't cut it out."

She blinked innocently while her hand slipped into his jersey pocket and closed around his keys. "What are you going to lose?" She held up his keys well out of his reach. "Your keys?" She raised her brows, trying to provoke him.

"Hey, now, those are the keys to my wheels." He swatted out to snatch them, but she scooted back in the grass, pulling her hand behind her back.

"All right, you're gonna get it now." He crawled toward her.

"Losing your patience?" She backed away, crab-style, his keys clutched in her hand.

His eyes lit mischievously as he advanced, despite the menacing growl that snarled from his mouth.

She giggled, "Losing your temper?"

"Losing my mind is more like it." He shot forward, catching her ankle.

She shrieked and flailed, but he held tight, crawling beside her and tickling her ribs. Their laughter floated on the wind, vibrating the air with joy, piercing the tranquillity around them with sounds of giddy pleasure.

CHAPTER
TWENTY-THREE

"Hi, come on in, Hanna." Natalie shut the door behind her sister, then gave her a quick hug. So much had happened in the last few weeks, and she was glad to see her only confidante. "Shh. I just put Taylor down."

"Where's Alex?"

"At a friend's house. That's why I asked you to come over after one, so we could talk in peace." They headed into the kitchen, where Natalie had brewed a pot of French vanilla coffee. "How's Gram doing?"

"Pretty good, really. You know Gram; she's using her sense of humor to help deal with it."

Natalie grunted. Her own sense of humor seemed to have disappeared lately. There was something about affairs, attorneys, and divorce papers that wasn't conducive to a sense of humor.

"Are you ready for the court date?"

"As ready as I can be." She set mugs down on the bar. "Even Carol, my lawyer, has been surprised at how fast we worked out the details. He's getting the bank; I'm getting the house. He's getting the other woman; I'm getting the boys." Ugly bitterness seeped into her tone. She couldn't seem to help it anymore.

Silence, normally welcomed this time of day, blossomed into awkwardness. So she was angry. It was easier than being hurt, and she wasn't going to apologize for her feelings. Not even to Hanna.

"I'm glad he's not vying for custody of the kids. And you said he's paying the bills, right?"

"How big of him."

"Are you still seeing Micah's dad?"

"And how would I pay for it? Right now, I'm living off a man who has deserted me. I can't exactly tell him he needs to pay for therapy, can I? On the other hand, he did cause this whole mess, why shouldn't he pay for it?"

Hanna ran a finger around the rim of her mug. "I can understand your anger, Nat. Anyone would be angry at what he's done and the way he's handled the whole thing."

"But?" She heard it coming, and irritation boiled up within her.

"It's just that, at some point, you're going to have get rid of all that. I know it must be hard, but you're going to have to forgive him, for your sake as well as the kids'."

"Forgive him? He left me for another woman, Hanna."

"I know, and I understand—"

"You can't possibly understand. You're not even married. What's ever happened to you that was so awful?" Nat's breath caught as she remembered, and she wished she'd left the last sentence unspoken.

"How can you say that? You watched me go through it."

"I know. I didn't mean—"

"You're not the only one who's suffered, Nat."

"I know; it's just . . . that was a long time ago. You're talking about forgiveness, but you've had, what? Six or seven years to get over it? I've had a matter of *weeks*. And your situation was different. It was a stranger who hurt you. My *husband* betrayed me, the one who was supposed to love me and care for me 'till death do us part.'"

"What he did is awful; I'm not saying it's not. But don't brush over what I went through. I was raped. It changed my life. I still sleep with the light on, for heaven's sake, and until Micah, I couldn't bear the touch of a man, so I'd hardly consider that 'over it.'"

Nat closed her eyes and sighed deeply. "I'm sorry, Hanna. I didn't mean to make light of what you went through, what you're going through." She offered her sister a wan smile. "Truth is, I'm angry and bitter and testy, and you happen to be here."

Hanna offered a reluctant smile.

"For the first time in my life, I feel like I have more pain than I can deal with. It's there all the time, and I wish it'd go away, for just a few minutes at least. I keep praying for God to take it away, but I can't even feel Him anymore. Where is He, Hanna?"

"He's still with you."

"I don't feel Him. I don't feel His comfort. I don't feel any comfort at all."

Hanna squeezed her hand. "Have you been going to church or to your women's Bible study?"

Guilt pricked Natalie's conscience, not for the first time. "I haven't been keeping up with my study guide, so I haven't been going to study group, but I have been going to church." *And my mind has been miles away from the message.* Maybe she should start her study again. She'd done a few days' worth before she'd found out about the affair, and she'd been enjoying it.

They talked awhile about Gram and the divorce proceedings before Hanna looked at her watch and said she needed to run.

After Natalie shut the door, she went to the bookshelf and scanned the titles. She might as well make use of the quiet moments before Taylor woke. Finally she found it, *A Woman's Heart* study guide. She went to the garage to get her Bible, feeling guilty again that it was still in the car from last Sunday.

She wondered why she was even bothering with the study. The women's group must be almost finished with it by now.

When she sat at the bar and began thumbing through the first finished pages, she saw she'd done a good job of keeping up with the daily worksheets, but on week two, day four, her penned-in answers stopped. She grabbed a pen from the junk drawer and went to work.

She began reading through the day's lesson about the manna the Israelites received from God every morning. Turning to Lamentations 3:22–23, she read the verse and then the question: How often are God's mercies new? She filled in the blank: every morning.

> Another characteristic of the manna spoke beautifully of God's mercy: It would always be given in perfect supply for the need. God's measure of mercy is offered according to the need. That is why we often say the words, "I could never endure it if that happened to me."

How many times had she wondered that when other women had found out their husbands were having an affair? It had always been her worst fear, next to losing one of her boys. She quickly read on.

> In the moment we say those words, our ratio of mercy matches our present need. True, on that exact amount of mercy, we could not survive. But when the time arises and the need escalates, so does the grace required for us to make it!

Then why didn't she feel God's presence, His mercy? She didn't feel like she was "making it" at all. Glancing down at the workbook, she looked up the next verse and wrote it in the blanks: "My grace is sufficient for you, for my power is made perfect in weakness."

Her eyes perked at the next paragraph in the guide.

> Although I rejoiced greatly over what God taught me about the manna, one thought kept occurring to me: "Precious Father, I've known a few Christians who did not appear to make it very well through their crises. If Your mercy is always sufficiently given according to the need, what happened to them? I have known Christians who had nervous breakdowns. I have even known Christians who committed suicide." In His great tenderness, God led me back to the wilderness and instructed me to do exactly what I am going to ask you to do.

Natalie's eyes skipped to the next blanks, where she was instructed to look through Exodus 16 and list every verse in which the word *gather* appeared. She listed seven verses, wondering about its purpose. What did gathering manna have to do with Christians finding strength to get through difficult circumstances? She read on, looking for an explanation.

> I finally understood the nature of God's mercy and grace. They are always there, available every day prior to our need, and in direct proportion to every moment's demand; but we must gather them. That part is completely our responsibility. What do you think would have happened to the Israelites if they had stayed inside their tents with their stomachs growling? They would have starved to death with the provision right outside the tent!

Natalie stared at the page. Why had she never seen it before? Of course. She needed to gather the manna. But what had she been doing all these weeks? She'd been cooped up in her tent complaining she was hungry. Didn't Jesus call Himself the "bread of life"?

She bowed her head. *Thank You, Father God, that You've opened my eyes to a new teaching. I will begin gathering, and only then will I expect to find the mercy and grace You intended me to have for this time in my life. Forgive me for forsaking Your provision. Amen.*

Natalie read through the next day's lesson, then the next, filling in blanks and gleaning nuggets of wisdom from the Scripture. By the time Taylor called to her from his crib, she'd read a week's worth of lessons and gained new insight that strengthened her and cloaked her in the grace and mercy of her Father.

Somewhere in the lodge, a door slammed shut, and the muffled sound pulled Hanna from the depths of sleep. She rolled over and tugged the comforter over her shoulders. A stray hair dangled over her nose, tickling her, and she swiped it away.

Then she started thinking about bills. Specifically those she'd received in the mail the day before. Had she received a bill for the magazine ads this month? She mentally reviewed the stack of mail on her desk tray and couldn't raise the image of the bill. Had she gotten last month's bills for the ads? She didn't remember paying them, but surely she had.

Hanna cracked open her eyes, blinking at the light from the bedside lamp and peering at her alarm clock. She groaned. Four thirty-seven. Why was she wide awake when it was practically the middle of the night?

She turned over and shut her eyes, but after ten minutes of trying to lull her brain to sleep, she gave up and tugged on a pair of sweats. She may as well get some things done before church.

The door made a loud click behind her as she turned into the hall, guided by the exit lights. She hadn't even brushed her hair or teeth, but then, she wasn't likely to see anyone at this hour.

A noise sounded in the lobby near her office. She stopped just short of the wide doorway, hugging the wall. What if it was the person who'd been breaking into her office? Her heart thumped heavily in her chest. Should she go back to her room? Go wake Micah?

Before she reached a decision, someone rounded the corner. Her breath caught. He turned the other direction, walking away from her.

It was Micah's silhouette, his build, his gait. She released a breath and started to call out to him, then stopped. What was he doing out here in the dark of night?

Suspicion crowded her mind. Could he have been doing it all along? He was here; he had the opportunity.

She watched him amble down the hall and slip inside his door. If he'd been up to no good, wouldn't he be in a hurry? Wouldn't he be looking around, sneaking around? He'd been walking as if he'd been out for a midnight stroll, not breaking and entering or stealing confidential information.

Discomforted and anxious, she turned back to her room. Her heart rejected the notion that Micah could be betraying her. That he could be feigning feelings just to secure his convenient position. She had initiated the relationship, she reminded herself. And he had fought the attraction at first.

She didn't know what to believe anymore. Closing the door behind her, she entered her bedroom and slid under the covers again. She thought of their last outing together, the day they'd spent fishing and hiking. The kisses by the lake, the frolicking in the grass. The moment she'd realized she loved him. Had she fallen in love with her betrayer? Her heart argued no, but her mind refused to ignore the compelling evidence that said otherwise.

CHAPTER
TWENTY-FOUR

Her sleeplessness showed at church later that morning. She'd had trouble keeping her mind on the sermon; instead, it was filled with bills, suspicions, and questions. She needed to resolve this whole mess. After lunch Hanna keyed the reservations into the computer, including names, addresses, and specifics about their room and shuttle service. Next, she deleted the two guests who'd called to cancel. As she keyed in shuttle-service information, she heard Devon enter the lodge.

"Hey, I'm back." He leaned against the doorframe. "Did you say you needed the keys to the van?"

"Yeah, just toss them on the counter. Your schedule for this week is over there too."

Hanna hit the shift key, but her finger slid off, and she inadvertently pressed a couple of keys at once. The program closed out without saving any of her changes.

"Shoot!" She looked at the keyboard, wondering how she'd made her work disappear.

"What's wrong?" Devon peeked in.

"I don't know. I accidentally hit one of these keys, and everything disappeared."

His footsteps neared as she stared at the screen in frustration. "What did you hit?"

She told him what had happened. He leaned over her with one hand on the mouse, the other on the keyboard, surrounding her with his body. The space grew claustrophobic. Her pulse drummed in her ear. The heavy scent he wore brushed her nostrils, and she turned her face away from his neck.

"Here. Just click here and do this," he said.

No longer was she concerned about the information she'd lost. She'd type it in ten times over if only he would remove himself from her space.

"Hanna, I have—" Micah's voice penetrated her senses.

She looked at the doorway as he stopped on the threshold.

"There we go." Devon straightened proudly. "All taken care of." He squeezed her shoulder.

"Hey, Micah," Devon said on his way out the door.

Micah jerked his chin upward in greeting and watched Devon saunter away before stepping inside the office and shutting the door. "You all right?"

She drew a deep breath and let out the tension. "I'm fine. He was helping me retrieve some documents."

"When do his classes start again?"

"Two more weeks. I'll be glad when he's gone, even though I'll have to start running the shuttle." She gave him a sad smile. "*If* there are any guests to pick up. Our reservations are dismal."

"I know. Hang in there, baby."

He squeezed her shoulders, and she relaxed under his hands.

"You look tired."

"Thanks." She smiled sarcastically. "Actually, I was up early. I mean very early. But then, you should be tired too. I saw you walking down the hall toward your room as I left my room."

His hands stopped and his eyebrows inched upward. "I didn't come out until just before church."

She felt as if she'd walked through a fuzzy web of confusion. Why would he deny it unless he had something to hide? "No, I saw you in the hallway at four-thirty."

"Hanna, I didn't come out of my room until eight-thirty."

She shook her head. "It had to be you. I even saw you going into your room."

His jaw slacked. "You saw someone going into my room?"

"Micah. It was you. I'm sure of it."

His gaze shifted around the office as if searching for the answer. "I guess I could have been sleepwalking."

She breathed a laugh. "Sleepwalking?"

"I don't do it very often, but I hope that's what it was. The alternative isn't very comforting."

"I'm sure it was you, so relax." Hadn't he mentioned before that he was a sleepwalker? That explained it all, didn't it? She pushed away the thread of doubt and rolled her chair closer to him. "So, you sleepwalk, huh? Got any interesting stories to tell?"

He laughed and pulled her chair even closer. "Well, there is the pizza story."

"Do tell."

He folded his arms across the back of the chair and laid his chin on his arm. "When I lived with Jim and Jan, they had this brown Lab named Snickers."

"Snickers?" She grinned.

"You know, like the candy bar. Anyway, Jan woke up one morning to find an empty pizza box on the kitchen floor—we'd had pizza delivered the night before. She knew Snickers couldn't open the refrigerator door, and Jim swore he didn't do it, so . . ."

"You fed the dog pizza in the middle of the night?"

"Hey, I didn't remember doing it, they just laid the blame at my feet."

"I think you ate the pizza in the middle of the night and laid the box on the floor so they'd blame the dog."

"And I think you need another good tickling."

The last days of August approached, and Hanna's mind was muddled with worry. Natalie's court date approached, and she prayed every day for God to give her sister peace. And there was Gram, who appeared to be doing fine, but Hanna knew she must be in turmoil about the months ahead. Then there was this business with the lodge. Soon she would need to do the bills, but a sense of dread had made her put off the task. Business was sluggish, and she knew when the last subtraction was punched into the calculator, there would be a minus sign in front of the numbers. Not a good place to be when skiing season was still two to three months away.

The one good thing was that Devon was gone. With his departure, there was one salary she wouldn't have to pay. But if business didn't pick up, it would be a moot point. Just the thought that someone might succeed in sabotaging their lodge made her heart seize with anger. If they did go under, she would make every effort to find out who it was and keep the property from their dirty hands.

Finally, on the last day of August, Hanna sat at her desk and pulled the bills from the tray. She did the payroll first, then proceeded to the dreaded expenses, starting with the mortgage payment and subtracting from their bank balance as she went. By the time she'd paid the mortgage, their money was gone. And she still had a stack of invoices.

She propped her elbows on the table and covered her face with her hands. Had it all come down to this? What had happened to her plan to save the lodge? It had started out so promising with reservations galore.

A sudden thought struck. Where were the bills from the magazines that were running her ad? She flipped through the ledger and looked for the last payment to those magazines. That was strange. She hadn't paid the monthly fee since June, which meant they hadn't billed her.

Should she call and straighten it out or count her blessings that she didn't have to pay those bills? She debated a moment, then flipped her Rolodex open to the *Travel America* card and dialed their number. After listening to messages and being transferred from one department to another, she finally got through to the right person.

"Hi, Cindy, this is Hanna Landin from Higher Grounds Mountain Lodge."

"Hi, Ms. Landin, what can I do for you?"

"I placed a full-page ad to be run in every issue until the end of the year, but I just realized I hadn't received a bill the past two months."

"Hold on a moment, and I'll pull up your account."

She heard Cindy tapping the keyboard for a moment, then silence.

"Yes, here it is. Your ad ran in June's edition, then you asked us to cancel the ad in mid-June—"

"What?"

"You canceled the ad in June, so it hasn't run since that first time, that's why you haven't been billed."

"But—but I didn't cancel the ad."

"I'm sorry. I have a notation right here on the screen, and I remember taking the call. Would you like to begin running the ads again?"

Hanna's mind spun. She hadn't called. Maybe Gram. "I know I didn't make that call. Did the caller identify herself? Maybe it was my grandmother."

"I'm sorry. I don't know what's happened."

Well, Hanna did. She clenched her jaw. Her pulse sped, and heat spread to her face. Their little interloper had done it again. This prank had no doubt cost them in reservations, but at least it could be remedied.

"Could you please restart the ad as soon as possible?" She'd have to worry later about how to pay for it. At this point, if the business didn't turn around, it was all over.

"Sure, I'll do that. The deadline for next issue is tomorrow, so we still have time to get it in there. I'm really sorry about the mistake."

"That's all right; it's not your fault."

She got off the phone and flipped through the Rolodex again, this time looking for the other magazine representative. She had the extension number for him, so she got through right away. Sure enough, the same thing had happened there. She requested that the ad begin running again and hung up the phone.

How long would this go on? How many other ways had this person interfered with their business that they hadn't discovered yet?

"Knock-knock." Micah's voice called from the doorway.

Hanna turned. "Hi there."

"What's wrong?"

She sat back in her chair. "Am I that transparent?"

She saw him take in the stack of bills, the payroll envelopes, and the desk calculator. "Uh-oh. It was as bad as you thought?"

"Worse. I haven't even paid two bills, and we're already in the red. And that's not all."

"Don't leave me in suspense."

"I just found out that someone canceled our magazine ads. Remember how we were busy through June, but business slacked off in July and August?"

"Yeah."

"Well, my ads ran in June, then someone phoned the magazines pretending to be me and canceled the ads. They haven't run the past two months."

"But can you start them again?" Micah asked.

"I did, but that doesn't solve this problem. I can't even pay the bills." She gestured to the desk.

Micah picked up the payroll envelopes and shuffled through them. "Paychecks?"

"Umm-hmm."

He pulled his own from the pile and tossed the rest on the desk. Then he ripped the envelope in half.

"Micah—"

"There's one you don't have to worry about." He pulled his wallet from his pocket and sifted through it.

She watched, confused.

He pulled two paychecks from his wallet and ripped them in half too.

"Micah, you can't do that!"

"I already did." He stuffed his wallet back in his pocket.

"That's your pay; you don't work here for free."

"Look at it as a loan then, if you want. Pay me back when the lodge is back on its feet."

"That may be never," she said.

He held out his hands and pulled her from the chair into his arms. "Not if I know you. Besides, the ads are running again. Use the money. I want you to."

She looked up at him, inhaling the musky scent of him. "Anyone ever tell you you're stubborn?"

His lips tipped in that crooked grin she loved. "Am not."

"Are too."

"Am not."

"See? Stubborn." She nuzzled his nose with her own.

"You love me that way."

She stilled, searching his eyes. Her heart lurched madly, and she swallowed tightly. "You're right." She planted her message in her expression. Let him make what he wanted of that.

He opened his mouth.

She laid a finger on his lips. He'd gotten her message. She could see it in the stirring of his smoky eyes. "You don't have to say anything."

Her finger fell as he stared at her lips. Then he slowly lowered his face to hers.

CHAPTER
TWENTY-FIVE

Natalie smoothed down her dove gray suit and sped to answer the ringing phone. "Hello?"

"Hey, Nat, it's me," Hanna said. "I just wanted to let you know I'll be praying for you today."

"Thanks. I'll need it."

"Are you sure you don't want me to come with you?"

It was tempting. But she needed to learn to rely on God, and she wanted to be strong enough to do this alone. "I'm sure, but thanks for asking."

"I'll be thinking about you."

The doorbell rang, and Natalie walked toward the door. "Thanks. I've got to go, Hanna. Mom's here."

She hung up the phone and opened the door to one of her mother's hugs. Natalie allowed herself a moment's consolation. Her mother patted and rocked as she was known to do, and Natalie gathered strength from the embrace.

"Grandma!" Alex came running from his room.

She gave her mom last-minute instructions before grabbing her purse and slipping out the door. As she pulled from the drive, she gripped the steering wheel with both hands and drew in a shaky breath. She couldn't believe her court date was here at last. Weeks ago, when she'd been served the papers, this day had seemed so far away.

Since that time, she'd had meetings with Carol, her attorney, and agreements with her soon-to-be ex-husband. Tensions had mounted whenever he'd come to pick up the boys for the weekend, but she had to admit he was being fair about their assets.

Still, the bitterness lingered, and she'd had to keep a tight rein on her tongue. Only once had she let the acrid emotions seep into her words, but one look at Alex's face had stopped the flow.

Not until this mess had she realized what it was to put her children first. It meant clamping your mouth shut when you wanted to scream and curse. It meant letting your husband have visitation rights every weekend when he didn't deserve to see the boys at all. It meant telling them their dad loved them when you wanted to tell them what he'd done to you. God had given her the courage to do what was right, but many times her thoughts sank to a level that stunned her.

Having Hanna with her today would have been comforting, but she feared her sister's presence would have unleashed the emotions. And that was her biggest fear, that today she would weep like a baby, showing Keith her vulnerability. She wanted him to watch her and admire her strength. She wanted to conceal from him the depth of her pain.

Please, God. Maybe it's pride, but please don't let me fall apart today. She wanted to add something to the prayer. She wanted to ask God to make Keith feel all the guilt and remorse he ought to feel. But she knew her motives were wrong. And she needed to concentrate on holding herself together, not worry about how he felt.

When she reached the courthouse, she pulled into a space and walked on legs that felt as wobbly as a three-legged table. She looked anxiously for Carol, needing to see her before she saw Keith. She spotted her on a bench in the hallway.

Carol rose as she approached and took Natalie's hand. "How are you doing?"

"So far, so good." And it was true, she realized. Through most of the recent weeks, she'd been on the verge of tears. But today she felt a strange sense of detachment, as if she couldn't squeeze out a tear if she wanted to.

"Are you sure you want to be present? It's not too late; you can turn around and go back home."

Natalie drew in a deep breath and blew it out through her mouth. "No. I need to be here."

"All right then; let's go over again what's going to happen."

Carol briefed her, but most of the words passed over Natalie without taking hold. She glanced at her watch more than once.

When Keith and his attorney entered the courthouse and took a seat down the hall, her heart hammered as it had when they'd first met. Keith saw her and quickly averted his eyes. In his presence, her new suit and French twist did little to boost her sagging confidence.

How had it all come down to this? To attorneys and courtrooms and evading glances? A deep sadness flowed through her. They were losing so much. She was losing her companion, her partner. The boys were losing their dad. And they were all losing their family, the feeling of oneness that came from knowing they belonged together.

Carol stood, and Natalie realized it was time. Her legs moved, carrying her to the seat at the front of the courtroom. She avoided looking at Keith. Though tears were nowhere near the surface, she wouldn't push her luck.

Natalie forced herself to pay attention as they were sworn in. The judge was a small man with a balding head and ears that stuck out elfishly. Not at all what she'd expected a judge to look like.

"Do you promise to tell the truth regarding the case now in question?"

They said, "I do," and Natalie noted the irony of the words, used both to seal their marriage and to tear it apart.

They stated their names and addresses for the record. Keith's voice was subdued. She looked at him and noticed his eyes turned downward. She felt a moment's vengeance at his apparent shame.

Carol read the questions, waiting after each one for Keith's answer. As they proceeded, a numbing fog settled around her. She was vaguely aware of the sadness and anger she felt, but the emotions were hazed over, giving her a welcome reprieve.

"Are you asking the court to give you a divorce today?" Carol asked.

"Yes." Keith's answer echoed through the room.

"Have you and your spouse reached an agreement regarding your divorce today?"

"Yes."

Carol handed the papers to the judge. The room grew quiet as he reviewed it. Coming to an agreement had happened fast, but it hadn't been easy. They both knew if they didn't reach one, they would lose money in attorney fees. And Keith, wonder of wonders, seemed to be making up for his betrayal with a generous settlement.

She kept her eyes turned forward. This is not how she had expected to feel on this day. She had expected violent emotions. She had expected to feel weepy and helpless. Instead there was numbness. Everything seemed surreal. *Thank You, Jesus.*

The judge asked some questions regarding their property. Keith's attorney answered. Then the judge asked if the agreement was entered into voluntarily. Both she and Keith replied in the affirmative.

"The state of Wyoming," the judge said, "grants me the right to order both spouses to attend classes regarding the impact of divorce on children. Because you have managed to reach an agreement without arbitration and because the agreement appears to put the children's best interests first, I will refrain from ordering said classes."

Natalie's heart sped as she realized they'd reached the end of the proceedings. The end of their marriage.

"By the authority granted me by the state of Wyoming, I hearby grant this divorce." He tapped his gavel on the stand.

Carol reached over and squeezed her hand. "You okay?" she whispered.

Natalie nodded her head. She was okay. Dazed and numb, but okay. She'd gotten through it without dissolving into a pathetic fit of tears.

Carol gathered her papers and stood. Natalie bent down to retrieve her purse.

When she looked up, Keith stood in front of the table. He looked at Carol, then back to Natalie.

"Can I, uh, can I talk to you a minute?"

She looked at Carol, then stood. "I guess so."

"I'll meet you out in the hallway," Carol said, before she turned and left.

The judge was getting ready for the next hearing, so they walked to the back of the room. Questions flew through her mind with the speed of an F-16. What did he want? Was he going to back out of their agreement? Wasn't it too late for that?

Pathetic hopes sprang into her heart. Had he changed his mind? Had the finalization of the divorce shaken him up? Just as quickly she smothered the thoughts. It was over.

They reached the back of the room and turned toward one another. Dark crescents underlined his eyes. She studied his face. Every feature was so familiar. The wayward eyebrow hairs, the thin upper lip, the receding hairline. She wanted to reach out and touch him, but she no longer had that right. Someone else did.

"I just—I wanted to say I'm sorry." He stuffed his hands in his pockets. "We've had our differences, but—I never meant to hurt you."

Shame coated his features. He *should* be ashamed. And part of her wanted to tell him that, but she'd gotten quite good at holding her tongue.

"I appreciate your agreeing to every weekend on the visitation rights." He rubbed his nose, a sign he was getting uncomfortable. He blinked rapidly, drawing her attention to his watery eyes. "I don't think I could bear to—" His voice cracked.

She watched his jaw tighten and knew he was struggling to control his emotions. And she knew with equal certainty that one day he'd regret what he'd done to them.

Natalie tugged her purse strap higher on her shoulder. "Well. Let's just continue to do what's best for the boys." Her stomach rolled, and her fingers trembled, but she stood straight and held her chin high.

"Yeah, well—" He looked over his shoulder at his attorney.

"I guess we'll talk soon," she said. "Take care."

He mumbled something as she passed him, walking tall on quaking legs. Legs that would have to carry her through the coming years. But they would make it. She and God and her two priceless boys.

CHAPTER
TWENTY-SIX

September arrived, and business slacked off further, just as Hanna had suspected it would. Kids were in school, vacations were over, and their guests consisted mostly of retirees and young families. Ski season wouldn't arrive until December, leaving them short of business—and cash—for just over two months. She knew it did no good to fret, but even with the ads kicking up again this month, she wondered how she could make the mortgage payment.

So far she'd seen no evidence of the continuing cancellations. Perhaps whoever had been responsible saw the lodge floundering and knew it was just a matter of time.

Hanna had kept in close contact with Natalie and was surprised at the change in her over the past few weeks. Natalie attributed the shift to a renewal of faith, but Hanna was just glad her sister seemed more hopeful and less angry.

Midway through September the temperatures dropped dramatically, and the weather forecasters began tracking a snowstorm across the Northwestern region. Micah left with two local men on an overnight climb, despite Hanna's misgivings. The storm wasn't expected to enter their area until the evening of their return, and he was confident they'd be back before the flurries began.

On the afternoon they were due, Hanna wished she felt as confident. In the recent past, experienced climbers had died in snowstorms on the Teton range. She stared out the window as the first snowflakes fell. They were predicting fifteen to eighteen inches of heavy snow, and all their guests had made arrangements to return home. Mrs. Eddlestein had agreed to stay with Gram while Hanna went to pick up Micah and his group.

The flurries had become thick, white specks, coming down like manna from heaven. She looked at her watch and decided to leave a few minutes early to allow for slippery roads.

"I'm leaving now, Gram."

"Drive carefully," she called from the kitchen.

The roads weren't yet slick, but as she pulled into the waiting spot, the visibility worsened, and she turned the wipers on high. A glance at the dashboard clock told her she was early, so she put the van in park and nudged the heat up a notch.

She looked out the snow-speckled windshield. What if they lost their way in the thick snow? It was easy to get turned around when you couldn't see ten feet in front of you. But Micah knew what he was doing. He always carried a compass. He'd been caught in snow before, he'd told her weeks ago. She played the reassurances in her mind. *Bring them back safely, Lord.*

The numbers on the digital clocked ticked away the minutes. The windows began fogging, and she turned on the defroster. It cleared slowly, but even so, it appeared that the van was sitting in the midst of a white cloud. There was no evidence of mountains or trees or even head-lights from other cars. How would Micah find the car once he got near?

She flicked on her lights, knowing that would only help if he got within twenty or thirty feet. The horn. Maybe he couldn't see her, but he would be able to hear.

She blasted three short beeps. Every few minutes she repeated the pattern. An hour later, when three snow-covered bodies emerged from the white tempest, Hanna gasped. Gathering her senses, she hit the button to unlock the doors. Stiffly, the men opened the car doors.

"Thank God! I was worried sick." She hopped out and helped them stow their gear in the back, urging them to get in the warm van.

Micah's lips chattered. "Good thing you were honking; that's how we found you."

Instead of bringing the men back to the lodge as planned, she offered to drop them at their houses, and they accepted readily. They could retrieve their belongings after the storm was over. All the while, she suppressed the urge to rail at Micah until she could do so in private. He'd given her a fright, and she wasn't about to let him off easy.

At last they unloaded the men from the van and eased away from the curb, going as fast as the low visibility would allow. Driving absorbed most of her concentration but not all. "You should have listened to me, Micah, and not gone on that trip."

"It worked out fine."

"You could've died up there." She spared him a glance, but even his red-tipped nose and rosy cheeks elicited sympathy. "What were you thinking?"

Micah warmed his fingers with his breath. "I was thinking we could make it back before the snow started."

"You were wrong." Her body began sweating under the thick coat, but she left on the heat for his sake.

"I'm sorry I made you worry."

"You should be."

"I'll listen to you from now on, boss lady."

She heard the smile in his voice and glanced his way in time to catch his wink. "You better."

The ride to the lodge seemed interminable at the slow speed, and Hanna felt her shoulders tensing. When they finally arrived, Mr. Eddlestein took his wife home.

"Drive carefully out there." Hanna shut the door behind them.

Micah went to warm up with a shower, and Hanna dropped her purse in the office, then went to gather wood from the stack outside. Even if the electricity didn't go out, a nice toasty fire always seemed comforting. They fixed sandwiches for dinner, then her grandma made homemade hot chocolate, a treat usually savored only during the winter months.

Gram called the Eddlesteins to make sure they'd arrived home safely, then they settled on the sofas to watch TV for a while. Every few minutes a blue bar swept across the bottom of the screen announcing the winter storm warning. The National Weather Service continued to predict a heavy snowfall with blizzardlike conditions, and they declared a snow emergency.

"Well, I guess it'll be quiet around here for a few days," Gram said.

Hanna rubbed her temples, trying to diminish the tension headache she'd had all evening. "Let's just try and enjoy the reprieve."

Gram stood. "You two sit here and enjoy it. I'm going to bed."

They said good night, then Hanna got up to flip off the old floor-model set, pressing a hand to her temple to abate the throbbing.

"Headache?"

She nodded, and he motioned her to sit on the floor between his knees. When she leaned back, he began massaging her tense shoulder muscles. "That feels heavenly."

He kissed her softly on top of her head. "Since I'm probably the one who stressed you out, it's the least I could do."

She smiled. "Good point."

"Have you taken anything?"

She leaned her head forward while he massaged her neck. "Mm-hmm." His strong fingers felt so good against her skin, and the heat from his hands seeped into her muscles.

By the time he finished, she felt a bit better. She stayed on the rug, leaning back against his knee while they talked for a long time. When the mantel clock struck eleven, Hanna stood up and stretched. "It's my bedtime."

Micah stood and gathered her to him. He rubbed her nose with his own, and she smiled at the endearing habit they'd formed. The smile left her face as his lips claimed hers, gently at first, then with controlled passion.

His touch never failed to stir a fire deep within her belly. By the time they parted, her legs felt shaky, like she'd gone days without a meal.

"Night-night." He gave her a soft peck on the lips.

"See you in the morning." As she walked to her room and readied for bed in her warmest flannel pajamas, she was unable to wipe the giddy grin from her face.

Something pulled Hanna from the depths of sleep. She tossed about the bed, her mind hovering somewhere between sleep and wakefulness. Finally, the throbbing in her head dragged her into consciousness. She peeked at the clock. Three-seventeen. The ibuprofen had worn off, leaving her with a full-sprung migraine. She turned over and closed her eyes, willing her body back to sleep.

After ten minutes she knew she wouldn't sleep until the pulsing pain stopped, so she stumbled to the bathroom for more medicine. She squinted against the florescent light and opened the medicine cabinet, searching the rows for the familiar teal label. Not finding it on the first pass, she scanned the rows again.

Where was it? Then she remembered tossing the empty bottle weeks ago. Her purse. She had another bottle in her purse. She walked to the dresser, stopping when she saw it wasn't there. Her gaze skittered across the room. Where had she put it?

The office. When she'd come in from picking up Micah, she'd dropped off her purse in the office. With one longing gaze at the bed, she reluctantly snapped the keys up off the nightstand and left her room. She held her temples as she walked and tried to keep her head steady to curb the throbbing.

Even with the heat on, the air had grown cold in the night, and she shivered. The keys jingled with each step, and she wondered briefly how much snow had fallen since she'd gone to bed. She considered pulling back the drapes for a peek, but decided she didn't want to wake herself by doing anything more than the bare minimum.

Silence filled the lobby, making her steps on the wooden plank floor seem loud. Her heart cringed from the darkness, but she was closer to her office than the light switch. She put the key into the door's lock and turned. The key twisted easily. Too easily. She thought she'd locked up last night.

She pushed open the door. The computer screen flickered, sending eerie shadows across the walls. She reached for the light switch.

A hand grabbed her from behind. She tried to scream, but a gloved hand muffled it. She kicked and fought. He grabbed her around the abdomen with his other hand and carried her from the office.

Oh, God! Help me! She kicked and thrashed, banging her foot into the counter wall, knocking over a Rubbermaid trash can. Screams escaped her lips only to be swallowed by his hand. She fought for breath, clawing at his hand. He carried her across the lobby toward the door. *Where is he taking me? Help me, Micah!* She had to get loose before he took her away.

She twisted and struggled, but her aggressor was too strong. When he removed the hand from her waist to open the door, she twisted and struck at his jaw with her elbow. In the cloak of darkness, he was a black monster from head to toe. A ski mask covered his head, but eyes glittered at her through the material.

He opened the door, then snatched her against him again. She kicked violently at the door as they passed.

"Stop it!" he hissed, then called her a vile name.

He half carried, half dragged her across the porch and down the steps. She fought all the way, pulled at his hands, tried to twist from his arms.

The snow bogged down his steps, and when her kick caught him in the shins, they fell forward.

His body collapsed on hers, crushing the air from her lungs and shoving her face into the cold, wet snow. He spat a string of curses and covered her mouth again before dragging her to her feet.

They stumbled forward. Her strength drained with each step. Where was he going? What was he going to do to her when he got there?

Dizziness overtook her. She couldn't faint. She stilled in his grasp, trying to pull in oxygen around the woolly glove. She could fight later, but for now, she had to stay conscious.

Where were they? Her eyes took in the snow-lit area, and she saw the lake to one side. *Think, Hanna, think!* There was nothing out here. Just a shed used for boat storage and maintenance.

He stumbled again, but caught them before they went down. His arm tightened around her midsection, cutting off her breath. They passed the docks. He was taking her to the shed.

There were only two things he could do to her there, and neither was an option she wanted to consider. She had to find a weapon. Her mind spun through the items in the shed. Gas can, oars, tools. Tools. If she could just get to the toolbox and get a screwdriver or saw. Anything.

He burst through the door and dragged her inside. The door hung ajar, allowing the reflection of the snow to illumine the shadowed interior. When he removed his hand from her mouth, she opened it to scream, but a rough, woolly cloth took its place. She thrashed and kicked, but he pushed her to the ground. Her face struck the rough, wooden slabs, and the cloth cut into her lips as he straddled her back and tied it behind her head.

CHAPTER
TWENTY-SEVEN

A muffled thump wrenched Micah from a pleasant dream, and his eyes snapped open. His sleep-hazed mind took a moment to clear. Had he heard a noise, or had he dreamed it? He rolled over to look at the clock, then groaned. It was the middle of the night.

He shivered in the night air. The last thing he wanted was to get out of bed and investigate some imagined noise. He turned over, pulled the sheet up to his chin, and closed his eyes. Slowly, the fog of slumber closed over him, enveloping him in a blanket of peace. He hovered on the brink of sleep, his thoughts still churning in a pleasant, quiet manner, the precursor of genuine rest.

A sound dragged him fully awake. His eyes popped open. Had he heard a squeal? His pulse jumped, and he lay frozen, listening. He threw off the sheet and pulled on the clothes he'd worn the day before.

When he opened the door, he paused on the threshold to listen. Silence hung heavily in the air. Only the high-pitched buzzing of the Exit light broke the stillness. It had probably been an animal. Or the cold air seeping through the windows. He should go back to bed. That's undoubtedly where Hanna was now, sleeping like an innocent newborn.

He wavered on the doorstep, peering down the shadowed corridor. Finally, he stepped out into the hall and walked to the lobby. In the darkness his foot connected with something that scuttled across the floor at impact. He flipped on the light. The trash can. What was it doing in the middle of the floor?

He saw papers at his feet that looked as if they'd fluttered to the floor from the counter. The front door was cracked open.

A shiver snaked up his spine. His arms prickled at the base of every tiny hair. Something wasn't right. In front of the door, he saw puddles of water spaced evenly apart on the wooden planks. A pea-size clump of snow sat melting in the middle of one puddle. Someone had been here, and it hadn't been long ago.

Indecision swamped him. He had an overwhelming urge to check on Hanna, but the clues left behind told him there may have been a struggle. He hurried to the phone and dialed 9-1-1. When the operator answered, he gave her the pertinent information, then set the phone on the counter. She'd told him to stay put, but there was no way he was going to sit and wait for help. He grabbed the flashlight from the battery pack on the wall.

Flipping off the porch light, he slid out the storm door and shined the light around. His eyes adjusted quickly to the night. At the base of the porch, he saw marks in the snow that looked as if something had been dragged through the snow.

He stopped and shined the beam out as far as he could see. The trail continued toward the lake. Again, he felt the urge to check on Hanna. But if Hanna was in danger, he had to act fast. He listened for a moment. Snowflakes batted about his head, falling from a clay-colored sky. The blanket of snow illumined the night, allowing him to see quite some distance even without the flashlight.

He rushed onward, following the path. As he neared the lake, he heard something. He stopped and listened.

At first he heard nothing. Then muted sounds of a struggle reached his ears. He flipped off the flashlight and followed the sounds. Why hadn't he gotten a weapon of some kind? What if the intruder had a knife or a gun?

His heart echoed heavily in his chest, booming violently in fear of what he would find. *Dear God, let her be all right.*

The sounds grew louder on his approach to the shed. He crept to the shed, conscious of the snow crunching under his shoes. At the door he waited for his eyes to adjust. Just then he heard a muffled cry and the shuffling sounds of struggle. It was Hanna; he knew it in his heart.

He wanted to charge in and protect her, but he knew he had to be smart. He peeked around the doorway. A black, shadowed body pushed her to the ground. He winced when he heard her smack the floor.

Just another second. When her attacker faced the other way, Micah would hit him from behind. His fists clenched in anticipation, and his face tightened in fury. Whoever was hurting Hanna would have no mercy from him.

At last the man knelt over Hanna's back. Micah sprang forward and hit him with a force that knocked his body across the room. The man's body thudded against the floor. Micah pulled his head up by the collar of his coat and slammed his head onto the floor. Once. Twice. Three times.

He got up and shoved the still body over. The man groaned.

Behind him, Hanna whimpered. He turned. The scarce light shimmered on her wet face. He came to her as she finished working the knot on the cloth and removed it from around her head.

She stepped into his arms and collapsed against him, shaking.

"Shh, it's okay now, honey." He held her tightly, relief washing over him like waves on the shore. "Are you all right?" She nodded against his chest. She was wet and cold, but unhurt, thank God. *Thank You, Jesus. Thank You.*

Groans from behind him warned him the man was coming to. "Where's that cloth that was around your head?" He found it on floor and asked her to hold the flashlight. She shone the light on the man's head. His eyes remained closed. A crimson spot bloomed through the ski mask at his forehead. Micah kicked him over onto his belly and tied his hands behind his back with what felt like a thin scarf. The light wavered.

"Shine it down here." Micah pushed the man back over, then he grabbed the top of the ski mask and yanked it off. Another moan sounded as the material slid over the wound.

"Devon!"

Hanna gasped.

Rage tore through him like a tornado. Hanna had provided the man with a job. Trusted him. Paid him. And how had he returned the favor? Micah grabbed Devon by the coat and drew back a fist.

"Don't, Micah." The light fell as Hanna grabbed his shoulder. "He's already unconscious. I'll go call the police."

Micah dropped Devon's weight. "I already did. They should be here soon."

"I was so scared." Her voice trembled.

He stood and held her, stroking her back. Her whole body quaked, and he knew it wasn't just the cold that made her tremble. "Go back to the lodge." He held her away. "You need to warm up. Send the police down here."

"I don't want to leave you."

He wondered whether she was afraid of being alone or afraid to leave him with Devon. He glanced down and noticed her bare feet. "Oh man, Hanna, your feet." He kicked off his tennis shoes and knelt down to slip her feet inside them. They looked like clown shoes on her.

"What about you?"

"I'll be fine." He held her to him again, overcome with gratitude for her safety. What would he have done if anything had happened to his Hanna? He clenched his jaw and squeezed his eyes shut. Swallowing the knot in his throat, he set her away from him. "Go on back. I'll be there as soon as I can." He stooped down for the flashlight and handed it to her.

She took it and nodded, then walked out the door. He watched her stumble through the snow and hoped the shoes didn't fall off.

Sounds of movement came from behind him, and he turned to see Devon stirring. His blood simmered with fury. What would Devon have done to Hanna if he hadn't shown up? The thoughts that tumbled through his mind sped his pulse and sent jabs of anger through his limbs. Somewhere in the distance a siren pealed.

From the window Micah watched the police cruiser pull slowly onto the road, tamping down the virgin snow. Still, the white flecks fell, swirling frantically around before settling onto the thick blanket on the ground.

He heard Hanna pad into the room and turned. She looked warmer now, dressed in fleece sweats, a multicolored quilt hugging her shoulders.

"Are they gone?" She stood before him looking alone and vulnerable, her tear-swollen eyes a tangible remnant of her ordeal.

"Yes. We'll need go to the station and fill out a formal complaint later." He longed to hold her. To erase the last hour and tell her he'd never let anything bad happen to her again. "Do you feel like going back to bed?"

She shook her head and pulled the quilt tighter around her shoulders.

"Is your grandmother back in bed?"

Hanna nodded. Gram had been frantic when she'd awakened during all the chaos. Only Hanna's assurances that she was fine expelled the panic from her eyes. But Micah knew Hanna wasn't fine. She had yet to show any emotion other than the tears that had leaked silently from her eyes.

"Want me to start a fire?" he asked.

She nodded.

He stacked fresh logs in the grate and worked to light them. Hanna stood behind him as if she didn't know what to do.

Finally, the logs flickered to life, and he took her hand, pulling her to the sofa. He sat first and gently pulled her into his lap. She let go of the blanket and wrapped her arms tightly around his neck. Her knees drew up protectively, and she lay her face in the curve of his neck.

What was she thinking? What was she feeling? He wanted to wipe it all away.

He wanted to beat Devon until his eyes were swollen and black and blue. His jaw clenched, and his breaths grew shallow. Why hadn't he done it while he'd had the chance? The man deserved it. Deserved worse.

Hanna sniffed, and he knew she was going to cry in earnest. The shock was wearing off. He fought to dispel his anger toward Devon. Hanna first. He would deal with his own emotions later.

"It's okay," he whispered, tightening his arms until their bodies were melded together. "He can't hurt you anymore."

Her body broke into sobs that sounded as if they were wrenched from the deepest part of her. "Shhh." The sobs came in waves, each one stabbing him with pain. He thanked God he'd awakened in time to prevent something worse but wished it had been him that had caught Devon in the lodge. "It's over," he murmured. The whole rotten farce was over. And Devon had been behind it all along.

"I—it just brought it all back . . . ," she choked out, then cried again.

He wondered what she was talking about but didn't ask. He curled his hand around her chin and turned her face toward him. Fear shadowed her eyes. He wiped away the tears on her face, but more trickled down in their place.

"It brought back the whole nightmare." She wiped her nose with a tissue she had wadded up in her fist.

He waited silently for her to continue, knowing something inside her desperately needed to come out.

"It happened when I was eighteen. I—I was on my way home from work. I knew I was low on gas, but it was late, and I thought I could make it home." She closed her eyes.

He thought she must be talking about whatever it was that gave her nightmares.

"I ran out of gas. It was so dark. But I got out and walked—didn't have a choice." She stopped and wiped her nose on the soggy tissue. "I came to a bar. It was lit up. I could hear the loud music from inside. I was afraid to go in." A blink sent another tear chasing down her cheek.

"I saw lights ahead, a gas station. So I passed the bar and kept walking."

Somewhere within Micah, a pebble of apprehension sent ripples through him.

"It got really dark once I passed the bar. There was no one around. I was scared. And then I heard footsteps behind me. I walked faster. And then I started running." She turned her fear-laden eyes on him. Her voice lowered to a whisper. "Someone grabbed me from behind. He—he pulled me away from the road—"

Icy fingers of dread spread through him. It was too familiar to be a coincidence.

No.

It couldn't be.

"I was so scared," she whispered.

Her words grazed across his frozen mind. *Please, God, no! It can't be true!*

"It was so dark."

No. It hadn't been Hanna. She'd had short hair. Curly hair. In his drunken state, he'd seen his mother. And he'd wanted to hurt her. His heart clenched painfully, and blood pulsed at his temples. *It's a mistake. A mistake.*

"Afterward, I just wanted to die." She buried her head in his chest, and his arms mechanically tightened.

She'd said she'd been eighteen. He tried to force his paralyzed brain to do the math. The slate of his mind went blank, and he tried again.

Eight years ago. Which would've made him—

Guilty.

The numbing blow choked off his breath. His heart skipped a beat, and his tongue stuck to the roof of his mouth as the realization echoed through him in waves of shock. *Oh, God. It was me.*

CHAPTER
TWENTY-EIGHT

Hanna stretched, her stiff muscles protesting loudly. She turned and opened her eyes. Morning light peeked through the curtains, chasing shadows from the lodge. She sat upright, confused for a moment to find herself on the sofa.

It all came back with brutal clarity. She ran a hand across her puffy eyes. She must've fallen asleep on Micah. She wondered where he was now. What did he think of all she'd shared with him last night? Was he horrified at her experience? Last night's ordeal with Devon had brought back all the shame she'd felt those years ago. How dirty she'd felt. She'd lost her virginity, a long-valued treasure she'd been saving for her husband.

Was Micah disappointed? He'd been quiet while she'd talked and cried, but she'd assumed he was simply allowing her to vent. Had she been wrong?

The quilt she'd been wrapped in the night before was now spread over her like the wings of an eagle, and she took comfort in the thought that Micah had covered her before he left. As she slid off the couch and walked to the kitchen, she became aware of soreness throughout her body. No doubt, she'd been bruised in last night's assault.

She started a pot of coffee and placed a bowl of oatmeal in the microwave, then walked to the window. Cold air seeped through the glass, adding to the winter-wonderland feeling the sight inspired. The earth was enshrouded with snow, as if someone had generously sprinkled confectioner's sugar from a God-sized sieve. Every branch was coated in white, and still the snow continued to fall. Judging by the stack of white atop the bird feeder, she figured they'd received eight or nine inches so far.

Despite the horror of the previous night, she rejoiced. The early snowfall meant skiers, and skiers meant customers. With Devon out of the way and the national ads running again, they could expect a strong fall.

The scene beyond the windowpane looked peaceful. The footprints from the night before had been covered completely. It was almost as if it hadn't happened. Micah had said Devon admitted to nothing, but his assault would see him in jail for a while at least.

The coffee maker silenced as the last drips filtered through, and the microwave beeped. Hanna stirred the oatmeal and set muffins and fruit on the table, then went to wake Gram, knowing she hated to sleep too long. Last night's debacle must've taken its toll to keep her in bed until nine.

After waking Gram she walked to Micah's door, feeling awkward about the night before. She was being silly, she assured herself. Micah had rescued her and held her until she'd fallen asleep. There was nothing to be embarrassed about.

She raised her hand and rapped quietly on the door in case he was still asleep.

She heard him clear his throat. "Who is it?"

"It's me." Her heart pounded in anticipation of seeing him.

"Oh, I-uh . . ."

Silence ensued. She wondered if he wasn't dressed. "I just wanted you to know breakfast is ready."

He paused a beat. "Go on without me; I'll be out in a while."

"All right." She hesitated a moment, hoping he'd say something else or open his door. When he didn't, she returned to the kitchen. He'd sounded strange. Not snappy or irritable. Just distant. She shook her head and berated herself for reading so much into a few words.

She and Gram ate together, and Hanna assured her once again that she was fine. While Gram loaded the dishes in the dishwasher, Hanna started a fire, then turned on the TV to check the latest forecast. Snow, snow and more snow. That, combined with the strong wind, amounted to a snow emergency. A couple of calls came in requesting reservations for the following weekend. Ski buffs, wanting to take advantage of the early snow and optimistic that several days of heavy snow would give them a good base. Hanna, on the other hand, wondered if they'd even have the roads cleared by then if they got all the snow that was forecasted.

After Gram went to the kitchen for another cup of coffee, Micah rounded the corner in full winter attire.

His gaze skimmed past hers without so much as an acknowledgment. "Thought I'd shovel some snow."

She stood. "There's a snow blower in the shed, but—"

"I'll get right on it." He opened the door.

"You may as well wait; they're forecasting—"

The door shut behind him.

"A lot more snow," she finished for the empty room. What was that about? Knots of apprehension coiled in the pit of her stomach. Was he feeling awkward about all the emotion of the night before? Or had his worst fear come true—he'd fallen in love with her and was scared silly?

Elation bloomed in her heart for just a moment before a dark cloud smothered the feeling. That wasn't it.

Maybe he was just in a bad mood. None of them had gotten a good night's sleep. He probably didn't function well on less than a full night's sleep. Natalie had always been that way. They'd teased her in the morning about having the grumpies. She smiled contentedly. She'd just discovered a new character trait in her beloved.

Later, she and Gram fixed soup and sandwiches and talked about Devon and his dirty work at the lodge.

"The thing I don't understand is why," Hanna said.

Gram set the ladle in the soup pot. "You know, I could call the police station. Maybe they got the story out of Devon."

"Really? Will they tell us?"

"Well, I don't know what the rules are, but Gerdy Feldner from church does paperwork down there, and I know she'd tell us."

It didn't take but a minute for Gram to get Gerdy on the phone.

It was all Hanna could do to sit still during all the "uh-huhs" and "oh goodness's." Gram's brows drew together, then apart, and finally she closed her eyes. "Oh, dear . . . all right. Yes, thank you, Gerdy . . . goodbye." Gram hung up the phone.

"What? What is it?"

"Well, you'd just never believe it. I can hardly believe—"

"What, Gram?"

"Keith!" Gram's brows bunched up tight, and her lips flattened.

"Keith? Natalie's Keith?" It didn't make sense. He'd helped them with the loan, the refinancing.

"You know how he'd told us we could lose the lodge if we missed payments? Well, apparently, he was trying to make sure we did miss those payments!"

"But why? That doesn't make sense. He wouldn't gain anything from that. If the bank repossesses a property, they have to auction it. That's the law. Besides, I can't believe Keith planned this. He was trying to help us. Maybe Devon's just trying to blame someone else."

"That's what I thought at first. Even the police thought it was bogus at first since Keith had nothing to gain from the lodge's failure. But once they started telling Devon what kind of time he faced in the pen, he cracked. Get this . . . the owner of the Majestic approached Keith about our property. Must've been sometime after our loan papers were signed. The owner must've wanted the property bad. He was willing to pay Keith a healthy sum to make sure he got it."

"So the Majestic owner paid Keith to arrange our failure," Hanna said. "He hired Devon to snoop around and get our customers' addresses, then gave them to the Majestic so they could steal our customers. And he cancelled my ads so business wouldn't improve." She gritted her teeth. "And all this time I've been thanking Keith for helping us. It makes me sick." Something flickered in her memory. "Hey, remember back in the spring when that Realtor called and said she had a client interested in our property? I'll bet that was the Majestic. And when they couldn't get the property fairly, they tried to finagle another way."

"I can hardly believe it. Gerdy said to keep this under wraps because the police are going to bring Keith in for questioning."

"I have to tell Nat. She's going to be so upset."

The soup and sandwiches were ready, but Hanna had lost her appetite. While Gram ate, she called Nat to tell her everything that had happened the night before. Her sister was concerned about her, but Hanna assured her she was fine and that Micah had been there for her.

"Sounds like he's your knight in shining armor," Nat said.

Finally, she had to break the news about Keith. At first Nat was reluctant to believe it, but once Hanna told her about the connection with the Majestic, she seemed to accept it.

"Oh no," Nat said. "Hanna, I'm so sorry. I can't believe this."

"Don't apologize, Nat. It's not your fault."

"It really stinks that he'd be so underhanded with his own sister-in-law. But then, he betrayed his own wife, so why not? I wonder what they paid him to do it? I guess the Majestic thought they could snag the lodge at auction for a song. And they probably would have. Things go pretty cheap at those auctions.

In the background Nat's boys were fussing loudly.

"I'd better go break that up," Nat said.

After the phone call, Hanna decided to go outside and tell Micah there was food on the table. What would he think of Keith's involvement in this? She felt so relieved that it was over and that the lodge would survive, but her heart broke for Nat and the boys. Surely Keith would go to jail for this. And he'd never work at a bank again. How would this affect child support for Natalie and the boys? She shook her head and said a quick prayer for her sister, hoping that this didn't make her life even harder. Then she slipped on her boots and coat and walked down the driveway. The snow blower's motor pierced the otherwise peaceful day. Wet flakes danced in the air around her, and she pulled her hood up over her head.

Micah glanced up and saw her coming. She waited patiently for him to kill the motor. Finally, he reached down and flipped the switch. The engine died.

She stopped a short distance away. "Lunch is ready."

He looked up the drive. "I . . . uh . . . I just have a few more swipes to go, and I'll be done."

Considering that the drive was over one hundred yards, a few swipes would take him an hour or more. "At least come in and warm up. I have news about Devon. You can finish later." It wasn't like they could go anywhere anyway, what with the roads still covered and more snow falling.

He looked everywhere but toward her. "All right."

They walked together, but tension hung heavily in the air between them.

He broke the silence. "You feeling okay today?"

"Sure." She tossed him a confident smile, which he missed entirely. "I'm just a little sore."

Their boots crunched alternately in the snow.

"So, what'd you hear about Devon?" he asked.

She told him the story Gram had gotten from Gerdy.

Micah seemed surprised, and his jaw clenched when she told him about Keith, but through the whole story, he never once looked at her.

When they approached the porch, she stopped him with a hand on his arm, her heart in her throat. "What's wrong, Micah?"

The corners of his mouth dipped low, and he shook his head. "Just a little shocked—about your brother-in-law and everything."

He continued up the porch steps, and she trailed behind.

Hanna and Gram carried the conversation through lunch, mostly about Keith and all the trouble he'd caused. Micah gulped down his food and was out the door before the tip of his nose lost the pink-nipped look.

Hanna and Gram passed the afternoon deep cleaning the guest rooms. The lampshades needed a good thorough cleaning, and they washed drapes and rehung them.

They called to check on Nat and the boys. Nat hadn't decided what to tell Alex yet about his dad, and Taylor was too young to be told anything.

A few more reservations were called in, cross-country skiers eager to hit the trails. Hanna finally felt the lodge was going to be okay.

When Micah came in from clearing the drive, he disappeared into his room until dinner. The snow still fell, and the drive was again covered.

Hanna's attempt at pulling Micah into the dinner conversation was a complete failure. He even seemed distant with Gram. Hanna observed his behavior carefully. He smiled at the appropriate times and responded to questions with short comments, but he wouldn't look at her, and he hadn't touched her since last night.

Worry clawed at her insides as the evening progressed. Something was definitely wrong. Something that wasn't going away on its own. She feared he was distancing himself from her, perhaps in another attempt to protect his heart. But they'd come so far over the past weeks. She'd seen glimpses of fear in his eyes, but he'd overcome them and continued to build their relationship.

What about last night had changed that? Had he feared losing her when he'd discovered her missing? Had her confiding in him scared him? Was he afraid her past was too much to deal with? She wanted to reassure him. She wanted to quell his fears and heal this part of him that was so vulnerable.

Now she peered at him from the corner of her eye. Gram had picked *It's a Wonderful Life* from their video library and had talked Micah into joining them. He stared at the screen, but Hanna wondered if he even followed the story. She wasn't doing such a good job of that herself.

When Gram announced she had to use the rest room, Hanna paused the tape.

Micah scooted to the edge of his chair. "I think I'll get another pop."

"Micah, wait." She wanted to utilize this opportunity while they were alone. "I was wondering—I mean, is something wrong? You've been quiet today and—"

"I'm fine." He stood and began walking toward the kitchen.

"Micah."

He stopped but didn't turn.

"Something's wrong." The dinner in her stomach gelled. "You're scaring me."

His head dropped forward, and he turned. When he raised his head, he wore an inscrutable mask. "I'm sorry. I'm not handling this well." He shifted, then stared at the screen. "I think it might be best if I work someplace else."

Her stomach dropped, taking her heart with it. The dread she'd felt before rose up in her throat. "If you mean because we're involved, that's not necessary."

Silence stretched between them. The fire snapped.

"I don't think we should see each other anymore."

No. He didn't mean this. It was fear talking. He was just afraid of loving. Her eyes burned.

His jaw flexed wildly, and his Adam's apple bobbed.

"You don't mean that."

Gram entered the room. "Let's get that tape rolling." She smiled, then seemed to sense the tension in the room. "Each time I see this movie, it's like the first time."

"Go ahead and start it; I'll be right back." Micah left the room with his glass, and Hanna stared after him, shock settling around her like a thick fog.

Gram started the tape, and the stilled crowd in the bank came to life. Hanna was fully aware of Micah's return but didn't look his way.

The rest of the movie passed as if in slow motion. Hanna's mind churned the whole time. She wanted badly to take Micah from the room and make him talk to her. She was certain she could change his mind if only he'd open up.

When the closing credits began rolling by, Micah stood. "Think I'll turn in. Good night."

Hanna's heart seized. She couldn't let him get away. "Wait, Micah—"

"Talk to you tomorrow," he slung the words over his shoulder and dashed from the room.

Micah hurried down the hall and slipped through his door. The last thing he needed was to get cornered by Hanna. He wasn't ready to explain why he was calling off their relationship. He hadn't meant to tell her that, but she'd been so insistent. He should've known that would lead to more questions. Questions he couldn't answer. *You're scaring me.* His gut tightened with guilt.

He kicked off his shoes and flung himself on the bed, not bothering to turn on a light. He'd have to give Hanna some reason for ending their relationship. But not the real reason. He could never tell her that.

Didn't even want to think about it. He shook the horror from his mind. *Don't think about it, Gallagher.* But try as he did, the blurry images from that night flashed through his mind. It had been so dark. But it had been Hanna kicking and struggling—Hanna whimpering.

Tell her.

His breath caught. Even his heart skipped a beat. Then his breath came in rasps, and bile rose in his throat. *I can't.* He turned his face into the pillow, wishing he could disappear. Wishing he could reverse time and change everything. *Oh, God, what have I done? And what will I tell Hanna?*

He had labored to think of some excuse, some reason she would believe. The only thing that came to him was the reason he'd given her before: that he wanted to remain single. That he couldn't stand the thought of needing a woman, loving a woman. Would she believe it? He'd have to make her believe it. Telling her the truth would only hurt her. And he'd already done plenty of that.

CHAPTER
TWENTY-NINE

When Hanna woke, she saw the snow had stopped sometime during the night. The white powder whipped through the air, driven by the vigorous wind. A thick pile of snow crowded the end of the drive, evidence that a plow had attempted to clear the road. Everything was once again covered, and judging by the forecast, it would be a couple of days before travel would be possible.

Physically, Hanna felt better, but Micah's words from the night before cast a shadow of fear over her heart. She had to convince him he was wrong, but first she had to find out what he was thinking. And that was proving to be as difficult today as it had been yesterday. Between his evasiveness and Gram's presence, it was after lunch before an opportunity arose.

Gram took her plate to the kitchen and returned for the other dishes.

"I'll get them," Hanna said.

Gram nudged her glasses up onto the bridge of her nose. "Well, all right. I think I might go take a nap."

Hanna's stomach stirred as she realized the moment had arrived.

Immediately after Gram left, Micah rose and carried his plate through the swinging doors.

Oh no, you don't. You're not getting away that easily. She swallowed the last bite of chicken salad and followed. Her knees weakened. What if he wouldn't listen? What if she lost him?

She came through the door just as he was leaving.

He stepped aside. "Sorry."

She remained still, blocking his escape. "Micah, we need to talk."

He leaned back against the counter and sighed. Twin commas formed between his brows.

She crossed her arms. "What's going on with you?" She searched his face for a clue to his thoughts. His lashes hung at half-mast; his gaze skated across the linoleum. He gave an almost imperceptible shake of his head. "It's like I said. I need out. I can't do this."

"We were doing fine." She hated the wobble in her voice. "What happened?"

"I told you a long time ago. I can't get involved with you—with anyone; it's all wrong." He looked everywhere but Hanna's face.

Was it fear? Had the intensity of his feelings frightened him? She grabbed at the thought. "You're scared. You're developing feelings, and sometimes it's—"

"No. That's not it." His jaw twitched.

"Then what?" Her pulse raced; her head pounded.

He looked away, finding the dishtowel hanging on the oven door. "It's like I said. It's over, that's all. I'm sorry."

The finality of the words, his deep voice, sent quivers of dread over her. It didn't make sense. Everything was fine until the night Devon had attacked her. She shook her head slowly, suspicion crawling up her spine. "There's something you're not telling me. You're not even looking at me."

His eyes swung to hers and clung. Tiny red veins squiggled through the whites of his eyes as if a toddler had taken a red ink pen to them. "I don't want to hurt you, Hanna."

She resisted the impulse to stamp her foot. "What do you think you're doing now?" She pleaded with her eyes. "Micah, don't you know, I love—"

"Don't! You don't know who I am. You don't know."

"Tell me then."

"I can't!" He pivoted away, clutching the edge of the steel sink, his wide shoulders tense. "You don't know what you're asking."

She stepped closer to him and grasped his arm, turning him around.

Pain glazed his eyes. When she saw the film of tears, her heart caught. She wanted to soothe his fears. She wanted to love him. She lifted a hand to his jaw. His skin was rough with stubble, and his jaw flexed.

"Tell me," she said.

Something—she wasn't sure what—shadowed his eyes.

"You don't know what you're asking," he whispered.

"Tell me." Her hand fell away.

He stared at her without blinking. She saw love flicker in his eyes. Her heart thrilled for just a moment.

He opened his mouth to speak.

She waited for the words that would explain, wished she could pull them from him. His mouth closed again. *Tell me.* She telegraphed the message with her eyes.

"It was me," he rasped.

Confusion ricocheted through her mind while the adrenaline of dread coursed through her veins. His behavior, more than his words, terrified her. "What was you?"

Suddenly she recognized the emotion she saw in his eyes. It was remorse.

"That night. All those years ago . . ."

His intensity scared her, and her heart lurched. She couldn't breathe. Fear kindled a fire in her midsection.

"I was leaving the bar. It was late. I'd had too much to drink." His voice droned on as though he was in another place, another time.

"It was dark. I saw someone walking beside the road."

Comprehension ignited the fuse of shock. *No! It can't be!*

"She looked like my mother. And suddenly—I wanted to hurt her. For all the times she—I wasn't thinking straight."

Hanna felt her teeth chatter. Her stomach rolled. Through a veil of tears, she saw his eyes narrow with fervor.

"I followed her. Attacked her." He blinked, and a tear rolled down his face.

She shook her head. *No! Please, God, no!* Her stomach clenched. Bile rose in her throat.

"It was me." His eyes closed. He turned his face from her.

The nightmare slashed like a dagger through her mind. The darkness. The terror. The monster. Revulsion burned like acid in her stomach.

It was him.

Micah, whom she'd confided in.

Micah, whom she'd kissed.

Micah, whom she'd loved.

White noise exploded inside her. A great roar, like a jet on takeoff. He was the monster who'd hurt her, left her terrified of the dark, left her terrified of men. Anger boiled, hot and furious. The man she'd feared, the man who'd shamed her and stolen her body, was standing in front of her.

Her hand lashed out, striking him across the face. The harsh crack seemed magnified.

Slowly, he lifted his hollow eyes to hers. *Do it again,* they seemed to beg.

Something in her shattered like glass, a thousand fragments piercing her soul. The force of it left her dizzy. Blackness closed in around her. The room swam. Her stomach heaved, setting her feet in motion.

CHAPTER
THIRTY

Hanna sat on the cold tile, her knees pulled up to her chest, her arms curled around them. She didn't know how much time had passed since Micah had ceased his pleading. She'd gotten up only once. To lock the door.

"I'm sorry, Hanna. I'm so sorry." His words haunted her. They'd seeped through the doorjamb as though he'd had his forehead pressed against the door. *"Open the door. Please."*

Her mouth had felt thick like it was stuffed with wool. After her stomach had emptied, she'd dry-heaved until it cramped in painful knots. *"Are you all right?"* Silence met his concern. She wiped her nose on a square of toilet paper. *"Hanna? Are you all right?"*

What right did he have to be concerned? He'd done this to her. *"Go away."*

And finally he had. Her buttocks had gone numb long ago, but she didn't want to leave the safe cocoon of the bathroom. She stared at the square pattern on the floor. Each one had marbling through it and gleamed with yesterday's fresh cleaning. Even now, the pine scent lingered, mixed with the acrid smell of regurgitated chicken salad. Her stomach rolled again.

A knock sounded at the door, startling her. "Hanna, are you all right, child?"

Gram. Had she been in here through Gram's nap?

She pulled herself up, catching herself on the vanity when her legs trembled like leaves on a tree.

She opened the door. "I'm fine."

Gram took her hand and tried to pull her from the room. "No, I don't want—Micah—"

"It's all right; he's in his room. Come on, we'll go to our room."

A barrage of emotions coursed through her. She wanted to see him again so she could finish what she started. She wanted to strike out at him. To hurt him the way he'd hurt her. She wanted him to go someplace far, far away. Her pulse accelerated again, making her dizzy and lightheaded. She put her hand on the wall beside her as she walked.

The fear was still there. Hiding like a cougar, ready to overtake her when she was least aware. The man who assaulted her was here. In her home. But was it the same man? Was Micah the man who'd attacked her, or was he the man she'd grown to love? He couldn't be both. It was a contradiction. She felt betrayed by him. As if the man he was now, the man she loved, had done this to her.

They entered the suite, and Hanna sat on the couch. How much should she tell Gram?

Gram poured her a glass of water and brought it to her. It felt good to swish the water around her mouth.

"Micah woke me. He was worried about you."

She clenched her teeth. Gram wouldn't feel so kindly toward Micah when she heard who he was.

"You must feel terribly shocked," Gram said.

Hanna looked at her. Why would she say that? There was sympathy in her small, glassy eyes.

"He told me, child." She drew Hanna into her arms.

Hanna went willingly. Grief erupted within her and manifested itself in the form of hot tears. She sobbed in wrenching jerks, crying for the pain she'd endured that night, for the fear she'd fought all these years. The fog of anguish covered her, blinding her to everything else. Time was lost, almost standing still.

Gram's gentle voice penetrated the haze, and Hanna realized she'd been talking all the time. Murmuring words of comfort with little meaning.

Suddenly she remembered what Gram had said. Gram knew who Micah was. Words spilled from Hanna's mouth. Her feelings, her thoughts, in a tumble of confusion. She hopped from the past to the present and back to the past again with no coherency or order. As thoughts came to her mind, they flowed out of her mouth. The hatred and bitterness she'd buried for years revealed itself with harsh words and savage tears.

And Gram listened quietly. Just listened. And it was as soothing as salve on Hanna's wounds.

⋯⋯

Something stirred Micah from his sleep. He opened his eyes. Light filtered in from the night sky, bathing the room in gray.

Then he remembered.

As it had each time he'd awakened during the night, the harsh reality crashed over him like a merciless tidal wave. He closed his eyes, trying to sink back into that blissful state of oblivion called sleep. Trying to escape reality for just a little while longer.

He wondered if Hanna was sleeping. He longed to go to her. To comfort her. The urge was almost too much to resist. But truth kept him pinned to the bed. She didn't want his comfort. She didn't even want to see his face.

And he couldn't blame her. He shouldn't have told her. It would've been better to leave. It would've been better for Hanna to feel confused and rejected than this. Anything was better than this. What had he been thinking when he'd let the words spill from his mouth?

He ran a hand over his swollen eyelids and down across the bristled plane of his jaw. His stomach rumbled, protesting the fast he'd unintentionally started the previous day. He'd wanted to stay out of Hanna's way, so he'd holed up in his room like a badger. Dinner had been three mints he'd gotten from a restaurant where he and Hanna had eaten a few weeks ago. He distinctly remembered scooping up the mints from the bill tray on the table. He'd offered them to Hanna, but she'd winked and said, "You're the one who had garlic."

Never could he have imagined the disastrous turn their relationship had taken. Who could have imagined this? It was over now, of this he was certain. How could he expect her to forgive him? He couldn't even forgive himself. And who was he to deserve someone like Hanna? What had she ever done to hurt anyone?

Unwelcome pictures from the past surged into his mind. He closed them off, unable to bear it. His bones ached when he thought about what he'd done. Could he have done anything more depraved? What kind of a person did that to a woman?

He remembered the thoughts he'd had about Devon after he'd attacked Hanna. He'd wanted to hurt him. He'd thought Devon deserved to be hurt. Deserved worse. The memory of his thoughts haunted him. Hadn't Micah thought Devon a despicable brute?

What a hypocrite He'd done worse himself. And now he was paying the price. He remembered vaguely something in the Bible about the consequences of sin not being removed. He'd done something evil, and now the price was his to pay. His and Hanna's.

He rolled over and buried his face into the pillow. All these years he'd avoided love, afraid of losing his heart, afraid of not being loved in return. But that wasn't the worst thing that could happen. He'd known it when he'd seen hurt and betrayal eclipse the shock and disbelief. Hurting the one you loved, hurting her down to the soul, was worse than losing her. Why hadn't he known that before?

He rubbed the sleep from his eyes and looked at the clock. Four thirty-two. A time that hovered between night and day. He sat up and reached for the remote, flicking on the TV. The national map covered the screen on the weather channel. Maybe the snow would let up today, and he could leave. His emotions teetered between relief and despair at the thought. Leaving was a necessity. A kindness. He owed it to her.

Where he would go was not a question. He'd decided sometime in the middle of the night what he would do.

The local weather flashed on the screen. Blizzardlike conditions over the next several hours, and the snow emergency was still in effect. The air left his body like a deflating balloon. At least it was going to taper to flurries later. Perhaps by lunch, then he could slip out and clear the drive while Hanna was eating.

His stomach constricted, and the hunger nudged him from the warm bed. Cold seeped from the planks through the soles of his feet. Quickly he dressed and left the room.

The air in the corridor felt thick with a heavy chill. When he entered the main room of the lodge, he flipped on the lamp and stacked the last three logs in the grate. After wadding up sections of newspaper, he stuffed them into the crevices. The lighter faltered, the grating sound of the switch echoing up the hollow chimney.

Finally, a fire lit the tip of the lighter and caught the wad of paper. Brown charring spread rapidly, consuming it until its edges were lacy and gray. The log above it caught the flame, leaving the paper a brittle skeleton.

Micah rose and went to the kitchen. He flipped the switch, and the florescent lights flickered on. He opened the refrigerator door and pulled out several Rubbermaid containers, last night's dinner, he presumed.

By the time he'd eaten, faint rays of light teased the distant sky. Snow blew and swirled in front of the windowpane, blocking everything but the approaching daylight. The fire popped and hissed in the lodge. He plucked his coat from the rack and went outside to gather more wood. Hanna would be waking soon, and he wanted to be out of the way when she did. He hoped she might come to him today. If only to curse him and vent her anger.

The fury had been a surprise. He'd expected disbelief. He'd expected hurt. But he hadn't expected the rage that radiated from her like steam off a hot spring.

With the last of the wood in his arms, he kicked off his shoes and took the load to the hearth. As they thudded onto the pile, he heard a door click open in the distance. There was a pause as the pneumatic closure caught, then a louder click as the door shut. It was too late to slip into his room.

Somehow he knew it was Hanna. His breathing constricted, choking off the oxygen. Something coiled in his gut. Fear, he thought. It sucked the moisture from his mouth. He heard no footsteps.

He added a log to the fire. Sparks danced upward, hissing as they went. When he turned, she was standing in the doorway.

Everything in him locked up, the way brakes do on ice. He might have thought she looked small, vulnerable, standing in a pair of pink, fluffy socks, wearing cow-spotted flannels. But the starch in her jaw, the way her eyes raked over him, told him differently. The air chilled in a way that had nothing to do with temperature. Taut silence stretched between them. She hated him. Loathed him. He could see it in her eyes, in the way her reddened nostrils flared.

He looked away. Staring at the naked rage was like trying to stare at the sun. He couldn't bear it.

He sensed when she left. His lungs filled with air again; his heart came to life. But something else in him died.

⋯✦⋯

After lunch Hanna and Gram began cleaning again. Their suite and Micah's room was overdue, and the stall in business was the perfect time to catch up. Hanna tackled the chores that hurt Gram's back while her grandmother handled the dusting. Mentally, Gram seemed to be doing better now that she was on medication. Hanna had only noticed one or two times that a word had slipped out of her grasp. They had agreed to take one day at a time and appreciate each one they had together.

She attacked the soap ring on the tub with vigor. The activity was a welcome release for the emotions locked away inside. She was tired of dwelling on Micah. Tired of trying to evade Micah. He seemed to be avoiding her too: a smart move on his part.

She would've vented her anger that morning if not for the way it had exploded in her mind when she'd seen him by the fire. The fragments had spurted in all directions, and she hadn't known which piece to chase first. Eventually they would settle into an ugly mosaic, and she would examine it in detail until the colors grew dull. By then Micah would be gone, and she could get on with her life.

She'd thought she'd forgiven the man who'd done this to her. Thought she'd forgiven him years ago. But apparently, the wound had never been cleansed, just crusted with a scab, healing on the surface while infection festered inside. How had she managed all these years thinking she was all right, when deep inside her was this hideous mass of bitterness?

She turned on the faucet and rinsed the cleanser down the drain. After stacking fresh towels, she gathered the sheets and carried the cleaning supplies into the living room.

"Gram, I'm finished. I'll be in Micah's room."

"All right."

Hanna set the carrier in the cart and pushed it down the hallway. She wished she could ask Gram to do Micah's room. But Micah was probably outside, anyway, still clearing the drive. And if she hurried, she would be finished before he returned.

She tapped lightly on the door. The wood felt cool on her knuckles. Her heart pushed against her chest in rapid spasms. She looked both ways down the hall, then knocked again, louder.

Only the buzzing fluorescent light interrupted the silence. Her ears strained for sounds behind the door. Hearing none, she inserted the master key in the door handle.

Micah stood still letting the hot water wash over him. His fingers, half frozen from being wrapped around the snow blower's handle, were finally starting to tingle with warmth. He'd finish clearing the drive later, and this time he'd remember his gloves.

He shut off the water and stepped onto the tile. Steam hung in the air, and he opened the door to clear it. After toweling off he donned a pair of jeans and plugged in his electric razor. With his fist he wiped away the film of moisture on the mirror.

The man who stared back looked a lot like the man he'd been eight years ago. Three days' worth of stubble coated his jaw, and his hair almost reached his bare shoulders.

He flicked on the razor, and it came to life with tiny vibrations. Why had it happened? Why had he done what he'd done all those years ago? He noticed he avoided the word. Even in his thoughts, he couldn't bring himself to say it.

Why, God? Why? Anger infused itself in the words. Of all the people in the world, why had it been Hanna on the road that night? Why had it been him leaving the bar at just that moment? Why had it been Hanna he'd fallen in love with? The "whys" were always there, like a mosquito that refused to be swatted away.

He flipped off the razor and set it on the counter, then opened the medicine cabinet at his side. He withdrew the toothpaste and shut the cabinet.

When he looked in the mirror, he saw her. Standing behind him, frozen.

His heart kicked in his chest. He watched as she slowly lowered the cleaning caddie to her side. Her gaze was fixed at some point below his eyes. He was suddenly aware of the bright fluorescents shining overhead.

His back. He flinched. She was staring at the grotesque scars, the many raised dots of whitened flesh.

She grimaced. The revulsion was in the crinkle of her nose, the squinting of her eyes.

Raw anger rose up in him. Was it not enough that she knew how vile he was? That she knew what he'd done? Did he have to fully expose every last shameful detail of his past?

Her eyes slid upward, meeting his in the mirror. He straightened his shoulders, refusing the powerful urge to turn his back from her. "What's wrong? Never seen a human ashtray?"

She gasped, and her gaze skimmed downward.

He cursed himself for taking his anger out on her.

"I was just—" She held up the supplies. "I knocked—"

He picked up a comb and dragged it through his dripping hair. "I'll be out in a minute."

She turned and fled.

CHAPTER
THIRTY-ONE

Hanna moved Micah's toiletries around, scrubbing the counter with quick swipes. When she'd heard the snow blower start up, she'd rushed to clean his room. If she hurried, she could have it done before he returned.

She took a breath and realized she'd been holding it. Micah's scent lingered in his room, but breathing in the bathroom was like inhaling the essence of him. Like he was getting inside her, in her blood, in her bones.

She left the bathroom and began tugging off the bedding. She would not think about Micah sleeping here, dreaming here. She would just do her job.

Never seen a human ashtray? His words sprang into her mind unbidden. She hadn't allowed herself to consider the words or their meaning. She'd shoved them into a dusty corner of her mind, not wanting to feel the sympathy she knew would follow. But here, where every breath, every object, summoned thoughts of Micah, she let herself consider it.

Who had done it? Who had burned his back with cigarettes? His father? Had he been taken from his home and put in foster care because of the abuse? How old had he been when it had happened? She pictured a miniature Micah at three or four. She tried to imagine someone jabbing the hot tip of a cigarette on his baby-soft skin. She winced. Had he smelled his own burning flesh? Had they held him down and burned him over and over?

Dear God, how could anyone do such a thing? She'd heard of it before. Read it in the paper or seen it on TV. But never had she seen the physical scars or imagined the emotional ones.

She remembered something he'd said in the kitchen. *"She looked like my mother—and suddenly I wanted to hurt her."*

Oh, Lord, his own mother?

Her heart pushed against her chest. She was feeling sorry for Micah, and she didn't want to. *He doesn't deserve your pity. Remember what he did to you.* Whatever had happened to him was no excuse for what he'd done to her.

She tugged off the pillowcase and went to stuff the bundle of linens in the cart, relieved to be finished before his return. Moments later she folded the white towels, transferred her sheets to the dryer, and pulled the knob on the washer, starting the flow of water. After adding a capful of detergent, she began stuffing Micah's bedding into the washer. Even the sheets smelled of him. She tried not to inhale the musky, woodsy scent.

Something clonked against the top of the washer, and she searched through the folds, trying to find what was wrapped up in the sheet. Through the wadded, twisted material, she felt a hard rectangular object. Finally, she uncovered the object: his journal, she thought. The one she'd seen in his room.

She laid it aside, on the washer, and finished loading the machine. Once the lid was down, she stacked the towels in the basket. As she stood her eyes encountered the brown book. It drew her. Like a warm day in early spring drew children outside, the journal beckoned.

She picked it up. It was bound with a leather spine, but the cover was of plain cloth and titleless. A man's journal. She glanced through the doorway and realized with a stab of guilt she was being nosy.

She opened the cover anyway. There was an inscription on the first page, scrawled in bold, black ink: *To Micah: May the words you write within begin to heal your heart.*

It was signed by his foster father and dated almost three years ago. She fanned through the pages, not quite daring to read the private words. The pages were filled, with only a few left blank at the back.

Her lungs constricted with each shallow breath. She felt the familiar rush of adrenaline in her veins. She wanted to read it. Read the words that were not meant for her eyes. She wavered uneasily. The weight of the book burned in her hands.

It would answer her questions about Micah's past; she knew it somehow. But it was wrong to read the private thoughts of another. Then why did it feel so right? Why did she feel this compelling need to—

The front door clicked open and shut. She realized belatedly that the snow blower's engine had hushed moments ago. Moving quickly, she tucked the journal under a stack of towels in the basket. She mentally traced the footfalls across the lodge. Logs thudded into the grate, making the fire sizzle and pop.

She held her breath and felt her pulse pounding in her temples. More footfalls, but she couldn't determine their direction. She flattened against the washer, not daring to push the door closed. It was silly, hiding in the laundry room like a naughty child, but she didn't want to see him.

Finally, a door shut in the distance, and she knew he'd returned to his room. She gathered up the basket of towels and carried them to her room, thinking every step of the way about the journal tucked inside.

· · ✦ · ·

As the daylight faded into the murky shadows of evening, Micah heard a truck rumbling in the distance. He pushed the heavy drapes aside. A snowplow barreled down the road, throwing snow off to the sides like twin geysers. He'd expected the roads would be cleared tonight. The snow had stopped, and the forecast for tonight was clear. Clear for him to leave in the morning.

Dread coiled into a knot in his gut, tightening painfully. Memories of Hanna were branded on his heart. Memories of her laughing by the fire. Memories of them kissing by the lake. Good memories. The best of his life.

He turned and surveyed the open duffel bags, half stuffed with clothing. How had it come to this? The good memories had burned away, leaving nothing but ashes. Nothing good had come of his experience here. He'd gained love, only to lose it. He'd hurt Hanna in an unforgivable way. He'd exposed to Hanna the humiliation of his scars. The memories of his time here had turned bitter, as if tossed in vinegar.

He gathered his socks and tucked them in the bag. He wished he could pack up all the damage he'd done and take it away. He felt the sting of regret. He would give anything to turn back time and change things. Even if he couldn't have Hanna, he wished he could remove the pain he'd caused her. He would give up Hanna, if only he could erase the past.

A tap at the door set his heart galloping. His hands, still clutching a T-shirt and belt, paused. Hope sprang like a spring crocus through the frozen crust of his heart. He tamped it down firmly. When he opened the door, the hope withered and died.

"I thought you might be hungry," Gram said. She passed by and set a plate on the dresser.

He knew the moment she noticed. You couldn't miss the gaping bags, the empty chest drawers hanging open in haphazard fashion.

"What are you doing?" she asked.

He resumed packing. "Leaving."

"Why, Micah?" She laid a hand on his arm. Her sparse, white brows pulled together and nearly met over her nose.

He laughed bitterly. "You know why. You should be helping me pack."

Her hands twitched as if they didn't know what to do.

He pressed down the clothes and pulled the zipper.

"She's just confused."

"She's angry."

"Yes, she's angry, but she needs time."

"She needs me to leave," he said.

"No. She needs you to stay."

His gut twisted. He filled the second bag and turned, pushing the drawers back into their slots. He faced Gram. Pain pulsed through his veins, hot and sluggish. He swallowed around the hard lump in his throat. "How will she ever get over it if I stay?"

Gram's eyes teared. They pierced him with intensity. "How will she get over it if you leave?"

The words hung in the air. He wanted to snatch them, tuck them away in his heart, believe them. He would stay if there was a chance. Hanna's face flashed in his mind. He remembered the rage that burned in her eyes whenever she saw him. He remembered the expression on her face in the bathroom mirror. The disgust. The revulsion.

He directed his attention to the plate of food, and he picked it up like a life preserver. "Thanks for the food." He removed the foil, and the aroma of roasted pork assailed his senses. His stomach turned. "Smells great." He gathered the silverware, hoping she'd leave. In his peripheral vision, he saw her dip her head in defeat. He walked to the door, and she followed.

When she crossed the threshold, she turned. "Where will you go?"

He shrugged.

"At least give me a number, in case she—"

"She won't."

Silence surrounded them.

Finally, Gram reached up and kissed him on the cheek.

As she walked away, he clamped his teeth together and stared at the carpet that had come unraveled at the threshold.

⊰——⋇——⊱

From its spot on the corner of her dresser, the journal beckoned. It had called to Hanna all evening, but she had resisted its pull. The shock and rage she'd felt upon learning Micah's identity had settled into a dull ache. The icy hardness of her heart was beginning to thaw, giving way to the bitter sting of disillusionment. She had found love only to lose it. And while she was still numb, she knew her love for Micah must wither and die eventually. No love could survive the storm they'd been through.

She brushed her teeth and walked toward the bed, stopping when she reached the spot where the journal lay. Had Micah noticed it missing? Was he searching his room for it even now? She picked it up and slid her finger along the gold edges. Her heart quickened. She bit the inside of her mouth. What would it hurt, really? Their relationship was over, and she would return the journal when she was finished.

She couldn't deny the urge within her. Making the decision, she carried the book to the bed and snuggled beneath the covers. Tension skittered along her nerves as she opened the journal to the first page. The bedside lamp glowed on the paper, tingeing the pages with yellow.

The handwriting slanted boldly on the lines, the ungraceful scrawl of a left-hander. As she began reading, she thought the tone of the first pages was awkward. As if he was giving an impromptu speech and didn't know what to say or how to say it. He wrote about a recovery group he was attending for children of alcoholics.

Ah, she thought, *the Thursday-night appointment.*

After several pages of vague rambling, the tone evolved into a more tangible form of storytelling. The writing, in flashback style, was strong and evocative and intermingled with prayers.

I know I was five, because I tripped over my kindergarten tote bag in the dark, and the bells I'd tied on the handle jingled. Sometimes I'd hear her late at night. She would laugh, and I could hear a man's voice through the walls of my bedroom.

But this time was different. She wasn't laughing, and the groans I heard scared me. I heard a man's voice that time, too, and I crept out of my bed. That alone took a mountain of courage because I wasn't allowed out of my bed. But I was worried about her.

So I went and looked out the door. The light was on in my mom's room across the hall. I could just see the end of her bed through her cracked door. Her bare feet, toes pointed upward, were all I could see of her.

I heard the man chuckle. It was not a happy kind of laugh. I could see his leg hanging off the end of the bed. I wondered who he was. I wondered if he was my dad. I used to wonder that about every man she brought home.

I crept silently along the way, evading the board that creaked.
Finally, I peeked around the doorjamb. My heart was pumping
like it did when I ran the whole way home from school. I didn't
know who I was most afraid of: the man or my mom. His back
was to me, and my eyes widened at what I saw. He had a green
dragon on his back, a tattoo, with orange fire coming from its
nostrils.

My mom moaned again, and I watched her toes curl.

"Stop it!" I'd said without thinking.

The man jerked around. He was naked, and I'd never seen a
naked man before. He looked back at my mom, who was hidden
by his massive body. "Hey, you didn't tell me you had a kid."

My mom sat up, clutching the blanket to her chest. "Get in
bed, Micah!" Her voice was raspy and ugly.

As I turned and ran, I heard her words. "He ain't mine. He's
my sister's. I'm just baby-sitting."

Hanna's heart twisted at her first peek inside Micah's boyhood. A
yawn sneaked out, and she glanced at the clock. It was well past her bedtime, but the journal had her in its clutches, gripped her like a fast-paced
novel. More so even, because these stories were true.

An hour passed, then two. She didn't get up, not even for a tissue. Her eyes grew heavy and swollen, but something was happening
inside her at the reading of his words. Something good, something
right.

A battle raged in her mind. Sympathy pulled at her heart for the boy
Micah had been. Each wounded word tugged at the door, but something in her strove to keep it shut. How could a mother abuse her own
child? Verbally, physically hurt the child she'd carried and given birth to?
It was beyond imagining.

The next pages were a flashback to a time when Micah had emptied
his mother's last bottle of beer.

She sniffed the bottle. "What did you do with the beer?"

"I . . . I poured it in the sink."

Her eyes narrowed, and her mouth twisted in that way I hated. "That was my last beer! I don't get paid 'til Thursday, you know that, and you wasted my last beer."

When she turned and strolled to her purse, I held my breath. She pulled out a cigarette and lit it. It was like this angry, orange light. My mother looked hard, like she could have killed me, as she puffed on it.

I was terrified, and I stood slowly. She was so angry, I could see it in her eyes. I backed up, staring at the cigarette. It blurred into a fiery glow. My breath came in short gasps. I squeezed my eyes shut, tried to push myself into the wall, scarcely feeling the wet flow down my legs.

Hanna had to stop reading. She couldn't see past the tears in her eyes. She wiped them away with the corner of the blanket, then finally got up to blow her nose. She remembered with disturbing clarity the scarred flesh of Micah's back. The many white dots that disappeared beneath the waistband of his jeans. It was true. His mother had put them there.

Horror dragged its talons along her spine. She couldn't even fathom doing that to any child, much less her own. If he hadn't been loved by his only parent, how had he survived? How had he become such an honorable—

He hadn't been an honorable man. He'd been a man who drank and assaulted a woman. His mother's violence had produced a son who behaved violently. It was a known fact that abused children often grow up to abuse.

But Micah wasn't the man he used to be. She *knew* that. She'd seen nothing but integrity and virtue since he'd come to Higher Grounds. Memories of him flashed like fireflies in her mind. Of the time he'd gone out to find Gram when she was lost. Of the time he'd refused to cash his paychecks so she could pay the lodge's bills. Of the times he'd held his passion in check when they'd kissed. On and on it went. Memory after memory affirming the person Micah was today. God had made the changes in him, for only God could change a person so completely.

Hanna settled back in bed, and feeling flushed, she pushed back the covers. Eagerly, she picked up the journal. There were only four pages remaining.

Dear Mom,

I know you'll never read this, but this is for me, not for you. I need to get past the anger and bitterness I feel toward you, and to do that, I know I have to forgive you.

I learned something new in group tonight. I learned that forgiving you doesn't mean what you did was okay. Because it wasn't, Mom. It was inexcusable. But I will no longer hold you responsible.

Only lately have I begun to understand how your choices influenced the person I became. And I wonder what your childhood was like. I wonder if your choices, your behavior, was a direct result of your parents' choices. It's like an ugly heirloom that gets passed from generation to generation. Nobody wants it, but it gets passed on anyway.

Well, Mom, I'm throwing it away. With God's help it's stopping with me. I grieve the mistakes I've already made. I can no more undo them than you can. But maybe if I forgive you I can find it within me to forgive myself, for I hurt someone too.

I forgive you, Mom.

Please, God. Be with the one I hurt. Help her to find peace and healing. Help me to find forgiveness.

Hanna wiped her eyes with the soggy tissue and looked at the date in the corner of the page. June eighth. He'd written it after he'd started at Higher Grounds but before they'd begun dating. He had been praying for her even before he knew who she was.

Forgive him.

The words were whispered into her heart. Her breath caught and held, and she knew it was a critical moment. She had carried the animosity in her heart for eight years, and it was time to let it go. With her body trembling and her blood surging, she turned loose of the door. She flung it open and asked God for a measure of grace to sustain her. The moment hung suspended like a bubble, floating with iridescent beauty. God communed with her quietly there in the stillness of the night and assured her His grace would be sufficient. She could forgive Micah with God's help.

Hanna's eyes flitted over the last few pages. The last entry was September twelfth, two days before Devon's assault. She read avidly the words he'd written about their relationship. At the end of the entry, she caught her breath.

I can deny it to myself no more. I love her. Dear God, I love her so much my heart is near exploding with the exquisite joy and fear I feel. It must radiate from my eyes when I look at her, and she must surely guess. But soon I'll put words to my feelings, and she will know.

Hanna's stomach clenched pleasantly, the way it used to whenever Micah was near. She longed to hear the words from his lips. She longed to say them in return. His desperate prayer for forgiveness surged to mind. He needed to know. He needed to know he was forgiven.

She twisted in bed, putting her feet on the floor. Only then did she realize it was two forty-five. She slumped in disappointment. Everything in her wanted to go to him, bang on his door, wake him up, and tell him. But common sense took hold. It was the middle of the night, for goodness' sakes. She lay down and cradled the journal to her chest. Morning would come soon enough.

CHAPTER
THIRTY-TWO

It seemed only moments later that she woke to the warm sun peeking through the drapes. Water dripped from the eaves outside, a sure sign the warmer temperatures were melting the roof snow.

The awareness of last night's decision had not left her even during sleep. She slipped from beneath the covers, feeling at peace about the choice she'd made.

In her eagerness to see Micah, she skipped her shower and simply washed her face and combed her hair. After brushing her teeth and dressing in jeans and a sweater, she grabbed the journal and walked toward Micah's room. Renewed hope put a spring in her steps, and soon she stood face to face with the wooden door.

She tapped lightly, then glanced at her watch. It was not yet eight o'clock, and she hoped he was awake. Tendrils of apprehension wove through her body, centering in her stomach where they knotted uneasily. Silence filled the hallway, and she strained to hear sounds of movement behind the door.

Maybe he was still in bed. Or in the shower, or shaving, like last time. Had it been just yesterday that she'd walked in and caught him unaware? It seemed like weeks ago, so much had changed in her heart. She knocked firmly and crossed her trembling arms, hugging her waist.

Nervous energy danced in her feet. Where was he? Was he avoiding her? She couldn't blame him.

"Micah?" She called loud enough for him to hear behind the doors.

Silence met her beckoning. Where could he be?

The snow—he's probably clearing the drive. She turned and scurried down the hall and into the lodge. Once there, she pulled aside the drapes and peered out. Her ears perked for the sound of the blower, but she heard nothing.

A clatter of pots and pans came from the kitchen. She followed the sounds, hoping to see Micah, but when she swung the louvered doors open, Gram was setting a pan on the stove.

"Good morning," Gram said.

"Morning. Have you seen Micah?"

Her grandmother raised her brows. "No . . . why?"

Hanna wondered at the stilted caution in Gram's voice. "I need to talk to him, but he's not in his room. I can't imagine where—"

"Oh my." Gram's wrinkled fingers covered her lips.

Trepidation poured like hot wax through her veins. "What is it?"

"Oh my. Oh dear." Gram's hand slid up to cover half her face as her eyes closed.

Hanna forced a note of patience in her voice. "Gram? What's wrong?"

She opened her eyes, revealing sad regret. "Oh, Hanna, last night he was packing—he must've left earlier this morning—I tried to—"

Chills of dread pumped through her veins. "Why didn't you—" She stopped the accusation and breathed deeply.

"I didn't want to meddle. I didn't think you'd want—" Her eyes glazed over.

Hanna felt a stab of remorse and took Gram's hand. "No, I'm sorry. I didn't mean to blame you. Do you know where he was going?"

Gram shook her head. "He wouldn't say. I asked, but he wouldn't say."

Hanna's gaze darted helplessly around the cubicle. She had to find him. But how? She didn't know any of his friends.

His foster father. She rushed to the office, leaving Gram to follow, and unlocked the door. She searched through the filing cabinet for the paper he'd scrawled on when he'd first arrived. That's when she remembered. She'd tossed it out when she'd searched through her files. Her fingers stilled over the file tabs.

"What is it, child?"

She shut the drawer in a slow, decisive move. "I thought I had his foster father's number in his file, but I don't. Wait a minute. Natalie knows Jim. She's seeing him for counseling." Hanna punched in Nat's number, and her sister answered the phone. Natalie had Jim's work number, but he wouldn't be in the office when the roads were barely passable. She called the number anyway, but it was just as she figured. Despair settled over her like a lead blanket. If Micah didn't want to be found, he'd make sure he couldn't be tracked. She met her grandmother's gaze. "How am I going to find him?"

Micah walked up the steps to the building's glass door. His feet felt heavy, as if weighted with sand. His fingers curled around the New Testament in the pocket of his coat, giving him a dash of comfort.

He walked with deliberate steps to the front desk. The man was filling out a form and continued doing so for what seemed like minutes. His thin salt-and-pepper hair swept across his scalp in a poor attempt to disguise a bald spot.

Finally he looked up. "Can I help you?"

Micah cleared his suddenly dry throat. His gut tightened in a hard knot, sending tremors of fear through his system. "My name is Micah Gallagher. I'd like to turn myself in for a crime I committed eight years ago."

CHAPTER
THIRTY-THREE

"I was going to tell him I forgive him, Gram," Hanna said.

Gram drew her into a warm embrace. "I'm so sorry. Oh, why didn't I tell you last night? All this could've been avoided."

"It's not your fault. The way I've acted the last two days, it's no wonder you thought I wouldn't care. I did want him to leave."

Gram pulled back. "We'll find him somehow."

She didn't know how. For the past two hours, she'd searched the files of her mind for ideas and had come up empty.

The phone rang, and Gram answered. It had been ringing steadily all morning with former guests who wanted to ski Teton Pass and potential guests who had seen their magazine ad. She should feel pleased that Higher Grounds was going to survive, but her sorrow at losing Micah coated everything with despair.

Her heart felt like it was in pieces. Micah was gone, and he didn't even know that she loved him. He thought she despised him. A heavy weight settled inside her, and she blinked back tears. She walked to the window and squinted at the glaring, white world. That was the worst of it. He was out there somewhere thinking he was beyond forgiveness. She'd read it in his eyes, in his posture over the past two days. And she'd let him think it. She'd wanted him to think it.

She swallowed around the achy lump in her throat. What would he do? Where would he go? She remembered she owed him three paychecks, and regret swelled within her. She closed her eyes. Why did it take so long to see the truth? To see that he'd changed? Why had it taken the horror of his past to shove her into the place of forgiving? It had been eight years ago. He hadn't even known her. He'd been drunk. He'd been abused. Who's to say that she wouldn't have done something just as despicable if her circumstances had mirrored his?

She, who'd been raised in a loving, Christian family. How could she even fathom the effects of an abusive childhood? Who was she to be the judge and jury of his actions? God was the only One qualified to do that, and He had forgiven Micah.

"Why did it take me so long?" she muttered to herself.

"To forgive?"

Hanna jumped. She hadn't heard Gram's approach. She nodded, aching in the marrow of her bones. "I thought I was over it years ago. I thought I had forgiven my attacker."

Gram shook her head. "I've been praying all these years that God would bring you to a place of forgiveness and peace."

How had Gram known when she hadn't known herself? *Well, I guess your prayers were answered. In an awful, harrowing way,* she added silently. *Please, Father, help me find Micah or bring him back to us.*

The phone trilled in the distance. Gram went to answer it.

"Hanna, it's for you. It's a Sergeant Whitco from the police station," Gram whispered.

Hanna sighed. Now that the snow had cleared, they must want her to fill out a formal complaint against Devon. She didn't feel like dealing with it right now.

She took the phone from Gram. "This is Hanna Landin."

The sergeant introduced himself. "Ms. Landin, you filled out a formal complaint about eight years ago against a man who assaulted you. Do you remember that?"

Her attention blurred at the unexpected topic, then snapped into focus. Every nerve in her body tingled with awareness. "Yes—I mean—yes, I remember."

"This may come as a shock, but we've apprehended the perpetrator."

"What?"

Gram turned at her tone.

He cleared his throat. "Actually, what I mean to say is, he turned himself in."

Her head buzzed with confusion. "What do you—who turned himself in?"

"The man who committed the crime. Or so he says."

Her mind spun as he went on about the unusual nature of the situation. What would drive a man to turn himself in after eight years? *Your anger. Your judgmental attitude. Your unforgiveness.* Dear God, was he trying to punish himself—trying to earn forgiveness? Her heart ached.

Silence filled the lines, and she realized belatedly he'd asked her about pressing charges. "No! No, I don't want to press charges."

A long pause filled the line. "Ms. Landin, I know it was a long time ago, but—"

"No," she said, as firmly as she could. "I won't press charges."

"We can set up a meeting with a victim's advocate if you like and—"

"That won't be necessary."

She needed Micah to know that she forgave him, that she didn't want him punished anymore. The sergeant was saying good-bye, and she muttered good-bye in return before she placed the receiver in the cradle.

Still in shock, she told Gram what had happened. Then it hit her. "He's there, at the police station." She had found him. Or rather, God had found him, and she could go to him and tell him everything.

She slipped on her boots and grabbed her coat. Turning, she snatched the journal off her desk. "I've got to catch him before they let him go."

"Drive carefully," Gram called before the door slammed behind her.

The van started reluctantly after sitting in the cold for three days. She maneuvered it out of the lot and onto the slick driveway, her whole body trembling with anxiety.

Micah's shirt clung to him, producing a sticky layer of heat under his coat, but he couldn't summon the will to remove it. His heart beat erratically under his clothing, and his legs felt weak and shaky, either a reminder of the breakfast he'd skipped or a hint at his emotional condition.

He saw a poster of wanted criminals, and he scanned the black-and-white photos. He was no better than they were. Hadn't he committed a crime and evaded the police for eight years? Hadn't he victimized an innocent woman and left her wounded? Remorse filled him, eating away at the soft coating of his heart. He tasted the pain—relished it.

His future stretched before him like a dark, dirty corridor. He hadn't forgotten what the inside of a jail cell looked like. But he needed to pay for his crime. Maybe then he would feel forgiven; maybe then he would forgive himself.

When a bead of sweat trickled down the back of his neck, he shrugged out of his coat, letting it fall behind him on the metal chair. The door opened, and he looked up hopefully at Sergeant Whitco. Micah searched the man's face. When Micah had given the sergeant his reason for being there, he'd looked at him suspiciously. Micah knew Whitco had thought him a nut case. One of those attention-seekers who confesses to crimes he didn't commit. If only that were true. But Micah had known the officer would change his mind when he checked the files.

The officer dropped a folder on his desk and seated himself across from Micah. His eyes had lost that suspicious look. Accusation and distaste had taken its place. It was there in the slightly curled-up corner of his nose, in the hardened jaw and rigid posture. He knew Micah was just what he'd said. Micah shifted in his seat and focused on the cluttered desk. It had been a long time since his presence had evoked disdain. He liked it even less now than he had then.

Micah wondered what would happen next. Would a court date be set in which Hanna would testify? He hoped she could be spared that. Surely, with his pleading guilty—

"I looked in the files for information on the crime to which you admit, and the original statement of Ms.—the victim—concurs with the information you've given us."

Micah waited, wanting to search the officer's eyes for more information, but unable to look at him directly.

Whitco leaned his elbows on the desk, and Micah felt his probing eyes. "I just got off the phone with the young woman."

Micah's heart lurched, and he looked at Whitco. He hadn't known they would contact her so soon.

"Contrary to my recommendation, she refuses to press charges." The sergeant folded his hands on top of the manila folder. He seemed disappointed.

Anxiety pressed on his chest, squeezing and wrenching. "What does that mean?"

He shrugged. "Unfortunately, it means you're free to go."

Micah's head tipped forward. "But—I'm turning myself in. I committed a crime—"

"Son, the DA is never going to pursue this kind of case without the victim's cooperation."

Dismay settled over him, mingled with a pinch of relief. Adrenaline pumped through his veins, and he used it to organize his thoughts. "But this is different. I'm turning myself in—that doesn't happen every day—"

"Not on my shift." The sergeant gave a wan smile.

"There must be something on the books, some way around this . . ."

He narrowed his eyes as if trying to figure Micah out. "Am I to understand that you *want* to be arrested?"

"That's why I came."

"Well, yes, I know, but—" He stopped and shook his head. "Apparently the young lady is past this—issue—or else she doesn't want to relive it. That's not uncommon; most rape victims don't even report it."

Micah closed his eyes, his hope dwindling fast. Then an idea formed, and he grabbed on to it like a lifeline. "Maybe you could go see her." He leaned forward, clutching the desk's edge with his fingers. "Don't you have some kind of counselor or something? Someone who can—"

Whitco was shaking his head. "I already offered that." Confusion coated the man's eyes as Micah saw him spot the WWJD bracelet he always wore.

In that moment Micah let all defenses down. He had nothing to hide. All pride had perished long ago. *Please God. I want this. I want to make it as right as I can.*

Whitco's chair creaked, and Micah blinked to see him leaning back in his chair, his chin nudging upward as if he'd just figured Micah out. "You're a Christian."

Micah's brows drew together.

"I saw your bracelet." The sergeant drew in a deep breath and let it out in one whoosh. "I get it. You did something wrong before—and now you want to pay for it."

"It's more than that . . ."

"Maybe it is, but you've got to get over it. I can't arrest you; the victim doesn't even want me to. She's beyond it; now you need to get beyond it too."

The man didn't understand. He couldn't possibly. Micah stared at a V-shaped scar on the oak desk. Where would he go now? What would he do? How could he get on with his life when his crime hung over him like a black thundercloud?

Sergeant Whitco's chair scraped across the floor as he stood. He extended a hand.

Numbly, Micah stood and took it.

"Good luck, son. Sorry I can't help you."

Micah turned mechanically and left the building. His cycle stood right where he'd left it, with two bags piled on its back. He remembered Hanna helping him fix it. He remembered Hanna clinging to his back as the wind ruffled their hair.

He remembered Hanna's expression when he'd told her who he was. The disbelief—the refusal to believe. Then the horror, the hurt, the anger that raked over her features. Her eyes turning an intense green with splinters of gold fire. Her skin stretched taut across her cheekbones.

He peeled out of the lot, giving no thought to direction. His heart pressed against his rib cage with the heavy load of guilt. Memories flashed like lightning in his mind. Hanna retching from the shock of his confession, Hanna singeing him with her eyes as he stoked the fire, Hanna staring in revulsion at his disfigured flesh.

He drove aimlessly, the pictures scalding him like acid. Why couldn't he escape the guilt? God had forgiven him. Why couldn't he forgive himself?

He hadn't known where he was headed until his cycle pulled to a stop alongside the road. He dismounted, tugged off his helmet, and scanned the place. A canopy of pine needles sheltered the white ground. The sun moved behind a cloud, casting a shadow over the area.

His feet moved forward, toward the place. He trudged through the shin-deep snow without a thought. He didn't feel the cold wetness against his ankles. He didn't feel the wind's chill on his skin. He felt only the driving need to get there.

The ground sloped suddenly downward, and his feet stopped. A picture flashed into his mind. Something he'd forgotten until now. It had been dark. The landscape had been painted in dark shades of gray. He hadn't seen the gully, and they'd fallen down it, rolling and twisting until they'd jammed against a tree. His hand had slipped off her mouth, and she'd screamed in the dark.

He could hear it even now. He closed his eyes, trying to block it out, but it replayed in his mind like a haunting nightmare.

I'm sorry.

He'd had no mercy on her, had given no thought to the person she was or to her pleas. He covered his face with his hands. *I'm so sorry.* His legs buckled. He sank to his knees in the cold, wet snow and sobbed.

⁂

Hanna drummed her fingers on the steering wheel, her foot aching to press harder on the accelerator. Although the plows had cleared the roads, a smooth glaze clung to the pavement, making it slick. White clouds of snow drifted across the road like knee-high ghosts.

At this rate she wasn't going to make it to the station before Micah left. Why hadn't she asked the sergeant to keep him there? Now she might miss him, and she had no idea where he'd go. He might leave town or leave the state, for all she knew.

She braked for a stop sign but didn't come to a complete stop before accelerating again. *Please, God, get me there in time.* The sun emerged from behind the clouds and reflected off the white surface, blinding her with its glare. She squinted and flipped down the visor.

What would she say to him? Would he listen to her? Would he believe she had forgiven him? What if he'd convinced himself he was no good for her? Hadn't she behaved in such a way the last two days? Hadn't she treated him like he was nothing? How could she explain that the story of his past had brought understanding and eventually forgiveness? She patted her coat pocket to reassure herself the journal was still there.

Her mind was so preoccupied, she nearly passed the motorcycle before she recognized it. She slowed and looked in her rearview mirror. It was his.

And it was *there.* Where it had happened. She pulled into an empty lot and got out of the car, jogging carefully back to the cycle. His two bags were stacked on the back, and his helmet lay carelessly on top.

Footprints cut through the deep snow, and she followed them, placing her own feet in the center of each one. Brambles and thickets pulled at her clothing, but she trudged ahead heedlessly. Her veins surged with trepidation at returning to the spot where the attack had happened, but it hardly seemed like the same place. The landscape was different than it had been that night. The air had been dark with shadows, and now it was crisp with light. The ground had been dry and hard, and now it was softened with a blanket of snow.

She walked on, around the trees and scrub, stepping in Micah's footprints. Her breath came in rapid puffs. The snow beneath her feet crunched softly with each step.

Through a cloud of vaporized breath, she saw him. Kneeling on the soft-packed ground, sitting back on his heels, his head bowed forward. She stopped. Her breath caught, and her heart clamored, urging her onward. Her eyes clung to his back, her footsteps made prints of their own. She could hear him now, whispering words she couldn't make out in a pleading tone that constricted her heart.

When she drew close, his head jerked toward her. His face was wet and drawn. His red-rimmed eyes looked dazedly at her as if not quite believing she was there.

She opened her mouth to speak and realized she didn't know what to say.

He didn't seem to either. His gaze fell to a spot at her feet and slid away to his own hands on his thighs.

Each breath of air snatched the moisture from her mouth. Her heart couldn't seem to keep up with her lungs. Why had he come here? Why had he gone to the police station to begin with? "Why did you do it?" The words tumbled out before she realized she was speaking.

He looked at her, then away, as if each glance cost him something.

"Why did you turn yourself in?"

He looked the other way, and she could tell he was wiping his face. "It was the right thing to do."

She stepped closer and pulled the journal from her pocket. For the first time, she worried he would be angry with her for invading his privacy. Guilt and fear prickled her skin, but she held out the journal anyway. "I have something that belongs to you."

He looked up then. His eyes narrowed, a crease marred his forehead.

"I read it." She bit the inside of her mouth. "I'm sorry."

He reached out and took the journal.

"I know I shouldn't have."

"Doesn't matter."

"Yes, it does." How could she explain what the lessons from his past had taught her? She wanted to make him understand, but she saw in his eyes that he didn't. "Why didn't you tell me? About your mom, your childhood?"

He gave a brittle laugh. "I try to forget."

"It's part of who you are."

He studied the snow-crusted ground. "Why are you here?"

His raw, tortured voice drew her. She looked at him kneeling in the wet snow, defeat lining his eyes, anguish etching lines in his face. Ribbons of regret curled tightly in her stomach. Wasn't she to blame for the way he felt? Hadn't she treated him with contempt? Hadn't she wanted him to feel worthless?

Somehow she had to convince him she'd been wrong. And she had the feeling she'd get only one chance. "I came to tell you I forgive you."

He looked up, and this time he kept his eyes on her. Hope shimmered in his eyes before a shadow fell over them.

She longed to touch him, to hold him. To kiss away every whisper of doubt and self-hatred. "I didn't understand how someone could be so—how a person could do what you did to me."

He turned the other way, and she saw his jaw clench.

"You know how I grew up. I had everything a little girl could want—loving parents, a safe home, a Christian upbringing." She wished she could see his face. The knot in her stomach coiled tighter. "I never even imagined how frightful a childhood could be until I read your journal. It gave me a small glimpse of how awful it must've been. It's no wonder—how could anyone raised under those conditions turn out wholesome and healthy? Your mother's violence "

"That's no excuse." He pinned her with his stare. "That's no excuse." He repeated firmly.

"But it helps me to understand. It helps me to forgive."

"I don't deserve your forgiveness."

"Your mom didn't deserve forgiveness, either, but you gave it to her."

He opened his mouth and shut it again, turning away. But not before she saw hope dawn in his eyes.

She stepped toward him and dropped to her knees in front of him. "God forgave you. And He made you a different person, Micah." She lifted a hand and caressed the rigid lines of his face. "'Therefore, if anyone is in Christ, he is a new creation.' Remember?"

He turned his face from her hand and closed his eyes. "I'm still the same man."

Her heart softened, became pliable mush as she watched him deny himself her touch. She put her hand under his chin and nudged it back until he met her eyes. "What if you saw me walking alone on the roadside tonight? What if you were coming out of the bar again, and there I was. Would you do the same thing?"

"I wouldn't hurt you for all the world." The words seemed to grate across his throat. His eyes blazed with fervor. His hands clenched into fists on his thighs.

The tenderness she felt pulled the corner of her lips upward. "I know that," she whispered. "I've seen the man you are. It's in everything you do. Everything you say. You're not the same man you were." She thought of Gram's support of Micah and breathed a laugh. "Do you think my own grandmother would take your side if you hadn't changed?"

Longing filled his eyes. He wanted to believe her—she could see it plainly.

"I thought I'd gotten over this long ago. I didn't know I hadn't forgiven you until—until the other night. Gram has been praying all these years, she said, and I hadn't even realized—" She paused and looked deep into his eyes. "And you—you've gone all this time carrying guilt for what you'd done."

She had been clinging to bitterness, and Micah had been clinging to guilt. God knew they needed to know one another, needed to love one another, for true forgiveness to take place. Maybe that's why their paths had crossed again. She had thought it an awful set of coincidences, but maybe it wasn't happenstance at all.

Micah took her face in his hands. Remorse brimmed his eyes. "I'm so sorry, Hanna," he rasped.

She turned her face into his palm and planted a kiss on the cool, soft flesh. "You're forgiven." With her thumb, she brushed a falling tear from his cheek.

His warm breath ruffled her hair. "It won't be easy, this relationship," he said. "We'll have things to deal with."

"I know."

"There'll be pain and fear and guilt and—"

"Forgiveness," she added.

"Yes. Forgiveness. It's a good start."

THE END

Dear Reader,

When the idea for *Mending Places* came to me, I pushed it firmly away. I didn't want to explore the painful issue of rape, and I wondered how I could get my characters to push past the pain enough to forgive. Mostly, I wondered if I could do justice to such a difficult topic. Had God given this story to the wrong author? Still, the story grew in my heart, and after a year of praying, I gave in.

For some, the issues in this book were difficult to read about. My prayer is that the message of forgiveness will offer hope. Hope to those who've been harmed and, yes, hope to those who've harmed others. The strength to forgive can always be found through Jesus Christ. It will not necessarily come quickly, and sometimes it's a long journey. If you've suffered at someone else's hand, my hope is that God will help you along the path toward the mending place. He is always there waiting for you.

Denise Hunter

He heals the brokenhearted.
And binds up their wounds.
—Psalm 147:3

DISCUSSION QUESTIONS

1. Hanna was violated in a terrible way and faced the difficult task of forgiving. What does it mean to forgive?

2. Years went by before Hanna realized she hadn't truly forgiven her attacker. Why do you think that was? What finally forced her to recognize her unresolved feelings?

3. Do you think it's easier to forgive a stranger or a loved one? Why?

4. The Bible says God won't forgive us if we refuse to forgive others. Why do you think that is?

5. Has someone ever wronged you in a way that felt impossible to forgive? How did you get through it?

6. Micah's mother was an abusive alcoholic. Often these behaviors continue in cycles from one generation to the next. How did Micah overcome them? Have any negative behaviors been passed down to you? How can you break the cycle?

7. Hanna realized how Micah was treated as a child when she read

his journal. Do you think understanding other people's pasts can enable us to forgive them?

8. When Natalie's husband left her for another woman, she couldn't feel God's presence. Why do you think that was? Has there ever been a time when you couldn't feel God's presence? How did you get past this?

9. As a result of feeling bereft of God's presence, Natalie began studying God's Word. What happened as a result?

10. Hanna, Micah, and Natalie each came to a crossroad in this story and had to make decisions that could set them on different paths. Have you ever come to such a crossroad? How can you be sure you make the right decisions?

READ MORE ABOUT THE LANDIN FAMILY!
PLEASE TURN THIS PAGE FOR A BONUS
EXCERPT FROM

SAVING GRACE

THE SECOND BOOK IN
THE NEW HEIGHTS SERIES
BY DENISE HUNTER

COMING MARCH 2005

C H A P T E R
O N E

"You won't tell my parents, will you?" she asked.

Natalie Coombs thought the girl across the desk appeared to be eighteen or nineteen. She had a world-weary look in her eyes that Natalie had seen before—deep pools of despair that reminded Natalie of someone else.

"No, everything is confidential." She extended her hand across the desk. "My name is Natalie."

"I'm Linn." She shook Natalie's hand. Her dark hair hung down on both sides of her face like a curtain. "Can I take a test here?"

"Sure. You'll just need to fill out a form, then answer some questions first. All right?"

Linn nodded, and Natalie handed her a clipboard with the intake form. "You can have a seat over there."

Linn settled into the farthest corner chair, and Natalie returned to the desk. She was glad she'd sent this morning's volunteer, Amanda, upstairs to sort through the batch of baby clothing they'd just received. She had a feeling God had called her to help this girl. Her resemblance to Dana was uncanny, and Natalie prayed things would turn out differently for Linn than they had for Natalie's first client. Even though a year had passed, Dana's face still burned like a brand on her heart.

Natalie sneaked a glimpse at Linn. As the girl read the form, she toyed with the collar of her shirt. It looked as if she'd snagged it from the bottom of the pile in a cold dryer. At least she looked older than a lot of girls who walked through the doors. But she was young enough to be scared. And she was scared. Natalie could see it in her eyes. *Lord, help me to show her Your love.*

The phone rang, and Natalie reached for it. "Crisis Pregnancy Center."

"Hi, it's me."

His voice was a punch in the gut. Keith still took her breath away, just in a different way. She walked into the storage room and shut the door behind her. "I've asked you not to call me here."

"I can't help it. My plans have changed."

"What are you talking about?"

"Picking up the boys, going camping. I can't do it this weekend."

She closed her eyes. She could feel her shoulder and neck muscles tightening. "Don't do this to them again. You know they—"

"I can't help it, all right? I have to work. Half my crew deserted me today."

Well, you're an expert at desertion, aren't you? Natalie rubbed her temple. In her mind she could see Taylor and Alex scrounging in their closet for their sleeping bags the night before. She could see them packing their clothes and filling baggies with Cheese Nips and pretzel sticks to take along.

"Will you quit it with the silent treatment? Tell them I'm sorry, all right? I'll take them next   ″

"No way. You call them and tell them. I'm not doing it this time. It had been almost a year since Keith had been released from jail. Inside, Natalie still felt the need to make up the time he'd lost with the boys. Sometimes she wondered if he felt the same way."

"Would you stop making it sound like I do this every week? I told you I've gotta work. Will you cut me some slack here?"

"Call them, Keith. I've got to go." She disconnected before he could argue. She could hear her pulse in her head, and her scalp felt two sizes too small. Maybe she could take the boys camping herself. She thought there was a tent in the basement somewhere.

But it wasn't the camping they'd looked so forward to; it was their dad's company. Besides, she wouldn't know a stake from a pole.

She stretched her neck, tilting her head to the side, feeling the pull of taut muscles. She couldn't think about Keith right now. There was a girl in the lobby who needed her. She drew in a breath and blew it out, letting her facial muscles relax, then opened the door.

Linn was still in the corner chair. The clipboard rested on her lap, and she stared out the picture window where the words Crisis Pregnancy Center played in reverse. In the distance, Wyoming's Tetons rose majestically through the summer haze.

"All finished?" Natalie asked.

Linn nodded, then stood and walked toward her. The rubber sole of her shoe was loose at the toe and flipped with each step. Linn handed her the clipboard.

"Great. If you'll just step into that room there, I'll be right with you."

Normally, the volunteer would help the client, but Amanda lacked the experience to counsel with Linn. Anyway, Natalie felt drawn to help the girl.

Natalie called up the stairs. "Amanda . . . can you come watch the desk again?"

Moments later, the volunteer bounded down the creaking steps. "Sure."

Natalie glanced at her watch. *Shoot.* "Could you do me a favor and call Paula?"

"No problem," Amanda said.

Natalie jotted down her sister's cell-phone number. "Tell her something came up, and I have to cancel our lunch plans."

Amanda began punching the numbers.

"Thanks a bunch." Natalie grabbed a questionnaire clipboard from her desk and entered the counseling room.

"Now then." She took a seat on the chair across from the girl. "I'll need to ask you some questions, and then I'll get you the pregnancy test. As I said before, all the information you give me is completely confidential, okay?"

"The test is free, right?" She blinked, and a stray hair caught in her lashes and bobbed down, then back up.

"That's right. There's no charge."

Linn looked around the room from chart to chart, as if she was afraid the walls might collapse.

"I know you're anxious right now, but we're here to help, Linn, all right?"

She nodded, and Natalie perused her intake form. "You've come because you think you're pregnant. Can you tell me why?"

She shrugged. "I'm late."

"When was your last period?"

"Seven, eight weeks ago, I think."

"Are you using any kind of birth control?"

She crossed her arms, cupping her elbows with her hands, the nails short and ragged. "Yes—well, usually."

"How long have you known the baby's father?"

She looked away. "Two years."

Natalie wrote it down. "Are you still seeing him?"

Linn's lashes fluttered down, and she shook her head.

"Have you ever been pregnant before?"

Her brows drew together. "No."

"I'm not making any assumptions about you, all right? I have to ask everyone these questions." When Linn nodded, Natalie continued. "What do you plan to do if you're pregnant?"

Her gaze fluttered to the floor. "I'll have to get rid of it. Have to. My parents would go postal if they found out."

Natalie carefully kept her expression blank, though her stomach clenched at the words. She zipped through countless other questions, from substance use to family relationships to dreams and goals. That's when Linn finally opened up.

"I'm going to college in the fall. I got a full scholarship to Indiana University, and I mean room and board and everything." Her chin came up a bit.

"That's great, Linn, congratulations. What will you be studying?"

"Psychology." She smiled for the first time and wiggled her brows up and down. "I want to see what makes people tick."

"Well, when you find out, let me know, okay?"

Natalie tried to draw her out for a few more minutes, tried to put her at ease. When Linn's shoulders curled forward and her hands lay loosely on her lap, Natalie asked the last questions, the most important ones.

"Can you tell me what your religious background is like? Do you belong to a church or synagogue?"

She shook her head. "No, I don't think so. My grandma is Catholic," she offered feebly.

Natalie jotted it down. "How is your relationship with God?"

Her leg stopped bouncing. "Oh. It's fine, good." She nodded her head vigorously.

Linn gave vague answers to the last questions concerning religion, and Natalie knew the girl needed Christ. *Use me, Father.*

"Well, you'll be happy to know we're finished playing Twenty Questions." She pulled a release form from the desk and handed it to Linn. "I'll need your signature on this form. Basically it says you understand this is not a medical facility and that the pregnancy test may be inconclusive."

As Linn read the form, Natalie retrieved the pregnancy test and slid its contents onto the table. When Linn handed her the signed form, Natalie gave her the instruction sheet and explained what to do. Linn went to the adjoining bathroom with the plastic cup in hand.

Natalie watched the door shut and closed her eyes. *Lord, my heart is burdened for this young woman. She doesn't know You, and she doesn't know right from wrong. Father, if it's possible, let the test be negative. I don't want to see another tiny life snuffed out, and I don't want to see another woman scarred with the consequences. Yet, not as I will, Lord, but as You will.*

A few moments later, Linn returned with the urine sample and set it on the paper towel Natalie had laid out. Next, she opened the foil wrapper and pulled out the test cassette and dropper. She dipped the dropper into the urine, releasing the bulb to pull up the liquid. Pausing, with her hand over the test cassette, she looked at Natalie. "Four drops?" Her voice quivered.

"Yes." Natalie indicated the correct spot on the cassette. "Right in there." She pointed to the test window. "This other one is the window to watch. If there's a pink line there in five minutes, it means you're pregnant."

Linn's hand shook as she squeezed out the drops. When she was finished, she straightened and looked at Natalie.

"All righty." Natalie grabbed the egg timer and set it for five minutes. It began ticking off time. "I'll set the test over here where we can forget about it. Want a soda?" She smiled sympathetically. "This can be the longest five minutes of your life if you don't have something to do."

"No, thanks." The girl sat back down, and Natalie sat across from her.

Linn tilted her head back against the wall. "I can't be pregnant; I just can't."

"Well, we'll know in a few minutes, and if you are, there's a lot we can do to help you."

"You know somewhere I could get an abortion cheap? I don't have much money."

Cold fingers squeezed Natalie's gut until it was compacted into a hard knot. "If there is a pregnancy, this is a time of crisis. You're scared, confused. I know you just want this to be over with, but abortion doesn't solve that problem. It only creates new ones.

The girl noticed a picture on the wall. It was a photo of a newly formed baby. Just as quickly, she looked away.

"All the organs have formed; the heart is beating. It's not what you'd expect so early, is it?"

The young woman focused her attention on the test, though she couldn't see the windows from her seat. "There's just no way I'm ready to be a parent, and my dad's been telling me since I was twelve what would happen if I ever got knocked up."

Natalie offered what she hoped was a comforting smile. She wanted so badly to reach out to Linn, but she felt Linn closing up and changed the topic. "Did you graduate this past spring?"

"Yeah. With high honors. That's how I got the scholarship."

"That's wonderful, Linn. Your parents must be very proud."

She snorted. "They're just glad I'm cutting out in the fall." Linn tossed her dark hair as if that didn't bother her.

Natalie knew better. "Did you participate in any activities in high school?"

Linn shrugged. "Didn't have time. I worked part-time and had to keep up with homework." Linn glanced toward the timer. "How much time left?"

"Three minutes." Natalie gave a sympathetic smile. "They creep by, don't they?"

Linn's leg bounced up and down as she looked around the room. Natalie didn't have to turn around to know what she was seeing. Charts of a baby's development from conception on, pamphlets on adoption, the bulletin board with pictures of clients and their babies. That was her favorite. Tangible evidence of the lives they'd helped touch and change.

"Do you have any brothers or sisters?" Natalie asked.

A faraway look entered her eye. "Nope. Just me."

Natalie smiled. "I always wanted to be an only child. Especially when my sisters were aggravating me."

"It's not all it's cracked up to be."

Natalie searched for a new topic. "What made you decide to be a psychology major?"

"I don't know. I like to guess what people are thinking, why they do things and stuff. I want a real job, you know? A career. I want to dress up when I go to work and have people respect me."

"Sure, that's understandable."

Linn's eyes flittered toward the timer.

"One minute left," Natalie said. "There'll be a pink line in the reference window, and if there's a pink line under it, the result is positive.

Also, understand that sometimes, if you're pregnant, but there's not enough of the pregnancy hormone, the test can still read negative."

"How accurate is it?"

"The instruction pamphlet says 99 percent."

Linn's brows ticked up, then down again, and she began twisting a ring on her finger.

"That's pretty. Can I see it?"

Linn held out her hand. A sapphire shimmered on the gold band. "It's beautiful. Is that your birthstone?"

Linn's eyes clouded. "No, I—"

The timer dinged, and Linn's startled gaze met Natalie's.

"Well, let's go see, shall we?"

They walked over to the table. The phone rang in the other room, and Natalie heard Amanda answer it. When they rounded the examination bed, Natalie could see the test cassette, could see clearly the test results. She stepped aside, allowing Linn to come near.

The girl's eyes fixed on the test. Natalie could see the moment she understood. Her eyes widened for just a moment before they closed. When she opened them, she looked at Natalie, her eyes lit with desperation. "I'm pregnant."

Use the following pages to journal the story of your own personal
experiences with forgiving others and being forgiven.

JOURNAL

_____

_____

_____

_____

_____

_____

_____

_____

_____

_____

_____

_____

_____

_____

_____

_____

_____

JOURNAL

JOURNAL

JOURNAL

JOURNAL

JOURNAL

JOURNAL

JOURNAL

JOURNAL

JOURNAL

JOURNAL

Shoofly Pie
—*Tim Downs*

Get to know Kathryn Guilford, from a remote North Carolina county, and Nick Polchak—a.k.a. the Bug Man. When Kathryn receives news that her long-time friend and one-time suitor is dead, she refuses to accept the coroner's finding that his death was by his own hand. Although she has a pathological fear of insects, she turns in desperation to Polchak, a forensic entomologist, to help her learn the truth. Gold Medallion award–winning author Tim Downs takes you on a thrill ride as Kathryn confronts her darkest fears to unearth a decade-long conspiracy that threatens to turn her entire world upside down.

ISBN: 1-58229-308-2

HOWARD
Fiction

Secret Tides
—*Gary E. Parker*

Step back into the Old South on the eve of the Civil War. Welcome to Oak Plantation, an expansive, rice plantation in the South Carolina lowlands. When the overseer's daughter, Camellia York, accidentally causes the death of the plantation owner, she is haunted by guilt. Trenton Tessier, the son of the plantation owner and the man Camellia expected to marry, faces hard choices. At last Camellia risks telling Josh Cain, her father's half-brother, what really happened in the cookhouse . . . and discovers a startling truth about her family's past—a secret that will forever change the path of her life.

ISBN· 1-58229-359-7

Betrayal in Paris
—*Doris Elaine Fell*

Get acquainted with twenty-seven-year-old Adrienne Winters, as Christy Award finalist Doris Elaine Fell weaves a tale of mystery and intrigue. Headstrong Ms. Winters is relentless in her pursuit to clear the names of her brother and father who were victims of a double betrayal on foreign soil. Travel along as Adrienne's adventure takes her from the streets of Paris to the hot sands of the Kuwaiti desert. Set on the backdrop of the September 11 Pentagon tragedy, Adrienne discovers a gentle romance as she sorts out her family's history and her faith in God.

ISBN: 1-58229-314-7

Sins of the Mother
—*Patricia H. Rushford*

You'll surely enjoy getting to know country music singer Shanna O'Brian, as award-winning author, speaker, and teacher Patricia Rushford draws you into a story of romance, mystery, and adventure. As dashed hopes are rekindled and a haunting past comes into the light of truth, you'll find yourself caught up in Shanna's complex world. And when the mysterious death of her mother turns Shanna's world upside down, you'll feel her conflicting emotions as she is forced to make sense of her life—despite her fledgling faith in herself, her God, and the man determined to reclaim her love.

ISBN: 1-58229-342-2

Enjoyment Guarantee

If you are not totally satisfied with this book, simply return it to us along with your receipt, a statement of what you didn't like about the book, and your name and address within 60 days of purchase to Howard Publishing, 3117 North 7th Street, West Monroe, LA 71291-2227, and we will gladly reimburse you for the cost of the book.